DUPLEX

ORSON SCOTT CARD

A Micropowers Novel

DUPLEX

BLACK STONE PUBLISHING

Copyright © 2021 by Orson Scott Card
Published in 2021 by Blackstone Publishing
Cover design by Luis Alejandro Cruz Castillo

Printed in the United States of America

First edition: 2021
ISBN 978-1-7999-0317-8
Young Adult Fiction / Fantasy / General

1 3 5 7 9 10 8 6 4 2

CIP data for this book is available
from the Library of Congress

Blackstone Publishing
31 Mistletoe Rd.
Ashland, OR 97520

www.BlackstonePublishing.com

To John Hammer,
Writer and fair-minded newsman
And to Elaine Hammer,
Watchful editor and Muse:
Thanks for giving me
a dozen years of
free speech.
It never was a tame Rhino.

1

Father had been gone for six months. He missed Labor Day. Which was no surprise, because he also missed the start of school and summer and the Fourth of July and Flag Day and Memorial Day and pretty much every family tradition or important family day, including Ryan's and Dianne's birthdays, not to mention Mom's birthday and their anniversary, which, apparently, didn't matter anymore.

Ryan wasn't really angry about it. Mother refused to say anything openly to him and Dianne, but Ryan was almost sixteen and definitely not stupid, so he gathered from her surly hinting that Mom believed Dad had another family he cared about more, and he wasn't coming back.

Of course, Dianne was being a complete butt about everything. The only thing she said about it was after Mom let slip about the other family, and Dianne quietly said to him, as soon as they were alone together, "You don't actually believe that, do you?"

Well, in fact Ryan *did* believe it, because why shouldn't he? His own mother said it. Or hinted at it. But at age fourteen, Dianne always thought she was so smart, she could see through anyone, you couldn't fool *her*.

But on the twenty-third of September, when Ryan got out of bed late because there was a teacher workday and school was canceled, Mom and Dianne were gone—no note, because, like, who could possibly imagine that Ryan would care to know why he was alone in the house?

Only Ryan *wasn't* alone in the house.

There was hammering. That's what must have wakened him.

He pulled on shorts and a T-shirt and padded barefoot down the stairs only to find that at the base of the stairs there was a new stud wall blocking the path from the dining room into the living room. And instead of the front door and vestibule leading into the whole house, there were two new doors framed in, so that when the wall was finished with drywall and the doors were installed, any visitor would have to choose, left or right, whether they were entering the kitchen side of the house or the library side.

Of course, the "library" was actually Dad's office, but the walls were lined with shelves filled with so many books on so many subjects that whenever he was supposed to do library research on something for school, Dad would say, "Well, before we drive all the way down to the library, why don't we see whether we already own a book on that subject?" And they always did.

Ryan walked through the framed-in door, into the vestibule, and then through the other door, into the library side of the house.

The living room was stacked with boxes, and a quick glance showed Ryan that they were all full of books. Enough books that Dad's office was probably empty.

Not only empty. Dad was in there ripping out the built-in shelf units with a crowbar. It made a squealing sound—nails and screws getting ripped out of wood—and the work was almost done. The library was demolished.

More than anything else, this convinced Ryan that Dad had really moved out. He couldn't live in a place that didn't have his books. The question was whether *Ryan* could live in such a place.

Dad stopped his demolition work when he saw Ryan.

"I bet you're wondering," said Dad.

No need to go further. Old family joke. Walk in on something weird or scary, and you say, "I bet you're wondering." Ryan couldn't remember if that came from some old movie or a book Dad read to them, or maybe it was just something somebody said once and the joke stuck.

Only this time it wasn't funny.

Dad paused only a moment before realizing that Ryan wasn't going to laugh or even smile.

"Ryan, this is the only place where I can put a kitchen and downstairs half bath. I've got a plumber coming in later in the day to start laying pipe."

"We *have* a kitchen," said Ryan.

"That side of the house has a kitchen," said Dad. "But your mother and I decided that we weren't going to sell the house in order to split the equity. You kids are going to keep living here so you can stay in your schools."

"Didn't you say that Vasco da Gama High was fecal beyond belief?"

"I'm sure I didn't say that," said Father.

"Fecal," said Ryan. "That is the elevated word you used, though you intended me to understand it in a cruder way."

"I suppose it made my statement memorable."

"No, it was the accuracy of your statement that made it memorable. And three months into my junior year, I'm happy to report that da Gama High still enjoys a place of special prominence on the defecatory list."

"'Special prominence,' Ryan?" said Dad. "Really?"

"It's how I talk, Dad. Because, like it or not, I'm your son, so I talk like you."

"In order for you to stay in this house, we have to be able to keep up the payments. Since I also have to pay rent on my new place, we're falling behind on pretty much everything. So we're cutting this monstrosity of a house into a duplex and renting out this side. They're going to want a kitchen—most people do—and a downstairs half bath."

"Which means *no* bath, just sink and crapper," said Ryan.

"Exactly," said Dad.

"Or you could move back in," said Ryan. "Tear down that stupid stud wall and put up new shelves. No new plumbing."

Dad looked down at the crowbar in his hands. "I waited six months hoping that such a thing might happen," he said. "But payments keep coming due."

Ryan wanted to call him on the lie—Mother already said that Dad absolutely refused to consider moving back home—but instead he turned around and left the room. Left that side of the house.

While the plumber crawled under the house and then came back out and put blue chalk marks all over the library floor, Dad put up plasterboard on both sides of the stud wall and taped and spackled it. Then he mounted a couple of Home Depot doors into the frames he had made, shimmed them level, and then put lock sets and dead bolts on both doors, so the two sides of the house were sealed off from each other. He also installed new lock sets on the back doors—the old one off the kitchen, and the new one leading out of what used to be the library, to a four-foot drop down to the side yard.

"Watch out for that first step," Dad said when Ryan opened the door.

"It's a doozy," Ryan muttered. Another old joke. Only this time true, and really not funny at all.

"This'll all be finished before Columbus Day."

"That's good," said Ryan. "In our half-house, we can have half a Thanksgiving and half a Christmas."

"It'll be a whole Christmas."

"In the dining room."

"In the great room."

"How does a dining room become a great room without adding a square inch to the floor plan?" asked Ryan.

"Because 'great room' is what real estate people call a combination living room, dining room, family room these days."

"This other side is bigger than our side," said Ryan.

"By about two hundred square feet total," said Dad. "But your mom said she wasn't going to have you and Dianne moved out of your rooms. And your rooms are on that side of the house."

"Mom's room isn't," said Ryan.

Dad shrugged. "She didn't say anything about that."

"Where's she supposed to sleep?"

"Son," said Dad, "I don't make any decisions on that side of the house."

"Who's going to be sleeping in your and Mom's old room?" asked Ryan.

"It's going to be divided into two rooms," said Dad, "and the tenants on this side can make their own decisions."

"They get the master bath?" asked Ryan.

"Yes," said Dad. "And you three will share the other bathroom."

"So we've got to fit Mom into our bathroom?" asked Ryan. "Have you *seen* how much crap Mom has in the bathroom?"

"Yes, Ryan," said Dad. "Every day for the past ten years that we've lived here."

"Except the last six months," said Ryan.

"Has the amount of your mom's stuff decreased during that time?"

"Expanded to fill the available space," said Ryan.

"Unsurprising," said Dad.

"New lock sets mean that my house key won't work anymore."

"Oh, right." Dad walked to the new back door, pulled two sets of keys from his pocket, and tested one key on the dead bolt. It worked, pushing the tongue out and pulling it back in. He handed Ryan a key from the other set. "Go test it and make sure it works on your front door."

"So I won't have a key to this side?"

Dad looked at him with his are-you-really-asking-that look. "I think the new tenants will be less than pleased if the neighbor children have keys to their house."

"Who gets the money the new tenants will pay as rent?" asked Ryan.

"The bank," said Dad. "I'm hoping we can get enough in rent to keep up the house payments."

"Are we behind?" asked Ryan.

"We are not," said Dad. "But when our savings run out in January, then we'll fall behind unless we have tenants."

"Mom says you're just cheap," said Ryan.

"Then it must be true," said Dad, turning his back on Ryan. "Go test the key in the lock."

"You already tested them all," said Ryan. "I saw you. I don't think anything has changed."

"Test it by locking it, with you on the other side," said Dad.

"So you're kicking me out?"

"I'm going to continue doing my work, which includes putting up more walls here and upstairs."

"You going to finish it all tonight?"

"I can only work certain hours of the day," said Dad.

"When Mom isn't home," said Ryan.

"Take this key and give it to your mother. And give this one to Dianne."

"Dianne thinks that Mom's lying and this is all *her* fault," said Ryan.

"I'm not responsible for what either of you kids believes or doesn't believe," said Dad. "I'm just responsible for making the house payment."

"Why don't *you* just move in here?" asked Ryan.

"We need a tenant to bring in outside money to make the house payment."

"If you moved out of your apartment," said Ryan, "you could use your rent money to make up the house payment."

"Since you don't know anything about anything at this moment," said Dad, "your calculations are bound to be off."

"If you told me more," said Ryan, "I'd know more."

"Sounds like your mother has already explained things."

"Is Dianne right? Is she lying to us?"

"That would depend on what your mother said," Dad replied.

"She doesn't say anything," said Ryan. "She just hints and clucks her tongue and shakes her head and cries a lot."

"Sounds like your mother," said Dad.

"Defend yourself," said Ryan.

"I made my choices," said Dad, "and I'm not going to go whining about the consequences down the road."

"I don't want to hate you," said Ryan.

"Then don't," said Dad.

"Too late," said Ryan.

"Then there's nothing for me to say, is there," said Dad.

"Without a key to this side, how can I get in to see you?" asked Ryan.

"I won't be here long. I'm paying professionals to do all the finish work."

And that was it. Ryan went out the front door of the library side and then went through the door into the kitchen side and locked it behind himself.

He set Mom's and Dianne's keys on the dining-room table, then picked them up and took them into the kitchen and set them on the study table. Which would certainly become the eating table, too, because the dining-room table would have to go if they were going to have living-room furniture in there.

Ryan walked from the front of the house to the back and locked the back door, then went up the stairs to the bedroom floor of the house. There was no stud wall blocking off half the hall, so he walked the breadth of the house, from his and Dianne's rooms into Mom and Dad's room. He looked in the bathrooms.

There was no stairway up to this floor from the library side of the house. Dad would have to build stairs. And that meant he would have to come up through *their* side of the house to cut a hole for the new stairway to enter. Where would he put it? Had to connect it to the hall, so it would probably run exactly parallel to the existing stairway, except with the wall between them. Right here.

The linen closet would have to go in order to make a place for the stairs to come up. Another thing they'd have to find space for: all the towels and sheets. Plus Mom and all her stuff. Mom had a lot of stuff.

Ryan could feel his own closet space slipping away. Mom would take his room because Dianne was Becoming A Young Woman Now, so she would need her privacy. Ryan would end up sleeping on the couch downstairs, using the half bath down there, dipping a washcloth into the toilet bowl to give himself sponge baths, for all that anybody cared. Ryan knew that he was going to be the main loser in all of this.

Not Dad, that was for sure, since he had his other family. And the books would go home with him, and Ryan would have to start going to the downtown library.

2

"So your dad not only left, but he took half the house with him."

Ryan could hear a note of sarcasm in Defense Fabron's words, but also sympathy. He wasn't really ridiculing anybody in particular. More like his standard posture of holding the universe to account for its many stupidities.

"He locked us out of that half, but he left it where it was," said Ryan.

"Except it's no longer inside *your* house, so . . . gone. Taken away."

"And I now get the distinct impression that everyone's lying to me," said Ryan.

"Because everybody *is* lying to you, and they always have, and it's shameful that it has taken you all the way to age almost-sixteen, as a junior in high school, to recognize the fact."

"Everybody?"

"Especially your teachers. And all the girls."

"Girls don't even talk to me. How could they lie?"

"They're all *dying* to talk to you, so when they ignore you, they're lying."

"I see that *you*, also lying to me, are trying to set me up to humiliate myself yet again with some nubile young creature with blue-and-orange hair."

"That would be a cheerleader, and you'd have nothing to say and nothing to hear from any of *them*, so no, I'm not lying to you. I just haven't yet *identified* any of the girls who are dying to talk to you."

"You said they're all *dying*—"

"Everybody's dying, Little King."

"But not everybody's house just got cut in half. Not everybody's mother just took over their bedroom and put them downstairs on the couch that's in plain view from the room where everybody eats breakfast."

"You're going to have to stop sleeping in the nude, Ryan."

"Think again, Monsieur Blacksmith le Defenseur." As usual, he pronounced it in his best French accent. "The nakeder I am, the less likely either my mom or my sister will strip the blanket off me to make me get out of bed."

"The *more* likely."

"Again, think. I have no body shame issues. Let them study every part of me. While I continue to recline upon the couch."

"They'll call your dad to come and get you up."

Ryan had no answer for that.

"You won't like being naked when he shows up," added Defense.

"Who are you defending, me or the women who rule my life now?"

"I'm helping you see the future and forestall the most nauseating possibilities."

"I'll see you at lunch, Nostradamus," said Ryan.

"Not if I can figure out how to split the lunchroom in half," said Defense.

"Someday I'll find the ass that's missing its hole ever since you got loose," said Ryan.

"Easy to find. Look for somebody really bloated yet unfailingly kind."

And then Ryan walked through the doorway into first period, which was also Homeroom, which was also AP European History, which was also inhabited entirely by the most intellectual kids in the school. All five contenders for valedictorian were in this class, and everybody listened closely to the teacher and took notes.

Ryan didn't feel like doing that today. He sat down and, in his open notebook, he inscribed, "A House Divided Against Itself Cannot Stand."

Then he closed his eyes and let the drone of the class wash over him.

"Ryan de Burg," said Mr. Hardesty. His voice seemed to be coming from somewhere very close to Ryan. Perhaps to his left, leaning over him.

Ryan uncurled his back and sat up straight. He wiped his face on his sleeve because a sudden chill on his skin told him he had been drooling. There was a pond on his desk that was nearly ready for frog eggs to be laid in it.

"The name," said Ryan, in a voice croaky with sleep, "is Burke. Irish, not French."

"De Burg," said Mr. Hardesty. "Norman French, came over with William the Conqueror. They were counted among the Old English, the original Hiberno-Norman settlers who asserted overlordship in Ireland."

Ah, yes. This was European History, and Mr. Hardesty was one of the few teachers who still cared about his subject matter twenty years into teaching it.

"Mr. Hardesty," said Ryan, "I concede the probability that you are correct, though nobody in my family would answer to de Burg, and half of them can't spell Burke. However, you deliberately interrupted me during a deep sleep phase, in which I was drooling copiously on my desk. May I get paper towels from the back of the room?"

"You may, as soon as you answer the question I was asking you."

"Unless your question also became part of my dream, sir, I don't believe I know what that question was."

"Then answer the question that you *think* you were asked in your dream."

Ryan was sure that Mr. Hardesty actually liked him and enjoyed these little contests of will. Ryan had no idea what, if anything, he had been dreaming. But he did know where they were in the coursework, more or less.

"The family name of the dynasty founded by Geoffrey of Anjou and Empress Matilda was Plantagenet." Ryan gave the name its French pronunciation, and a couple of other kids emitted sighs or glottal stops to show their disdain for his showing off.

"Excellent information, which we stopped talking about some three minutes into your nap," said Mr. Hardesty.

"The three sons of Geoffrey and Matilda were Henry, who would become Henry the Second, the first Angevin king of England; Geoffrey Junior, the Count of Nantes, which is in Brittany; and the youngest, William

FitzEmpress. William may have been the smartest of the Angevin boys, since he studied Vegetius and actually followed his advice during military campaigns."

"You have a remarkable ability, Mr. Burke, to pronounce your semicolons so that they can be distinguished from commas without ever sounding like a full stop."

"Thank you, sir."

"You need to come home from the local bar much earlier in the future, so you can get the sleep you need at home. And yes, your answer did include the information I asked for, along with much extraneous but interesting material. Clearly you have decided to emulate me and learn everything there is to know about European history, preparatory to becoming that pinnacle of educational attainment and authority, a teacher of AP European History in a second-rate high school in the greater Charlottesville area."

"Third-rate, I submit, sir," said Ryan.

"Do not take unseemly pride in the low status of your high school," said Hardesty. "The cheerleaders in this class will report your lack of school pride to the jocks and you'll be beaten."

"There are no cheerleaders in this class," said Ryan.

"Are you sure of that, Mr. Burke?" asked Hardesty.

Ryan gestured around the class. "Just look," he said. "There's no cheerleader material here."

"And once again," said Hardesty, "you manage simultaneously to show off to and insult the rest of the class."

Hardesty was right, of course. But Ryan also knew that all but a few of the students were happy when he was able to distract Mr. Hardesty for five minutes at a time. Which he figured he had just done.

"I'll get more sleep at home, sir," said Ryan. "I truly want to excel in this course."

"Thank you, Mr. Haskell," said Hardesty. Ryan had Googled it once and found out that "Haskell" was a reference to an old TV show about beavers, but he never bothered to YouTube it.

Ryan had almost blurted out that his lack of sleep came from trying to sleep on the hideous couch in the dining room, which now was the "great room" in their half of the duplex that had once been a united house. But he decided that there was no reason for his domestic arrangements to become the subject of gossip around the school.

Hardesty apparently wasn't done with him, though. When he got to the front of the room, he gestured toward a girl sitting in the New Kid seat, nearest the door. "I imagine you slept through the introduction of our newest student, Ms. Bizzy Horvat. Please stand, Ms. Horvat, so you can get a look at Ryan Burke, a student so proficient that he can pass this class in his sleep."

The new girl stood up. She was pretty, so she would never have spoken to Ryan without being forced to by a teacher. She also looked a little awkward and uncertain, probably because she knew that she was being enlisted in Hardesty's attempt to heap ridicule on Ryan and had no way of knowing whether this was going to make her life in this new school harder.

So, out of compassion and solidarity, Ryan rose to his feet. "I'm honored to make your acquaintance, Ms. Horvat. Would you be so kind as to spell your first name, since it is cognate with the English word 'busy'?"

Other kids rolled their eyes.

"She has already done so, Mr. Burke," said Hardesty.

"Then I assume the spelling is 'B-I-Z-Z-I-E,'" said Ryan.

"There's a 'y' at the end," she said. "Not 'i-e.'"

"So you don't have a small 'i' to dot with a little hollow heart," said Ryan, trying to sound crestfallen.

"But I have the small 'i' before the 'z's,'" said Bizzy Horvat. "If I should wish to draw hollow hearts."

Several of the other students clapped at that, since Bizzy had sounded triumphant, as if she had somehow bested Ryan in a duel of wits. Which, perhaps, she had. She had matched his intellectual pretension with verve, and he respected that.

Maybe the social aspects of first period were about to become interesting. Because Bizzy had actually spoken directly to Ryan and had responded to his words *and* his tone. Something no girl had done since sophomore year, when Sylvia Creason had pretended to be Ryan's girlfriend for a week to annoy the boyfriend she had just broken up with. Ryan had been such an inconsequential threat that the boyfriend didn't even bother to beat him up. In fact, he paid for Ryan's lunch in the cafeteria every day until Sylvia dropped Ryan and went back to the guy without letting Ryan know about the status change until he saw her clinging to the jock-of-her-dreams after school.

Ryan hadn't realized until now that the sound of a female voice speaking to him, even sarcastically, could be so pleasant, as long as it wasn't either his mother or his sister Dianne.

So after Ryan bowed to her slightly and sat down, he occasionally glanced at her and mapped out his strategy to make friends with her. Not that any of his strategies had ever worked before; Sylvia had picked *him*, presumably for maximum annoyance to her boyfriend.

He quickly settled on the strategy of *not* walking up to Bizzy after class and certainly not finding out where she lived, her mobile number for texting, or whether she found sleepy, wet-faced droolers attractive as long as they could name the three sons of Geoffrey of Anjou and Empress Matilda.

Thus, he was, as usual, the last person to shoulder his backpack and head for the door of the room. Hardesty was already gone—he was always the first person out the door because, as he explained, "Getting older does not increase the capacity of one's bladder."

So when Ryan passed through the door of the room and turned right to head toward Hell—or Calculus, as others called it—he was surprised that not only was Bizzy Horvat waiting for him, she fell in step beside him. "You have Calculus next," she said.

"Thank you," said Ryan. "I'm awake now, so I knew that, but it was kind of you to wait for me and make sure."

"They told me in the office that I have all the same classes as you," said Bizzy, "and once I identified you, you'd show me where to go."

Ryan's first instinct was to be annoyed at the front office for saddling him with an assignment without even asking him if he minded. But since that instinct would include being needlessly rude to her, and since he realized that if he behaved that way she probably wouldn't speak to him again, he changed his tone before saying anything. "My pleasure, Ms. Horvat," he said.

"Mr. Burke," she said, "perhaps you would call me Bizzy?"

"I might," said Ryan, "if you tell me what Bizzy is short for, what nationality or language 'Horvat' comes from, and why you moved here in the middle of the school year."

"My first name is Bojana, spelled with a 'j' that's pronounced like a 'y.' It's a Slovenian name that's the feminized version of Bojan, which means 'warrior.' I narrowly escaped being named Brina, which means 'protector.'"

Ryan thought of telling her about Defense, whose name, Defenseur, also meant "protector." Then he thought about not telling her about Defenseur until he had cemented a friendship with her first.

"My last name is also Slovene," she went on, "because my parents are Slovenians who immigrated to the United States as soon as Yugoslavia broke apart. My father was a world-famous tennis player, or so we thought until he lost a few tournaments. Apparently he only played brilliantly as a Communist. Capitalism destroyed him, and now he's working on a doctorate so that he can teach Slovenian culture, history, and language at a university that has students who want to study Slovenian culture, history, and language. There is no such university outside Slovenia, so my mother supports us as an emergency room nurse, a job she just took so she could get away from oncology, which was too depressing."

"That's the job you moved here for?" asked Ryan.

"Father is staying close to the University of Virginia till he finishes his dissertation, because he has to teach classes every semester to keep his fellowship."

"I assume you're fluent in Slovenian yourself," said Ryan.

"I don't ever demonstrate my fluency to people who don't speak Slovenian," she said, "so please don't ask."

"You also speak Italian and Serbian."

"Croatian. Same language as Serbian, pretty much, except it's spelled with the Latin alphabet instead of the Cyrillic. How did you know?"

"Because Slovenia is close to Italy and used to be part of Yugoslavia."

She tossed her head a little. "It's also close to Austria."

"German is a hard language to learn and it sounds ugly even when you're fluent. Plus, the Austrian version is the language that gave Arnold Schwarzenegger his baby-talk accent."

"I never lived in Slovenia," she said. "I was born here in the US. But Slovene, Croatian, and Italian were all spoken in my house growing up, especially when my two grandmas lived with us—at separate times, thank heaven, since one was Italian and the other Croatian and they hated each other as only Catholic biddies can."

"So the whole family came to America," said Ryan.

"Is Calculus actually taught at *this* high school," she asked, "or are we walking to another?"

Ryan realized they were nearing the front entrance of the school. He had missed the turn to the math wing. "Sorry," he said. "Got too interested in the conversation."

As they retraced their steps and turned into the math wing, she said, "I don't think that was a conversation. I think that was an interview."

"I thought it was a conversation, because I was interested," he said.

"I thought it was an interview, because all I did was answer questions."

Ryan could feel himself blushing, and it made him angry. At himself, but he couldn't keep the edge out of his voice. "I answered every question I was asked."

"Ah," she said. "*My* fault, then."

Your fault for being so interesting, he didn't say. Your fault for having just the tiniest trace of an accent and for forming your words and sentences so charmingly and also your fault for being somewhat attractive-looking and for treating me as a person because you're so new here you don't know that it's everybody's job to ignore me or treat me like something they scraped off their shoe.

"Yes," he said. "Your fault, but I enjoyed listening to you."

They were at the door of the room, so he stopped. "Do you want me to introduce you?" he asked.

"Would that improve my social standing in the class?"

"I call this class 'Hell,'" he said. "Nobody likes me in there. So no, you should enter the room before me by about three seconds."

"Several people, as in about two hundred, saw us walking to class together. Am I already socially dead?"

"I'd administer CPR but I'm not actually trained in it," said Ryan.

"Don't worry," she said. "I like how well you faked being interested in my nattering, so I'll continue to speak to you after class and even eat lunch with you, if there's any room where you sit for lunch."

"I would be honored, Punca Bizzy," said Ryan, using the Slovenian word for "Miss" that he once noticed when he was reading a book about Slavic languages.

"I am not your girlfriend, Ryan Burke, but it's sweet that you think you actually know a word in Slovene."

"It means girlfriend?" asked Ryan. "I thought I was saying 'Miss Bizzy.'"

"And 'fant' means boyfriend," said Bizzy. "Now I'm going inside. The Slovenian lessons will continue after we've logarithmed our brains out."

Lunch was fine, even with Defense joining them and trying to conduct pretty much the same interview that Ryan had conducted. Only Ryan already knew all the answers because he had paid close attention to Bizzy's conversation and so he preemptively told Defense everything she had told Ryan.

And he told it in the form of a long monologue, leaving neither Defense nor Bizzy a chance to say a thing.

"A-plus," said Bizzy when he stopped.

"Did I leave anything out?" asked Ryan.

"Was anything you said actually true, or were you just doing your guessing thing?" asked Defense. To Bizzy, he said, "He tries to do a Sherlock Holmes thing and know everything before anybody speaks."

"In this case," said Bizzy, "he actually listened, he actually heard what I said, and then he remembered it and repeated it to you with complete accuracy, without leaping to any additional conclusions. It was an amazing performance."

Defense smiled at Ryan. "It's an act of God, you can't deny it. A girl comes here, and just by being your obnoxious self, you impress her."

"I don't know if God should get the blame," said Ryan.

"It can't be the devil," said Defense, "because she's also pretty."

"Pretty *what*?" asked Bizzy.

"Pretty cute," said Defense. "That's what Ryan's going to tell me when we talk about you after school."

"Not *pretty*," said Ryan, feeling extravagant and bold. *"Very."*

"This lunch is surprisingly close to being edible, for cafeteria food," said Bizzy, her mouth full.

"The old subject change," said Defense.

"But a truthful statement," said Bizzy. "Play along, boys, so I can stop blushing."

Yeah, Bizzy did everything right. So much so that she actually stayed with him at the end of the school day and Ryan actually had the confidence to say, "Can I walk you home?"

"I'm not sure how close I live to the school," she said, "because I haven't actually been to my house yet. In fact, we may still be in a motel tonight for all I know—that's where I started the day—and my mom is picking me up. Another time?"

"Anytime you want," said Ryan. He didn't say, "For as long as we both shall live," because that sounded both presumptuous and like plagiarism from Mom's and Dianne's favorite movie, *You've Got Mail.*

When Ryan left Defense at his apartment building and then walked on home, he was surprised to see a small moving van in front of the house. The new family was moving in.

Then an SUV pulled up behind the van, and a woman got out and went to the back and started pulling out suitcases. A moment later, two other people got out and started helping her. One of them was a boy who looked both athletic and handsome but probably attended middle school, so Ryan wouldn't have to deal with him.

The other person was Bizzy. Of course, of course, of course.

This was either the best thing that ever happened in his whole life, or the worst.

Definitely the worst.

Because if Mom was right, Dad might somehow be involved with the Horvat family in some despicable and unmentionable way. And even if Mom was lying and they just happened to be the new tenants, Mom was bound to either treat them as if her stories were true—i.e., as enemies—or else take Mrs. Horvat into her confidence and tell her *everything* about *everything*, which would totally destroy Ryan in the eyes of the new neighbors.

If only he lived alone in his side of the duplex. Or if only Dad were the one he lived with. Dad never embarrassed him. Dad never told horrible stories about his childhood to strangers.

And the most horrible thing of all was that without realizing he was doing it, Ryan had sidled over to the corner of his family's side of the house and was surreptitiously watching them haul their suitcases up the walk. As if he were spying.

Naturally, Bizzy spotted him. "Come on, Ryan Burke, man up and carry one of these suitcases, okay?"

He did. But from that moment, he knew that his chances of actually having a real girlfriend in high school had just disappeared. He wasn't ever going to be her fant, because she had just appointed him her bellboy.

3

Ryan phoned his dad. Dad actually answered. "Everything okay?"

"I got something I need to talk to you about."

Dad told him where his job was that day.

"Can you come by after work?"

"Not happening," said Dad.

"Mom can't take me, you know she won't."

"Such a dilemma. Good thing you're not a smart kid, or you'd figure it out for yourself."

"The *bus*?"

"Charlottesville Area Transit allows poor people to get where they need to go. You're poor."

"I didn't used to be," said Ryan.

"You were always poor," said Dad. "You were born poor. You still live completely from the charity of others."

"That's what I want to talk to you about."

"Well, poor relative of mine, do what poor people do when they need to talk to somebody with a job. Go to his place of work. On your own dime."

"If I had a Youth Smart Card, I could ride for free."

"You can only get those at the Downtown Transit Station on Water Street."

"I'd have to pay to ride the bus there, too, and you're the one I need to talk to."

"Break open your piggy bank, lad. A one-way ride only costs seventy-five cents. An all-day pass is a buck fifty. Come before quitting time or I won't be there."

"When's quitting time?"

"When I tell the guys we're done for the day."

"When will that be?"

"With luck, not till after you get here."

So Ryan looked up bus routes and schedules online and found that to get to Dad's actual job site would take two buses, and he'd arrive around seven P.M. if traffic didn't suck, which it would at that time of day, or he could ride one bus for a much shorter distance, but the nearest stop on that route was a half mile away.

Google told him he could walk half a mile in about twenty minutes. Ryan realized that this meant he only lived a quarter mile from school, because it always took him about ten to get home on days Mom came late because Dianne had some kind of practice or after-school activity or detention or whatever.

Ryan caught the one bus, which took him to a neighborhood where actual sidewalks led all the way to Dad's job site, except for the last block, which didn't even have a paved road yet.

Ryan walked onto the site, and somebody yelled, "Hard-hat area, moron!" and Ryan said, "I'm just here to see my dad," and the guy who yelled said, "Okay, all you hammers and boards and other junk that might drop from above, be really soft when you hit this clown in the head, because he's here to see his *dad*."

Another guy walked over and lifted a yellow hard hat off a small stack in the garage of the house they were putting a roof on. Ryan put it on. "My dad is—"

"Your dad's the only guy on this job who has a kid your size," said the man. "He's in the office."

Ryan looked around.

"This is a half-built house. It doesn't have an office," said the guy. He gestured toward the street. "Guess you don't come here often," he said, "or you'd know." Then he went back to whatever he had been doing with a nail gun. Reloading it, Ryan guessed.

The "office" was the camper on the back of Dad's pickup truck. Ryan knocked and Dad's voice said, "It isn't locked." Ryan climbed up into the thing and realized that it really was an office, every inch of it. Nowhere to sleep, except if you dozed off sitting at the worktable and dropped your forehead onto a blueprint.

"So you came," said Dad. "Bus, or did you wangle a ride after all?"

"No wangling," said Ryan. "Feet, then bus, then feet."

Dad reached over and pressed a button. While he was pressing it, a loud BLAT came from a horn on top of the camper. "I arrive, you end the workday?"

"It's four forty-five, that's the fifteen-minute horn. It means, Finish up and pack up, boys, we're walking off in a quarter of an hour."

"Very eloquent horn," said Ryan.

"It's a message they're always glad to hear, so they remember the meaning. I've got fifteen minutes till I drive away, and a lot of guys will be coming by to sign out, so what was it you wanted to talk to me about?"

"My driver's license," said Ryan.

"We couldn't do this on the phone?"

"You would have told me no because, you know, insurance rates, and hung up on me."

"So you still get the no because, you know, insurance rates, but I can't hang up. Very clever."

"Without a driver's license, I'm going to look pretty stupid for buying a car, aren't I?"

"Can't drive it without insurance, if you can actually afford to buy a car that runs."

"Can't drive it without a license," said Ryan. "And if I can buy the car and pay for gas, I can pay for insurance."

"Not necessarily. How well is McDonald's paying these days?"

"Better than no job at all, thanks for asking. But I have a plan."

"How much does having-a-plan pay these days?"

"I apprentice construction, I work my way up to journeyman, I make twenty bucks an hour, and—"

"That's twenty-one thirty for a journeyman electrician, twenty-three fifty for a journeyman plumber, twenty fifty for a drywall finisher, sixteen seventy-seven for a carpenter. There's no such job as 'construction.' But you won't be a journeyman anything till three or four years after you start your apprenticeship, and that's a long time to wait for a car, especially considering you'll be going to college long before your apprenticeship ends."

"I thought maybe working for my dad, it might not take as long."

"Sure, I can start paying you like a journeyman right away, except for the part where all my other journeymen quit on me, and you aren't worth anything because you're completely unskilled, and I'm not hiring you anyway, because you're lazy and irresponsible. I'm not sure this is better than hanging up on you."

Ryan felt slapped. Punched. He actually had to take a couple of deep breaths before he could speak. "I'm not lazy. I work hard."

"You work hard at whatever you feel like working at. Because you're a kid. I get it. I was a kid once. 'Lazy' is just redundant, talking about a kid."

"I work hard at school."

"You fall asleep in class whenever you feel like it, because school comes easy to you."

"Not math."

"And you're getting a B-minus in Calculus first quarter, according to your teacher's email, so yeah, you're sleeping there, too. And besides, that's school, where you *do* have skills. At construction, you'll be worthless."

"I can drive a nail."

"With a hammer. We almost never use hammers anymore. Ryan, skill doesn't matter if you don't show up at work every day, on time, and do whatever job you're assigned to do, and do it with energy and commitment and concentration, and don't stop till it's finished. Guys who lean or sit or stand around and take breathers on my site don't have a job the next day."

"I can do that."

"How do you know?" asked Dad. "You've never tried it. It's hard. Most grownups do it, but they had to train themselves to. Force themselves to. Most of them because they have babies to pay for and it keeps them concentrated. Your imaginary *car* costs as much as a baby, but it doesn't smile up at you and say 'Da-da,' so it's not enough of an incentive."

"So I'm the only kid in the world whose dad is the *boss* of his own company and I can't get a job with you."

"You can get a job with me," said Dad. "Just show me that you're worth hiring."

"How can I show you if you won't let me on your job site to prove it?"

"Money is at stake every single day here, Ryan. I'd be insane to let you on the job site, even *with* a hard hat, because anything you did wrong— which would be everything at first—would cost me money to undo or redo, and there goes my profit margin, which is, by the way, the *only* source of income for the family."

"Mom has a job."

"Fascinating. Her lawyer says she doesn't, so my child support and alimony provide the entire household budget for you."

"It's not a household," said Ryan. "It's a half-household."

"You're eating half as much, because you live in a duplex now? You're wearing half as many clothes? That must be getting chilly, what with the weather turning."

"You're just being snotty and mean," said Ryan. "I'm asking what I can do, and you're telling me . . . nothing, really, except no, no, no."

"On the contrary. I have observed your character for almost sixteen years—"

"Minus the past six months," said Ryan.

"Sixteen damn years," said Dad, "and I have never seen you take on a responsibility and carry it out like a grownup."

"I do my homework. I study for tests!"

"When you feel like it, but that's not what I'm talking about. You do that stuff to impress your teachers and your friends and make a name for yourself at school. I'm talking about onerous responsibilities. Physical labor responsibilities."

"Like what?" asked Ryan.

"The fact that I have to tell you is a complete proof of my point. Who takes out the garbage at your house?"

"I do," said Ryan.

"When?"

"Every week."

"You mean the kitchen garbage takes a whole week to fill up? The bathroom trash cans? The recycling?"

"I don't know," said Ryan.

"Why don't you know?"

"I take the big can to the street every week and the little can every other week, no earlier than six P.M., and I take them back within twelve hours of collection the next evening, which means as soon as I get home from school."

"Really," said Dad.

"Those are the city rules, by law, and I don't want to go to jail for doing it wrong."

"And you think that's 'taking out the garbage.'"

"That's all Mom ever asks me to do."

"So you're blind. You can't see when the kitchen garbage is full. You can't pull the bag out, tie it off, take it out to the big can, then replace it with a clean bag."

"Nobody ever told me to!"

"And that's why you'll be worthless to *any* employer on God's green Earth."

"People get trained when they get a job. McDonald's trains their people!"

"People *keep* a job and get *raises* when they show initiative, when they take responsibility. Once a week, when your mother asks you—Once? Twice? Eight times?—to take out the garbage, you go take the cans to the street. They have *wheels*. This is a job you did as a toddler, pulling that stupid quacking duck toy around the house. Pulling wheeled cans! So once a week, you save your mom a ten-minute job. But every week, how many times does *she* have to take garbage bags from inside the house out to the wheeled vehicles you deal with? How many minutes, while you're playing video games or texting or reading or watching TV or—"

"Doing homework or studying—"

"I'll tell you when you'll be ready to get a job—not with me, with *anybody*. It's when your mother never needs to *think* about the garbage. She never has to remind you to take the cans to the street, because it's already done. She never has to take a bag out to the cans, because it's already done. She never has to put a new liner in a trash can, because it's already done."

"I get it, yes, I can do that, I'll do that."

"I'll believe it when I see it."

"How will you see it, what with you not living there?"

"And it's not just the garbage."

"Of course not," said Ryan.

"Why does your mother have to take dishes out of the dishwasher and put them away? How does she put away things that go on the top shelves? You can reach them without even standing on tiptoe. Why aren't you already doing it?"

"I do it whenever she asks!"

"Why should she ask? Why should she *ever* take clean dishes out of the dishwasher?"

"Doesn't Dianne come into this sometimes?"

"Dianne is fourteen and she isn't asking me for a job so she can buy a car."

"And I bet she gets her license at sixteen."

"Of course, because you'll be rich by then and you'll volunteer to help her out by paying for her insurance yourself."

"I'm not that nice a brother."

"I know. Which brings me to another thing you have to do to make you employable."

"Oh, man," said Ryan.

"Your fighting with your sister makes that house a hellish place to be. No matter how annoying your sister is—and I know she is, but so are you—"

"I'm not the one who—"

"You're annoying *me* right now by being deliberately stupid when I know that when you *care* about it, you can be resourceful and smart."

"And you're mad at me."

"No, I allowed you to trap me into this waste-of-time conversation because you didn't want me to have the option of hanging up and ending the irritation."

"So this is all about persuading me never to bother you at work again."

"When you get a job—and eventually you probably will, what with the college degree you're going to get—you're going to be working on jobs with *real people* working over you and alongside you and, God help us, *under* you someday, and they will *all* be irritating. Annoying. Many of them infuriating. Some people can be patient and kind in dealing with them, unfailingly polite, never talking bad about them behind their back, helping them when they need it even if they've been rude before. Those people are suited to becoming management. Leaders. But a kid who can't let *any* annoying thing his fourteen-year-old sister does pass by without getting ridiculously, embarrassingly red-faced-and-screaming *angry* at her—that kid is not leadership material."

"She's my sister. I'm not her *leader*. She wouldn't follow me out of the house if it was on fire."

"Of course not, because you'd be carrying her," said Dad. "Because you love her and you care about her."

Ryan was stopped cold. It was a long time since he had even thought about whether he loved his sister. But yes, he cared about her, he had proof. He just didn't *like* her.

"On the job, you need to treat your coworkers like family," said Dad. "But, unfortunately, that's what you would probably do—whining and moaning and disappointing your supervisors, and yelling and screaming at anybody else who annoys you. Just like you treat family."

"I'm not that bad!"

"There are worse kids than you. But I don't plan on hiring any kids. I plan on hiring men and women who behave like grownups, even in their own families."

"You hire *angels*, apparently. How do you get them to apply for jobs?"

"I hire ordinary young men, mostly, who apply for jobs because they actually need the money—not for a car, but for a *life*. For food and rent for them and their family. Whom they love. Then I find out whether they're worth keeping on, and whether they're worth promoting. For instance, have we once been interrupted by guys signing out?"

"No," said Ryan.

"Do you have any idea why?"

"They haven't finished their jobs and put away their tools yet?"

"Seven guys have already signed out, Ryan. Because Niddy Adams is standing at the back door, signing them out on a random sheet of paper, because he can hear us talking, and he knows that family is the most important thing to me, as it is to him and all the guys on this site. So he's telling them, 'Boss is talking to his son,' and handing them the sheet, and they sign out and put down the time and go on home. Do you know why that works?"

"Because you hire grownups."

"Because they all trust Niddy. They know he won't lose the sheet, they know it will be copied faithfully onto my master time sheet, they trust Niddy. He's not a foreman, he's just a guy, like them, but he saw a need and he took action without waiting to be asked, and the other guys know that Niddy is right as rain, that whatever he says he'll do, he does, faithfully, every damn time. These are all good guys, but right now Niddy is showing me why I'm not going to have him working for me long—not because I'd ever let him go, because I'm not crazy. Not even because somebody else will hire him away, because he knows I'll match their offer and top it. He won't be here long, because he should be running his own damn company, and when he thinks it's time to do that, I'll help him finance the equipment he needs, and I'll guarantee him with suppliers and rental companies, and I'll let him know that he can offer jobs to a couple of my employees, and not the worst ones, and I'll help him get set up in business."

"In competition with you?"

"Ryan, *nobody's* in competition with me. I'm the best. I get the best workers. I get the best jobs. And when Niddy starts up on his own, he and I will *both* be crushing the companies run by people who aren't as good as their word, who inflate their charges, who don't finish on time, who don't provide as good a wage to their men, who yell and scream when things don't go right. We'll both *crush* those guys, and some of *them* will either wise up and get better at their jobs, or they'll wise up and go work as Walmart shopping-trolley collectors."

"So because you've got Niddy, you don't need me."

Dad shook his head. "When you *act* like Niddy, *then* I'll need you."

"But, Dad," said Ryan, so hurt and angry now that he decided to say this terrible thing. "*You're* not as good as your word."

Dad fell silent.

"Wasn't there something about 'till death do us part'?" asked Ryan.

Father stood up. "Walk on back to the bus now, Ryan."

"I'm sorry."

"No you're not," said Dad. "I have to get the time sheet from Niddy so *he* can go home."

"I don't have the bus fare home," said Ryan.

"That's not very good planning," said Dad.

"I was hoping you'd give me bus fare."

"I never said I would," said Dad.

"But . . . you're my father."

"Not judging from what you just said to me," said Dad. "You've got a longish walk ahead of you, and night comes pretty early these days, so you'd better get started."

"I don't know the way."

"Man," said Dad. "You've got a problem."

"Can I use your phone to call Mom?"

"My phone doesn't call your mother. It *receives* calls from her, but it doesn't *initiate* those calls."

"It wouldn't be *you* calling, it would be—"

"It would be my name popping up on her phone, and if experience is our teacher, that means she will not answer, she'll just text something unpleasant to me."

"Oh, come on," said Ryan.

Dad handed him the phone, then opened the door and stepped down and quietly thanked Niddy, who was the guy who had brought Ryan the hard hat, not the one who yelled at him.

Ryan punched in Mom's number. It rang a few times. Then it stopped. It didn't go to voicemail. Instead, a text message appeared. "Die," it said.

Oh. That was illuminating. Dad was telling the truth. Mom was not just freezing him out. She was cruel. It had never crossed Ryan's mind that maybe Dad was putting up with some hard things in the dissolution of their marriage. Mom's version of everything made it Dad's fault that they would never be getting back together. Dad who had another family he liked better. Dad who left home to please himself instead of keeping his marriage vows.

And suddenly Ryan wondered if Dianne might be right about whose fault this whole divorce thing was.

No. One mean-spirited text message wasn't "the truth" as Dianne saw it.

Ryan climbed down from the camper and walked over to Dad, who was still talking to Niddy. Ryan handed him the phone. Dad took it, saying nothing. Except to Niddy. "See you tomorrow, Nid. And thanks again."

Niddy grinned. "Have a good night, sir."

Dad went back up into the camper.

Ryan stood there looking at Niddy.

"Something I can do for you?" asked Niddy.

"Thanks for the hard hat," said Ryan. He took it off and handed it over.

Niddy set it down on the ground, then got his wallet out of his pocket and pulled a few bucks out. "Your dad doesn't want you walking home the whole way after dark."

Ryan took the money, then looked at Niddy again. "This isn't from my dad, this is from you."

"It *will* be from him, when I tell him I gave it to you, before he takes off looking for you on the street."

"He's not going to do that."

"He talks hard, kid, but he loves you more than life. This is from him."

Then Niddy trotted back into the garage of the half-built house and put the hard hat back on the stack. Ryan watched him and thought, this is a guy who doesn't have to be reminded to take out the garbage. This is a guy who puts things away where they belong.

Suddenly Ryan felt an urgent need to get home and check how full the kitchen and bathroom trash cans were. He pocketed the bills Niddy gave him and took off walking toward the bus stop. His watch told him that if he really booked it, he could catch the next bus instead of waiting an hour for the one after. He started jogging.

4

So it was a sure thing. Ryan would never be able to go out with a girl, because he was never going to have a driver's license or a car, and he was never going to have a car, because he was never going to get the kind of job that would allow him to pay for a car. Besides, if he made that kind of money, he'd contribute most of it to helping pay for food and stuff, because now that he was noticing things around the house, it was more than overflowing garbage cans that blighted the place. The upstairs bathroom and the half-bath downstairs each had exactly one roll of toilet paper. It made him more careful about pulling off too much paper for each job, because he didn't want to be stuck with too little paper to finish. The rolls disappeared more slowly, but rationing was the kind of thing you did when buying toilet paper was something you had to think about. And that was even true when you were using some generic sandpapery toilet paper brand that wasn't good enough to be used in a gas station restroom.

Garbage cans, toilet paper, and paper towels. Ha. Paper towels were a distant memory. Apparently, they had used them too freely before, and now there weren't any. Spill something? Grab a rag from the rag drawer and wipe it up, then put the wet and dirty rags in a laundry basket in the basement so they could be washed and dried and folded and put back for next time. Or, if you were a lazy kid, drop the rag on the back of the sink.

Seeing how endless the whole laundry situation looked, Ryan took a bunch of stiff, mostly dried rags and ran them through the washer and dryer. Before they were fully dry, Mother called him and led him down into the basement. "Your heart was in the right place," she said, "but we can't afford to use soap and water and wear and tear on the washing machine on a tiny load like a dozen rags. Plus, the rags need bleach to make sure they're sterile. Plus, putting them through the drier uses a lot of electricity, and you put a whole drier sheet in with them."

Only then did Ryan remember that when drier sheets got accidentally left in with a batch of his clothes—sometimes hiding in his underwear, sometimes in a T-shirt—it was always about a quarter of a sheet. So he had used four loads' worth of drier sheets on a single tiny load of rags.

"We don't use drier sheets on rags," said Mother.

"I didn't know," said Ryan.

"Therefore, I'm telling you," she said, with an edge of "duh" in her tone. "But I'm so glad that you did your trial laundry run with rags, because you washed in hot water and dried at top temperature. What if you had tried to wash a batch of clothes? My clothes, Dianne's clothes, even *your* clothes? On those settings, only your T-shirts and underwear would have come out okay. *Nothing* of mine would have survived. Dianne's clothes would be too small for a Barbie doll, if she owned such a thing."

Then Ryan remembered how annoying it was that there was always a drying rack set up in the basement, festooned with Dianne's and Mom's jeans and tops as well as their underwear, which he shouldn't have to look at. They were drying there because the actual drier would have killed them.

"I won't wash anything of yours or Dianne's," said Ryan.

"I could teach you how to wash them—cold wash, cold rinse, Woolite for the woolens, soak this, don't spin that, knits laid flat to dry because you can't hang them wet. I could teach you, but I won't, because you wouldn't remember."

"I remember things," said Ryan, a little sullen now.

"You remember things that you care about," said Mother, "like every other human. Dianne and I remember which clothes have to be treated in certain ways, because we're going to wear them. We *have* to remember. But you'll *think* you remember, you'll *think* you got it right, but we'll be out some clothes that we can't afford to replace. So here's the deal. When you find your socks and underwear and T-shirts and pants running low or smelling so bad that even *you* are offended, then you are free to wash your own clothes. But if you put something red in with a bunch of whites, then you'll just have to wear pink T-shirts and socks and underwear because we can't afford to replace them."

"Got it," said Ryan.

"You can go upstairs now," said Mother. "The lecture's over."

As he headed up the stairs, he heard her mutter, "Or you can take all your clothes to your father and see if he can get someone else to wash them for you."

So with garbage, sure, take initiative. But with important things, Ryan, you are not trustworthy or even worth training.

I should have tried to get Dad to let me live with him.

But that wasn't the problem, not really. He was doing better already at *always* noticing the garbage and never taking out a bag until he filled it completely from the bathroom and bedroom trash cans, so their supply of plastic trash bags didn't get depleted too fast. He noticed when it was time to sweep in the kitchen and vacuum in the great room or the bedrooms. He noticed when he got splashes of urine on the lip of the toilet, and he wiped it up and even sometimes put some cleansing powder onto the toilet and then used some dampened toilet paper to give a more thorough scrubbing.

There was probably a better way, but at least he could flush the toilet paper when the job was done, and he didn't have to see Mom on her hands and knees, scrubbing the floor around the toilet. He never wanted to see that again, because there was only one man in the house splashing urine onto the floor around the toilet because you couldn't always aim right on the first squirt, and besides, piss came out whatever direction it felt like and it splashed everywhere anyway.

He was doing better at all those things, and the reward was that every now and then Mom had time to sit and watch TV or even, like, converse with Ryan and Dianne at night. And *he* dropped hints to Dianne and then sat her down and talked to her so she would do her homework without

Mom having to nag her all the time. When she gave him snotty answers, he just let it flow past him. The house was a quieter place, even if it didn't actually make Dianne nice to him.

With all this stuff, he knew he was doing what Dad wanted him to do. But he didn't congratulate himself about it, because he understood now that this was the bare minimum. He didn't deserve a medal for doing stuff that he should have been doing all along.

He also didn't allow himself to wonder where Mother went all day if her lawyer was telling the court that she needed child support and stuff from Dad because she was unemployed. Of course she had a job. He just didn't know what it was.

Yet with all of this new adult-style watchfulness sucking time out of his life and still not making him proud of himself, the thing that bothered him most was that the nicest, smartest, funniest, and, yes, prettiest girl who had ever talked to him on purpose lived on the other side of the wall running down the middle of the house, and he knew he would never be able to take her out on a date, because they only had one car and Mom had it and couldn't pay for insurance if Ryan got a license, so he would never be able to drive anybody anywhere.

Sometimes, though, in spite of the fact that Ryan would never be girlfriend-ready, she came out onto the back deck of her half of the house and he would come sit on the second-from-bottom step off her deck down to the shared lawn, and they would talk. About nothing. About something. Some weird metaphysical idea that occurred to him in science or math, or some historical thing that he had read about in the library at school, and she would listen and then answer in a way that showed she understood what he was talking about, even when she disagreed, and he'd get this sad yearning sickness in the pit of his stomach that he finally decided to call "love" for lack of a better word.

"You love her," said Dianne one evening when Ryan came back inside when it was pitch dark.

Ryan didn't want to fight with her, so he didn't say, "Shut up." He didn't say anything, just walked past her, heading for the kitchen sink for a drink of water.

"I think it's kind of cool," said Dianne. "I mean, *she's* cool, and if she thinks *you're* cool enough to talk to, that makes you, not cool, really, but sort of . . ."

"Cool-adjacent," said Ryan, echoing a term Dad used when making fun of the way pretentious wannabe neighborhoods were described in real estate ads.

"Naw," said Dianne. "I've listened to you guys talking, and I'll just admit it, you're killer smart and so is she and you're both cool. Even if nobody at school knows it."

"You don't go to my school," said Ryan. "How do you know we're not the coolest kids there?"

"Maybe you are, but, like, if nobody knows it, Ry, then what good does it do you?"

After that, instead of being the enemy—albeit one that Ryan was keeping a one-sided truce with—when it came to Bizzy, Dianne was his ally. Something he would never have thought possible.

It was Dianne who broached the idea of dating. "Why don't you take her out?"

"All I can afford to do is bring a couple of Dad's scrapers and the two of us can scrape gum off the bottom of the school bleachers and then dispose of it in regular garbage bags destined for the landfill, since chewing gum is mostly plastic and isn't biodegradable or recyclable."

"So . . . a service project date," said Dianne.

"No, Dee. Not a date."

Dianne laughed. Since he no longer reacted to her with rage, he just silently heard her laugh and decided the conversation was over.

"She likes you, bonehead," said Dianne. "What do you think a date with her has to be? Car? Dinner? Movie? That's for people with money. She doesn't have any money, she knows you don't have any money."

Ryan didn't say, because Dad won't hire me so I can earn money and pay for those things.

"Ryan, she has feet. The same number of feet that you have."

Ryan imitated a female voice. "I have the *best* boyfriend. We walk *every-where* together. None of that automobile stuff for *us*."

Dianne just shook her head, looking sad. "You've talked to her for, like, a hundred or two hundred hours this fall, and you still don't know her at all."

"And you do?" said Ryan.

"How many other guys do you see her hanging out with and talking about deep stuff with? Is there a long line of them? Does she have a hard time fitting you into her packed schedule? You're the only name on her dance card, dimwit."

"So it must be love," said Ryan.

"Eventually, some older guy is going to realize what a looker she is," said Dianne, "and then you'll be S.O.L. Right now you've got this narrow little window in which you just might be able to get yourself out of the friend zone into the boyfriend zone, if you just show her that you *like* her."

"Boyfriend zone" made him think of the Slovenian word "fant," which made him think, "fant zone," and therefore "phantom zone," but this wasn't a Superman comic. "So, I'm supposed to know she likes me just because she talks to me and makes time for me, but my going out into the back-yard in the cold, just to wait for her to come out onto her deck and talk to me, *that* isn't enough to tell her I like her?"

"Life is so unfair, Ry," said Dianne. "You're going to die childless and alone, wondering why nothing ever happened between you and Bizzy."

Ryan wanted to say, Why don't you tell her *for* me?

Because he knew Dianne would go all innocent and say, Tell her what, that you like her? Speak for yourself, John Alden.

No, Dianne would say, she's three years older than me. It's actually illegal for me to talk to a high school student without being invited. Especially not as a go-between for my cowardly big brother who thinks big thoughts but can't do the small things that would make his life worth living.

Dianne wouldn't say any of those things. It was Ryan saying them to himself, all the time. It was part of the agony, the ache of being in love with a girl who thought of him as some kind of brother.

There was one other person who apparently took his relationship with Bizzy at all seriously: Mother.

"That girl next door," said Mother.

"Bizzy Horvat," said Ryan, knowing that Mother perfectly well knew all the names of the family through the wall from them.

"You spend a lot of time on her."

"I get my homework done," said Ryan. "I do my chores."

"I know that," said Mother. "But you are both bags of undifferentiated hormones as volatile as nitroglycerin. So I'm warning you. Keep your clothes on, buster. Keep your fly zipped. Don't get that girl pregnant."

Ryan blushed with shame, as if he had actually planned to do exactly what Mom accused him of. He had no such plan.

The thought *had* occurred to him. Not getting her pregnant—that would be crazy—but doing the stuff that might lead down that road. Kissing, anyway. He thought a lot about kissing her. If he could just stop talking once in a while, so there was time to do something else with his mouth besides trying to dazzle her with words.

"I see you blushing and I know it only means that you're embarrassed, because if you were actually fooling around with her, you would have started right in lying to me and saying you never *touched* her."

"I never touched her," said Ryan. "It's not a lie."

"Come on, Ryan, how old do you think I am? You think about her all the time. In bed at night. In the shower. Sitting at your desk pretending to study."

"What makes you think you know anything about me?" asked Ryan.

"Because you've got testicles that pump out testosterone every second of every day," said Mother. "Like all the other men."

"You really have no mercy, do you, Mom?" said Ryan, his voice getting so soft he could barely hear it himself.

"I tell the truth," said Mother.

"No, you don't," said Ryan. "You just say what you think will hurt me and make me embarrassed to spend time with Bizzy."

"I know how men think," said Mother. "And you're a man. You'd be pretty worthless as a man if you *didn't* think that way."

"Bizzy is the most interesting person I know. The smartest kid in school who isn't me. Go ahead and believe that I'm a bunny rabbit with only one idea in its mind, Mom. It just shows you don't know half as much as you think you do."

"No," said Mother. "You don't know half as much as *you* think you do. Just remember, I warned you. And when your hands are going places they have no business going, you're going to hear my voice in your head, saying, 'Get control of yourself, don't ruin her life—or yours, for that matter.'"

"We've got to have more of these lovely talks, Mom," said Ryan.

Mom gave a little hoot of laughter and left the great room so he could get undressed and go to bed. He lay awake trying desperately not to think of Bizzy in a sexual way, and failing; but then every time he did, he would imagine his mother right there watching them, and he thought: If I'm going to think of my mother whenever I'm hugging or kissing some girl, then I really am living in hell.

I need to get a job so I can move out of the house and not have other people watching every single thing I do.

And then he thought: What am I worried about? Like Dianne said, I don't need a car, and I don't have to scrape gum off the bleachers to be with her.

Bizzy's mom drove her to school every morning, but Ryan *could* walk her home every night. All he had to do was wait till the after-school play practices and chorus practices were over, and then just walk home with her. He'd say, Why don't I walk you home from school so your mom doesn't have to come and wait for you?

The next day, when he said that, Bizzy grinned. "So it's somehow better for *you* to wait till my practices are over?"

"I can read. Do homework. Listen to the practices. Or all at once," said Ryan. "My time is pretty well worthless, and your mom has stuff to do."

"Like casting spells using the toes of frogs," said Bizzy. "Double double, toil and trouble."

"Just let her know I can get you home safely."

"Because nobody would dare attack me with *you* as my giant guard dog."

"So I have to earn a black belt or buy a gun before I qualify as your escort?"

"I'll tell her not to pick me up tomorrow. Tonight, you stay after and show her that you really will be here, reliably, and that you're sort of respectable—no tin, no ink—and she'll give her verdict about you walking me home."

"Isn't it enough that I live on the other side of the same house as you?"

"Of course not."

"It isn't enough that I'm my father's son?"

She looked at him as if he were crazy. "Why would that matter? We don't even know your father."

And that was what kept nagging at Ryan even after Bizzy's mother gave him a long stare and then said yes, he could walk her home the next day. Bizzy's family really didn't know Dad? Then who had Mom been talking about when she dropped all those remarks about a family that Dad liked better than them?

5

Walking Bizzy home started out weird. Not because of anything Bizzy said or did, but because of other people. Not other kids, necessarily—not that many kids were even at school that late, except whoever was in the same activity that Bizzy had stayed for.

The first night, it was play practice, and so when the drama kids acted a little weird, what of it? They were always weird, anyway. But yes, they *did* kind of keep an eye on Ryan and Bizzy, looking at them covertly, like in a spy movie. Never actually facing them and staring, but tilting their heads, glancing over their shoulders, in one case even looking into a makeup mirror.

Were they feeling protective of Bizzy? Making sure that Ryan wasn't, what, abducting her? As if he could. Ryan lived in a house with a nice big bathroom mirror. He had looked at himself often enough, dressed *and* naked, and he knew that nobody would worry about his having the strength to subdue a cockroach. He had clear memories of Dianne once shouting at him *not* to stomp a cricket on the back porch, because if he got its attention it might eat him. He didn't even get mad at her that time, because he knew that it was kind of true and he couldn't think of anything more pathetic than a weak kid like him getting red-faced screaming mad. Just one more thing to put on his Why-am-I-not-an-only-child checklist.

So why would they think they needed to keep her safe from him?

No, no, that wasn't it at all. They weren't protecting her. They weren't looking out for her.

They were simply looking *at* her. Ryan might as well not exist. Their eyes were following her and only her.

"You must be really popular with the drama kids," said Ryan.

"Oh, yeah," she said in a very sarcastic tone.

"Well, yeah," he answered.

"New girl comes into school, tries out for the school play and gets the lead right off, beating out six girls who've been in drama from freshman year, all of whom felt entitled to get the part."

"So . . . admiration?"

She gave a little bark of a laugh. "Yeah, they admire me. They want to grow up to be just like me."

"I don't see them hating you," said Ryan.

Bizzy shrugged. "Your mind-reading skills are apparently deficient."

No point in arguing, because she was right. He could see where the other kids were looking, but he had no idea what they were thinking. He never knew what anybody was thinking. Sometimes not even himself, especially when he caught himself thinking some thought that retreated out of his head the moment he realized he was thinking it. And above all, he could never outguess Bizzy. He had learned that several times during back-porch conversations.

However, once they got away from the school grounds and the looks still continued, not just from kids but from adults walking or cycling or driving by, Ryan started getting curious. They were still taking semi-clandestine looks—eyes glancing then darting away—and nobody seemed to be angry or suspicious or hostile at all. Just furtive.

Finally he said, "Can we stop for a second?"

"You need a *rest*?" Bizzy asked, bewildered.

"I just need to look at you. And while we're at it, you look at me."

"Yep, you're still visible," she said.

"People are staring at us," said Ryan.

"An early symptom of paranoid schizophrenia is the certainty that people are spying on you."

"I know," he said. "But I'm pretty sure they're spying on *you*."

"Paranoia by proxy?" she said. "I don't think that's a thing."

"You look completely normal."

"And I try so hard to be special."

"Well, you *are*," said Ryan.

Her eyebrows rose.

"Don't read anything into that," he said. "I'm just saying, I know *I* think you're extraordinary, but I didn't expect total strangers in passing cars to be distracted by you just because you're walking down the street."

"I have such a special walk," she said.

And then, before he could make any kind of retort, she added, "I know they look, Ryan. And maybe someday we'll talk about why."

"You know about it? And you know why?"

"Just not today," she said. "This is what I was worried about. What Mom was worried about. That you'd notice and ask questions and make life hard for me all over again."

"I'm not here to make life hard for you," he said, though he was dying of curiosity now. "I thought I'd make it easier."

"And that *is* what you're doing," said Bizzy. "Just . . . please don't notice people noticing us. Or at least, don't make me talk about it."

"Fine," said Ryan. "I actually thought I was being really clever to notice them noticing you. You, by the way, not 'us.'"

"You *are* clever. And observant. You're looking out for me, and I appreciate it."

Slight as it was, her smile was so sweet and genuine that he felt his heart leap, and warmth overspread his face. Am I blushing? he wondered. The way he felt made him want to reach out and touch her.

"Can we walk again now?" she asked. "We've been standing here so long that I'm beginning to feel like I grew out of a crack in the sidewalk."

"Sure," he said, turning and letting her pass him so he could walk beside her again. Wanting so badly to take her hand.

"I appreciate especially that you aren't turning this into some kind of boyfriend-girlfriend thing," Bizzy said.

"Not a good move, then?"

"I saw you wanting to take my hand, and I don't want any kind of outward symbol of something that isn't really there."

"You saw me *wanting* to take your hand?"

"Was I wrong?" she asked softly, still walking forward, still watching where she was going.

He didn't want to answer. But he also didn't want her to think he was trying to fool her. "You weren't wrong," said Ryan. "But it wasn't a plot, like that's why I offered to walk you home. It just sort of came up."

"I'm not offended by your wanting to, Ryan. I'm kind of flattered by it. It might be nice to hold hands. Less lonely. But people read things into anything that happens between a girl and a boy."

Meaning, thought Ryan, that you don't want *me* to read things into holding hands with you.

"There's nothing wrong with you, Ryan. We've had some great talks. I like you a lot. I consider you my best friend at this school. I don't have anybody like your Defenseur Fabron."

"Defense? What do you think he *is*?"

"A brother," said Bizzy. "For a guy who needs a brother and doesn't have one."

Ryan thought about this a little. "And is that what you want *me* to be? To you?"

"Too late," said Bizzy. "We already passed that point a few back-porch conversations ago."

"Then what are we?"

"Walking home together," said Bizzy. "Since we live, literally, next door."

"Thank you for using 'literally' correctly," said Ryan.

"I literally always do that," she said. "To help make English a better language."

He laughed. She was funny, and laughing was way better than showing any of his feelings, since he didn't know whether to be hurt that she didn't want to hold hands, uneasy that she could see that he wanted to, or thrilled that she had said "we already passed that point," so he was already more than a brother. Whatever more-than-a-brother meant.

This walking-her-home business was going to be very bad for his nerves.

Because now that he was paying such close attention to her—looking at her, trying to see what the passersby saw in her—he was reaching the conclusion that she might be the most beautiful girl he had ever seen. Was that just because he was falling in love with her? No; self-honesty time. He had already fallen in love with her, head-over-heels, dreaming of her at night, thinking of her whenever he wasn't actively reading something or watching something or talking to somebody. And sometimes even when he *was* doing those things.

"Don't get silly on me, Ryan," she said.

Could she really read his mind?

Then he felt her hand slip into his. She held his hand lightly and not for long. It slipped away after just a few steps. He did not try to hold on or to reconnect. That hand-holding thing—it had quieted him, eased the aching feeling in the pit of his stomach. Why did that happen? Shouldn't her touch have heightened all his feelings?

He was going to make himself crazy with all this.

It was pretty late in October, but this was Virginia, not Minnesota, so only a few leaves were beginning to turn, and the air wasn't brisk enough even to require a jacket or sweater. Not while the sun was up, anyway.

There were still insects out and about. Now and then, bees wandering across dandelion blossoms in lawns they passed. Butterflies here and there. No winter kill-off yet. Mom said that was one of the best things about living in Virginia. Not far enough south for the insects to live through winter and get gigantic.

Now and then, a bee rose from the flowers and headed out, sometimes in a wiggly path, as if it were still randomly scouting for more pollen, and sometimes in a rapid, direct flight, probably home to the hive to do a little dance and tell everyone where good pollen could be found.

There was one bee, however, that didn't seem to have any rational purpose. It began to circle Ryan and Bizzy. It made a couple of close passes. Ryan saw her flinch a little each time.

"Not a fan of bees?"

"Wish they weren't fans of mine," she said. "The curse of blonde hair. They think I'm a really big flower."

Ryan thought of Dianne's long hair, back when she wore it that way. The time when Mom dragged her into the house while Dianne was screaming, "Get it off me, get it off, it's stinging me!" Dianne flailed at her own hair, and Mother called to Ryan, "Help, Ryan! The bee is tangled in her hair!"

And Ryan did what seemed quickest and best to him at the moment. He scooped up the kitchen shears from the knife box on top of the counter, ran into the living room, saw where the bee was squirming in Dianne's hair, right near her neck and just under her ear. Then he pushed Mother's hands out of the way, pulled Dianne's hair straight, and cut the hair just above the bee.

"Who said to *cut* her hair?" demanded Mom, even though he had already been brandishing the scissors when he pushed Mom's hands away.

The bee just tumbled to the ground, already dying or maybe dead from having stung Dianne.

Ryan knew that the stinger might still be in his little sister's skin, so he pulled the remaining hair out of the way, and yes, there it was, standing up from her skin. He knew better than to pinch it—that would be like pumping more poison into her through a syringe. Instead he flicked the stinger away.

Dianne's skin was already swelling under the spot where the stinger had been. She said, "I can't swallow, Mom." And then she opened her mouth and gasped for air.

"Call nine-one-one," said Mom.

Ryan was already at the phone, or so it seemed, he moved so fast. "Bee sting," he said. "She's having trouble breathing."

The 911 operator already had their address from the phone display. Dad once said, this is why we need a landline: so that when we call from home, emergency people will know where we are. Smart man, Ryan thought right then.

Dianne was turning blue and Mother was blowing air into her throat while pinching off her nose, but Ryan knew that his job was to stand in the doorway and wave the EMTs into the house. So he did that and they came in, one of them already holding a syringe and needle. The anti-sting, thought Ryan. A sting just like the bee's, only to save her life this time.

A few seconds after he injected Dianne with whatever it was, the anaphylactic shock eased off and then just seemed to end. Dianne was breathing readily enough, but there was still a high whimper in her voice. And they took her to the hospital, Mother riding in the ambulance with her, and Ryan staying home to call Dad and tell him where they were and what was happening.

Ryan had never felt so helpless in his life. And yet when he thought back over the event, he felt like the thing to do had come straight into his mind, and when he did the thing, he moved so fast, so accurately—he reached for the scissors before he even looked for them—because the decision to cut her hair had already been made, somewhere in the back of his brain. And his hand came away with the scissors, and he switched the scissors to his right hand and moved Mom's hands away and then *whick*, one neat cut, and a thick sheaf of hair was falling and the bee was falling and *instantly* he spotted the sting and his hand was already reaching to brush it off and . . .

And even though no one said it at the time, Ryan knew that he had been *superb* in that crisis. He had been quick and he had been right. Because later, when Mom groused about how the only way to deal with the cut he had made in Dianne's hair was for her to get a bob and wear it short for a while, Dad said, "The doctor said that if Ry hadn't gotten to the sting so fast, she probably would have died."

The doctor said that and nobody bothered to tell Ryan? The doctor had said that Ryan's quick action probably saved her life, and Mom was complaining about Dianne having to wear her hair short?

That was the only acknowledgment he got.

That and the fact that Dianne *never* grew her hair long again. It was always so short on the sides that it never reached past the bottoms of her ears, and never touched her collar in back. A catch-no-bees strategy. She must still remember the terror of the bee in her hair and the sting and the anaphylactic shock. And maybe somewhere in there she remembered how somebody saved her life by cutting a major tress from her head.

Or maybe she resented his intrusion into her hairspace. They didn't discuss it. But might that have been the foundation of the better relationship they were starting to have lately? Her knowing that when push came to shove, he cared about her and did whatever it took to save her?

So that whole memory was there in the back of Ryan's mind as the bee darted in at Bizzy for a third time. Bizzy was fairly blonde all right, and her hair didn't quite reach her shoulders, so it swung free, and that's why she caught the bee in the web of her hair. As she flipped her head away from the bee, her hair floated out and suddenly the bee was in it and couldn't get out.

No scissors, but that was fine, because Ryan already knew what he was going to do and he did it. His left hand flashed out almost before he realized it, and gripped the bee-trapping lock of hair just above the bee. He slid his fingers down smoothly with just the right amount of tension to move the bee out of her hair without tangling his own fingers in it.

He could feel the bee writhing even as he pulled it out of her hair. Because his touch was light enough to not actually pull on Bizzy's hair, the bee was undamaged. Ryan knew that the moment it got out of her hair, the bee would be enraged and would go into sting-anything mode. He couldn't let the bee fly loose or it might sting Bizzy after all.

He didn't dare hold the bee in his hands—he knew from Defense's stories that catching bees gave you lots of experience with stung palms and fingers. But he knew exactly what to do. Without any break in the motion of pulling on the bee, he bent to his hand and brought his hand up toward his face and popped the bee right into his mouth.

It wasn't that he thought bees couldn't sting you inside your mouth—of course they could. But his mental picture was of a whole set of unstingable teeth, upper and lower, and himself chomping down on the bee, killing it immediately. He had put the bee into a place fully armed with his own weapons—cuspids and bicuspids and . . .

And the bee wasn't stinging him or even trying to. He could feel it moving inside his mouth, but there was no pain.

So he thought, maybe the bee doesn't have to die this time. It hasn't injected venom into anybody, so it might live through this, and who am I to kill it? It was only doing what nature shaped it to do. It was Bizzy's hair that had trapped it. The bee was—so far, at least—an innocent victim. And if Ryan had pulled it away so gently that it was still trying to buzz and fly in his mouth, maybe he had known that all along. Minimal violence—that's what he had used.

Ryan turned his face away from Bizzy and opened his mouth and exhaled hard, blowing the bee out of his mouth.

It flew away. Maybe it was going to have an amazing story to dance about to the other bees in the hive. Maybe it was going to huddle in a corner somewhere and rethink its career choices.

But it was gone, no longer divebombing Bizzy.

He turned back to her, and she looked at him with a still-panicked expression and said, "Did you pull my hair?"

There would be no explaining what had actually happened. Even if she believed him, the weirdness of having put the bee into his mouth might bring an end to any thought of hand-holding with a bee biter.

"Sorry," said Ryan. "I might have brushed against your hair when I was swatting the bee away."

"Oh, good. Swatting bees *always* calms them down and makes them fly away," said Bizzy.

"In this case, it did. It flew away."

"Are you sure you didn't just stun it and it's on the ground, waiting to get even?"

"I saw it fly away," he said.

"You're sure it was that same bee?"

He shrugged. "Pretty sure." He did not add, I had it straight from your hair into my mouth, kid, so yeah, I'm sure. It was enough that she was safe.

"That really scared you, eh?" she asked.

It was her fake-Canadian "eh," so he chuckled.

"It was tense. My little sister almost died from a bee sting a long time ago. I take bees seriously."

"Anaphylactic shock?"

"Her first-ever sting, and it was nearly fatal," said Ryan.

"I've never been stung, so I don't know. But I saw the movie *My Girl* and it just about killed me when Macaulay Culkin died, especially after my mother explained about anaphylactic shock. I decided I never wanted to find out whether I was allergic to bee stings."

"Wise choice," said Ryan. "I've never been stung, either."

"Lucky," said Bizzy.

"Short hair," said Ryan.

"You think so?"

"Bee got caught in my sister's hair and stung her on the neck. And your hair . . . pretty much caught the bee before I managed to brush it away."

"Felt like you grabbed my hair."

"Brushed your hair," said Ryan. "Or, you know, kind of combed it with my fingers."

Bizzy shuddered. "That puts your hand awfully close to the bee," she said.

"I'm walking you home for a reason," said Ryan.

"To fight bees?"

"To keep you safe, if it's in my power." He said it simply, but he was trembling inside. I can't keep her safe. I can't keep anybody safe. I'm weak and slow and I have no skills and . . .

And he had acted instantly, got the bee out of her hair and away from her skin without any regard for his own safety, and put the stupid thing in his *mouth*, and . . .

Surely it didn't happen. Surely he just imagined it and then remembered what he imagined as if it had been real.

But if bee-sting allergies ran in families, he might well have been risking his own life. He would never say anything so tacky, but if he said, I'd die for you, Bizzy, he had already proved that such a statement was true. He wouldn't *choose* to die, but he would do ridiculously perilous things to keep her from harm.

That was something that people did when they loved somebody, right?

But Bizzy started talking about something from math class, and Ryan paid attention and all his self-gratulation about jousting with bees retreated into the back of his mind.

That night, he found that he was dying to tell somebody what he had done—even the put-the-bee-in-the-mouth part—but who would he tell? Not Dianne, in case she still wasn't over her own bee episode, and not Mom, because she'd mock him and accuse him of lying, because the idea of him being brave could never enter her head. Not Dad, either, because Ryan didn't want to claim credit for brave actions that his father hadn't actually seen.

Defense? He would never stop teasing Ryan about bees and saving damsels in distress.

No, the only person he could tell was Bizzy. And she had been there—and saw nothing.

Still, he went out on the back porch in the dark and waited for a while, in case she came out on her deck. But she didn't.

Just as well. He might have become too fervent about seeing her. Might have said something that gave away too much about his feelings. Might have cried with relief that she was okay, and that would have sunk him forever. He cried way too easily. It was his downfall. Cried when he was sad, sure, but also when he was relieved or proud or angry, and pretty much anytime he felt something strong. Girls don't like guys who are weepers. Dad told him long ago, look away and think of something important that doesn't make you cry. What Ryan had *not* said was, can you give me a hint about what won't make me cry?

Not feeling anything, if he could help it. That was how he got by. Laugh at everything. And everybody. Keep your distance.

But there was no distance between him and Bizzy, not in his own mind and heart. This was love. Sickening, crippling, humiliating love.

She had held his hand today. For about three steps. And he maybe saved her life, so he knew inside himself that his love was real. This was a red-letter day. Worth writing about in his diary. If he kept a diary.

6

Mrs. Horvat met Bizzy at the door with a smile, but the smile vanished when she looked at Ryan.

"Just leaving," he said, backing away.

"No you're not," said Mrs. Horvat.

"Mother," said Bizzy softly. Like a little prayer.

"If he's going to be useful, he has to know."

Apparently Ryan was supposed to be useful.

"Come inside," said Mrs. Horvat.

"I'm going to go upstairs and study," said Bizzy.

"You'd only sit and stare at yourself in the mirror," said Mrs. Horvat.

"Where did you put your broom?" asked Bizzy quietly. "I don't see it."

Mrs. Horvat's gaze never left Ryan. "When I don't obey her," she said, "Bojana teases me about being a witch."

"Not teasing," said Bizzy softly.

"Escorting Bojana out in the world is not a trivial task," said Mrs. Horvat.

Ryan nodded. Bizzy rolled her eyes.

"She thinks she is in no danger, because she's young and stupid," said Mrs. Horvat. "People watch her."

Ryan nodded again. Bizzy did not roll her eyes. She got a faraway look, as if she were watching a movie instead of taking part in the conversation.

"If you see the same person in different places," said Mrs. Horvat, "you are to inform me. Take a picture of him if you can."

"What are they looking at her for?" asked Ryan.

"Have you seen such a person?" asked Mrs. Horvat.

"A couple of people, maybe," said Ryan. "I didn't take pictures, so I can't be sure."

"You see someone like that, you will point him out to Bojana, yes?"

"Sure," said Ryan, glancing at Bizzy, who gave no response at all.

"She is in danger."

Ryan was puzzled. "What's so special about her? Why is everybody always looking at her?"

Mrs. Horvat looked at him as if he were insane. And Bizzy turned to her mother with a look that seemed to say, Told you so.

"You have to ask?"

"I've been trying to figure it out," said Ryan. "I see all the people staring at her but trying not to look like they're doing it, and I thought maybe Witness Protection, but if somebody had recognized her, the Marshals Service would have relocated you and renamed you already. I mean, if your moving in *here* was part of your most recent relo, it's already kind of failed."

Mrs. Horvat turned to look at Bizzy. "I didn't believe you," she said.

Believe what? Ryan wanted to demand. But he just looked at Bizzy, waiting for an explanation.

"You really don't see it?" Mrs. Horvat asked him.

"See what?" asked Ryan.

Mrs. Horvat seemed not to believe him, but she didn't interrogate him any further.

That night, when they both were on the back porch talking, Ryan sitting on the lowest step and Bizzy in a cheap lawn chair on the small deck, he asked, "So what is it that I was supposed to see?"

Bizzy didn't answer. But Ryan didn't go on talking. He let the question hang there.

"Most people find me . . . remarkable."

"So do I," said Ryan, feeling very bold.

Bizzy shook her head.

"What is it that your mother thought I didn't see?" he said again.

"If you really don't see it," she said.

"I probably do. I see a lot of things, I just don't know what thing I'm supposed to see."

Bizzy covered her face with her hands. She mumbled something behind that mask.

"What?" asked Ryan.

She took her hands away from her face. "Mother says that when I was a baby, a Gypsy woman got so angry at Mom that she cursed *me* with something that would cause my mother grief for the rest of her life. Quite a vicious curse when you think about it."

"If you believe in curses," said Ryan.

"Oh, being the daughter of a witch, I absolutely *do* believe in curses."

"I'm assuming you're speaking with humor. Or irony. About your mother."

"Of course I am," said Bizzy. "No such things as witches."

"Cursed you how?" he asked.

"She put a glamor on me. A look."

"No she didn't. You're pretty, that's all. How can that be a curse?"

Bizzy shook her head. "It's one of the things I like about you," she said. "You really don't see it."

Ryan shook his head. "Okay, *don't* tell me."

"I'm not just pretty, Ryan. The glamor is one of astonishing beauty. I'm heartbreakingly beautiful."

"Oh," he said. "That."

"Don't pretend you can see it," said Bizzy, "because I know you can't. If you did see it, you wouldn't have been able to talk to me. The only boys who will ever talk to somebody as beautiful as this *glamor* makes me are the kind of boys who think they're such hot stuff that every girl is dying to have them talk to her. That's not you."

Ryan was trying to understand whether she was teasing him or not. "I'm not that kind of guy," said Ryan.

"That's just it," said Bizzy. "Boys sort themselves. Most guys know that if a girl is extraordinarily beautiful, then she won't like an ordinary guy like them, so they never talk to her, they just ignore her, so she can't hurt them by putting them down."

Ryan had to laugh. "Come on, Bizzy, I never would have taken you for having this level of conceit."

She got up out of the chair and came down the stairs and stepped a little way out onto the lawn. The light over the back door softly illuminated her face. She did not even look at Ryan. But a change came over her face—something subtle, so that he couldn't say what it was she actually did, but he knew that there was a change. And now she was so amazingly beautiful that it brought tears to his eyes. Heartbreakingly beautiful—that was right.

Why hadn't he seen it before?

"Mother's story about the angry Gypsy woman is hogwash, of course," said Bizzy softly. "It's not something that's been put on me. I put it on myself, when I want to. And take it away when I don't want it."

And suddenly her face changed again, and she was back to being Bizzy—pretty and intelligent but not *astonishing*.

"So everybody stares at you because you show them that face?"

"I don't really understand how it works," she said. "I can see myself make the transition when I look in the mirror. When I came into European History class that first morning, I was deliberately *not* showing the glamor. Or you wouldn't have talked to me as naturally as you did—the way you would talk to a regular person."

She still sounded vain, and yet, after seeing that transition, that desperate beauty, he knew it was true. He could never have talked naturally to that face, to that girl.

"But on the street—" he began.

"For some reason, people who are a little farther away, I can't control what they see. They see the beautiful face. They have to look back, several times, in order to believe it was real. And they still can't believe it."

Ryan hardly knew what to say, because it did sound as if Bizzy believed she had some kind of magical power.

"Mother is afraid some maniac will abduct me and use me in some hideous perverted way."

"To cook for him? Do his laundry?" asked Ryan.

"That's why I like you, Ryan. You're an idiot."

"I'm glad you hold me in such esteem," said Ryan.

"If Mother had her way, I'd wear a mask or a veil or a bag over my head all the time."

"I see how pretty you are," said Ryan. "I can hardly take my eyes off you."

"That's because you're a shy nerd," she said. "But you talked to me, you joked with me, and you know perfectly well you never saw the face I just showed you."

"I did in my dreams," said Ryan.

It sounded so cheesy to him that he put his hand to his forehead to cover his face.

She stepped over and sat down next to him, put her arm across his back, holding him by the shoulder. "Do you think you're in love with me?" she asked.

"I don't *think* it," he said.

"I'm sorry, I didn't mean to sound patronizing," she said. "I'm so honored that you feel that way. Really."

"But everybody says they love you," he said.

"They love that face."

"I don't believe in magic or curses," said Ryan.

"But you saw me make the transition," she said.

He nodded.

"You're wondering which one is really me," she said.

He nodded again.

"They both are," she said. "Still me, all the time."

"So you really *are* out of my league," said Ryan.

"You already knew that," said Bizzy. "But somehow you still had the courage to talk to me. I liked that. Still do. It means that you're really my friend."

"Friend?" he asked.

"We're in high school," said Bizzy. "Of course I'm going to keep you in the friend zone."

Astonishing himself with his bravery, he reached out and touched her cheek.

She grimaced. "Checking to see if I have horrible acne scars under my makeup?"

"You're not wearing makeup," said Ryan.

"I never do. It gets in my pores and starts to itch."

"Bizzy, I think about you all the time. It's not about your looks, though sure, you look nice, way out of my league. But I like talking to you, being with you."

"That's how I feel about you."

"But you can do better," he said.

She smiled. "Not so far," she said. "Lots of offers, but no one better than you."

She reached out and touched *his* cheek. It sent an electric thrill through him. "I'm not crazy," said Bizzy. "I just have the gift of making people look at me."

"Did you make *me* look at you?"

"It was the school secretary's idea to have me follow you from class to class," she said. "And when I came to class, you were the only one who *didn't* look at me. Because you were asleep and drooling on your desk."

"What gave me immunity to your glamor? Was it the sleeping or the drooling?"

"The drooling gave me immunity to *your* glamor," she said. "Ryan, don't make this weird. Mother worries that one day somebody will kidnap me. It really scares her, whether there was truly a Gypsy curse or not. But I want to have a life, as close to a regular life as I can. You're helping with that, and I'm glad I have you as a friend. Please don't make it weird."

"So my telling you that I'm in love with you hasn't already done that?"

"I've always hoped that somebody could fall in love with me. Not my looks. Not the glamor. But *me*."

"I don't mind your looks," said Ryan.

"I don't mind yours, either," she said.

"I'm going back inside now," said Ryan, "because what you showed me, and what you've been saying—it makes me want to hold you and kiss you and all kinds of stuff that would require me *not* to be in the friend zone."

"You actually said that out loud?" she asked.

"Should I lie and pretend I don't want what I want?" asked Ryan.

"Yeah, you'd better go inside now," she said. "But please keep walking me to school and back. It's giving my mom so much more time during the day."

"For her," said Ryan. "I'll do that for her."

* * *

A few mornings later, when Ryan and Bizzy got to school, Defense bounded up to them and announced, "I've got the greatest costume for Halloween!"

Ryan knew his old friend well enough to dread the announcement, because Defense never looked quite this happy unless he was about to lay a zinger on somebody—most often Ryan.

"I'm going as you," said Defense.

Bizzy gave one small hoot of laughter.

"Nobody will know who you're dressed up as," said Ryan. "So nobody will get the joke."

"Joke?" asked Defense. "*Everybody* will know it's you, because I'm going to put a picture of Bizzy on a broom, and then I'll go around staring at the Bizzy-broom and saying sweet lovey things to her. *Everybody* will know it's you."

Bizzy looked like she was going to answer, but Ryan forestalled her. "He's not going to do it," said Ryan, "because he wants to remain my friend. So he'll get all his pleasure from teasing me about it, but then he'll do what he always does, and go as Yoda's handsome older brother."

"Correct he is," said Defense, "but tell him not, or spoil my fun it will."

Bizzy shook her head. "Why have I been committed to the same asylum as you two?"

"Excuse me, what have *I* done that's insane?" asked Ryan.

Bizzy seemed disposed to answer, and Defense certainly had that idea in mind. They both opened their mouths at once to speak, then waited for the other. During the pause, Ryan jogged away. Bizzy didn't need him to escort her once they were on school grounds, and Ryan had no need to stick around and face any more humiliation, like Defense's assertion that he was in love with Bizzy. Of course it was true, but Ryan wished sometimes that he had a best friend who actually cared about his feelings, at least now and then.

Once he was inside the main doors of the school, Ryan looked back outside and glanced across the crowds of students yammering and walking and taking selfies. That's when he noticed a guy who looked a little too old for high school, standing near the school buses and covertly watching Bizzy.

Ryan had seen him before. Near the house, once. And another time, he couldn't be sure when, but this guy had shown up to stare at Bizzy several different times. The guy knew where she lived, he knew where she went to school. This was exactly the kind of person that Ryan was walking home with Bizzy to protect her from. A stalker.

But the moment Ryan stepped back outside—pushing past a group of inconsiderate girls who thought they owned the whole width of both doors—the guy was gone. Did he know that Ryan meant to confront him? He couldn't have been afraid Ryan would beat him up or something, because nothing about Ryan would intimidate anything bigger than a bee. Maybe the guy was still hoping he wouldn't be recognized. But I *will* recognize you from now on, thought Ryan.

There was going to be a history test this morning, probably a pop essay—a kind of quiz that nobody but Mr. Hardesty would give students, because that would mean he'd have to grade the papers himself, which meant reading a whole bunch of really stupid short essays. But as Mr. Hardesty had said more than once, "The only tests worth giving are oral and essay, even if it means I have to read all the drivel you write." Ryan regarded that as a challenge, so he tried to write jewellike essays that covered all the points so economically that he never had to use a second paragraph.

But he couldn't resist putting a completely extraneous statement—a gibe at the principal or the president or some celebrity, or an absurd stand on some issue—in the middle of his answer. Then he would draw a couple of lines through that sentence, leaving it perfectly legible but marking it as *not* part of the essay. He figured that Hardesty couldn't come down on him for adding stuff to the essay, as long as he crossed it out.

So today, in the middle of a clear disquisition on the War of the Roses, its causes, and its impact on England, he inserted, "~~The problem with keeping hamsters as pets is that they're always snarling at bigger rodents when you walk them through the neighborhood.~~" Hardesty had never commented on Ryan's gratuitous observations, but Ryan was sure he read them, and hoped he was either amused or annoyed.

By the time the test was over, Ryan had forgotten about Stalker Dude for a while. But when he looked at Bizzy, he was reminded that she might actually be in some kind of danger. When she was paying no attention to him, he could see how the glamor poked through, stabbing at the hearts of strangers. Unlike people who had resting-angry-face or resting-bitch-face or whatever, Bizzy had resting-beautiful-face. It was all he could see, now that he knew what to look for. Her talent wasn't that she could make herself beautiful, it was that she could make herself *less* beautiful in order to have a friendship with an easily intimidated regular guy like Ryan.

At the end of history class, when Mr. Hardesty picked up the essay tests, Ryan had already decided to see if he could avoid walking with Bizzy, so that people couldn't see what a puppy dog he was around her. But instead, Mr. Lindquist, the guidance counselor, appeared in the door of the classroom and said, "I need to see Ryan Burke."

"After school?" asked Ryan.

Lindquist looked at him. "*Now* was more what I had in mind."

Ryan followed him through the crowded corridors during the class changeover until they got to Small Group Room B, which had chairs around a table. Apparently, it had been reserved for Lindquist and Ryan.

"Have a seat," said Lindquist.

Ryan turned a chair around so its back was against the table, then sat down on it.

"You couldn't just sit up to the table? Or is that how you sit at the dinner table at home?" asked Lindquist.

"We don't use a table," said Ryan. "We stand at the kitchen counter."

Lindquist got a pained look. "Oh, you're one of *those*."

"On the contrary," said Ryan. "I'm one of *these*. Much better than any of *those*."

"Mr. Burke," said Lindquist, "you've been recommended to take part in a research group."

"Recommended by whom?" Ryan asked.

"The recommender," said Lindquist.

"No need to keep it a secret," said a voice at the door to the room. "He knows it's me."

Ryan jumped backward from the chair and turned to face the door. It was Stalker Dude.

"You," said Ryan.

"I saw you notice me today," said the guy.

"I'm not going anywhere with him," said Ryan.

7

Stalker Dude came into the room and sat across from Ryan at the table. He had a limp. Ryan noticed that one leg was a little shorter than the other. He knew that they made shoes with one sole thicker than the other, to compensate for that. But this guy didn't wear shoes like that. Just regular shoes, and a limp.

Lindquist headed for the door.

"You're leaving me alone in here with this weirdo?" asked Ryan.

Lindquist stopped. "He would be entitled to ask the same question."

Ryan was stung. Weirdo? What had he ever done that would make Lindquist think of him as a weirdo?

"No offense," said Lindquist.

"Wrong," said Ryan. "I'm definitely offended."

"So am I," said Stalker Dude.

"You're the one who asked for this meeting," said Ryan.

"Why don't we talk for a while before you decide whether to continue regarding me as your enemy," said Stalker Dude. He looked at Lindquist. Lindquist left and closed the door behind him.

Ryan got up and walked toward the door.

"Not even curious?" asked Stalker Dude. "If I had stayed by the bus when you headed back out of the school, wouldn't you have talked to me then? Even though you know I could beat the crap out of you without even trying?"

Ryan stopped, his hand on the doorknob.

"For instance, I have a name. I can tell it to you, if you want."

"Dying to hear it," said Ryan.

"Aaron Withunga," said Stalker Dude.

"Withunga," said Ryan. "You must have to spell that a lot."

"Every time I write it down," said Aaron.

Ryan was tired of this. "What's this research group I'm supposed to join? Because I'm not a researcher."

"My mother founded it and she's in charge of it. She's got a doctorate and she's a scientist, but she'll be the first to tell you that what she's doing isn't actually science, because almost everything we learn is unrepeatable—it deals with only one case."

"So, scientific but not science, and still I have no idea what the group does."

"It's called GRUT, G-R-U-T—the Group of Rare and Useless Talents," said Aaron. "Only we found out last year that the talents aren't really useless, though they really are rare. Anyway, Mom tried to change the name, and when she writes about the things we learn, she doesn't say 'useless talents'; she says 'micropowers.' And members of the group are called 'micropotents,' or 'micropots,' or sometimes just 'mops.'"

Ryan waited for some kind of clarity.

"The opposite of superpowers," said Aaron. "Which don't actually exist outside of movies and comic books. But the micropowers are real."

"And you think I have one."

"I know you do," said Aaron. "And I know what it is. Because I saw you with the bee."

Ryan sat and thought about that. He must surely mean the bee that was in Bizzy's hair, the bee that he put in his mouth and then blew out again.

"I don't know what you think you saw," said Ryan, "but the only thing you can conclude from that is that I'm so dumb, I put a bee in my mouth."

"I wasn't inside your head," said Aaron, "so I don't know what you *think* you did. I only know what I saw, and that was a mental process so phenomenally fast that you made all your moves as if you had spent ten thousand hours practicing them. You were reaching for the bee before it got caught up in Bizzy's hair, and you didn't reach for where it was when it started. You reached for where it was when it got tangled. You already seemed to know. You reached, you slid your hand down her hair, but you were already reaching your hand to your mouth and your mouth to your hand before the bee was even free. A single movement—reach for the bee and put it in your mouth as if that was already your only goal. Like you had a real craving for fresh bee."

"Like I said, phenomenally dumb. If that's a micropower—"

"For all I know, it is, but you don't have it. At first I thought your only micropower was to resist other people's micropowers, but you don't have that at all. You have your own. Your brain just makes a connection and you *act*, flawlessly, smoothly, so that the whole bee-catching took about a second. Maybe less than a second. No lag time. Even opening your mouth to let the bee out again—"

"I blew it out," said Ryan.

"Happened immediately, so you put in the bee and blew it back out as if your only purpose was to catch a bee and blow it out into the air."

Ryan hated knowing he had been spied on, but he also felt a thrill at knowing that someone had actually *seen* what he did.

"So my micropower is bee catching?" asked Ryan. He did not add, Why couldn't I catch the bee that stung my sister before it did the stinging?

"I don't know," said Aaron. "I don't know what's actually going on. I just know that no other human I've seen has reflexes like yours. I don't even know if you think of what you're going to do before you do it—there doesn't seem to be enough time. You just *act*, and you make no mistakes at all. Everything works as it's supposed to. The bee didn't get tangled in Bizzy's hair, it didn't have time to sting your hand, you didn't yank on Bizzy's hair hard enough to hurt her, and when it was all done and the bee flew away harmless and unharmed, you didn't seem to think you had even *done* anything. No adrenaline rush, no panting, and no apparent need to brag to Bizzy about what you had just done for her. I don't think she has a clue how close she came to being stung."

"I was just looking out for her," said Ryan.

"I think that might be part of your power. Looking out for somebody you love. Or maybe somebody you have responsibility for. Some condition internal to your own mind, which has to be met for this micropower to assert itself. But that's why you come to GRUT: to have the group help you understand the rules of your own micropower."

"I don't come to GRUT," said Ryan.

"I know," said Aaron. "And if I'm reading you right, you have no intention of doing so. That's fine, there's nothing compulsory about it. We have no plan to study *you*, but we can be helpful when you decide you need to study yourself. I could tell you stories, but I won't, because the stories are fairly private, and you aren't part of the group. So here's where I'm going to leave things. Mr. Lindquist has my contact information. When something happens that makes you decide you might need our help, our experience, whatever—when that happens, you go to Lindquist and ask him to call me."

"I'd ask him to give me your number," said Ryan.

"He wouldn't give it to you. I have to protect myself, don't I?"

"Seriously? Like you said, you could beat me to a pulp."

"I could, sure. Unless you were in your hyperactive mode. Then it's quite possible you'd move so fast I couldn't defend myself. With micropowers, all things are possible. And neither you nor I know the limits of yours. I just know that if you ever come to think of me as a bee about to sting Bizzy, I might not be able to get away in time."

"And that's why you hid from me when I came back out of the school," said Ryan.

"Because I was afraid of you, yes, if I triggered your hyperprotective mode."

"And that's your message," said Ryan.

"Yep," said Aaron as he rose to his feet.

"You're not going to try to persuade me to come to your therapy group?"

"Not a therapy group," said Aaron. "And why should I care whether you come or not?"

"If you don't care, then why would you—"

"Because you got yourself chosen to be Bizzy's protector," said Aaron, "and *she* matters." Then he was out the door and striding—well, limping very quickly—along the corridor.

Ryan didn't try to go after him, because he wanted Aaron gone and now that had happened. Mission accomplished.

Except that nothing had been accomplished. Aaron might have been watching Ryan and saw his thing with the bee, but it was Bizzy that this guy was stalking. Nothing he said gave Ryan any assurance that he and this group he was with had good intentions toward Bizzy. Mrs. Horvat was right to worry. And Ryan was right to stay with Bizzy and look out for her.

Any more attacks by insects, Ryan could probably deal with. He was the right man to call if bees were out to get you. Anybody tougher than a bee, though, he wasn't sure what he could do.

Boxing lessons? Kickboxing? Karate? None of those would make him any bigger. Well, no, all of them would get him working hard, putting on muscle. And getting some skills, that would help. Might even intimidate somebody into backing off.

Except people with weapons. Knives, guns—what would Ryan do if they came at Bizzy with tools like those?

Witness protection. International espionage. Deep cover. Talking with Aaron Withunga didn't rule out any of that. In fact, Ryan was starting to think that maybe this ridiculous GRUT thing was just a distraction, meant to get him away from Bizzy so they could do . . .

Whatever. Kidnapping? If they wanted her dead, a sniper could take her out at any time. Or maybe this was a conspiracy of predatory fashion magazines to force her into sweatshop employment as a fashion model. Every idea he thought of sounded more and more absurd. And any idea of protecting her sounded even stupider.

He needed to find a way to earn money and get a car. Get Bizzy off the street.

Of course, Ryan was the one who put her *on* the street. She had been safely in her mother's car before he started walking with her.

So he should tell Bizzy and Mrs. Horvat that he couldn't walk her home anymore. Get Bizzy back into the car.

But he liked being with her. He *loved* her. Could he give up a half hour a day walking with her even if other kids mocked him for it? He loved her more than he feared their ridicule, that was for sure. But did he love her so much that he would keep exposing her to greater danger by walking with her every day at predictable times?

Nothing he did would take her out of danger, if she *was* in danger.

Nothing he did would make any difference at all, except to him. If he stopped having conversations with her, then his life would reduce like soup stock, leaving only his miserable existence as a child of a marriage that was breaking up, a house that had been divided, sleeping on the couch and hating himself and his life and, to be honest, both his parents for not being able to work things out like grownups.

At least he had the adventure of taking out the garbage and putting away the clean dishes from the dishwasher.

He knocked on Mr. Lindquist's door.

"Come in, Ryan," said Mr. Lindquist.

There was no window in the door. It was not ajar. Had Lindquist attached a tracking device to him?

Ryan opened the door and saw that someone was sitting in a chair across from Lindquist.

"Dad," said Ryan.

His father turned and looked at him. He was holding a pen, and there was a form on Lindquist's desk, filled out with Ryan's name at the top. A permission slip.

"I hoped you'd stop by before you returned to class," said Lindquist.

"I came to tell you never to do that to me again."

Father was still holding the pen, hovering over the parent-or-guardian signature line. He was also studying Ryan's face.

"The group that is soliciting your involvement," said Lindquist, "is fully sanctioned within the school district and in all the other local school districts. As such, they require all minor participants to have parental permission to take part."

"And you called my dad?" asked Ryan.

"I called your home," said Lindquist, "and your mother suggested that I should call your father."

Ryan looked questioningly at Dad.

"Your mother said, I believe, that it was about time for me to start taking some interest in my own children," said Dad.

Lindquist rotated his chair to face the narrow vertical window in one wall.

"Come on, Mr. Lindquist," said Ryan, "we can't be the first family you've dealt with where the parents are behaving like petulant children."

"Or where the children are also petulant and have no sense of discretion," said Dad.

"They want to study me," said Ryan, "because I ate a bee."

"If that's true," said Dad, "I would want someone to study you."

"It didn't sting me inside my mouth," said Ryan. "Or anywhere. I think it kind of felt like it had a Jonah moment. It flew right off to call Nineveh to repentance."

"You know the Jonah story?" asked Father.

"You and Mom took me to church, remember?" said Ryan.

"About six times," said Father.

"Two of the times they did Jonah," said Ryan. "It must be a favorite with children's Sunday school teachers."

"Do you intend to go to these meetings?" asked Father.

"Less often than I intend to go to church," said Ryan.

Father turned to the desk and signed the form. And the one behind it.

"Why did you do that, when I said—"

"If you're not going to attend, then my permission slip does you no harm," said Father.

"It does me no good, either," said Ryan.

"It does *me* good," said Father.

Ryan waited.

"When you decide you *do* want to go after all, and you need a permission slip, your mother won't have to go into a diatribe about how I couldn't carry out one simple task for the benefit of my children."

Father was, of course, right. It would do Ryan no harm, and it would save Father grief. He could picture his mother saying or texting, did you take care of Ryan's permission? And now Dad could answer yes.

"When do they meet?" asked Father.

"At a time when I'll be doing something else," said Ryan.

"They usually meet after school, in a classroom," said Lindquist.

"If you're ever kept late because of it, or you need a ride, or whatever, call *me*, not your mother, and I'll smooth it over. I'll take care of it."

"Very kind of you to take care of anything that might go wrong at home because of a thing I am never going to do," said Ryan.

"You'll do it," said Father.

"Is that an order?" asked Ryan.

"It's a prediction," said Father.

"You do know that I now am honor bound to make sure your prediction is wrong," said Ryan.

"You're not an idiot," said Dad. "You'll do it when you see a good reason for doing it, and you won't care about some petulant desire to show me."

Ryan said nothing, just looked at his father, wondering whether he was right, and if he was, whether saying it meant that Dad had respect for Ryan, or none at all.

Dad got out of his chair. "I've got to go back and get a bunch of lazy guys to pick up their tools again."

"I thought you didn't hire lazy guys," said Ryan.

"I never said that," said Dad. "I only said I don't hire lazy fifteen-year-olds who are close relatives of mine."

Dad brushed past him and went out the door. Ryan toyed with the idea of tearing the permission form in half.

Lindquist slid the form toward himself. "I'll tear it up when you ask me to," he said, "but only after you've actually attended once so you know what you're talking about."

How did Lindquist know that Ryan was thinking of tearing it up?

He wished his micropower was having an unreadable mind. Or at least an unreadable face.

* * *

"So what were you called out of class for?" asked Bizzy the next morning on the way to school.

"Silly, stupid counselor stuff," said Ryan.

"If you don't want to tell me, say so," said Bizzy. "Don't treat me like a child."

He wanted to argue the point, insist that he wasn't treating her like a child. But he was. Just like his parents treated him and Dianne. This is grownup stuff. You wouldn't understand. Well, why not give us a try and *see* if we understand? That was a conversation that would never happen. At least not with Mom.

"There was a guy who saw something I did once, and thought I had a skill that needed training."

"What skill?"

"Bee catching."

"Oh, be serious."

"Specifically, catching a bee in my mouth and then blowing it out again unharmed."

"Who was unharmed? You or the bee?"

"Both. Neither. No harm."

"You caught a bee in your *mouth?*" said Bizzy. "That's just pointless."

"It's a place where you can store a bee to keep it from stinging anybody."

"Except you," said Bizzy. "I don't think there's anything in the bee rule-book that says they face a ten-yard penalty for stinging somebody inside their mouth."

"I'd say only five yards," said Ryan. "Except that stinging somebody, inside or outside the mouth, carries the death penalty for the bee."

"Good point. You're talking about the bee that was buzz-bombing me and you tugged on my hair and the bee was gone. You put it in your mouth?"

"It spent a little time there."

"Did you have any kind of *plan* when you did that?"

"Yes," said Ryan. "I figured one chomp would put an end to its career as a sting-carrier."

"So how do people get anything between their teeth?" said Bizzy. "They move it with their tongue. Their nice, soft, stingable tongue."

"I didn't end up chomping it anyway."

"Why not?"

"Because I would have had to move it with my nice soft stingable tongue."

"You were saving me from the bee," she said. "And you didn't even tell me you had done it."

"The bee was gone. It just flew away. Didn't mess with us anymore. Now, chances are that about a week from now, a whole hive of bees is going to track us down and swarm us, and you'll curse the day you agreed to walk home with a guy who starts feuds with stinging insects."

"The bee started it."

"That's not the way she's going to tell it to her friends."

"They'll just mock her for having human spit all over her," said Bizzy. "Bees are very sensitive about substances that get carried back into the hive."

"My spit will only increase their intelligence," said Ryan. "Or rather, that of the *next* generation of bees, after my spit gets ingested by the queen."

"What was this training the guy was offering?"

Trust Bizzy not to stay distracted by the empty chatter, and come back to the real question.

"He thought I dealt with the bee very quickly. Just pulled it out of your hair and it was already in my mouth—some of your hair with it, so if you feel smarter suddenly, that's because I got a bit of spit onto your tresses."

"He didn't come for samples of your spit."

"He thinks I have a micropower," said Ryan. "Like a superpower, only kind of trivial. Can't pick up the Golden Gate Bridge and move it to Alcatraz, but I can grab a bee, terrorize it by putting it into the deep cave of my mouth, and then set it free. He says they can train me to be better at my micropower. Like, two bees at a time, or a dragonfly. Or a rabid dog, if I can fit it into my mouth."

"Protecting *me*," said Bizzy. "He saw you protecting me, and he wanted to train you to be a better protector."

"Or get me to do something that takes me away from school after hours so I can't walk you home."

"Mom can come and get me again. She's been glad to have a few weeks off, but she'll also be fine with picking me up."

"I told him no," said Ryan.

"Because you don't want to get better at your micropower."

"Because I don't have a micropower. There's no such thing as a micropower."

She stopped, which forced him to turn around and face her.

"Do you *want* to be late to school?" said Ryan.

"I don't care a rat's petoot about being on time to first-period European History, especially since we're going to have to sit through Hardesty's theories about what really happened to the poor little princes. Personally, I think it was Henry Tudor who had the boys murdered, and not Richard the Third at all. But I'm sure he's all set to shatter that hypothesis."

"Nobody knows, so it's just his opinion against yours and mine and Thomas More's."

"I know about these people, Ryan," said Bizzy. "They approached us years ago. Dr. Withunga came to our house, back where we used to live. Said that my 'amazing good looks' were a micropower, and my mother said, drop dead, and that was that."

"So you knew about them?"

"They seem pretty harmless. They aren't the ones my mom was worried about. They're kind of like the people who try to get photographs of Bigfoot, or people who remember being abducted by aliens."

"Do you think they're right? That there really are micropowers?"

"Ryan," she said, "you've seen what I can do." And as she said it, right there beside the road, about a block from the high school, she turned herself so beautiful that it almost stopped Ryan's heart.

And then she switched it off, and she was just Bizzy again—very pretty and smart and kind, but nothing to make some group of scientists take notice.

"Okay, yeah, only I don't know if what you do is a *micro*power."

"They say it is," said Bizzy. "And now you seem to have one, too."

"Nothing like yours."

"Rapid bee-eating is way more impressive than being able to put on a face without using makeup."

"Here we are," said Ryan. "This is the high school where we are required by law to show up every day."

"Aren't you even curious about these micropower people?" asked Bizzy.

"I just assumed that they were loons."

"Me too," said Bizzy. "Mom thinks they're sinister somehow. But look, you and I are proof that they aren't loons."

"You didn't even see me take the bee," said Ryan. "You don't know if I actually did anything."

"I didn't get stung. The bee went away."

"Look, you're not getting stung right now, too, so is my micropower really that good? Having saved you from one bee, *if* I did—does that warn all the other bees to stay away?"

"Why don't you go and find out what their group is really about?"

"Leaving you to be assaulted on the way home by teams of ruffian bees?"

"I'll roll up the windows in Mom's car and I think I'll be safe enough."

"I'm walking you home. Every day."

"Okay, here's another plan. I drop out of the play and go to this rare-and-useless-talents group *with* you. Then we still get home before Mom knows we did anything unusual."

"You can't drop out of the play," said Ryan. "They're counting on you."

"Every other girl in the cast has been memorizing my part in case I got hospitalized for, you know, anaphylactic shock or something."

"So the show would go on without you."

"All the girls would be so glad I was gone. I'm sick of them sniping at me during rehearsals, anyway."

"What makes you think this group meets in the afternoon?" asked Ryan.

"Because I think they'll meet whenever I tell them I can come."

"Why would you think that?"

"Because Dr. Withunga said so. She'd assemble a group meeting at whatever time and place I could attend."

"Wow," said Ryan. "They must think you're really hot stuff."

"You know of any reason why they shouldn't?"

Ryan thought about his feelings toward Bizzy and answered honestly enough, "Nope. Very rational plan."

"Wanna do it?" asked Bizzy, with fake eagerness.

"If we could really get back without worrying your mom."

"Mom always knows everything without anybody telling her. I think she's got a palantír or a crystal iPad or something."

"Because she's a witch," said Ryan. "Come on, that's a joke."

"It's not a joke," said Bizzy. "I think if these GRUT people had any actual knowledge, they'd be after *her*, not me."

Ryan knew that it *was* a joke, because that's the way Bizzy always talked when calling her mother a witch.

"Next time I catch Aaron spying on us," said Ryan, "should I tell him we're in?"

"Not the boy," said Bizzy. "We're going right to the top."

"Dr. Withunga?" asked Ryan. "How will we find out—"

"How many Withungas are on the faculty of a university somewhere around here?"

"I don't want to do detective work," said Ryan. "Mr. Lindquist has Aaron's contact information. If it includes a home number, Dr. Withunga probably lives there too."

"So your micropower is creative laziness?"

"I don't think I have a micropower. It's you they want anyway, but if we go together, then either we can be witnesses to make sure nothing bad happens, or it'll happen to both of us."

Bizzy rolled her eyes. "Then there'll be two families causing grief to the police until they find us."

"Nothing bad will happen," said Ryan.

"Why not?" asked Bizzy. "You sound so sure."

"Because Aaron Withunga has one leg shorter than the other. We can probably outrun him."

"I hope they really know something," said Bizzy. "I hope they can help me understand this stupid ability I have."

Ryan wanted to say, It's not stupid, it's amazing, it's wonderful. But then he'd get a lecture about how it's sickening that her micropower only affects something as stupid and evanescent as personal beauty. And she'd be right. He didn't love her for her beauty, because he had seen it at full blast only a couple of times. He loved her for all the right reasons: her intelligence, her wit, her sass, her lively curiosity, and the fact that she wasn't repulsed by his attention.

By the end of second period, Ryan had gotten Dr. Withunga on the phone. By the end of school, he was able to tell Bizzy that there would be a group meeting the next day right after school, in the same conference room where he had met with Aaron.

"She can assemble a group *here* on one day's notice?" said Bizzy. "Very odd for a bureaucracy. Things are always supposed to take a week."

"And you're sure you want to quit the play?" asked Ryan.

"I already told the drama teacher. GRUT or no GRUT, I was done with it. He's posted the notice for auditions for my former part. Ten signatures on the lines under the notice. Already. They were *so* ready for me to get lost."

"But I'm not," said Ryan. "I don't want to lose you."

She laughed. "You don't *have* me, Ryan."

Yes I do, he thought. I have you tightly sequestered where only I can see you. It's just that the prison of my heart has invisible walls and you don't know that you're my captive. Or wait. No, that's backward. I'm *your* captive. Bummer.

8

Ryan had expected that the next morning would be the usual: walk out the front door, sidle over to the Horvats' door, knock, and then he and Bizzy walk to school.

Not quite. The Horvats' door opened, but it wasn't Bizzy standing there. It was Jake Horvat, who was not only athletic but was getting almost as tall as Ryan.

Jake didn't look happy. "Mother wants to talk with you."

"After school," said Ryan. "Or we'll be late."

"You know that you're planning to meet with those psycho bastards this afternoon, so you're going to talk with Mother now. Or Bizzy never walks anywhere with you again."

Ryan knew inevitability when he saw it. He stepped past Jake into what used to be the living-room side of the house. Where Mom and Dad used to share the master bedroom upstairs. Where Father had his book-lined office, and where they used to gather to watch television, back when entertainment was a family goal.

Now it had slightly tatty rental furniture, and Mrs. Horvat and Bizzy were having a very quiet standoff. "Why should I have told you?" asked Bizzy—her voice quiet and reasonable sounding, but her stance and expression pretty much what they would have been if she had been screaming.

"We already discussed this," said Mrs. Horvat.

"No, Mother, *we* never discussed anything," said Bizzy.

"Watch how you talk to me," said Mrs. Horvat.

Bizzy noticed Ryan. "I'm ready to go, Ryan. I don't think it'll matter if we're a couple of minutes late."

"You're not attending that meeting this afternoon, Bojana," said Mrs. Horvat.

"Probably not," said Bizzy, "but it's not your call."

"It's not *his* call, either," said Mrs. Horvat.

"Correct, Mother," said Bizzy. "It's up to me."

"Why do you waste your time on this *norček*?"

Bizzy hesitated a moment, glanced at Ryan, and said, "He saved me from a bee." She started walking toward Ryan.

"You look so pretty today, Bojana," said her mother.

Instantly Ryan saw Bizzy slip into her beauty mode. It stabbed him to the heart, to see her looking so breathtakingly gorgeous while still being herself, still able to show the full range of human expression, including her absolute fury at her mother.

Bizzy stood still. "Mother," she said, keeping her voice level. "I already showed him this face. He already knows."

"But does everyone else at school? Are you ready to go out in public this way?"

A beat. Two beats.

Mrs. Horvat began to talk again exactly as Bizzy said, "Yes. Let's go, Ryan."

"Don't do it!" said Mrs. Horvat.

"Maybe they can help me learn how to control it," said Bizzy. "Maybe they can help me learn how to keep *you* from controlling *me*."

Bizzy took Ryan's hand and pulled him out the front door.

Jake followed them out onto the porch. "Stupid move, Ryan Burke!"

Ryan hurled back at him, "Like I have any choice about what's going on here!"

"Do you have a baseball cap?" asked Bizzy as she dragged him quickly to the street and then along the sidewalk toward the school.

"Because I like having jocks grab hats off my head and stomp on them because I'm not worthy to wear clothing that is associated with an actual sport," said Ryan.

"A beekeeper's veil, then," said Bizzy.

"You know that I don't actually keep bees," said Ryan.

"How am I going to make it through the day looking like this?" demanded Bizzy.

"You mean, wearing the face that every girl believes or at least hopes her makeup is going to give her?" said Ryan.

"It'll ruin me at school, you know it will."

"Just change faces again. Go back. Like you did before."

"When my mother triggers me, it takes hours before I can make it go away."

"Are you saying she has some kind of magical power over you?"

"All mothers do," said Bizzy. "She just makes it obvious. She does it on purpose."

"By saying that you look pretty?"

"Exactly that way."

A car pulled up beside them. Mrs. Horvat was driving. "Get in!" she shouted through the open passenger-side window.

"Go away, witch!" Bizzy answered, but not loudly. Not shouting. Just . . . intense.

"You're still a minor child," said Mrs. Horvat.

"Why not persecute Jake for a while?" asked Bizzy. "Why do you let him do whatever he wants?"

"Because nobody's trying to kill Jake. Because Jake isn't *special*."

To Ryan, this seemed like a sad inversion of favorite-child syndrome. Was Jake a victim here? Or was his unspecialness a blessing for him?

"You know what I can do," said Mrs. Horvat.

Bizzy let go of Ryan's hand, took one step toward the car, then dropped her backpack off her shoulder, sprinted to the chain-link fence beside the sidewalk, and vaulted over it into the stand of poplars that made a visual barrier shielding the neighborhood from prying eyes.

Bizzy was already over the fence and beyond the trees when Mrs. Horvat began to shout, "You can't do that, Bojana, because you're so . . ."

The last word wasn't said, though clearly Mrs. Horvat had been building up to some clincher. Instead she looked at Ryan. "Pick up her backpack, *norček*, and put it in the car."

"I don't speak Slovenian," said Ryan, "but I'm pretty sure '*norček*' means something between 'ass-face' and 'idiot.'"

"It means 'ass-faced idiot,'" said Mrs. Horvat.

Ryan, who had already picked up the backpack, dropped it back onto the sidewalk. He turned and walked away. He could hear Mrs. Horvat call after him, "You dropped the backpack, *norček*! You are so . . ."

But again Mrs. Horvat didn't finish the sentence.

You are so . . . You look so pretty . . . A formula. When she said it to Bizzy, Bizzy's face did indeed go pretty, if that was even a good word for how she looked. So what word was she going to say to Ryan just now? Or to Bizzy when she jumped the fence?

The car pulled up beside him. "Please listen to me," said Mrs. Horvat.

"So you can curse me, too?" asked Ryan. "I'm not afraid that you have the power to make me pretty, so I'm figuring you've got something much worse to lay on me."

"Looking the way she does right now," said Mrs. Horvat, "she's in danger. Surely you know that, yes? There are people in the world who would try to take that girl, with that face. So do your job, Ryan Burke. Go after her and keep her safe."

"Okay," said Ryan. "I'll get her backpack."

Mrs. Horvat screeched something about the backpack that seemed to have the f-word in it. Was it possible that Slovenian had the same word?

Not a good time for linguistic inquiry. Ryan scrambled up and over the fence—not as gracefully as Bizzy had, but efficiently enough. He dodged through the poplars and saw Bizzy striding down one of the streets in the gated development. He had to catch her before her face could dazzle the security guy who patrolled the neighborhood. He would never get that image out of his mind, poor man.

Bizzy let Ryan catch her before they got to the gate. Ryan stepped on ahead to be sure Mrs. Horvat wasn't waiting just outside. She wasn't. Of course, the sentry in the gatehouse watched them approach. He called out, "I didn't sign you in, and you don't live here!"

"Sorry!" called Ryan.

"Get over here!"

"We are minor children!" Ryan called back. "You have no right to detain us. We're going to be late to school! I will claim you made me drop my pants while you did a cavity search!"

By now they were beyond the gate. Clearly the guy wasn't going to follow them. Nor was he phoning anybody.

Maybe he had caught a glimpse of Bizzy's face, even though she was looking away from him. Maybe he was lying unconscious in his booth, suffering a concussion and a migraine—not from seeing Bizzy, but from having to look away again.

"You do look pretty good," said Ryan. "Just in case you were wondering whether it had worn off yet."

"I know how long it takes after Mother curses me," said Bizzy. "I'm trying to think of a way to stay in the library. Or the bathroom."

"Here's my idea. Go to the library. Or go to the bathroom. Can't stay there till you actually *arrive* there."

"You don't keep a ski mask in your locker, do you?" asked Bizzy.

"Nobody would look at you with a ski mask on," said Ryan.

"I don't care if they look," said Bizzy. "I just care what they see."

"People always look at you, Bojana," said Ryan.

"Bizzy," she said angrily.

"Bizzy, your drop-dead-gorgeous face is always leaking out no matter what you do. People look and they *think* they see that face, and they look again and no, just a regular pretty girl, but then, like the twinkle of a star, a glimpse of *that* face again."

"I know how it works," said Bizzy.

"Does Jake ever see that face?"

"I don't know what Jake sees," said Bizzy. "He's never bothered me about it."

"And what was your mother almost going to curse you with after you hopped the fence?"

"She didn't say it?" asked Bizzy.

"Almost said the same curse to me," said Ryan. "But she didn't even finish cursing the *norček*. Unless '*norček*' is the curse."

"*Norček* is just what she calls any boy or man who falls in love with me."

"I didn't fall in love with you because of that face."

"I know," she said. "That face would have caused you to never come near me. But Mother doesn't understand that."

"Because she doesn't know *me*," said Ryan.

"Nobody knows anybody," said Bizzy.

"Your mother apparently knows you well enough to force you to wear your glamor," said Ryan.

They were still outside the school, and other late kids were rushing inside, but instead of joining them, Bizzy stood in front of Ryan, holding his face between her hands, forcing him to look her right in the eye. "My mother *is* a witch. Or, in more scientific terms, her micropower is one that would have gotten her burned as a witch in 1680. Because if she mutters a certain formula under her breath, things go wrong for that person for a few days."

"What kind of thing goes wrong?"

"They drop things. Like heavy tools on bare feet. Or the baby they're carrying. Or the file folder they absolutely have to get to the boss's desk *right now*. Or they trip over things, or trip over nothing, and fall flat on their face. Or they walk into a glass wall thinking it's an open door."

"Tripping and glass-banging can be dangerous," said Ryan.

"They are. She says not, but I think she's probably caused people to have fatal accidents."

"What's the formula she mutters under her breath?" asked Ryan.

"It's like what she said to me."

"'You're so pretty'?"

"Only it's, 'You're so clumsy.' Said with all the pity and understanding in the world. Not really a curse at all, just an observation. But it makes them clumsy for a few days. Really clumsy at first, and fading till it's finally gone."

Yeah, that would have gotten her burnt during any village witch trial. Mutter mutter, and then somebody drops their baby into the stewpot and it drowns or boils.

"I assume she doesn't curse people very often."

"What if somebody heard her yell at me that I was clumsy while I was climbing that fence? What if I fell and broke a leg? She doesn't want to rile up the natives, get them suspicious."

"Nobody believes in witches anymore," said Ryan.

"Of course nobody believes in witches, until they watch one curse somebody," said Bizzy.

"'You're so pretty' doesn't sound like much of a curse," said Ryan. And then he thought of something. "What if somebody else says it? Does it trigger you?"

"They say it all the time," said Bizzy. "Has no effect on me. Only when Mom does it."

"And if I say, 'Wow, you look ordinary today, Bizzy,' that doesn't help you get out of the spell, either?"

"I think your power is bee extraction," said Bizzy.

"Pretty limited, really. Because, for one thing, it requires a bee."

"How am I going to get to the library?"

"First, we go inside the building," said Ryan.

"And some hall monitor nabs us for—"

"We're not that late yet," said Ryan. "The monitors are all in homeroom and if they saw you they'd just stare at you anyway."

"I don't want them to see me."

"Be like a New Yorker," said Ryan. "Just stare straight ahead. Make no eye contact."

"That doesn't work," said Bizzy.

"It works better than *not* doing it, because it's your direct gaze that puts the last nail in the coffin."

"So that's your whole plan?"

"And if anybody starts heading toward us," said Ryan, "you plant a long, fervent kiss on my amazing face and keep it there till we get yelled at for public displays of affection. Then you use your hands to cover your face in shame and walk away."

"You're not amazing, Ryan, but I wouldn't be ashamed to kiss you."

"You have to *act* ashamed of getting caught kissing a guy who's in the running for valedictorian. Like normal girls would."

"Okay, I can do that," said Bizzy.

To Ryan's disappointment, it only took one kiss to get them to the library. And even *that* kiss was kind of a false alarm, because the person didn't actually approach them. Worse yet, Ryan felt like he had wasted their first kiss on what amounted to camouflage. Their first kiss should have been one that she *meant*, not just a pose to keep somebody from seeing her face.

Ryan led Bizzy to one of the carrels that long experimentation had proved were not in line of sight from the desk librarian and were almost always overlooked by people browsing the stacks.

"Somebody's going to ask me why I'm not in class," said Bizzy.

"I'm going to take care of that," said Ryan. "You'll be left alone."

He walked away from her and took a roundabout way to the main desk. He leaned over it and spoke to the librarian. "You know the girl I brought in with me?" he said.

"New girl," said the librarian. "The pretty one."

"Bizzy Horvat," said Ryan. "Look, she has all the same classes as me. I'm going to tell her all the assignments and let her read my class notes. But right now she's in no condition to go to class."

"If she's sick, she belongs with the nurse, not in the library."

"She isn't sick. But her mom and her had a nasty fight before she left for school. Some really ugly, hurtful things were said."

"If every kid who has a fight with her mother—"

"I agree," said Ryan. "But this was a really vicious, hurtful fight. You have no idea. And Bizzy is fragile."

Ryan could see the librarian's eyes glazing over.

"You seem to believe that the problems of pretty girls aren't actually real," said Ryan.

As he had expected, he hit the nail right on the head. The librarian looked startled and defensive.

"But being pretty doesn't make her immune to her mother saying things that make her ashamed to go out in public."

"She really told you that?"

"No," said Ryan. "I saw it. I saw her mother say something that made Bizzy change completely. It was a wreck of a girl I helped make it here today. I told her she could hide in the library until she was ready to face other people."

"Why would you say that?"

"Because she's going to get the lecture notes of the best student in the junior class," said Ryan, "and because I know for a fact that you have never narked on a student who hid out in the library crying."

"She's crying?"

"I don't know," said Ryan. "My guess is, not. My guess is that she's such a total introvert that if you try to go comfort her she'll run right out of the library and back out of the school and *then* where will she go? What will happen to her? Books are her safe haven, at home and here at school. Please let her hide in the books for a while, knowing that she won't lose a day of school."

"They'll look for her when she's reported absent."

"Let me take that up with Hardesty. *Mr.* Hardesty. Okay?"

"Why do I let students walk all over me?"

That's between you and your therapist, Ryan did not say. The words that actually came out of his mouth were, "Because you're a good person." He would have said her name if he could remember what it was. But he didn't dare look at the nameplate on the desk. Should have done that when he first walked up.

"Good person, pushover," she said, waggling her hand as if to show there was no difference.

"Good person," said Ryan, as if it were the answer to a serious question. "But now *I* need to get to class."

"Yes, you do," said the librarian. Mrs. Medena, said her nameplate.

"Thanks for looking after my friend, Mrs. Medena," he said.

"You're welcome for being such a doormat," said Mrs. Medena.

"She and her mother are too close, Mrs. Medena," said Ryan. "And a thousand miles apart. They know how to hurt each other. But Bizzy needs her mother to figure out how to love her."

Mrs. Medena's eyes teared up a little.

"Get to class, you rotten little con man," she said.

Ryan didn't stick around to argue. Because despite her joking tone, she had nailed what he was, and if he stayed any longer she'd get ticked off enough to go confront Bizzy.

Ryan made it to class before attendance was reported at ten after. He took just a moment to con Hardesty into not reporting Bizzy absent. "If the nurse sends her home," whispered Ryan, "then *she'll* report her absence. And either way, I'll be sharing my notes with her."

"That's no compensation for not being in class."

Ryan grinned. "Come on, Mr. Hardesty, you know my notes are better than yours."

"You're a sphincter, de Burg," said Hardesty. But he didn't mark Bizzy absent. So Mrs. Horvat would not be phoned, would not have an excuse to come down to the school and raise a stink about her missing daughter.

I'm fooling good people by playing on their kindness and compassion, thought Ryan. I'm using their virtues against them.

And I feel just fine about it.

9

Ryan led the way into the conference room, with Bizzy, head tipped downward, following behind. The only adult in the room had to be Dr. Withunga; the others must be the kids in GRUT, the ones with micropowers. The micropots. Aaron was not among them. Ryan asked about him.

"He doesn't usually come to the meetings," Dr. Withunga explained. Only it wasn't an explanation.

"Why not?" asked Ryan.

"He doesn't think he has a micropower," said Dr. Withunga.

"Then how did he identify me?" asked Ryan. "I thought that was his micropower."

"He calls it a secondhand micropower," said a teenage girl. "Like, it's a powerful thing to build an airplane, and a powerful thing to fly one. But to *see* one in the sky and know what it is, that's nothing. Says Aaron."

"And that's all that needs to be said about someone who is not here," said Dr. Withunga, sounding a little testy. "We have a new member. His name is Ryan Burke."

"Hello, Ryan," said the others, in good twelve-step program form.

"And this is—" Ryan began, but Dr. Withunga cut him off.

"We all know Bizzy Horvat," she said. "I see she's pretending to be invisible today."

"How do you all know her?" asked Ryan.

Nobody answered.

"I've met with them before," said Bizzy quietly.

Ryan was irritated. That would have been useful information. But he didn't pursue the point. "I don't even know why I'm here," he said.

"Because you aren't anywhere else," said the same girl. "You have to be *somewhere*."

"So this is a very basic philosophy course?" asked Ryan.

"Allow me to introduce Dahlia," said Dr. Withunga.

Dahlia smiled. It wasn't a nice smile.

"I'm thrilled to make your acquaintance," said Ryan, looking at her with dead eyes.

And then he was yawning. A deep, long yawn, like a lion preening as it rises to its feet after a nap.

"Stop it, Dahlia," said Dr. Withunga. "We don't use our micropowers against each other."

"As if *you* haven't already determined whether he's an innie or an outie," said Dahlia.

"She made me yawn?" asked Ryan.

"I did not," said Dahlia. "Not *every* yawn is mine."

"That one was," said Dr. Withunga. "Don't insult my intelligence. Dahlia makes people yawn, which partially incapacitates them."

"Good for you," said Ryan mildly.

"My own micropower is pathetic," said Dr. Withunga.

"Not," said a boy.

"She can tell whether your belly button is an innie or an outie," said Dahlia. "And it *is* pathetic."

"She knows that information whether she can see you or not," said the boy. "So you can't sneak up on her, because she's aware that a belly button is approaching her from behind."

Ryan could see that it might be useful, after all. It just *sounded* silly.

"We all took a drive of up to an hour to get to this meeting, so what's the big deal?" asked another girl, who looked old enough to be in college. "What can *he* do?"

"According to Aaron," said Dr. Withunga, "Ryan Burke does the exact right thing, very quickly and accurately."

"He hasn't done anything right yet," said the college girl.

"In an emergency, Jannis. When someone he cares about is in dire need. He saved somebody from a bee sting recently. He saw the danger and took action that involved putting the bee in his own mouth," said Dr. Withunga. She looked to Ryan for confirmation. He didn't give any sign.

"So he does the exact right thing for an idiot," said Jannis.

"What do *you* do?" asked Ryan.

"I always know high E," said Jannis. "That's very useful when tuning a guitar."

"You know it, but can you *produce* that pitch?" asked Ryan.

"Oh, now you're testing *us*?" asked Jannis.

"Yes," said Ryan.

"Enough," said Dr. Withunga.

"No ma'am," said Ryan. "She *says* she can do something, but why should I believe it?"

"I've never heard her do it," said Dahlia.

"How would we verify it if she did?" asked the boy.

"Find a piano?" said Dahlia.

"I've heard her," said Dr. Withunga, "and I've verified it with a pitch pipe and a church organ." She said it with finality. "Can we stop the competitive challenges and move ahead?"

"What are we moving *toward*?" asked Ryan. "What's the point of meeting? I don't need Dahlia to teach me how to yawn. I'm not tuning a guitar. What do *you* do?" Ryan asked the boy.

"I know where the spiders are," he answered. "I'm Mitch. Please don't step on spiders around me. I can feel their pain. I know when they die, and I know whether it was deliberate arachnicide or not."

"Do you *like* spiders?" asked Ryan.

"I don't keep them as pets or take them for walks through the neighborhood," said Mitch. "But I care about them and their well-being. And before you ask, there are nine spiders in this room, but eight of them are very small—just little red dots on the wall."

"Thanks for the information. If I ever need to yawn or get a spider census or find out if my navel pokes out or in, I know where to come." Ryan rose to his feet. "This isn't a club I want to join."

To his surprise, Bizzy spoke quietly. "I do," she said.

"Your mother denied us permission to talk with you," said Dr. Withunga. "I'm not supposed to allow you to attend a meeting."

"I gave myself permission to be here," said Bizzy, still speaking very softly.

"You're a minor," said Dr. Withunga. "I have to respect the rights of your parent—"

Bizzy interrupted her. "When she triggers me to have one of these pretty-fits, she has no further rights."

"Pretty-fit?" asked Mitch.

Bizzy lifted her face and looked at him full on. Mitch gasped audibly and recoiled a little as if he had been slapped. But he couldn't take his eyes off her.

Even the girls in the room were riveted.

"She triggered me this morning as I was leaving the house. She did it on purpose, as a punishment, knowing that it would make it impossible for me to function at school."

Nobody said anything. They all understood why she wouldn't be able to function. Nobody *around* her would be able to function.

Ryan realized that yes, he saw her beauty, but it didn't actually increase his feelings toward her. His devotion to her, his *love* for her, wasn't about beauty. It was about knowing her. Talking with her. So the beauty was just an extra. Like a wardrobe item.

Except that it left him gasping just like everybody else. If he didn't already know her, this face she was wearing today would instantly convince him that she was so far out of his league that he would never approach her.

That was when Aaron Withunga showed up. Door opened, there he was. He stood there, holding the door open, staring at Bizzy.

"Please come in and sit down, Aaron," said Dr. Withunga. "You're defeating the air-conditioning in this room."

Aaron deliberately closed his eyes, then turned his head away from Bizzy and made a show of blindly groping for his seat. His limp made it seem especially random, until Dahlia said, "Aaron, if you use this as an excuse to pretend to accidentally grope me or anybody else, you will yawn continually for the rest of your miserable life."

"With *that* in the room, you imagine that *you* are somehow irresistible to cripples?" Aaron took a seat against the wall, not with the others.

Dr. Withunga turned to Bizzy, squinting a little, as if the sight dazzled her eyes. "Bizzy, could you, um, put that away?" asked Dr. Withunga.

"Ordinarily I can switch it off at will," said Bizzy. "But when my mother the witch triggers me, I'm stuck like this for at least a day, usually longer." But then she looked downward, ducked her head, put a hand up to half-conceal her face. It helped.

"Can somebody explain," said Ryan, "what the point of a meeting like this is supposed to be?"

"Yes," said Dr. Withunga. "Jannis, will you do the honors?"

"Why me?" said Jannis. "I'm not the expert here."

"None of us is," said Dr. Withunga. "Why do we meet?"

"We're pretty sure," said Jannis, "that being around other micropots increases our power. We get stronger effects. Mitch can notice spiders that are farther away. Dahlia can make you yawn so wide you not only cry, you also wet your pants."

Bizzy gave a low chuckle. "That's serious yawning," she said softly.

"So if there's ever a urine shortage," said Ryan, "you all get together and Dahlia presses the urine out of you with a yawn."

"Several lives have been saved," said Dr. Withunga, "by people using their micropowers. So it's better to listen and learn than to show off your clever skepticism."

Ryan clammed up.

"We also help each other by scientifically testing each other's powers. Their limitations and possibilities. We've done some sessions where we tested Dahlia's range. She can yawn somebody up to about fifty yards away."

"Forty-one meters," said Dahlia. "I try to live metrically."

"Beyond that," Dr. Withunga continued, "her power drops off pretty quickly."

"It took a few sessions to get that information," said Jannis.

"There's no way to test me," said Ryan. "Because if what I do is really a micropower, I can't fake it. Either there's really an emergency affecting somebody I care about, or there isn't."

"That's a potential problem," said Dr. Withunga. "But that's why we meet. Because at some point, somebody might think of a way to measure your potential."

"But I don't care about measuring it," said Ryan, "because whatever I've done during a time like that turned out to be right, so it's already working well enough."

"Confident, aren't we," murmured Jannis.

"It's only happened twice, so yes," said Ryan. "Both those times, I just did stuff and it was right."

"So what if the third time you *aren't* right?" asked Jannis.

"Then it's a pretty lousy little micropower, isn't it?" said Ryan.

Again a short laugh from Bizzy. And from Mitch, too. "He's got a point," said Mitch. "We've never actually tested any of our powers for basic lousiness."

"Yes we have," said Dahlia. "All the time."

"No one knows your mental process during an episode, Ryan," said Dr. Withunga. "But the next time it happens, it might be good to try to remember exactly what it felt like. And how quickly you figured out what to do, for instance. And whether you 'know' to take actions that you've never heard of before, like palming your bee into your mouth."

"It wasn't *my* bee," said Ryan.

"It was mine," said Bizzy softly. "He was saving me."

"Because you're so beautiful," said Mitch, only a little mockingly.

"Because he's my friend," said Bizzy.

Ryan nodded. In his own heart, he was far more than a friend. But "friend" would do for now.

"So how often do you meet?" Ryan asked. "What sort of homework should I do?"

"If you don't have an emergency to solve, then you can't do any homework, can you," said Dr. Withunga. "But you can think back on how it was when you did it before. See if you can figure out how it works. What the rules are."

"It's a game now?" asked Ryan.

"There are always rules. Gravity. Inertia. All those natural laws are boundaries," said Dr. Withunga. "We can use the boundaries to figure out just how far we can push things."

"I can make spiders dance like the Rockettes," said Mitch.

"*Make* them?" asked Jannis.

"Entreat them to invade a room and scare the crap out of everybody," said Mitch.

"And they do whatever you ask," said Ryan.

"Not really," Aaron said to Ryan, shaking his head. "Rockettes."

"So far, I got them to do everything I thought of that was possible. Can't make a spider fly or swim." Mitch grinned. "At least, not so far."

"So we meet," said Ryan, "to strengthen our micropowers and then to demonstrate them and test them and find out the limits."

"And maybe stretch them to do more than we thought we could do," said Dahlia. "I've done ride-alongs with police guys on patrol, and they found it a lot easier to subdue drunks who were yawning. Even though yawning is sometimes a trigger for vomiting."

"The whole group didn't come?" asked Ryan.

"Only so much room in a cop car," said Dahlia. "All that mattered was we proved the point—we weaponized yawning."

"Sounds great, if you're trying to help one side in a war," said Ryan.

"We're not the Avengers or the X-Men," said Dr. Withunga.

"Not even the Justice League," said Aaron.

"But we'd like to find practical real-world uses for our micropowers," said Dr. Withunga.

"Some are easier to do that with than others," said Jannis.

"Sometimes one of us has saved lives," said Mitch.

"But he's not here," said Dahlia. "He lives in North Carolina, and it's a three-hour drive for him to get up to Charlottesville."

"Unlike our superconvenient one- or two-hour drives," said Aaron.

"We only have a select few authorities in the regular world that we can work with," said Dahlia. "Most of them would regard us as too ridiculous to take seriously."

To which Mitch added, gesturing toward Bizzy, "But none of them would think *she's* ridiculous."

"None of them would be able to think straight, with her in the room," said Aaron.

"When she has her glamor," said Dr. Withunga. "Since it's come up, let's talk about that."

"Let's not," said Bizzy.

"When we're first discussing someone's micropower," said Dr. Withunga, "we need to ascertain the rules. How it works, when it works, what parts are under control. A methodical approach. We can't call it *scientific*, because every micropower is different."

"Let's discuss Ryan's micropower," said Bizzy. "He's actually interested."

"Not much to discuss," said Ryan. "I've been trying to think it through. It's only happened twice, and both times involved bees. So I don't know if I have some ability related to bees, or if it's about a sense of emergency that triggers it."

"What are we talking about here?" asked Jannis.

"He gets really fast," said Aaron. "And he seems to know *exactly* the right thing to do. No hesitation."

"Believe me, that's not my usual pattern," said Ryan. "I never know the right thing to do or say."

"Like regular people," said Bizzy. "And you say the right thing a lot of the time."

"I'm not stupid or completely inept," said Ryan. Then he thought of how tongue-tied he sometimes was around Bizzy. "Not usually, anyway. But the two times this thing kicked in, it had to do with a bee getting tangled in the hair of somebody I was responsible for." Whereupon Ryan told them about the time he cut his sister's hair and flicked the stinger off her neck, and the time he pulled a living bee out of Bizzy's hair and put it in his mouth.

"Wow," said Mitch. "How did *that* feel, a bee in your mouth?"

"Pretty good," said Ryan, "compared to having it sting me."

"Can't believe it didn't," said Dahlia.

"That's why I wondered if I had some kind of a knack with bees," said Ryan. "If that's my micropower, it has pretty limited application. But I've never been able to, like, control bees. Or I would have made the bee leave Bizzy alone, instead of having to pull it out of her hair."

"Or you just haven't found your ability to control bees yet," said Dahlia. "It took me a while to figure out I could make people yawn without yawning myself."

"That's right," said Dr. Withunga. "It takes time and experimentation."

"If my micropower is only triggered by emergencies," said Ryan, "then it's hard to set up an experiment. I'm not interested in putting people into emergency situations to see if I can save them. Especially if it's a non-bee emergency and I can't actually help them."

"If you can go into your hyperspeed mode with other stuff," said Mitch, "you'd make a great cop."

"A career I do not aspire to," said Ryan.

"Civilization needs cops," said Mitch.

"I agree," said Ryan. "That doesn't mean I want to be one."

"What do you plan to become?" asked Dr. Withunga.

"A dad," said Ryan. "And a husband."

"So, plenty of emergency work in *those* jobs," said Dr. Withunga.

"And plenty of ways to screw it up," said Ryan.

"You're independently wealthy?" asked Jannis. "Or do you plan to marry a wealthy woman?"

"I'll have a job," said Ryan. "When I learn a skill that's more complicated and valuable than taking out the garbage and doing my own laundry."

"I think we're getting personal without being productive," said Dr. Withunga, to Ryan's gratitude. "Ryan's micropower seems to be such that he'll simply have to be observant the next time he has an emergency. There are questions, though, that he can think about. For instance, does this micropower kick in only when somebody *else* needs your help, or can you do it to save yourself?"

Ryan shrugged. "I don't have a lot of emergencies. Like, none so far, that I know of. I've had some—falling out of a tree I was climbing, tripping on things—but I haven't noticed any particular ability to get out of stuff like that."

"So maybe your ability only deals with helping other people," said Dr. Withunga.

"Who, though?" asked Dahlia. "Anybody? Or people you know?"

"Or people you like?" asked Jannis.

"Or people you love?" asked Mitch, looking pointedly at Bizzy. But it didn't sound like he was taunting Ryan.

"I was thinking," said Ryan, "maybe it's people I have responsibility for. Bizzy's mother charged me to look after her on the way home. Keep her from getting hurt."

"Not in those words," said Bizzy.

"The meaning was clear enough," said Ryan. "And my mom asked me to help with Dianne when she got stung. I just figured out the right things to do because it was my job. I kind of *knew*."

"And that 'kind of' knowing—that's your micropower," said Dr. Withunga.

"Not completely," said Aaron. "I saw him. He was amazingly smooth and quick. He not only knew, he just *did* it, without hesitation."

"Nobody's ever called me smooth before," said Ryan. A few people chuckled at that.

"Our micropowers," said Dr. Withunga, "fall into three categories, with plenty of overlap. First, there are things we just know, like my ability to know about people's belly buttons. I don't do anything, the knowledge is just there in my mind. Is that how it is for you, Mitch?"

"Yep," said Mitch. "I just know, without looking, without even thinking about it."

"Then there's the stuff we can do with our own bodies," said Dr. Withunga. "Like Lanny."

Ryan looked around.

"He couldn't come today," said Dr. Withunga.

"He makes everything around him smell better," said Dahlia.

Jannis corrected her. "He neutralizes odors. He makes it not smell at all."

"The important thing is that he doesn't choose to do it," said Dr.

Withunga. "He's aware of it, especially when it wears him out. But his skin seems to respond without any information even going to his brain about it. Totally a reflex of his own body."

"He must have been great as a baby," said Bizzy. "Diapers that didn't stink."

Dr. Withunga didn't take it as a joke. "We don't know when his micro-power kicked in. With most people, it happens near the time of puberty, but other people get their micropowers when they're younger."

"I was about ten the first time," said Ryan.

Bizzy looked like she was about to say something, but she stopped herself.

"Come on, Bizzy," said Dr. Withunga kindly. "It's okay to tell us."

She considered for a moment more and then said, "Mine was triggered when I was three." Again she hesitated, on the verge of saying something else.

Dr. Withunga held up a hand to keep others from speaking. And she waited for Bizzy.

"Mine wasn't born in me," said Bizzy. "Mine came as a curse."

Dr. Withunga didn't say anything, though Ryan could see that she was considering the idea.

"Who or what was it that cursed you?" asked Dr. Withunga.

"Her mother," said Ryan softly, because he knew Bizzy would have a hard time saying it.

"Interesting," said Dr. Withunga. "She cursed you with great beauty?"

"Her curses are temporary," said Bizzy.

"But your glamor persists," said Dr. Withunga.

"She only has one curse, usually," said Bizzy. "She says to somebody, 'You're so clumsy,' or 'You're such a klutz,' and then for the next few hours or the next couple of days, they trip and fall, or drop things, or cut them-selves, or bump into things."

"Dangerous," said Jannis.

"Very," said Bizzy. "But she's never done that one on me or my brother."

"You're saying that's your mother's micropower?" asked Dr. Withunga.

"I don't know," said Bizzy. "She told me she was a witch, and that's always been as good an explanation as any other."

"It's a micropower," said Aaron. "She clumsied me once. I was just passing by her, but I could feel that she had a micropower. A strong one. And then she said, 'Clumsy of you,' and I fell flat on my face. The effect lasted all the next day. I had to be *so* careful."

"Sorry," said Bizzy.

"And she cursed you with beauty?" asked Dr. Withunga.

"I don't know if she meant to," said Bizzy. "But I came into the room wearing a new dress that we just got from Goodwill, and I twirled in it, and she said, 'You're so pretty.' And then she gasped, looking at me."

"This is so helpful," said Dr. Withunga. "How clear are your memories of that time?"

"Very," said Bizzy.

"So let's think of a few things, all right?" asked Dr. Withunga. "For instance, could you feel your face changing?"

Bizzy closed her eyes and thought.

"Can you feel your face changing even now, when the glamor comes over you?" Dr. Withunga persisted.

"It's usually under my control. I work on keeping my face relaxed. Regular. But if I want to wear that face, I can choose to do it. A bunch of muscles tightening in certain ways."

"And did that happen the first time?"

"Yes," said Bizzy. "Not as clearly as now, not as quickly, but yes. That was the first time I realized I even *had* those muscles."

"Did you practice with them?"

Bizzy blushed, which only made her more beguiling. "After it wore off. The third day, I looked in the mirror and it was gone. I was just regular again. And so I tried to flex those same muscles again."

"Like learning to wiggle my ear," said Ryan. "I noticed that when I smiled really broadly, my ears went up. So I tried to isolate those muscles and I practiced until I could raise my left ear without smiling at all."

"Just *one* ear?"

Ryan shrugged. "It's the one I controlled first, and that was enough to establish me as a genuinely weird kid."

"A status you aspired to," said Jannis.

"I was a five-year-old boy," said Ryan. "You always want to be able to do something that makes your friends go, 'Wow.'"

"Like that, I suppose," said Bizzy. For the first time, she was deliberately drawing the attention back to herself. "I worked on it, until I could pretty much get the effect on my own. Whenever I wanted. And over the years, it got better. Smoother."

"Until it stuck that way," said Ryan.

Bizzy whirled on him. "It never," she said sharply.

"I figured you didn't know," said Ryan. "It's not usually full-on drop-dead stunning like *this*, but all the time, when you're walking along the street, through the halls at school, it's like your face is flickering on the edge of looking like this. People stare, and I think that's why."

Bizzy shook her head. "When I'm not doing it, it isn't there."

"You haven't seen yourself," said Ryan. "I'm only telling you because you need to know. It's like your face *wants* to go this way and kind of tries to. I bet you keep reminding yourself to relax your face."

Bizzy was about to make some retort, but she stopped. "Maybe," she said.

"I'm not making it up," said Ryan. "I'm not the only one who notices. People glance at you and see the glamor, and then watch you to see if it happens again."

"That happened to you?"

"Weirdly, not at all on the first day I knew you," said Ryan. "You were just a girl I was leading to class and kind of talking to."

"You wouldn't know what my face was like that first day," said Bizzy. "You barely ever looked at me."

The other kids chuckled.

Ryan nodded. "I didn't have much experience talking to pretty girls."

"Or *any* girls," said Dahlia.

"Yeah, like that," Ryan answered. Dahlia *was* taunting him, but she was also correct, so there was no point in taking umbrage. "I didn't really notice it until I saw you moving into the house that night."

"What, you're neighbors?" asked Dahlia.

"Next door?" asked Mitch.

"Next *wall*," said Ryan. "They're in the other side of the duplex."

Mitch rolled his eyes, and Ryan imagined he knew why. Living in the same *house* as all that beauty? Insane. Even if there was a wall between them. Since it drove Ryan crazy sometimes, he assumed Mitch was imagining the situation. Only what Mitch didn't know was that Ryan fell in love with her for her conversation and kindness and humor and all, not her face. Her regular face was pretty enough, but it wasn't distracting. He felt as though he loved the *person* Bizzy, not the glamor.

"So you think your mother caused this?" asked Dr. Withunga, bringing them back to the methodical discussion.

Bizzy shrugged. "When I was three, I was sure of it. Since then, I've learned that when she tells other people things like 'You're so pretty,' or—my brother, for instance—'You're so strong,' or 'You're so athletic,' it doesn't have any particular effect. Only 'You're so clumsy' or 'What a klutz.'"

"But she can still trigger Bizzy's glamor," said Ryan, using Dr. Withunga's term for it. "She did it this morning, as a kind of punishment. 'You're so beautiful.'"

"It switched it on," said Bizzy, "and it'll last all day. Maybe tonight I can sleep it off and have a more normal day tomorrow."

"So she uses it as a punishment?" said Dr. Withunga.

"It's a curse," said Bizzy, "and she knows it."

"But safer than making you clumsy," said Dr. Withunga.

"I think she actually loves me," said Bizzy, "so she doesn't want me damaged. But a witch like her—what does she know of love?"

Dr. Withunga didn't contradict her. She just nodded.

"She's not really a witch," said Jannis. "No such thing."

"You're so sure of that?" asked Dr. Withunga. "Oh, the kind of witch they looked for in Salem—that's just silly. Trafficking with the devil? I don't think so. But witches were usually identified because they muttered curses that came true. 'No milk,' and a nursing mother's dugs would dry up."

"'Dugs'?" asked Aaron.

"The word they used in court documents from the period," said Dr. Withunga.

"You've researched witchcraft?" asked Ryan.

"Micropowers would be interpreted different ways in different times.

Most so-called wizards and witches were charlatans, of course, using illusion and misdirection to *seem* to do transformations and curses. Maybe even hypnosis and suggestion. But some of the things people saw might have been real. The result of micropowers. So of course I researched it, once I became convinced that micropowers existed."

In a quavering voice, Jannis asked, "Are you a good witch or a bad witch?"

"I'm a witch with a very small and barely useful power," said Dr. Withunga. "But right now we're talking about Bizzy, who has a very strong power. She's able to change herself, her face in particular, in a way that is extraordinarily pleasing and attractive to other members of her species."

"We used to have a dog," said Bizzy, "and she whined whenever I had the face on."

"Interesting," said Dr. Withunga. "Because that raises another question."

The others waited only a moment before Dahlia said, "What?"

"Just trying to phrase it clearly," said Dr. Withunga. "We don't actually know yet whether Bizzy's micropower is just something she does to herself, changing her face, or whether there's also something that emanates from her, like the way Dahlia makes other people yawn. It might just be that it's her face changes alone that make people regard her with . . . let's call it 'astonishment.'"

"Yes, let's," said Jannis.

"Or maybe 'worship,'" said Mitch.

"Please no," said Bizzy.

"Or is it an emotional thing also, something that even a dog can feel?" said Dr. Withunga. "For instance, Aaron has told me, and Ryan has implied, that passersby look at you even when you're not wearing your glamor. Could that be an emotional thing that you give off all the time, to one degree or another? It's hard to test for that, but you already have some observational data. From Ryan and Aaron."

"Mine's pretty clear," said Aaron. "People who aren't looking at her turn and stare when she comes within range. I think your hypothesis of an emotional connection is spot-on."

"But you're immune?" asked Ryan.

"Heck no," said Aaron. "But I'm trying to be scientific, so I force myself to look at other people instead of her. They stare, with or without the glamor. Well, not *stare*, but keep looking at her covertly, pretending that they're not, because they know it's rude to stare."

"Sounds like I'm a traffic hazard," said Bizzy. She said it in kind of a joking way, but she also sounded worried and hurt.

"That's right," said Aaron. "But when you're not full-on stunning, people can still operate heavy machinery."

"Maybe she could quell a riot," said Mitch. "Just by standing there looking pretty."

"Or cause one," said Jannis.

"We're not going to get answers today," said Dr. Withunga. "It's just like with all the rest of us. We ask questions, we wonder about possibilities, and then we work on figuring out how it works and how to get more control over it. Learn to switch it on or off, which Bizzy has already done— at least the on-switch part. But it's up to her now for a while. When she knows more, we'll discuss her micropower again."

"Next time," said Mitch, "would it be okay if she either comes without the, um, glamor, or, like—"

"Wears a bag over her head?" said Dahlia.

"A mask," said Mitch.

"No mask, no bag," said Dr. Withunga. "We learn to bear each other's micropowers. Even if it takes a lot of gratuitous yawning before some people get control of themselves." She raised her eyebrows at Dahlia, who looked defiantly unrepentant.

"I only yawned people who deserved it," said Dahlia.

"In your ignorant opinion," said Jannis.

Dahlia turned languidly toward her. "Are you feeling really relaxed, Jannis?" she asked.

"You really don't want to get into a micropower battle with Jannis," said Dr. Withunga.

"I'm tired of nobody knowing what Jannis's *real* micropower is," said Dahlia. "It isn't fair. And that bull about knowing high E is just . . ."

Jannis gave a tight little smile. Then she parted her lips and emitted a soft high-pitched note, like the chirping of a shy bird.

"I'm sure that's a high E," said Ryan, "give or take six tones."

"It isn't fair that she doesn't tell," said Dr. Withunga. "But if Jannis is wise, she will continue not to tell. I certainly won't tell on her."

"And we're not trusted," said Mitch.

"For all we know," said Dahlia, "she uses her power on us all the time."

"I know that she has never used it on any of you, because there has never been either a need or a provocation," said Dr. Withunga.

Jannis sat stiffly in her chair, not looking at anybody.

Ryan thought that made Jannis the most interesting person here. After Bizzy, of course.

"I think," said Dr. Withunga, "that we've gone as far as we can today, with both Ryan and Bizzy. We'll have to look into forming a group here in Charlottesville, because we can't expect all of you to make this trip on a regular basis."

"I can do it," said Jannis.

"Because you go to school here," said Dr. Withunga. "It would be kind of you to help form the nucleus of the new group."

"If my mother lets me take part," said Bizzy.

"That's between you and her," said Dr. Withunga. "I wish you could get her to take part in the group, because her micropower sounds fascinating."

"There's more than one sense in which she's a witch," said Bizzy.

Ryan couldn't help but agree. Mrs. Horvat didn't *look* like Margaret Hamilton in *The Wizard of Oz*, but she carried the same attitude of general malevolence. She was definitely not like Glinda, the good witch of the north.

"We'll figure out what's possible," said Ryan. "But I don't know if my micropower is going to be worth studying, or even *possible* to study. I kind of hope I never find out, because I don't want any more emergencies."

"Because you're not sure you will always be able to save the person you have responsibility for," said Dr. Withunga.

"Yes," said Ryan. He did not add that it was also because he clearly remembered putting that bee in his mouth, and he was afraid his micropower would require him to take a bullet for somebody or stand between them and a speeding car. He wasn't sure how ready he was to die for love. Or even to get stung for it.

10

Errol Dell was the kicker for the Vasco da Gama High School football team, and such was their offense that he was called upon often in every game. Because he was strong and fairly accurate, he was the team's top scorer by a wide margin, and there was talk that he would be scouted by some major colleges.

So it was not surprising that he moved through Vasco da Gama High School like a god, followed by worshipers and worshipful glances.

It was also not surprising that he became a particular target of Defenseur Fabron, Ryan's best friend.

Defenseur wasn't really a bully. He never picked on anybody weaker than himself. Instead, he singled out people of arrogance and authority. Principals and teachers and counselors hated him because of his mastery of the pointed remark—usually nothing that could get him expelled or even sent to the office, but nevertheless a barb that stuck and stung and often got repeated by other kids around school.

He got people to call one English teacher "Professor True-or-False" because of his reliance on that easiest-to-grade and most worthless type of exam. The remark, though, was simply this, while yet another test was being passed out: "Wow, Mr. Pritchard, you really really love true-false tests. I bet they take almost *no* time or thought to grade."

The voice was enthusiastic and cheerful. The class didn't even laugh. But the new nickname spread through the school very quickly, and Pritchard overheard "Professor True-or-False" being spoken even in the faculty lounge, more than once. But how could he send Defense to the office for making a statement that sounded rather admiring and that was also demonstrably true?

Defense, however, did not have much experience with the vanity of athletes, who did not have the kind of boundaries and self-discipline that teachers were required to have. Errol Dell's godlike saunter through the halls of Vasco da Gama was an irresistible provocation for Defense, whose attempts to humiliate without provoking punishment were not quite as successful with athletes as they were with teachers, counselors, and the principal.

There was the matter of "Foot-Man," the nickname that Defense attached to Errol after the first game in which Errol was the top scorer for the da Gama Explorers. It was actually a good nickname for a kicker, and Errol took it that way for quite a while, until he started hearing that it was being used to imply that the only functioning part of Errol was his foot, or that Errol had an unnatural fondness for his own and other people's feet.

There was no way to prove that such weirdness was Defense's doing or his intent, but Errol began to get a chip on his shoulder about the nick-name, so Defense's persistent use of it became a provocation.

When this became obvious, Defense switched to just calling him, and referring to him, as "Foot." It soon became a chant at games, the entire da Gama side of the stadium chanting, "Foot! Foot! Foot!" whenever Errol came out to kick.

Errol claimed it was distracting, and if he ever missed, he blamed it on the chant. Defense claimed that Errol's completion average had improved since the chanting began.

"Statistics don't lie," Defense said when Errol began haranguing him one day. After that, Errol knew he would look stupid for complaining to Defense about the chant. It wasn't as if Defense could have stopped it, anyway.

But the day after Ryan's first meeting with GRUT, Defense got all excited about the possibilities of his micropower. "So is it just bees and girls, or is it, like, anybody you really, truly love?"

"I didn't even *like* my sister when I unstung her, so no, I don't think so."

"Not liking your sister doesn't mean you don't love her," said Defense. "And anyway, I know you love *me*. You do love me, don't you, Ryan? Oh, admit it, Ryan, you love me!"

Since they were in the cafeteria at lunch, and Defense was getting louder and louder, Ryan had to say yes just to shut him up. And it was true, as long as everyone understood that it was a friendship kind of love.

"So I'm betting," said Defense, "that we can put your micropower to a test. For instance, if something bigger than a bee is threatening to harm me, I bet you'll know exactly how to prevent it, and you'll do it, even if it's a kind of thing you normally wouldn't do, like putting a bee in your mouth."

"Defense, I wouldn't put a bee in my mouth to keep you from being run through a car compactor."

"That's what you say right now, when I'm nowhere near a car compactor. And besides, bee-mouthing probably wouldn't be the correct action to take in order to save me in such a case."

"What I'm saying, Defense, is that if you get yourself into a dangerous situation on purpose just to test me, I won't help you. Neither my sister nor Bizzy did anything to attract the bee."

"That you know of."

"Period."

"Tell you what. You meet me after school and we'll discuss it further."

"I'm walking Bizzy home tonight."

"No you're not," said Defense. "Not till play practice is over."

"She dropped out of the play."

"If she did, she hasn't told anybody," said Defense. "It would have been all over the school, and it isn't."

"Whatever," said Ryan. "If you do something to get yourself killed, I don't plan to be there to watch it."

Defense put on his mock-weepy face and said, "You'd make me die alone? Like a death-row inmate who killed all his friends and family so there's nobody left?"

"That's exactly right."

Defense pretended to be in a huff as he carried his tray to the return.

But at the end of the day, Ryan made it a point to intercept Defense at their adjacent lockers in order to keep him from doing something stupid.

Unfortunately, Defense had already started his provocation of Errol Dell before even opening his locker. It happened that Errol was swanning his way through the after-school crowd when Defense called out to him, "Hey, it's Athlete's Foot, the Hero Fungus!"

Errol stopped cold and turned to face Defense from twenty feet away. "Take that back," he said.

"Sorry," said Defense. "*Not* a hero fungus. Just a regular fungus. Treatable with Tinactin—no need for Lamisil."

"Don't ever call me that again," said Errol. The menacing edge to his voice was making people start to back away.

"Sure," said Defense. "'Athlete's Foot' is such a pedestrian name. The scientific name is tinea pedis. Or is it tidea penis? I'm always getting that confused."

Errol lunged toward Defense, but some of Errol's friends restrained him.

"He's not worth it." "Nobody cares what he says." "He's nothing." "No reason to get yourself in trouble over him."

The voices of reason restrained him for now, but Defense saw Ryan arriving right then and grinned at him. "It's sad that Mr. Foot never learned the poem 'Sticks and stones may break my bones, but—'"

"You want broken bones?" shouted Errol.

"Well, not *now*," said Defense. "Not here, inside my beloved high school, with all these witnesses."

"So you want to die alone?"

"No, he doesn't," shouted Ryan. "Don't let him get to you, man."

"When did I start needing advice from *you*, loser?" Errol shot at Ryan.

Ryan realized that he was just making it worse. Errol could take such advice from his friends, but not from a nobody like Ryan. Even though he was in the running for valedictorian of his class. That only made him more of a loser in Errol's eyes.

In the end, as Defense strode boldly past Errol and his entourage, Ryan had no choice but to try to catch up with him. He reached him at the door and grabbed his arm. "Come on, idiot," he pleaded. "Go back inside and hang around with me near the principal's office until Errol gives up and goes home."

"I don't think he'll ever give up now," said Defense. "But it's sweet of you to care."

Ryan tried to talk softly enough that other people wouldn't overhear. "My micropower won't work if you—"

Defense certainly didn't act as if *he* could hear Ryan.

That's when Errol reached the door and shoved Defense hard, tearing him out of Ryan's grasp. Defense staggered and finally fell onto the pavement of the walkway toward the buses.

Errol's friends rushed past Ryan, trying to prevent him from getting anywhere near Defense. But Ryan managed to get off to the side, where he had a perfect view as Errol, instead of letting Defense get up and make some kind of fight out of it, simply kicked him in the ribs.

Kicked him with all the force of a game-winning field goal.

Defense gave a horrible *oof!* that sounded as if all the air he had ever inhaled was discharged at once. That was followed by a high gasp and then a whine that told Ryan that Defense probably had some broken ribs.

So much for my knowing how to save Defense and then doing it. Mine must be a bees-only micropower.

Then he saw Errol getting set to kick Defense again. This time in the face.

It wasn't about keeping Defense pretty. His face was attached to his head, and that kick could cause major brain damage, if it didn't actually kill him outright.

Before he had consciously registered that thought, however, Ryan was already moving, taking three running steps and then launching himself into the air directly toward Errol.

Ryan's right arm was already extended, his fist formed. But instead of presenting the flat of his gathered fingers, he was aiming with the first knuckles of his index and middle fingers, as if to make a precision strike.

And his leap had not had enough loft to allow him to aim at Errol's face. He was at exactly the right position to strike Errol on the Adam's apple.

Ryan had heard somewhere that a direct strike to the larynx could be fatal. He had just enough time and control to aim a bit lower and strike below the larynx.

The blow landed with Ryan's full mass behind it. Errol's body instantly went limp and he fell straight down, with Ryan landing atop him. Ryan expected to be pummeled immediately, to be pushed off Errol.

Instead, it took a few moments before people began to *pull* Ryan off and shove him back. But nobody was trying to hit him or even hurt him. They were trying to look after Errol, who wasn't moving.

Wasn't breathing.

It took a few minutes for the school nurse to be summoned, but she had been an EMT for several years, and within a couple of minutes she had performed an emergency tracheotomy and had Errol breathing again.

By that time, Ryan had helped a groaning, panting Defense to his feet and helped him limp a few yards away.

A few minutes later, the official EMTs arrived in an ambulance, along with a cop car. The cops got all the bystanders into one place and questioned people. The EMTs surrounded Errol and got him into the ambulance, and they were about to leave with him while the school nurse tried to tell them what to do.

Ryan interrupted. "My friend, guys. Defense Fabron. That guy kicked him in the ribs and I think they might be broken."

"In a schoolyard fight?" said the nurse. "I don't think so."

"Errol is the kicker for the football team," said Ryan, "and he can kick a field goal from the forty, they say."

One of the EMTs stayed to look at Defense, and despite the nurse's constant skepticism, he called for another ambulance while he bound up Defense's chest on the outside of his clothes. Ryan insisted on riding in the ambulance with Defense, and when the school nurse protested, the EMTs told her that it would be an excellent plan. Ryan figured they said yes only to annoy the nurse, but motive didn't matter. He got to be in the hospital with Defense and call Defense's mom from there.

By the time she got there, Defense had real bandages around his ribs, and Ryan had used Defense's phone to take a couple of pictures of the massive bruising underneath and how his ribs looked caved in.

"I don't need a picture of that," said Defense. "I can feel it from the inside."

"In case we need it for the trial."

"You think they're going to try Foot for assaulting me?" asked Defense.

"From this moment on, the *only* name you use for him is Errol, got it?"
Defense blinked. "Um."

"Because you picked this fight, you moron. You goaded him."

"Well, words against kicks, man. He shoved me from behind and put
me on the ground and then he kicked me."

"Yeah, he's a kicker. I'm sorry you never thought of that."

"You laid him out, man."

"And that's the trial I'm talking about," said Ryan. "Mine."

"Yours! That was self-defense, man!" said Defense.

"No it wasn't. I wasn't being threatened in any way. I jumped in and
punched him in the throat because he was about to kick *you* in the head."

"Well, duh," said Defense.

"But is that the story that all those kids watching the so-called fight
are going to tell? All those kids who worship Errol and who see you and
me as complete nothings?"

"Who would believe I would pick a fight with Errol Dell?" Defense
asked scornfully.

"Everyone at school," said Ryan.

"Well. Yeah."

Then Defense's mother got there.

And a few minutes later, there were cops. One to question Defense,
the other to talk to Ryan.

Or, as far as Ryan knew, to arrest him. Was fifteen old enough to try him
as an adult? Just in case Errol died and it was going to be a murder charge?

As the cops were approaching, Defense whispered, "What do I tell
'em, Ryan?"

"The same thing I'm going to tell them," Ryan answered. Out loud.
"The whole, honest truth. That way we don't have to get our stories straight."

"Good advice, kid," said Cop A.

Cop B took Ryan by the shoulder and steered him off to somebody's
office, which the hospital people had opened up for him.

Cop B soon became Detective Sergeant Wilbur Nix, and he set down a stack of four cell phones on the desk in front of him. "Before I ask you anything, I'm going to show you what the cell phone videos I confiscated as evidence have to say."

Nix played him the first one. Pretty good angle. It caught Errol's first kick—even showed the toe denting Defense's rib cage. It was an excruciating sight. Not for *America's Funniest.*

Then it was very, very clear that Errol was going to kick Defense even harder in the face. Until Ryan appeared in midair, flying in from out of frame, and straight-armed Errol in the throat. Ryan went back and replayed it and paused right at the point of impact. He nodded. "I tried not to hit him right on the larynx," he said. "And it looks like I did that."

"Yes," said Nix. "The doctors working on Errol Dell say that if your blow had landed on his larynx, it would have been beyond reconstruction. But you did some serious damage, kid. He had to have an emergency trake right there at school. And he's still not breathing through his mouth and nose. He won't be swallowing anything for a while, either."

"But he'll be okay, right?" asked Ryan.

"It depends on how you define 'okay,'" said Nix.

"You can see that he was going to do some serious damage to Defense, right?" asked Ryan.

"Kid. These videos all tell the same story. If you hadn't poked the kid, he'd be facing murder charges, because I don't think your friend on the ground would have survived that kick. Okay? So nobody's going to charge *you* with anything. If the kicker's parents protest, we'll play the videos for them. If there's some kind of community protest, we'll put the videos on television. You saved a life today, kid."

"That was all I hoped for," said Ryan. "Please don't put the videos on TV, though."

"I know, people think you're a fighter, they want to pick fights and take you on," said Nix.

Ryan hadn't thought of that at all. He had only thought how the way he flew in there with his fist extended had a definite Superman vibe to it, as if he could actually fly, and the last thing he needed was for morons to think he actually had a superpower.

But Ryan held his tongue and let Nix think that he was worried about people picking fights.

"So you're not charged with anything," said Nix, "and unless you want police protection against mob violence for taking the top scorer on the Vasco da Gama Explorers out of football for the rest of the year, you won't be seeing us after today."

"I don't think I'll need protection," said Ryan.

A silence hung in the air for a long moment.

"I still want to ask you something," said Nix.

"Okay," said Ryan.

"I've looked at these videos, including the one that actually shows you from the moment you started moving. And here's the thing. You started moving the moment the kicker turned back around to face the kid on the ground. You were *already* moving when the kicking motion first started. Even then, kid, there's no way you could have launched yourself into the air and punched him in the throat before the kick even landed."

"But I did," said Ryan.

"It's like you knew it was going to happen," said Nix.

"Of course I did," said Ryan. "Errol was crazy angry, and what he does is kick. When he turned around, it was clear he wasn't going to go for the ribs again."

"Maybe. But come on, where's the deciding time? You immediately launched yourself at exactly the point where his throat was going to be. Why did you go for the throat?"

"I didn't know I was going for his throat until I was in the air, and his throat was the only thing I could reach with my full strength. So maybe I unconsciously decided that, but I didn't *know* it, like, with my actual brain, until I was almost on him. And all I could do was aim a little lower so I didn't shatter his Adam's apple."

"So you knew you could really mess him up, and you decided not to," said Nix. "Guy was ready to kill your friend, and you decide to take it easy on him?"

"I knew hitting his throat would take him down and stop the kick. That's all I cared about. You think I wanted him dead?"

"Why didn't you?" asked Nix.

Ryan sighed. "Because except for the kick in the head, Defense was begging for it."

Nix sat back. "You're saying Defense picked this fight?"

"He's been riding Errol all year, nicknaming him 'Foot-Man' and then just 'Foot,' and all the other kids took to chanting 'Foot' from the stands, and Errol hated it. But today Defense just pulled out all the stops, in the hallway after school, in front of everybody. Called him 'Athlete's Foot,' which everybody knew would catch on and make Errol's life a living hell. And then when Errol told him to take it back—like that would actually happen—Defense said, 'How about the scientific name,' which is something like tinea pedis, only Defense made all the "E's" long, so it was 'tee-nee-a PEE-dis,' and then he switched it to 'tee-dee-a PEE-nis, and—"

Nix shook his head. "And you think other kids would have picked that up?"

"It would have become 'Teeny Penis' by the third repetition," said Ryan. "And that's the thing about Defense—when he tags you with a nickname, it sticks, everybody hears it, everybody remembers it. He's kind of famous for it, and Errol knew that."

Nix put his hands behind his head. "So he's the football hero of da Gama High, only some pissant kid can tag him with humiliating nicknames whenever he wants."

"I don't think knocking Defense down and kicking him was right," said Ryan, "and he's still my friend. But, Sergeant Nix, Defenseur Fabron can be a real ass-face, and I don't blame Errol for losing it. I only hit him because Defense didn't deserve to die for it."

Nix chuckled wryly. "I never thought I'd hear a story like that from you."

"It's the truth, sir."

"Oh, I believe it," said Nix. "It's just, you were so even-handed. You're supposed to tell me how horrible the kicker was, always kicking sand in your friend's face. But instead, your friend was the sand kicker, am I right?"

"Metaphorically speaking," said Ryan.

"Yeah, I went to high school, too," said Nix. "Metaphorically speaking."

"Sir, did you really mean it when you said I'm not being charged or held or anything?"

"Yes, I did. Even if you had confessed to planning the whole thing, I didn't read you your rights, I didn't have your parents present, and I didn't record the interrogation, so you'd be off on a technicality no matter what. But I saw the videos, and look, I still have to ask you my original question."

"I don't remember what that was."

"I didn't actually ask it yet," said Nix. "Your response was so quick, your leap was so perfectly timed and aimed with just the right amount of thrust, and look, Ryan, I was Army Rangers and I fought in savage special ops and I saw the best of the best, and look, kid, nobody makes a leap like that. Perfect aim. Powerful, when your arms aren't anything, no offense. Buggy whips, that's what they look like. I wouldn't have been surprised if you *broke* your arm punching him like that."

"My elbow is kind of sore."

"Put ice on it. Listen. I need to know. Who the hell did you train with?"

"What?"

"Who taught you moves like that?"

Ryan shook his head. "I've never—I don't train. If I trained, would I have buggy-whip arms?"

"Maybe you're one of those people, those ectomorphs who can't pack on muscle so they're just wiry strong, and they—"

Ryan held out his arm for Nix to palpate. Which he did.

"There's nothing here," said the detective.

"I don't train," said Ryan.

"I don't know how you can lift a fork to your mouth," said Nix.

"Oh, come on," said Ryan. "I think I'm pretty much normal for a kid whose most strenuous activities are walking to school and playing video games."

"You have reflexes like that, accuracy like that, strength in your thighs to make you airborne, and you—"

"My thighs and my calves and my feet are pretty sore, too, now that you mention it," said Ryan.

"You're telling me that all of that was pure adrenaline?"

"I'm telling you that I saw what needed doing and I did it. I didn't stop and think, I didn't know if I *could* do it, I just did it and it worked and I really hope it doesn't lay Errol out for too long because he was totally goaded into it and I don't think it's really in his nature to be, like, murderous."

"But your friend, Defensooer?"

"Defenseur. We call him Defense."

"He's kind of a bully."

"He normally only picks on people in authority. The principal. Teachers. Pokes them, and sure, they hate him, but they aren't going to punch him out. Usually he's subtler, so they can't even get angry with him. Usually."

"Still a bully," said Nix.

"I really am trying to work with him about that," said Ryan.

"Keep trying. Succeed. Because someday he's going to goad the wrong guy, and you won't be there to rescue him."

"Maybe if I'd started the day by punching Defense in the throat," said Ryan.

"Not a bad idea," said Nix.

"The thing is," said Ryan, "I've never punched anybody in the throat before. I've never punched anybody anywhere."

Nix raised his eyebrows.

"I'm a lover, not a fighter," said Ryan, doing his best Rodney Dangerfield from *Back to School*. Which wasn't a good imitation. But Nix seemed to get it.

"Stick with love, then," said Nix. "Because however you did it, you're scary dangerous, my man."

"The world is safe, except when somebody's trying to kill my friend."

By then Nix was standing at the door, about to open it. "Ryan Burke, the kid I saw in that video, if I were going into combat today, I'd want you beside me."

"I don't want to go into combat, sir. Ever."

"Good choice," said Nix. "Because if somebody trained you, you'd be seriously scary."

Then Nix was out the door.

And Ryan was off in search of a way to get back to school in time to walk Bizzy home from play practice. If she was still going to play practice. Didn't she tell him they had already cast somebody else in her part? Why would Defense tell him that she was still in the play?

Was Defense just lying to get Ryan to be there when Errol creamed him?

Or was Bizzy lying when she said she had dropped out?

The buses took a long time. Play practice was over before Ryan got back to school. So whether Bizzy had been at practice or not made no difference. She must have called her mother.

Ryan walked home alone.

Mrs. Horvat met him on the sidewalk in front of the duplex. She looked angry, but she was containing it. "I thought you would be reliable," she said.

"Something came up," said Ryan.

"Bojana told me about the fight," said Mrs. Horvat.

"I tried to prevent it," said Ryan.

"She told me that, too," said Mrs. Horvat.

How had Bizzy known? Maybe she was close enough to hear Ryan begging Defense to go to the principal's office instead of facing Errol.

"She also told me you made one flying leap and laid out that kicking boy with one blow. She told me you saved your friend's life because the kicker was going to break his head."

Ryan said nothing. Because now he realized that Mrs. Horvat wasn't actually angry. She was just being intense.

"I don't know what you are or why you can do such a thing, and I don't need to know. I have just one question. Do you love my daughter as much as you love your friend?"

Ryan nodded. He didn't say, way more, because he didn't really know how to measure two different kinds of love against each other.

"If somebody was attacking her, you defend her like that?" asked Mrs. Horvat.

"I'd do . . . whatever I thought of in the moment," said Ryan.

"Would you die for her?"

Ryan was taken aback by that. "If I'm dead, I can't protect her," he said.

"Good answer," said Mrs. Horvat. "No foolish gestures. Real, practical saving of my daughter, that's what I expect from you."

"That's what I hope to be able to give her," said Ryan.

"Keep walking her home from school," said Mrs. Horvat. "I feel safe about her for the first time in years."

Ryan didn't think now was a good time to ask if Bizzy was still in the play. Best to just go inside his own house and maybe talk to her later tonight, on her back deck.

And then talk to the people at GRUT and see what they thought. See if they could give him some idea of what was going on, and what he should do to maybe get some kind of control over this ability to do the necessary thing even if maybe it might kill somebody.

11

Ryan didn't want to wait a week for the next GRUT meeting. He called Dr. Withunga the next morning before school.

"I've got to talk this out," Ryan told her.

"Fine," she said. "I'll be there right at the close of school today. But it won't be a big group. Probably just me, and Aaron if he feels like it, and I think Jannis will want to come. Will Bizzy be with you?"

"I can't predict. Should I invite her?"

"Your call. And hers, of course. Sure, ask her."

So it was a smaller meeting indeed, since Aaron was not there. Just Jannis and Dr. Withunga, plus Ryan and Bizzy. Because Bizzy had actually brought it up, asking Ryan at lunchtime whether he was going to be at a GRUT meeting soon.

"I think we can safely say that Ryan's micropower isn't about bees," said Bizzy.

Her face was back to normal, which meant pretty and a bit distracting, but not stunning.

"I got Bizzy's mom's seal of approval," said Ryan.

"I'm so happy to hear that," said Bizzy. "Did she ask if you would die for me?"

"I told her I couldn't save you if I was dead," said Ryan.

"Very logical, but that usually doesn't cut much ice with her."

"She took it well," said Ryan. "Look, this isn't about her, it's about what I can do. The problem is that Defenseur absolutely provoked the fight. He *made* it happen. He wanted it to happen, because he thought if he was threatened, my micropower would kick in."

"Which it did," said Jannis.

"But it shouldn't have!" cried Ryan. "I mean, what am I? My friend picks a fight by making really ugly and damaging taunts, and his purpose was to get me to save him. What am I, to nearly kill another kid because my friend provoked him?"

"He was going to kill your friend," said Jannis.

"I thought so, yes, but I didn't *know*. I changed my aim at the last second. Maybe Errol would have changed his. Maybe he planned not to really kick Defense at all."

"Maybe indeed," said Dr. Withunga.

"So I didn't save Defense from the *first* kick, which didn't just break his ribs, it caved them in, and they *haven't* bounced back out, so I think Defense is going to heal up wrong. And I have no idea what's happening to Errol, but Detective Nix said he was in bad shape."

"How was any of this your fault?" asked Jannis.

"I don't think it was, really," said Ryan. "It was Defense's fault, and he was setting me up on purpose, and I *begged* him not to do it, I begged him to *stop*, so—"

"You still feel guilty because you feel responsible," said Dr. Withunga.

"That's just me," said Ryan. "I was actually worried about the bee I had in my mouth. I watched to make sure it was actually flying well, in case my saliva or mucus from my mouth or something was making it impossible for her to fly straight."

"A very active conscience," said Dr. Withunga. "That means you're probably civilized beyond your years. But since there's nothing you can do to repair the physical damage that Defense and Errol have suffered—"

"Dr. Withunga," said Jannis. "Are you planning to go with Ryan to visit Defense in the hospital?"

Dr. Withunga looked at her steadily for a couple of beats and then said, "That's really a very nice idea. I think Ryan plans to go visit his friend anyway, and if you want to come . . ."

Ryan definitely did *not* want either Dr. Withunga *or* Jannis there. But then it occurred to him that something else was going on here. Maybe something connected with Jannis's real micropower. Jannis must have a reason for going along, and Dr. Withunga must also have a reason for letting her.

You've got to trust people, Ryan, he told himself. Jannis doesn't want to talk about her micropower, but maybe she's offering to use it, and that's a big deal. If her micropower was destructive, Dr. Withunga wouldn't let her come along, right?

"As long as we're making it a field trip," said Ryan, "do you want to come along, Bizzy?"

"There's no need for her to come," said Dr. Withunga. "But I have enough room in my car to take all of you, and we can drop Bizzy off at home along the way."

Bizzy looked sharply at Ryan. He could only give a tiny hint of a shrug. How can I know what they're doing, but can you play along as if it made sense?

Maybe she got his silent message, maybe she didn't. What mattered was that she said, "I don't like hospitals, so I'll be just as happy to get started on my homework. And, for what it's worth, I didn't learn *anything* about my own micropower since our last meeting, so I'm glad we're breaking up the meeting without discussing it."

Nobody said anything during the drive home, but about a block away Bizzy asked Dr. Withunga to stop the car. "Just so Mom doesn't see me get out of your car."

"She'll know anyway," said Jannis.

"She's not that kind of a witch," said Bizzy.

"But she's that kind of a mother. Right?" said Jannis.

Bizzy got out of the car and started walking up the block. Dr. Withunga turned the other way so she wouldn't drive past the duplex.

At the hospital, Ryan led Jannis and Dr. Withunga to Defense's room. Defense, whose shirt had been replaced by an open-backed hospital gown, looked annoyed. "I'm glad they left me my pants," he said.

"Sorry to bother you," said Ryan. "I'll set up an appointment with your secretary next time."

"Who is this?" asked Defense. "Your superhero group?"

"Micropower," said Ryan.

"Rare and useless talents," said Jannis.

"Ryan's was useful to *me*," said Defense. "Though it would have been nice if you had stepped in before he caved in my chest. Doctor said the only way to push my ribs back into place is through surgery, and since none of the bone fragments are in a threatening position, he prefers to leave them where they are for now and see what they do."

"Is it really dented in?" asked Jannis. "I've never seen that."

Defense rolled his eyes. "It's the only interesting thing about me now, so I should probably thank Errol for giving me a declivity in my rib cage."

"Declivity," said Jannis. "Oh my." It should have been taken as a taunt— it was just the kind of snotty thing that Defense liked to say. But Defense took it calmly. In fact, he pulled his hospital gown across his body to show where, even under the bandages, there was a pretty deep and obvious dent in the left side of his rib cage.

Without even asking, Jannis reached out and started stroking the bandages over the dent, tracing the outline and then running her fingers *through* the dent. "Lots of pieces," said Jannis. "I bet it would take a doctor hours to get them all back together."

"What are you doing?" asked Defense. But he didn't sound worried. Just curious.

"I plan on a kind of medical career," said Jannis, "and I'm fascinated by the ways that injury can remake the human body without losing any critical function. But I'm surprised your doctor isn't worried about bone fragments working their way to other parts of your body. I mean, what if a bone chip punctured your lung? What if one got over to your heart? Have you gotten a second opinion?"

"My mom asked for one," said Defense. "I was just thinking, Pain doesn't last forever, and chicks dig scars."

"Chicks," said Jannis, shaking her head.

"I didn't make up the saying," said Defense.

"I know," said Jannis. "But you're quoting it wrong."

"I'm quoting the parts that apply," said Defense, a little resentfully.

Jannis pulled her hand away from Defense's bandage and drew his gown back over his chest. But as she did that, Ryan got the weird idea that Defense's dent was nowhere near as deep as it had been when Jannis first reached out to touch it.

They made their goodbyes then, as if the only thing they were there for was for Jannis to touch Defense's injury.

"No, you stay," said Dr. Withunga to Ryan. "You and your friend have things to talk about, I'm sure."

"I'm pretty much fed up with Defense today," said Ryan, "and what I want to say to him will probably use up most of my list of Tourette's words."

"I already know your pathetic Tourette's list," said Defense. "You keep refusing to let me teach you more bad words."

"For a guy who hurts when he breathes, you sure talk a lot," said Ryan.

When he looked around, Jannis and Dr. Withunga were just going out the door.

"That's not cool," said Ryan. "I thought they were going to be my ride home."

But Defense didn't answer. His eyelids were fluttering and then they stopped. Closed. He was asleep.

Ryan sat there thinking. What had Jannis done? What was her micropower? It hadn't caused Defense any pain, apparently, when she stroked his injury. And she talked about the bone fragments as if she knew a lot about that kind of thing.

Sitting in the chair by Defenseur's bed, Ryan kept thinking about Jannis's micropower for a long time, or maybe just for ten seconds because he must have fallen asleep. He woke up because the door to Defense's room opened a little, and Dr. Withunga leaned in and beckoned him.

Ryan got up. Defense was still asleep, so Ryan didn't wake him up. He wanted to lift the hospital robe and look again at the dent in the bandages, but he didn't. He just went out into the corridor and watched Dr. Withunga carefully close the door without making any noise that might wake Defense.

"You're a good friend," Dr. Withunga said.

"I try to be," said Ryan.

"Saving his life and all," added Jannis.

"Where did you guys go? How long was it, about half an hour?"

"Only nine minutes, actually," said Jannis.

"We visited your other friend," said Dr. Withunga. "Errol Dell. His room is also on this floor."

"You really did a number on his throat," said Jannis.

"I didn't invite you to come along," said Dr. Withunga, "because I didn't think the guard at his door would let the kid who punched his throat come in with us."

"He has a guard at his door?"

"The league champion kicker on the football team has a constant stream of visitors who have no regard for the official visiting hours," said Dr. Withunga. "The hospital put a security guy at the door so people wouldn't keep bothering the nurses, trying to wheedle their way in."

"But you got in," said Ryan.

"The hospital staff here," said Jannis, "they kind of know me because I follow them around sometimes, trying to learn medicine and all."

Somehow Ryan thought that was unlikely. Jannis didn't seem to be the following-around kind.

"I think you like to stroke people's injuries," said Ryan.

Jannis looked away, and Dr. Withunga stared off into the distance. "If word gets out about what Jannis does," said Dr. Withunga softly.

"I won't tell," said Ryan. "She would get no rest, I think."

"I think some of the nurses in the trauma center have a pretty good idea," said Dr. Withunga, "but they don't know about micropowers, so whether they think it's the power of prayer or some kind of weird hill-country magic, I can't begin to guess."

"I help put things in order," said Jannis. "But nothing deep inside the body. I'm good with broken bones just under the skin, and I was able to do some work on the mess you made of Errol's throat."

"How effective are you?" asked Ryan.

"She's effective," said Dr. Withunga. "But not predictably so. If a wound is too deep, she can't reach it. She can't fix cancer or, really, anything except trauma. A concussion, many broken bones, sutures, you heal without a scar—that kind of thing."

"So Defense's ribs?" asked Ryan.

Jannis shrugged. "They were such a mess. I think I did some good. I corralled all the chips of bone, got them back in place. I think he'll heal up fine."

"Without a dent?" Ryan asked.

"We'll see," said Jannis. "I help with superficial injuries, which, thank God, all of Defense's and Errol's were. Just under the skin. So things look pretty bright for both of them."

"You undid the damage," said Ryan.

"Tried to," said Jannis. "Did my best."

"Do you let people hug you?" asked Ryan.

"As rarely as possible," said Jannis.

"Is this one of the times?" asked Ryan.

"If you can do it without copping a feel," said Jannis.

What a jerk, thought Ryan. And then he thought of her stroking Defense's wound and he reached out and hugged her. Not really tightly or really closely, but he held her like that for kind of a long time.

"If you're trying to turn me on, it's not working," said Jannis.

Ryan pulled away. "I'm really grateful," said Ryan. "You weren't just healing them."

"I don't know if I actually healed anybody. I think I just help speed up the body's natural process."

"And putting bone fragments where they belong," said Ryan.

"If they stay where I put them," said Jannis.

"I get it," said Ryan. "No promises. But I'm grateful. And in my family, strong feelings get hugged on. I wasn't trying to do anything . . ." He was about to say "sexual," but that just felt ugly.

"She knows that," said Dr. Withunga. "But she tries to turn away gratitude because it embarrasses her and she doesn't know how to respond to it."

"Thanks for the translation," said Jannis.

"I needed it," said Ryan. "You kind of give off mixed signals."

"I'm pretty sure I conveyed a general hostility toward you," said Jannis.

"Yes, you're good at that, message received."

"So . . . no translation needed, right?"

Dr. Withunga laughed. "Ryan, not a word to anyone, not even a hint that you *know* her micropower."

"I already promised, and I promise again," said Ryan.

"She and I work together on strengthening her micropower. And having you here along with me—that helped intensify the power. Another micropot—that really makes a difference to her."

"But you didn't want Bizzy?" asked Ryan.

"She still doesn't trust us," said Dr. Withunga.

"This today might have helped with that," said Ryan.

"And we don't know how much to trust *her*," said Jannis.

Instead of leaping to Bizzy's defense, Ryan realized that they probably didn't fully trust *him*, either, but they came here partly to help him, and he needed to be along. If Ryan's friend and Ryan's victim were both helped to heal faster and more completely, then Ryan didn't have to feel so bad about the things he had and hadn't done at school.

"Thank you," said Ryan.

"See how much better than a hug it is when you use your words?" said Jannis.

Ryan didn't bother to answer or argue. If Jannis wanted to keep him at arm's length, he didn't mind at all.

I'd rather have her micropower than mine, thought Ryan. Healing instead of hurting. Even if I only hurt bees, I still don't like it. And I messed Errol up even though this was a fight someone else picked. I punished him for losing his temper, when he would have to have been a saint *not* to. But now he's not going to suffer for years or forever because I took a poke at his throat. Thanks, Jannis, even if you're kind of a jerk about it with me. You were kind to Defense and I bet you were kind with Errol.

"Errol wasn't actually awake," said Dr. Withunga, as if she felt a need to explain. "He won't remember that we visited. Nor will anybody else. So perhaps if you don't ever refer to our visit today?"

"Errol and I never, never, never talk," said Ryan.

"I think that might be a healthy trend in your relationship," said Dr. Withunga.

"I've got nothing to say to him," said Ryan. "Because I'm not sorry I punched his neck. If he really meant to deliver that kick—and I still believe that he did—then I saved him from murder."

"Micropowers have their uses," said Dr. Withunga.

"I'd rather have the power to heal."

Jannis gave a low chuckle. "You have no idea yet what your power really is or what it can do."

"Why, do *you* have an idea?" demanded Ryan.

"Nobody has an idea, until they work on it and study it for a pretty long time," said Jannis.

"Then teach me," said Ryan.

"That's the second thing people ask me, when they suspect what I can do," said Jannis. "But it can't be taught, unless I actually understand what I'm doing, and I don't, so I can't."

"Got it," said Ryan.

It was dark when they dropped him off at the duplex. He went inside, checked the garbage situation, changed the bag in the kitchen, and in general did his chores. His mother came into the kitchen when he came back inside the house. Without saying anything, she heated up some of the lasagna she had made for dinner. Ryan thanked her.

"You were with Next-Door Girl?" asked Mom.

"You mean Bizzy?" asked Ryan.

"That's not a name," said Mom. "It's hard for me to remember."

Ryan didn't argue with her. Fine with him if she wanted to pretend not to remember Bizzy's name.

"We dropped her off a couple of hours ago," said Ryan. "I visited Defense in the hospital."

"You're a good friend," said Mother.

"I try," said Ryan.

"Try not to kill anybody," said Mother.

"I took some pains not to kill anyone," said Ryan. "I intend to keep making such efforts."

"I know," said Mom. "Just . . . succeed at not killing."

"You got it, Mom," he said. "Not much homework tonight, but I've got to get it done."

"Eat the lasagna first," she said.

"You didn't have to heat it for me, you know. Your lasagna is also really good cold."

"That's more than a little disgusting," Mom said. "Even if *you* don't mind."

"Yeah, it is," Ryan said. "But I don't mind."

"My son who I'm so proud of doesn't have to eat lasagna straight from the fridge tonight."

Ryan didn't say anything, but her words gave him an inward glow that momentarily blinded him.

Her words also gave him a stab of pain. Because Father wasn't there to hear what she said. And, perhaps, to agree with her.

Despite such contradictory feelings, the hot lasagna tasted great.

12

Defense was in school the next day. "What are you doing here?" asked Ryan.

"Passing my classes, if I can," said Defense.

"Why did they let you out of the hospital? I thought they were watching to see what happened with your—"

"They already saw what happened," said Defense. Ryan waited for the explanation.

"Your friend with the stroky-stroky fingers," said Defense.

"Not my *friend*," said Ryan.

"You brought her," said Defense.

"Dr. Withunga brought her. And me."

"I didn't tell the hospital people anything about her, all right?" said Defense. "You can relax."

And Ryan realized that he *had* been tense, and that knowing that Defense had not blown Jannis's secret did indeed allow him to relax.

"So?" asked Ryan. "What did they think happened? Did *anything* happen?"

"They had serious doubts about the accuracy of the original X-rays," said Defense. "And if they had thought it was safe to expose me to radiation again, they would have retaken the new ones. They wanted to do an MRI, but my parents weren't interested in testing their insurance coverage with unnecessary procedures."

"Unnecessary," said Ryan.

"Because I don't have a dent anymore. And they don't think I have any bone chips floating around in my chest. The diagnosis was 'complete recovery.'"

Ryan said nothing. He was really impressed with Jannis now. If you can heal people like that, nobody gives a rat's petoot whether you're a jerk.

"Your micropower is pretty damn fine," said Defense. "But hers? Miracle Max from *Princess Bride*."

"Not a miracle," said Ryan. "And not to be discussed here in a crowded corridor."

"Nobody listens to us," said Defense.

"Used to be true, but a lot of people saw videos of your ribs caving in, and here you are at school."

Defense glanced around, saw how many people were openly or covertly watching them. "Well, whaddya know," he said.

"Let's not do anything to feed your fame," said Ryan.

"*Your* fame," said Defense. "I didn't fly over and jab Athlete's Foot in the neck."

"No more nicknames," said Ryan. "Period. Ever."

"Errol Dell," said Defense.

"No nicknames for anybody. That phase of your life is over."

"Says who and what army?" said Defense.

"Says me," said Ryan. "Your days of tormenting people with cruel nicknames are over."

"Cruel *accurate* nicknames," Defense corrected him.

"Time for you to stop leaving a swath of pain and humiliation wherever you go," said Ryan.

"Not your decision."

"No," said Ryan. "My decision is whether we remain friends."

Defense looked at him soberly, then took him by the elbow and drew him into an alcove near the entrance, where nobody else was lurking long enough to overhear them. "Are you giving me an ultimatum?" he asked.

Ryan nodded. "Yes, I am. And in case you think I'm being arbitrary here, let me remind you: I almost killed a guy two days ago. A guy that you goaded mercilessly into attacking you, in order to *force* me, because I was your friend, to jab him in the throat. Is that a fair description of what happened? Am I misrepresenting your motives?"

"You're so impressive when you talk like the Declaration of Independence," said Defense.

"When you use my love for you—shut up and listen—when you use my love for you to maneuver me into doing something unconscionable (my conscience, not yours), then I will remove that power from you by ceasing to love you. Get it? I will never again rescue you from a danger you deliberately brought on yourself to control me."

"I get it, man. I would never do that."

"You did it two days ago. So if you continue to be the same rectal constriction with your name-calling, you'll be doing it as not-my-friend. My ex-friend."

"Your enemy?" asked Defense.

"The enemy of all civilized people. You're not a child anymore. You're a full-sized person—"

"*Mon dieu*, I hope not," said Defense. "I'm still hoping for six inches more. In *height*."

"And the trouble you get yourself and others into can have permanent, real-world consequences. The fact that Jannis was able to use her . . . *attention* to speed up your healing should not lead you to think you can play these games with impunity. The next time someone is kicking you to death because you taunted them into it, I will not step in to help you. Clear?"

"What if I didn't provoke them?"

"You provoke everybody," said Ryan. "So let's see a fundamental change in your relationship with, let's say, the entire human race, or there won't be enough friendship between us for me to care whether you provoked this particular attacker this particular time."

"Wow," said Defense. "I really pissed you off."

"It took you this long to reach that conclusion?"

"So the only person you'll be protecting from now on is, like, Bizzy?"

"If I'm not protecting *you*, Defense, it'll be none of your business who I might be protecting."

"Ryan," said Defense. "I'm really sorry. I really am."

"Sorry enough to change?" asked Ryan.

"It would really help me if a lot of other people stopped being pomp-ous asses, bullies, and fools."

"You can't control them. But has your ridicule ever caused *any* of them to be less pompous, less bullying, less foolish?"

Defense grinned foolishly. "Usually makes them worse."

"Start trying to heal the world around you instead of sticking your fingers into the open sores," said Ryan.

"You're so poetic," said Defense. "I'd have a new nickname for you right now, except that I suspect your new rule about how I can't ridicule people probably includes ridiculing you."

"Yes," said Ryan.

"So if even *you* are out of reach of my unspeakable—no, my *speakable*—wit, can you explain what I will gain from continuing to be *your* friend?"

Ryan gazed at Defense and finally said, "Have I done something to damage our friendship, Defense?"

"You mean besides giving me an ultimatum and requiring me to completely change my character and all my habits? No, not really."

"Haven't you had proof enough of my love and friendship in the past forty-eight hours?" asked Ryan.

"I think so, yes," said Defense.

"So are you still my friend?" asked Ryan.

"If I can be," said Defense. "If I can measure up."

"You can," said Ryan. "All you have to do is start regarding the people around you as humans who deserve compassion."

"I wasn't doing all my taunting of other people alone, you know."

"I know," said Ryan. "I was right there with you. I am also trying to change."

"Because you found real beauty in the world," said Defense.

"Maybe," said Ryan. "But it isn't in the way she looks."

Defense grinned. "I know. It's in the way other people look at *her*."

"It's in her soul. It's in her kindness. She sees everything you and I have always seen, but she forgives people for it."

"Does she really?" asked Defense. "Or does she just try not to be mean?"

"Trying not to be mean is good enough for me. Good enough for now. Let's do that, too."

"We're going to be late to class," said Defense.

"You're the one who called this meeting," said Ryan.

"Adjourned," said Defense.

"Let's go learn some more truth and beauty."

"It's still high school, bonehead," said Defense. "And 'bonehead' wasn't a nickname. It was just an accurate description."

"I know," said Ryan. "I bet you'll beat me there."

Defense squinted his eyes. "Is that some kind of reverse psychology to get me to walk slower than you so you lose the bet by arriving first?"

"Is it working?"

"Suck rocks, *mon ami*," said Defense as he took off at an Olympic fast-walking pace.

Ryan let him take a long lead. It just didn't feel right to try to compete with Defense right now. Besides, Ryan wasn't sure that the things he said to Defense were actually true. And the part he wasn't sure about was whether Ryan had already cut off the friendship. It might not have been a conscious decision—no, it definitely wasn't—but he still didn't feel anything like the closeness and easiness he had felt with Defense up until the time Defense rejected all of Ryan's pleas and provoked Errol Dell.

Maybe if Ryan had given him the same ultimatum in the first place . . . But no. Today's ultimatum had come *after* Defense's ploy worked, exposing the fact that Ryan's micropower was not just about bees. Defense had already proved his point, had carried the day, had won the battle. The ultimatum was closing the barn door after all the rats had run out, or whatever the saying was. After all the cows were gone. But nobody kept cows in a barn. Except milk cows.

Get control of your thoughts, Ryan told himself. Images of milking machines plugged into udders aren't helpful right now.

But what *would* be helpful?

As Defense had said, the only person Ryan was protecting now was Bizzy. But protecting her from what, exactly? Yes, someone had been stalking her, but it was Aaron Withunga, and GRUT posed no threat to Bizzy or, really, anybody.

Of course, Ryan would also protect Mother, and he had already proved that he had sufficient love for Dianne to save her from a bee sting, or at least flick it off and call the EMTs. It was hard to imagine what Ryan might ever need to save Father from, but if there was something, he knew that he would do it. But his list of beloved people was kind of small.

Could his list have people grafted on? Ryan had no particular feelings toward Mrs. Horvat, except for a general dread of getting on her bad side. But because Bizzy loved her, did that mean that Ryan's micropower would kick in to protect Mrs. Horvat? If Mom fell in love with some post-Dad clown and, like, married him, would Ryan have to defend the interloper as if he himself didn't want the guy dead? Because if Mom brought some other man into the house, Ryan would definitely hate him with a fiery rage.

And if Dad supposedly preferred another family to Mom and Dianne and Ryan, where was that family? It wasn't the Horvats, and Ryan couldn't think who the other family might be. If they existed and Dad loved them, though, would Ryan's micropower also be triggered to protect *them*?

If there was no other family that Dad was seeing or supporting or whatever, then what did Mother's mutterings about them mean? Why would she talk about a family that Dad loved better than them? There was no reason for her to lie, was there? Her resentment and grief and anger seemed real enough. There was nothing calculated about it as far as Ryan could tell, back when the rift between Mom and Dad first came into view.

How do married people who loved each other so much they moved in together—how do they get so *angry* that they completely reject the life they built? How could Dad stand to cut their house in half?

Of course, having seen much of the process of framing in the new walls, Ryan knew that the houses weren't as separate as they seemed. For instance, Dad had cut a little storage closet into the walls framing the base of the stairs. Once when Ryan was alone in the house, he opened that door and crept in with a flashlight. He saw that Dad had *not* put wallboard between the old stairs and the framework underpinning the new stairs on the other side. They weren't exactly parallel—the new stairs started closer to the front door—but it was still possible to slither from the space under the Burkes' stairway into the space under the Horvats' stairs.

Dad hadn't installed a nice hinged door on the Horvats' side, but there was a removable panel, and the Horvats had put a couple of empty suitcases and some boxes into the space. Not so much that Ryan couldn't have popped that panel open and gotten into the Horvats' house any time he wanted.

But he wasn't a burglar or a stalker or a peeping tom. He didn't need to see anything on the Horvats' side, because if he walked into the Horvats' kitchen, it would only make him sad that it wasn't Dad's book-lined office anymore.

And if the Horvats found him skulking around in their house, he would probably lose their friendship and any access to Bizzy. Also, when they told Dad, he would come back and completely seal off any points of passage between the houses.

It occurred to Ryan that the fact that Father hadn't walled off the two understairs closets from each other meant that Dad trusted him. Because he must have known that Ryan would notice the omission and that Ryan would know that he could get from one side of the duplex to the other. But he also knew that Ryan would not take advantage of the opening.

Bizzy was on the other side of the walls of the house. The permeable, vincible walls.

Stop thinking of it as a military problem with an easy solution, Ryan told himself when he lay awake at night, imagining Bizzy lying in her own bed. Or getting ready for bed. That was not a useful thing for him to think about. Better to think of her on the back deck, looking down at where he perched on the bottom steps. *That* was their relationship, their friendship, their love story. That was probably all it would ever be.

When Mother and Dianne watched the Rebel Wilson movie *Isn't It Romantic*, the part that really got to Ryan was the way she thought Adam DeVine was always staring at the sexy billboard outside the window, until, near the end, he finally made her sit in his chair and see that a reflection made that billboard invisible. Instead, he had been gazing all the time at her reflection.

Would there ever be a moment when Ryan could make Bizzy see how he saw her?

But of course she already knew, and not just because Ryan had told her more than once. Bizzy had spent her life being admired, from afar and otherwise. She probably learned how to beat suitors back with a stick before she was six. The beginning of that was learning how to turn glamor-face on and off.

The fact that she had never used glamor-face on Ryan until her mother forced her—what did that mean? That she didn't want Ryan to be attracted to her? Or that she didn't want Ryan to be attracted to glamor-face, and she valued his friendship because it wasn't based on that?

Did she value him because he was permanently in the "friend zone," as the romantic comedies called it? Would it wreck everything if he tried to move into a different kind of relationship? Or did the fact that she had actually held his hand for three seconds that one time mean that they were already moving that way?

And nobody *forced* her to kiss him in order to hide her face on the way to the library that day. She had made it a pretty convincing kiss. Lips parted. Some movement. It sure felt like an actual kiss, regardless of the motive. Did that mean he *wasn't* trapped forever in the friend zone? Or did it mean that an occasional insincere but convincing kiss was part of what the friend zone meant to Bizzy?

Naturally, all this was occupying his mind whenever Hardesty called on him in class. It was Hardesty's micropower, if he had one, to know which students had completely spaced out and weren't listening in class. And ever since Bizzy moved in, Ryan had pretty much always been spaced out in class. But Hardesty didn't pick on him very often—probably because Ryan was so good at pretending to know what Hardesty had been talking about, and also because he had a knack for getting Hardesty off on tangents, so that he didn't finish whatever the day's lesson was supposed to cover. Better not to call on Ryan. Better to let him brood about the girl next door.

The girl next door! Could Ryan be any more of a cliche?

At lunch, Ryan saw that Bizzy was sitting by herself. So was Defense, and they weren't near each other.

Today, Ryan chose Bizzy, partly because he was still pissed off at Defense—though he also knew that if he wanted to keep Defense as a friend, he needed to make sure Defense didn't feel as if Ryan had already cut him off.

As he sat down across from Bizzy, he said, "I got distracted and was thinking about other stuff. When did goose-face wear off?"

"It wore off?" she said.

Ryan gave her a twisted smile.

"I got distracted, too," said Bizzy. "The glamor already wore off before you began your mixed martial arts event. That's why I could be there to see it."

Somebody walked along behind Ryan and he felt a fist thump against his back. The anonymous male person commented on his dorsal sphincter.

"I see your fan club won't leave you alone at lunch," said Bizzy. "Lots of football fans in school think it would have been better for Defense to have died than to lose the inimitable foot of Errol Dell."

"Defense was back in school today," said Ryan.

"Seems impossible."

"Yet true," said Ryan. "Maybe Errol Dell will have a remarkably fast recovery, too."

Bizzy gazed at him. "You know something."

"As I plan to prove on the SATs," he said. "Or maybe I should take the GED and just test my way out of high school now."

"They won't let you," said Bizzy. "Because the school system gets its funding based on the number of students attending every day."

"But by leaving," said Ryan, "I'd relieve the overcrowding problem."

"But by leaving," said Bizzy, "you'd lower the cumulative grade point average of Vasco da Gama High School."

"But by leaving," said Ryan, "I'd ease up the pressure on the curve and make everybody else look better."

"You are a philanthropist at heart," said Bizzy.

"At this moment, I'm only a philogynist," said Ryan. Then they fell into some meaningless banter on Greek words that Ryan didn't know, and ended up with Bizzy accusing him of thinking he was somehow like Shakespeare. They were just making foolish chat, and Ryan gave up on it.

"Lunch today tastes like it was made from feet," said Ryan.

"Made *by* feet," said Bizzy. "Why didn't you sit with Defense? He looks sad, and I don't."

"I didn't choose my lunch companion by *their* need, but by my own."

"Ah," said Bizzy. "And what do you need from me?"

"Dr. Withunga is assembling a GRUT meeting after school today. Are you in or out of the play?"

"Out," said Bizzy, looking annoyed. "Did someone tell you that I was still in it?"

"Defense."

"Because he's an idiot," said Bizzy. "You've known him all these years without discovering that?"

"Sorry," said Ryan. "He said it back when I thought he had a brain."

"When I told you I was quitting the play, I quit the play. I do what I say I'll do."

"Knowing that, I ask you: Will you come to GRUT after school this afternoon?"

Bizzy cocked her head. "Mother says I never should again. Too dangerous."

"Nobody there has the power to hurt you. Some have the power to help."

"She's not saying it's dangerous for *me*," said Bizzy.

"For who, then?"

"For all the rest of you. For the micropotents. The micropots. Whatever you call yourselves."

"Why would *we* be in danger from having *you* show up?" asked Ryan.

"She would have to explain why," said Bizzy, "because it only makes sense while she's talking."

"I can't just walk up to your mom and ask her a question like that," said Ryan.

"You're not scared of my drop-dead glamorous self, but you're still scared of my timid mouse of a mother?"

"Sorry, I thought we were talking about Mrs. Horvat, the next-door dragon lady."

"My scared-of-everything, always-hiding mother," said Bizzy. "My mother who fled Slovenia and lives here in the United States as if she's in witness relocation. My mother who sees a stalker in everyone who looks at me."

"She's protective," said Ryan. "I can understand that."

"It's not *me* she's protecting," said Bizzy, with a wry smile. "I mean, yes, she does look out for me. But she's afraid of the people who are after *her*."

Ryan tried to make sense of that. "Is there a Slovenian mafia? I didn't know Slovenia was big enough to have organized crime."

"Charlottesville is *large* enough to have organized crime," said Bizzy. "It just isn't organized enough. Really, I'll talk to her. I'll tell her that if you're going to protect me, you ought to have some idea of what you're up against."

"Will she tell me?"

"I think she probably will," said Bizzy. "But will you believe it? Will it even make sense?"

"Let's find out," said Ryan.

"I'll be at GRUT this afternoon," said Bizzy. "But only if you tell me how Defense healed up so fast."

There was a sudden increase of chatter in the room, and then somebody started clapping, and pretty soon a lot of people were clapping. Ryan turned to look. Bizzy was already in a position to see.

People near the north entrance to the cafeteria were standing—some of them on chairs and tables—and applauding.

And then Ryan saw why. Errol Dell had walked into the cafeteria. Wearing no bandages, no neck brace, showing no sign of any injury. He'd had an emergency tracheotomy right there in the grass in back of the school, and Jannis had apparently healed that injury right down to the root. Her healing power was a lot more than skin deep.

"Well," said Ryan, turning back to Bizzy, "I guess Errol will still be kicking in the game this Friday."

"So *both* Defense and Errol got completely healed incredibly fast," said Bizzy.

"Miracles of modern medicine," said Ryan.

"What's miraculous is that neither of them thought of staying home and milking their injuries for as many days off as possible," said Bizzy.

"Defense is an idiot, somebody once told me," said Ryan, "and Errol has to show people that he's fit to play on Friday."

"You're sticking with 'miracles of modern medicine'?" asked Bizzy.

"You're not going to tell me how they healed so fast? Because those were massive injuries. I'm betting this is somebody's micropower at work."

Ryan could feel himself blushing. He almost never blushed, but Father had told him long ago that it was his sure "tell" when he was lying. "Never play poker, kid," Father told him then. "You can't bluff for crap."

"And you're about to lie to me," said Bizzy. So she already knew that about him. Even though he didn't remember when he lied to her before.

"No," said Ryan. "I'm about to not tell you anything, because of a promise that I made."

"A promise not to tell anybody? Or not to tell *me*?"

"Anybody," said Ryan.

"And in this case that includes me?" asked Bizzy.

"Ordinarily it wouldn't," said Ryan. "I'd rather tell you everything I know about everything. You know I don't keep anything private. But this isn't my secret. I've already told you too much because I promised not to say that there even *was* a secret."

"Thanks for telling me more than you meant to," said Bizzy.

"I always do," said Ryan.

"Yeah," said Bizzy. "That's one of the things I like about you."

"The fact that you can see right through me?"

"The fact that you don't have a lying heart."

13

The GRUT meeting started a little late because Dr. Withunga and Jannis weren't there, and neither Mitch nor Dahlia knew when they might arrive. Ryan wondered if Jannis and Dr. Withunga were doing rounds, like a regular doctor—did Jannis have patients that she worked with? Did they just drop in on hospital trauma units and see which patients might benefit from a little therapeutic stroking?

But with a micropower like Jannis's, where would she draw the line? Did she confine herself to healing people inside Albemarle County? Along US 29 from Danville to Gainesville? Did she go up to DC, where there were way more traumas than in any Virginia hospital? Or was that too much for her?

What would it be like to feel so *useful*? To know that wherever you went, you were needed?

To not have to wait for someone you loved to get into some kind of scrape that needed the help of a really violent guy. Or a guy who would put a bee in his mouth.

No point in comparing micropowers. That video of Ryan jabbing his knuckles into Errol's neck—it looked as if he was flying like Superman. Of course, he wasn't, but it was pretty spectacular all the same. So Ryan knew that it was stupid of him to denigrate his own micropower for no other reason than that it was his own.

It didn't heal people, it just hurt them.

No, he protected Bizzy from the bee, and he possibly saved Dianne's life. His power wasn't nothing. He absolutely *did* save Defense's worthless hide. So . . . not as cool as Jannis, because she never had to hurt anybody. But way cooler than, like, knowing where the spiders were.

Well, maybe not. Knowing about spiders was also really useful. In order to avoid them. To keep from walking into random invisible spider webs while taking a path through the woods.

And then the door opened, and it wasn't Dr. Withunga and Jannis. It was Bizzy, and following her into the room was Mrs. Horvat herself.

Mrs. Horvat looked around as if she was searching for a clean place to sit. It was all clean—school custodians did their job. But Mrs. Horvat clearly had disdain for everything and everybody in the room.

Maybe not disdain. Just a total lack of interest. She must have seen Ryan, but she didn't show a flicker of recognition.

Only after Mrs. Horvat was sitting down—not beside Bizzy, who had immediately walked over and sat by Ryan—did the door open again for Dr. Withunga and Jannis to come in. Dr. Withunga stopped in the doorway because she saw Mrs. Horvat. Jannis only saw that Mrs. Horvat was sitting in what Jannis apparently regarded as *her* chair, and said, "Oh. You." So Mrs. Horvat *had* come before, and Jannis had been there, and it didn't look as if they had formed a deep and abiding friendship.

"I'm trying not to extrapolate anything from your presence here today, Mrs. Horvat," said Dr. Withunga.

"I'm not going to pursue any action against you for working with my minor daughter without my permission," said Mrs. Horvat. "For now."

"What a relief," said Dr. Withunga. "For now."

Mrs. Horvat, who recognized irony when she heard it, shot a sharp glance at Dr. Withunga, who ignored her.

"Some of you remember Mrs. Horvat, Bizzy's mother," said Dr. Withunga.

"Just me," said Jannis. "Several years ago."

"Before the Horvat family moved to Charlottesville," said Dr. Withunga.

Mrs. Horvat said nothing and looked at no one except Dr. Withunga.

"Since Mrs. Horvat was very clear at that time about not wishing to explore whatever micropower she might have," said Dr. Withunga, "I expect that she has her own agenda, and we might save time by letting her take care of whatever errand brought her here."

"You're very kind," said Mrs. Horvat, not sounding as if she thought kindly of anyone. Ryan wondered if there was some kind of weird curse bound up in those words, the way Bizzy said her mother could curse with "How clumsy of you." But what would the curse be? Obsessive kindness for a couple of days? Not much of a curse, really.

"I'm here," said Mrs. Horvat, "to give you a warning."

"Why would you want to threaten us?" asked Jannis.

Mrs. Horvat stopped talking and stared at Jannis. "What do you mean?" she asked, and then apparently understood. "I shouldn't have said 'warning,' apparently. I should have said, I'm here to alert you to a danger that is quite likely to spill over from my family to affect this group."

"Danger?" asked Dr. Withunga.

"I am quite aware that what I'm going to tell you will sound paranoid, but I've lived with this for most of my life. This is what caused my parents to bring me to America, and it's why I have been ready to move at a moment's notice ever since."

"Can you possibly be any vaguer?" asked Jannis. Mitch snickered.

"My birth country was Slovenia," said Mrs. Horvat, "though when I was born it was still part of Yugoslavia. A very minor part, which was mostly ignored by the Serbs and Croats, who thought they ran everything. But Slovenia has an ancient history, and it includes a group of people who watched out for *čarôvnice*. A poor translation of the word is 'witches.' I was labeled a *čarôvnica* at an early age, because I could curse people."

"Watched out for witches?" said Dr. Withunga. "Protectively? Or with hostility?"

"Hostility," said Mrs. Horvat. "But in Slovenia, this group, the *lovece*, 'loveks,' began before there was any nonsense about witches being servants of some imaginary devil. What the word used to mean, what the group used to search for, was people who could affect other people in a magical way."

"Like making them yawn?" asked Dahlia.

"That would be hard to detect, don't you think?" said Mrs. Horvat. "*I* could be heard to mutter things, and then the person I was saying it to would have accidents. Nothing awful, mostly, but a degree of, a *frequency* of misfortunes that pointed a finger at me. Under the influence of Puritans in England, such people might have been burnt alive. In Slovenia, knives and swords were regarded as sufficient, though hanging and drowning and throwing from high places, of which there are many in Slovenia, were sometimes used."

Mitch said, "And you think they would interpret our micropowers as—"

"I don't *think*," said Mrs. Horvat. "I know. I could not understand why, having discovered where my family went, they have been content to stalk Bojana and me without ever taking action."

"Maybe they were afraid of getting cursed," said Jannis.

"Whatever else these *lovece* are, they are not cowards," said Mrs. Horvat. "Many have died over the years, but when they want a *čarôvnica* dead, the *čarôvnica* dies."

"So this is a secret society of witch hunters," said Jannis. "I feel like I'm trapped in the ending of *Peggy Sue Got Married*."

"I don't know what that means," said Mrs. Horvat.

"It's a movie," said Mitch. "One where Nicolas Cage gets really weird."

"He's always weird," said Jannis.

"You are amused by what?" asked Mrs. Horvat.

"The whole idea of a secret society that believes in witches and goes around killing them," said Mitch. "Come on."

"How long did you live in Slovenia?" asked Mrs. Horvat defiantly.

"It's a modern European country," said Jannis. "They have, like, cars and flush toilets."

"And here in America, there are people who play with snakes because they think God protects them from snakebites."

"Every country has its loons," said Dr. Withunga.

"In Slovenia, one group of loons got organized and passed on their lunacy from generation to generation. I know what I am talking about, and you do not, so stop ridiculing and start listening."

"We're all ears," said Jannis dryly.

"Still ridiculing," said Mrs. Horvat.

"But listening all the same," said Bizzy.

Mrs. Horvat froze for a moment but did not look at Bizzy. Then she went on. "I believe that they did *not* attack me or Bojana because they were looking for you."

"We're not Slovenian," said Dr. Withunga.

"They have no reason to confine their activities to searching for Slovenian *čaróvnice*."

"Can you spell that?" asked Mitch. Ryan had been wishing to know the same thing, but he didn't want to get on Mrs. Horvat's bad side.

"It would be a waste of time, because you don't have a letter that makes the sound 'tsuh.'"

"We use two letters for that," said Jannis. "As in the word 'tsar.'"

"Are you philologists?" asked Mrs. Horvat. "Am I here to acquaint you with Slovenian orthography?"

"You're alerting us to danger," said Dr. Withunga, "and I'm sorry if my young compatriots are too full of their own certainties to understand that historically, micropowers were bound to be misunderstood. As, for that matter, they continue to be misunderstood today."

"I have delivered my message," said Mrs. Horvat, "and one person here has understood it. I will go now."

"Wait," said Jannis. "I mean, come on. What does 'danger' consist of?"

"Sudden death. Or maybe kidnapping, or a car out of control, or a large object falling from above."

"Like a *Road Runner* cartoon," said Mitch.

"Apparently another reference to some American entertainment," said Mrs. Horvat, rising to her feet.

"What are we supposed to *do*?" asked Jannis.

"Are you taking me seriously now?" asked Mrs. Horvat.

"You *are* serious, aren't you?" asked Jannis.

"I came here as a kindness, because Bojana seems to value her time with you, and I did not want her to lose all her new friends. Especially because when they start killing, it means they no longer think Bojana and I have any further use, and we will probably die along with you."

"It sounds like you've moved before," said Dr. Withunga. "But you aren't going to move again?"

"Where?" asked Mrs. Horvat. "They found us here within a week. I don't know how."

"So you're giving up?" asked Mitch.

"I am not giving up," said Mrs. Horvat. "My daughter keeps company with a *čarôvnik* who has the power to protect her. My own micropower, to use your term, is a fairly effective defense if I see them coming in time."

"So you're safe enough," said Dr. Withunga.

"But you are not," said Mrs. Horvat. "Still, you are safer knowing than not knowing."

"*What* do we know? What should we be looking out for?"

"I don't know who will come for you. Or when, or how." Mrs. Horvat shrugged. "Be paranoid."

"Thanks," said Mitch. "Mission accomplished. At least if I die, I can make sure my killers are covered with spiders."

"A tiny vengeance, but perhaps it will ease your final moments," said Mrs. Horvat.

"Thank you for coming," said Dr. Withunga.

"I think you should stop assembling like this," said Mrs. Horvat. "It puts you all in danger, and young Mr. Burke will only be able to protect one person."

"Bizzy," said Mitch.

"Bojana is her name," said Mrs. Horvat. "And if he loves one of you more than he loves my Bojana, he will protect that person first."

Jannis looked at Ryan with a wry smile. "Do you love me, Ryan?"

"You have my respect," said Ryan. "And I don't wish anything bad to happen to you."

"Sounds like love to me," said Dahlia.

"God be with you all," said Mrs. Horvat, and she was out the door.

"That was . . . illuminating," said Dr. Withunga.

"Not really," said Ryan. "We don't know anything useful, except if somebody stabs us in the back or shoots us from a half-mile away like in *American Sniper*, we'll have a moment of understanding what we're being killed for, and then we'll be dead."

"How seriously should we take this?" Dr. Withunga asked Bizzy.

Bizzy shook her head. "People look at me on the street, but they always have. Maybe some of them are these loveks, but I don't know who is what. *If* they're even here. I don't understand my mother. Do any of you understand your mothers?"

"Not me," said Ryan.

Nobody volunteered as a mother-understander.

"Should we stop meeting?" asked Jannis.

"Nobody is required to be here," said Dr. Withunga. "But there are two ways of responding to this. One is to go into hiding, which may or may not work at all, since if anybody wanted to, they could have already identified every one of us."

"The other way of responding?" asked Bizzy.

"Keep meeting and try to understand our micropowers. Try to weaponize them if we can."

"Mission accomplished," said Ryan.

"A very narrow weapon, with only one shot in the chamber, but a powerful one all the same," said Dr. Withunga. "And my own micropower tells me that if somebody's planning to kill us, they aren't within fifty meters, or else they don't have navels."

"What do the spiders say, Mitch?" asked Jannis.

"Silent as always," said Mitch. "Nor do I think they'd care if I lived or died."

"Unrequited love is so sad and lonely," said Jannis.

"Can *your* micropower be weaponized?" Mitch asked Jannis.

Jannis shrugged. "I'm not going to try to find out," she said. "Nor am I going to tell anybody what it is, because I don't want you brainstorming ways that I can, like, kill people or cause bad weather or something."

"Dr. Withunga," said Ryan, "do you think there's a way for Bizzy to weaponize her . . ."

"Glamor?" asked Dr. Withunga. "I wonder if these . . . loveks? . . . have ever seen her in all her glory."

"Have *we*?" asked Jannis. "I mean, yes, she's dazzling, but what if she goes into glamor mode with us close by? Being with a group of micropots can supposedly intensify our powers."

"I can't imagine her becoming any *more* beautiful," said Mitch. "Not that I mean anything by that."

Bizzy waved him off. "It's not about beauty. We talked last time about how maybe I'm also giving off some kind of . . . attraction pheromone or psychic blast or something."

"And maybe *that* gets more intense when you've got other micropots around," said Dr. Withunga.

"I don't want to test it to find out," said Bizzy. "Because how would that even help? We don't want to *attract* these *lovece*. Loveks."

"Attract or *dis*tract?" said Ryan.

"I don't know," said Bizzy. "I don't really even want to know."

"I know *I* find it distracting," said Mitch. "And it didn't make me run to you in slow motion like in a rom-com."

"Well, then," said Ryan, "Bizzy is safe from any Mitch-like loveks."

"Nobody's like me," said Mitch.

Jannis whispered something that Ryan guessed was along the lines of "Thank God."

"It's also distracting to have spiders crawling all over you," said Bizzy.

"Sure," said Mitch, "but my micropower doesn't make spiders move any faster. Somebody coming in with a machete to wipe us out would have all our heads off before any significant number of spiders got halfway here."

"So most of them aren't close?" asked Jannis.

"I try to keep them out of your way," said Mitch, "because none of them deserve to die under your big feet."

"The discussion is deteriorating," said Dr. Withunga. From then on, they stayed on track but didn't come up with anything useful except that Mitch should maybe try getting the spiders to race each other, in order to speed them up. And Ryan thought, if Jannis could stroke to draw bone fragments together, could she stroke somebody to make their bones, or at least one bone, crumble into powder?

No. That's not what it's for.

"What are these micropowers *for*, anyway?" asked Ryan. "Why do we even have them?"

"The puzzle that dominates my thinking for the past ten years or so," said Dr. Withunga. "I don't mean, why did God give us these talents, but rather, why is evolution spraying out what may be nascent superpowers? Is there a chance that some of them will have a real impact on our survival? And are such micropowers transferable to the next generation?"

"Your son has a micropower," said Bizzy.

"My son is a micropower *detector*. Neither of us is sure whether that's actually a micropower."

"Of course it is," said Ryan impatiently.

"Such certainty," said Dr. Withunga.

"Minute distinctions aren't helpful," said Ryan. "Finding ways to augment our powers might be."

"What if two micropots mate?" asked Jannis. "Perhaps you and Bizzy are an experiment in the making."

Ryan blushed, of course; Bizzy, on the other hand, made no sign of having heard. At least she didn't make a gagging gesture with her finger down her throat.

"I think we ignore Mrs. Horvat's warning at our own peril," said Dr. Withunga. "So I think there's some urgency in trying to figure out ways to defend ourselves. And each other. Meanwhile . . ."

"Meanwhile?" asked Mitch.

"Try not to go anywhere alone," said Dr. Withunga.

"So they can be sure to get two at one whack?" asked Jannis.

"So we can try to protect each other. Augment each other's powers just by being close by. And if worse comes to worst, maybe serve as a witness, to notify others."

"Worse coming to worst would mean that we'd both be dead," said Jannis.

"Worse coming to second worst," said Dr. Withunga.

"If there's any danger at all," said Mitch.

"That's exactly what Aaron is going to say when I tell him."

"Where is he?" asked Ryan.

"You miss him?" asked Jannis.

"He's one of us," said Ryan.

"He's interviewing for a job," said Dr. Withunga.

Ryan had nothing to say to that. *He* wanted a job, but his own father wouldn't hire him.

"I've got to get home and take out the garbage," said Ryan. "It's a pickup day in the morning."

"Such a responsible young man," said Bizzy.

Ryan didn't take it as a snotty joke, even though if Defense had said it, that's what it would have been. "I try to be," he answered her.

"That's why Mother trusted you to be a reliable companion for me," said Bizzy. "Because she saw you taking out the garbage almost every day. And taking it to the street. And bringing it back in. Very impressive."

Thanks, Dad, thought Ryan.

"We learn so much about character by watching garbage-oriented behaviors," said Jannis.

"Not really a joke," said Bizzy.

"Not really joking," said Jannis. "I didn't know that about Ryan. A dependable garbageman. There are worse things to be at, what, fourteen?"

"Almost sixteen," said Ryan.

"You look young," said Jannis. "That will work well for you when you're forty."

If I live to be forty, thought Ryan. If I don't have to die to protect Bizzy.

"But it's not doing much for you now," said Jannis.

"He's doing fine," said Bizzy. "The most beautiful girl in the county is keeping him company."

She said it with a self-mocking tone, but it also happened to be true.

"More than that," said Ryan, "she sleeps under the same roof as me."

Not a good thing to say. Bizzy gathered her things and stood up. "Ryan," she said, "can you walk me back to that roof we share?"

"As you wish," said Ryan, deliberately invoking *The Princess Bride*. Though he doubted Bizzy had ever seen or read it.

"Her Westley," said Mitch, in a fake sentimental voice. So *somebody* knew the movie.

"You can explain who Westley is on the way home," said Bizzy.

"Thank your mother for coming, would you, Bojana?" said Dr. Withunga.

"My name is Bizzy," said Bizzy. "Bojana is what old Slovenian witches call me."

14

Ryan left the meeting with a sense of foreboding. He was especially alert—and apparently it was obvious to Bizzy, because, as they were leaving the school grounds, she said, "Ryan, the fact that Mother came to the meeting did not actually increase whatever danger there might be."

"It might have, if they saw her come, and put it all together."

"They watch me as much as her, or at least somebody does, and I've been to the meetings before, so they already know about GRUT."

"So I'm not supposed to be more careful?"

"Ryan, dear boy, you've always been insanely careful of me, capturing filthy bees, cleaning them in the bee-wash of your mouth, and setting them free, shiny and fresh, into the world."

"Bee-wash. Like a carwash," said Ryan.

"An intelligent boy. A remarkable boy," said Bizzy.

"So now we're captive in the final chapter of *A Christmas Carol*?"

"You're twice the size of Tiny Tim," said Bizzy.

"Which I suppose makes me the prize turkey. Not the little one, the big one."

"Have you memorized it?" asked Bizzy.

"Have you?" replied Ryan. "I had it read to me every Christmas for the past ten years, and this Christmas, Mother is probably going to make *me* read it, the way she makes me read anything that needs to be read out loud."

"Your father used to read it?"

"And maybe they'll grow up enough by Christmastime that he can come back and read it again himself. Sparing me the bother."

"Oh, so you've finally found a reason for your father to come home?" asked Bizzy.

"One that might convince my mother to relent."

"You're sure she's the one that needs convincing?"

"I used Dad's phone to call her a while ago, and because his name came up on her phone, her complete answer was to text the word 'Die.'"

"Ouch," said Bizzy.

"I suppose your parents get along perfectly," said Ryan.

"When one of them is a witch who can wreck the next couple of days of your life with a curse, sure, they get along fine. Or they would if Dad wasn't up at the university from six A.M. to midnight."

"That's a killer schedule."

"He says he doesn't sleep anyway," said Bizzy.

"Which is why I've never seen him," said Ryan.

"You saw him the day we moved in," said Bizzy. "When you were leaning against the wall watching us work."

"I helped as soon as I was invited."

"That's weak, lad," said Bizzy. "You saw we were carrying heavy things into the house."

"I also knew that it was *your* stuff, and you might take umbrage if a strange kid from the neighborhood came up and started picking things up."

"Are Americans really that suspicious?" asked Bizzy.

"I thought you were born here. When you say 'Americans,' that includes you. And yes, there are people who would scream at you and threaten to call the cops if you started picking their stuff up without being asked."

"You weren't a stranger," said Bizzy.

"Strange enough," said Ryan.

"Well, yes. Maybe my mother would have barked at you and I would have told her, I know him, he's a friend."

"But not your fant," said Ryan, thinking back to the word for "boyfriend" that Bizzy taught him on the day they met.

"To Slovenians," said Bizzy, "if a boy and girl are on a first-name basis and they aren't siblings, they're practically engaged."

"Engaged, but not punca and fant," said Ryan.

"'Punca' and 'fant' are not parallel words like 'girlfriend' and 'boyfriend,'" said Bizzy. "'Lahka punca' can carry overtones of being sexually easy. 'Fant' has no such connotation."

"Because all boys are assumed to be sexually easy," said Ryan.

"Are they?" asked Bizzy.

"Sexually easy? Or assumed to be so?"

"Whichever," said Bizzy.

"Both," said Ryan. "As a general rule."

"'Fant' doesn't carry overtones of professional involvement in being sexually easy," said Bizzy.

"I can't believe I thought 'punca' just meant 'miss.'"

"It was amazing that you knew any words of Slovenian at all," said Bizzy. "I forgave the inadvertent insult and respected the effort."

"You're a generous person," said Ryan. "But please note that through-out this charmingly distracting conversation, I have kept close scrutiny on everyone we passed, including the people in passing cars. The normal number are watching you covertly, but there have been no repeaters, and no cars that I recognize from previous trips except the cars of parents pick-ing up their kids from school."

"And look," said Bizzy. "There is the charming old house that your father cut in half so that we could live in such close proximity to each other."

It *was* still a charming house, because only the two mailboxes on either side of the front door showed that it was a duplex. And the two metal house numbers on the outside walls. And the fact that the Horvat family's side of the house had a neatly mown lawn, while the Burke side was getting long and dandelion infested.

"Why do dandelions keep growing all through the winter?" asked Ryan.

"It isn't winter yet," said Bizzy.

"It will be. It's hit freezing a couple of nights already."

"I know," said Bizzy. "That's why our basil on the back deck died."

"Sorry," said Ryan. His mother didn't cook with basil, so he hadn't recognized the herb among the pots on the Horvats' deck.

"It was way too overgrown," said Bizzy. "It grows faster than we can use it. And we always grow basil inside the house on a south-facing window-sill. So . . . fresh basil all winter."

"So what do you use it for?"

Bizzy stopped on the sidewalk and stared at him, making a show of being shocked.

"I've never had basil in my life," said Ryan. "What does it do? Is it hot? Is it minty? Does it have a nauseating flavor like nutmeg? Is it licorice-y like anise?"

"Well, you're a regular encyclopedia of herbs," said Bizzy.

"Mom makes a spice cake and she likes to mince fresh herbs. Well, fresh from the supermarket produce department. Not from a McCormick tin."

"Basil wouldn't work in a cake," said Bizzy.

"So what does it work in?"

"Pesto," said Bizzy.

Ryan shrugged. "I thought pesto was my younger sister."

"Also, it's vital on a caprese salad. Mozzarella, tomato, oil, and basil."

"I won't recognize it from foods I've never eaten or even seen," said Ryan. "What does it taste like?"

"It tastes fresh," said Bizzy.

"Do you want to know something interesting?" asked Ryan.

"Anything would be better than trying to explain a taste," said Bizzy.

"That's the third time that car has passed us. Don't look. It's a Toyota RAV4, which is weird-enough-looking that it's memorable, which makes it a terrible choice for surveillance."

"Are you sure it was the same one?"

"White with the same spatters of red mud on the right side."

"But not on the left?" asked Bizzy.

"I've only seen the left side once," said Ryan. "But better than mud spatters is the face of the driver, and the two car seats in the back."

"So it's a family car," said Bizzy, looking relieved.

"So I thought, the first time it passed. Heading for school. Except nobody at the high school needs car seats in the back, right? And it came *back* from the high school remarkably soon, with no additional passengers. And then it came back heading *toward* the high school. Also quite soon."

"So whoever it is has not been subtle," said Bizzy.

"Or it has nothing to do with us," said Ryan.

"Mother made us paranoid, is that it?"

"Wasn't that her purpose?" asked Ryan.

"Yes," said Bizzy. "Only I'm used to ignoring most of her dire warnings because in all the years she's been warning me, nothing bad has happened. Unless you count invitations from strangers to get into their white van to help them hunt for a lost kitten."

"Come on," said Ryan. "Really?"

"Only once, and Mother had trained me well. My only answer was to stand there and scream at the top of my lungs, 'I will not get in your stupid car!'"

"Did that work?"

"He drove away fast, without closing the van door. So yes, I guess it did. I also don't think he was a Slovene witch hunter."

"And you were what, five?"

"I was such a lovely child," said Bizzy. "Everybody wanted me to help them hunt for kittens."

It was Ryan's first glimpse at what Bizzy's life must have been like. Always attracting attention even when she wasn't wearing her glamor face.

Always a target for predators. Who needed Slovenian loveks when there were regular pedophiles around all the time?

"It's really your mother the loveks want, isn't it," said Ryan.

"I have dangers of my own, yes," said Bizzy. "But what better way to get control of my mother than by first kidnapping and sequestering *me*?"

Ryan shuddered. "So . . . nobody wants to kill you. *Or* your mother. They want to use her, and use you to get her to cooperate."

"We don't know," said Bizzy. "I've heard about the loveks my whole life, the way other kids hear about Santa Claus and the Tooth Fairy. About five years ago, I started wondering if they were all in the same category of important imaginary beings. But it's clear Mother really does believe in them. She's really scared of them. And we have no idea what they want. There's lore of loveks who kill witches as soon as they're sure they have a magical power—and sometimes way before they're sure. But the fact that they haven't killed her already makes us wonder if maybe they have something else in mind. Me, I'm just a pawn in this game. Maybe Mother is, too."

"What does your father think?"

"Mother doesn't talk about it much with him. If the subject comes up when he's home, he rolls his eyes and leaves the room, so I think he doesn't believe in it or doesn't think it's a big deal, but he also doesn't want to fight with Mom, because who in his right mind *would*?"

"And here it comes again," said Ryan.

The white RAV4 drove toward them. Definitely the same SUV, definitely the same driver. Same child car seats in back. But the driver didn't so much as glance at them. Just concentrating on the road.

"Still, maybe he just forgot something and had to go back and get it," said Bizzy.

"The likeliest explanation."

"Don't tell Mom about it when we get home."

"I don't report to your mom unless she comes out to meet me, which she's only done, like, twice, so it's *your* job to not tell her about it."

"Fine," said Bizzy. "Leave all the heavy lifting up to me. Again."

"You'll never let me off the hook for that one, will you."

"Of course not," said Bizzy. "It's always good for a woman to identify the lazy men so she doesn't end up stuck with one."

"You're stuck with me for now," said Ryan.

"Fortunately, you're still a boy," said Bizzy.

"And you're not a woman," said Ryan. "So my laziness isn't an issue for you. As long as you're around to give me orders—which, you'll notice, I always obey promptly."

"Good evening, Mr. Burke," said Bizzy as she headed up the steps toward the Horvats' door.

"Good evening, Punca Horvat," said Ryan, not loudly, but still loud enough to be heard.

Bizzy swished her butt back and forth at the door to show that she heard him but didn't much care. Though the more Ryan thought of it, inside the house and later that night as he tried to get to sleep, the more he wondered why twitching her butt at him was her answer to his calling her "punca." Wasn't a butt-swish kind of like acting out the negative implications of "punca"? Or were those implications *always* negative? What did Bizzy mean by it?

Ryan knew perfectly well that the game of "What Did Bizzy Mean?" was a terrible one, because it led him down many miserable and lonely roads, all of them leading to despair.

If Dad were home, Ryan could ask him about women. Of course, if Dad actually knew anything about women, he'd probably still be living at home. Or he wouldn't have married Mom in the first place, which would certainly have had unfortunate consequences for Ryan and Dianne. But he could sure ask Dad more comfortably than he could ask Mom, because then he'd get her nightmare lecture about never getting involved with the Serbian family next door because Serbians were genocidal slaughterers, and she just couldn't hear Ryan when he endlessly repeated, "Slovenian, Slovenian, not Serbian."

He finally did fall asleep, thinking of a white RAV4 with a sturdy-looking man driving. Was he an assassin? A spy? Or a machinist picking up somebody after school but he got the time or place wrong and had to go back and look up the note his wife had left him?

* * *

The next morning, Ryan was outside sitting on the steps, watching cars drive past. What would it mean if he saw that RAV4 again? That he was still doing surveillance, or that he just had a regular errand that required him to drive past their house?

And what would it mean if he *didn't* see the RAV4? That the surveillance had ended? Or that they had switched vehicles?

The RAV4 drove by. The guy didn't glance at their house. He still had mud spatter on the side of the car. If they were doing surveillance, they were really bad at it, because they left random identifying marks on their car.

Or maybe they *meant* Ryan to notice, while the *real* dangerous car slipped past him unidentified.

For that matter, maybe the guy didn't glance at the duplex, because there were cameras on both sides of the car uploading images to the cloud.

The door behind him opened. Please be Bizzy. Please don't be Mrs. Horvat or Mother. Nor either her sibling or mine.

It was Bizzy. She sat beside him and put her arm on his back, hooking her hand over his near shoulder, in what Ryan could only assume was a convivial gesture. Putting her arm *around* him would have been at least affectionate and maybe even possessive. So of course she did the brotherly friend-zone thing.

Her hand is on your shoulder, bonehead, the voice inside his head pointed out. Enjoy it while it lasts.

"So you're checking out for lovek spy cars?" she asked.

"The same RAV4 drove past, heading toward school."

"So he has to drop off a kid."

"No high school kid in the car. No little kids in the car seats."

"So he's on his way to work," said Bizzy.

"Maybe," said Ryan. "But there he is, coming right back toward us."

"Well. That's bad news," said Bizzy.

Without really thinking about it, Ryan leapt to his feet and ran out into the street. Fortunately, nobody was coming from the left at that moment. Ryan stopped in the middle of the lane so that the RAV4 would either hit him or stop. Or go around, but Ryan could hear a phalanx of cars coming from behind him, so going around was probably off the table.

Either I die here or the car stops.

And what then? I pull out my .45 and start shooting through the windshield? What kind of stupid action movie do I think I'm in?

Running out here came to him like his micropower—doing what was necessary. But what in hell was it necessary for him to *do*? Every time before, he knew what he was about to do when he started acting instinctively. Where was that knowledge now?

Maybe I have to actually *think* this time, he thought. But if I actually think, I probably won't go through with it.

The guy stopped the RAV4. Then he just sat there, staring straight forward. Not even looking at Ryan, just staring off into space. No honking. No opening the window and yelling for this weird teenager to get out of the road.

So this was not just a guy with errands to run. Even in Virginia, where Dad said drivers tended to be polite, this was taking patience and courtesy *way* too far.

Ryan started walking toward the car.

Why am I walking toward the car? I'm unarmed, I have no martial arts training, and I don't know what I'm supposed to say.

Ryan walked up to the driver's-side window and signaled for the guy to lower the glass.

The guy lowered the glass and actually turned his face toward Ryan. "Why are you driving back and forth in front of our house and when we're walking on the street?"

"That's just the way I'm going."

"Back and forth?" asked Ryan. "What do you want?"

"I want to talk to the woman," said the guy.

"My mother?"

"Her mother."

"Talk to her? Or kill her?"

"I don't kill people," said the man.

"You personally? Or the group you belong to?"

"There are people who might want to kill her," said the man. "But I am not one of them. I want to help her."

"So driving back and forth and creeping us out—that's helping?"

"That's making sure nobody *else* does anything to the girl or the mother."

Ryan shook his head. "There's a front door. A concrete walkway leads right to the porch. Ring the doorbell. Either one. Then you say, 'I'd like to have a peaceful conversation with the mother of the pretty girl who goes to Vasco da Gama High.' Now, my sister is rather pretty, so there might be a moment's misunderstanding, but eventually you'll end up talking to the pretty girl you're looking for. And her mother."

The man closed his eyes and turned his face toward the front again. "She will call me clumsy and I'll probably trip and break my neck coming down the porch stairs."

"There is that danger," said Ryan. "What if I tell her that you *say* you only want to talk and you are trying to protect her."

"Will she believe you?" asked the man, still facing front.

"The only way to find out," said Ryan, "is to try."

Somebody in a car in the line waiting for the RAV4 to move honked a long blast.

The RAV4 suddenly patched out, accelerating rapidly away from Ryan.

Ryan stood there on the double yellow line as the other cars roared past. Several drivers flipped him off. Ryan agreed with them and therefore did not flip back.

When traffic coming the other way cleared again, Ryan jogged back to the porch, where Bizzy had *not* waited. Instead, she had gone inside and watched from a window. Now she came back out.

"Did you tell him to go away?" she asked.

"He says he isn't trying to kill you or your mother."

"And killers never lie," said Bizzy.

"He says he's driving back and forth to protect you. He says he only wants to talk to your mother. I pointed out that you have a doorbell beside the door, and he suggested that he didn't want your mother to inform him that he's clumsy and cause him to break his neck."

"Not an irrational fear," said Bizzy.

"I told him that I would tell your mother what he said."

"And then what?"

"Then we'd find out if she believed me."

"And how," said Bizzy, "will we find that out?"

"First," said Ryan, "I'll tell her. Then she'll say whether she believes me."

"She'll believe *you*. But will she believe what he told you?"

"When he asked me the same question—"

"It's a good question, isn't it?" said Bizzy.

"I told him, the only way to find out is to try."

"And so he said he'd come back later and ring the doorbell?"

"Somebody behind him honked and he peeled out like he thought he was driving a Maserati instead of a Toyota."

"So now let's walk to school," said Bizzy.

"It's still a little early," said Ryan.

"I want to see if he keeps passing us in order to protect us, or if your little confrontation discouraged him," said Bizzy.

"We have time for me to tell your mother," said Ryan.

"We don't have time for you to spend the next two days hiding out in your house because my mother told you that confronting that man was clumsy of you," said Bizzy.

"She wouldn't," said Ryan.

"I know her better than you do," said Bizzy.

"If she cursed me, my mother would kill her," said Ryan.

"She'd curse her too, and then your mother would trip and fall on her own knife," said Bizzy.

"Then she'd stand up and keep making stabbing motions until one of them killed your mother. Really, you don't know what *my* mother is capable of."

Bizzy stood and looked at him, shaking her head slightly. "You think this is funny?"

"I think I need to tell her. I kind of promised the guy that I'd at least try."

Bizzy walked to the door and opened it. She stepped inside. Ryan followed her.

Jake was inside, eating what looked like a tortilla with jam on it. "What's *he* doing inside here?" asked Jake, with a lot more hostility than Ryan would have expected.

"I invited him," said Bizzy.

"You know Mother said—"

"Please tell Ryan," said Bizzy, "whether he can talk to Mother right now."

Jake's eyes went wide. "Are you insane?"

"I'm not afraid of her," said Ryan mildly.

"Because you think she needs you to protect her *preciousss*?" Jake asked. He elongated the hissing sound so it reminded Ryan of Gollum in the Lord of the Rings movies.

"Yes," said Ryan. "Or are you ready to step up and do it?"

Jake took a menacing step toward Ryan, but Ryan decided not to back down. He just looked at Jake with mild interest.

Jake stopped. "Mother's not here. She went to work."

"Not till nine o'clock," said Ryan.

"She's covering somebody else's shift," said Jake. "No lie."

"No lie," said Bizzy. "I brought you in so you could see that we have nothing to hide, except for Jake's ridiculously bad manners."

"Suck rocks," said Jake to his sister.

"You always offer," said Bizzy, "but you never provide the rocks."

"Why couldn't you just tell me that she wasn't home?" Ryan asked Bizzy.

"I thought it was better for you to see for yourself."

"I can't *see* that she isn't home, because, like, I can only see this room," said Ryan. "And I would have taken your word for it on the porch."

"I also thought it would be good for you to see how well my strong and beautiful brother watches over me," said Bizzy.

"Let's head for school," said Ryan.

"I'm taking classes in mixed martial arts," said Jake.

"If you took classes in baking," said Bizzy, "you'd make some lucky girl a wonderful wife someday."

Jake grimaced at her and headed back into the new kitchen that used to be Dad's office.

"Your dad's gone, too?" asked Ryan.

"He pulled another all-nighter at the library," said Bizzy.

"Why aren't you guys worried the loveks will take *him* hostage."

"Why do you think we're *not*?" asked Bizzy.

"Who watches over him?" asked Ryan.

"My father is a dangerous man," said Bizzy. "He learned many skills of his own in Slovenia. Now, let's go."

Ryan followed her out of the house and pulled the door shut behind him. The RAV4 passed them twice on the way to school.

If it had been doing that before yesterday, Ryan would have noticed, and so would Bizzy. What changed? What made the watchers become so obvious?

What would happen if the guy rang the Horvats' doorbell before Ryan had a chance to talk to Mrs. Horvat?

Not my worry, thought Ryan. The watchers probably knew already that Mrs. Horvat wasn't there. For all Ryan knew, they had bugged the house, or had one of those directional microphones pointed at their window so that they could listen in on everything said there. So they should know that Ryan hadn't told Mrs. Horvat anything about the RAV4 guy.

Or maybe they were really incompetent and the guy would get cursed. So what? Clumsy people survived all the time. It wasn't always fatal.

15

On the way to school, Bizzy suddenly veered off the sidewalk and headed for the fence. It took a moment for Ryan to realize that it was the exact place where Bizzy had taken off from her mother that time, and so he did the same thing he had done then—he followed her. Only this time he was right behind her, and they ended up going down the hill and getting on the other street together.

"Any particular reason for this detour?" asked Ryan.

"Not a detour," said Bizzy. "I like this route."

"Going downhill here means we have to go uphill to get to the school, and it adds about a quarter mile to the trip."

"We're early. And isn't it fun to think of spy cars having to go all the way around?"

Ryan knew that wasn't really her motive. Bizzy could be playful, but the fact that she didn't warn him what she was doing meant that *this* reason wasn't invented until she had already led him this way.

"You're just being romantic," said Ryan. "This is *our* detour."

Bizzy gave one hoot of laughter. "Are you also going to keep the anniversary of our first kiss?"

"Did that count as an actual kiss?" asked Ryan.

"I was really kissing *you*," said Bizzy. "And it sure felt like you were really kissing me. Even if there had been a layer of plastic cling wrap between us it would have counted as a real kiss."

"It's only a first kiss if there's also a second," said Ryan. "Otherwise, it's just an only kiss."

She stopped, swiveled to him, grabbed his head, and planted a kiss on him that was so passionate it blew the previous one out of the water. Since it came without warning, he hadn't taken a breath, and when it ended he had to gasp for air.

"Hello," said Ryan, when he could breathe again.

"You walked in front of a moving car for me," said Bizzy.

"He stopped."

"You didn't know he would."

"He had plenty of time to stop, I could see that."

"You didn't know that he would stop," said Bizzy.

"If I'd known it would earn me a kiss like that, from you specifically, I would have been stepping in front of cars for the past three weeks."

"Not all of them would have stopped," said Bizzy.

"I bet you'd visit me in the hospital, though," said Ryan.

"Or in the morgue," said Bizzy. "Enough with the kissing. I have something to show you."

They were in a gap between houses on this road, just a sidewalk and woods on both sides of the street. She turned her back on him. "Okay," she said, "I've got it, but you have to walk around me to see."

Ryan walked around her, looked her up and down.

"My face," she said. "I didn't do anything with my *knees*, you idiot."

He looked at her face.

It wasn't Bizzy.

Well, it was, but things had changed. Nothing huge. A little tighter here, a little slacker there. Her eyes were somehow different—bigger? Smaller? More or less slanted or squinty? Ryan couldn't decide about anything, and yet it was everything, her whole face was changed, and if this were the face on her driver's license, nobody would believe it was her ID.

"This is what," Ryan said, "your anti-glamor?"

"Exactly," said Bizzy.

"Well, it didn't make you ugly. So if that was the goal, failure."

"I didn't know what it would do. But I followed your advice. You know, learning how to wiggle your ear. I looked at my face when I did glamor, and felt how each muscle changed, tightening, loosening, and then I worked on each one of them, doing the opposite."

"How many separate moves was that?"

"About eleven, on each side of my face. There were some that were too hard to isolate, so the real total, when I do the glamor, is about thirty. But these eleven were enough to make me . . ." Her voice trailed off. She didn't know what to call this new look.

"A completely different person," said Ryan.

"Except, you know, hair and clothes. If I really wanted to pass for somebody else, I'd need a different walk, but not anything distinctive. I don't want a limp like Aaron Withunga's. Just different from what I usually do."

"But still a girl walk, not a boy walk."

"Right," said Bizzy. "I've never really looked at girl walks, except the idiot girls who try to do a sexy walk. They end up looking like beginner prostitutes."

"You've studied the difference between beginner and—"

Bizzy sighed. "I've never knowingly seen a prostitute except in movies or on TV. I'm just saying—"

"That's not a walk you're going for anyway, that's what you were saying."

"This is just the beginning. And it's beginning to hurt a little."

"Well, let it go."

"So get behind me again," said Bizzy.

"I want to watch the change."

"It's going to be weird," she said.

"I hope so," said Ryan.

"I don't want you having nightmares with my face in them," said Bizzy.

"Your face is in all my other dreams," he said. "Let's make it a complete set."

As he watched her face, it started changing. It happened asymmetrically, a few things on the right side, different things on the left. And when the changes stopped, it still wasn't right.

"I was afraid of this," said Bizzy. "I'm afraid the only way I can get out of weird-face is to go to glamor-face."

"I like glamor-face," said Ryan. "I don't mind seeing it again."

"You do *not* like glamor-face," said Bizzy.

"My first kiss was with glamor-face," said Ryan.

"But the *best* kiss was with my regular face," said Bizzy.

"That's the best? I've got nothing more to look forward to?"

"Do *I* have anything better to look forward to?" asked Bizzy.

"Come on, you're the first female human I've ever kissed who wasn't a relative, and I didn't kiss any relatives like *that*."

"Such a relief," said Bizzy.

"I need practice. And who do I have to practice on except you?"

"You have no access to a CPR dummy?"

"They don't kiss back," said Ryan.

"The expensive ones do," said Bizzy.

"We're at Vasco da Gama High," said Ryan. "And besides, no they don't. Why would they ever make a CPR dummy that would—" Her face went to full glamor and he couldn't talk. And then she relaxed into her regular face. "Bizzy," he whispered.

"You were saying?" she said.

"That was not the same glamor-face that you did when your mom triggered you."

"My mom-triggered glamor is one thing. It's another when I do it. It's a third thing when I go from weird-face to glamor-face."

"That's not it," said Ryan.

Bizzy put a finger on his lips.

He talked anyway. "That was the glamor-face that appears when you're talking to the guy that you just kissed like you meant it."

"You're saying it's not my glamor-face, it's my lovey-face, is that it?" asked Bizzy.

"I'm saying it was different."

"Better?"

"Every version of your glamor-face is perfect. Beyond perfect. You know that."

"But this one? That I just showed you?"

"It felt like it was just for me," said Ryan.

"It was," said Bizzy. "That's why I took you on this detour—'*our* detour,' s'il vous plaît."

"Is that Slovenian?"

"'Please' in Slovenian is '*prosim*,'" said Bizzy.

"You took me here to show me my private version of your glamor-face?"

"I took you here to show you that I'm taking GRUT seriously and I'm trying to turn my micropower into something more versatile. You say that when I'm walking along with my regular face, glamor-face keeps blinking on and off, and it makes people notice me. Right?"

"That's what it looks like to me."

"But if I walk along with weird-face, maybe only my regular face will blink on and off, and nobody will look. I mean, my weird face isn't freakish, is it? I don't look like the Elephant Man?"

"No," said Ryan. "You look like . . . a regular girl. Kind of pretty. The kind of pretty that could use a little help from makeup. Like most girls."

"So my weird-face is actually more of a regular face than my regular face."

"I guess so. Yes. But apparently, you can't walk or even turn around when doing weird-face."

"Not yet. I lose concentration. But the more I practice, the better I'll be at holding that face while walking."

"You do fine while talking," said Ryan.

"Because I've had more practice doing that."

"Has your mother seen that face?" asked Ryan.

"*You* have seen that face. My mirror has seen that face."

"We're going to be so late to school," said Ryan.

"I'll just tell the principal I had to stop and kiss you because you're so damn cute," said Bizzy.

"I'm sure he'll believe *that*," said Ryan.

"I think you are," said Bizzy.

"Apparently, I have a face that only looks good to second-generation Slovenian immigrant girls."

"That's good enough for me," said Bizzy. She kissed him again. This time it was a real girlfriend kiss. Not long, not passionate, just quick. A declaration of ownership. A little more lingering than a husband-wife kiss. A little more possessive. But still brief enough not to get teased about it by other people in the halls at school.

"What am I?" asked Ryan.

"Start walking," she said. They started walking briskly along the sidewalk.

"What am I?" Ryan asked again.

"I'm not sure what you're asking. You Ryan, me Bizzy?"

"Am I your . . ." He didn't finish the question.

"You are," she said.

"Say it," he said.

"Say what?"

"You have to say it before I'll believe it."

"Tell me what to say," said Bizzy.

"No," said Ryan. "You say it, if it's true."

She put her hand in his and they walked about five steps before she said, "You're my fant."

Ryan almost cried. The emotion that swept over him—relief, triumph, joy, love, he couldn't name all of the feelings—it was nothing he had ever felt before.

"You're such a sap. Do you watch all the new Hallmark movies every Christmas?" said Bizzy.

"Hallmark movies aren't just at Christmas anymore," said Ryan, trying to sound ironically informative.

"You sound like a boy in love," said Bizzy.

"I've sounded like that since about six minutes after we met," said Ryan.

"What took you so long?"

"That's how long it took for me to realize that you're actually smarter than me."

She squeezed his hand. "I know that was hard for you to say."

"Saying it would be easy, except that it's true."

"You stepped in front of a car for me," said Bizzy softly.

He had nothing to say to that. So he said something stupid. "After putting a bee in my mouth, what's a car?"

"Bigger," said Bizzy.

"No stinger," said Ryan. And then, because he really was too emotional to stay on this subject, he said, "If you want the new weird-face to really be weird. You know, ugly. Make it asymmetrical."

She didn't say anything.

"Not a complete half-and-half—glamor one side, weird on the other."

"That would be way too memorable," she said.

"Just one thing. Or two."

"I practiced symmetry," she said.

"I wiggle only one ear," said Ryan. "It can be done."

"That's actually a good idea," she said. "Most people aren't symmetrical."

"That's part of what works with glamor-face," said Ryan. "It really is perfectly symmetrical."

"More mirror time," said Bizzy. "It's a good thing I'm not actually narcissistic."

16

All day, Ryan kept getting impatient with all the rituals of high school. Changing classes, walking the halls, stopping at his locker. Why am I doing this? What does it matter?

He knew all the standard reasons. So he could get fine grades and get into a good school, though as far as Ryan could see, most adults said "good school" when they meant "university that you can brag about having attended." Ryan had once read that any university with a decent library will get you the education you want, as long as you take initiative and apply yourself. He recognized his own laziness in the idea of "getting through" school—which is what he was doing with high school. Get a diploma. Have a high grade point average so you can get into a "good school." Ace the SAT and the ACT. But all that really mattered was getting through and moving on to something real.

None of it was real. Mr. Hardesty tried to be real, tried to get his students to conceive of history as something substantial, a lens through which the world could be viewed. But it wasn't a lens, it wasn't polished, it couldn't be focused. When it came to things like that, Ryan was on his own. Everybody was on their own, but almost nobody understood that. They all thought they were "getting an education." It was like they were all being taught one set of dance moves, a single piece of choreography. If they worked hard and really got it down, would they be dancers? Absolutely not.

Knowing one dance doesn't mean you know how to dance. All these high school students, including him, weren't becoming "educated." They were being trained. For what? To perform tasks that only had meaning when they were performed *at school.* We are learning the dance of public secondary education. Unless we become high school teachers, God forbid, we will never have to perform that dance again, or even think about it.

Such thoughts roiled through Ryan's mind, but he knew he had thought them before, without feeling any anxiety about it. I'm marking time, yes, he had told himself for a couple of years now, but so is everyone else. As Dad says, it's just a way of keeping adolescents out of the labor pool precisely when minds and muscles are at their most creative and flexible, so that kids don't get into the workforce until they're more nearly untrainable and unadaptable.

But Dad was an eccentric. Nobody else thought like him.

Except me, thought Ryan. I think like him, and not just because he talks like that. Other kids tune out their father or mother or both, and learn to think only what their teachers or siblings or peers think. Everybody joins into somebody's collective opinion. Except Dad. And if I join in with his collective opinion, it's not like it provides me with ready answers. It just provides me with difficult questions and leaves me to make up my own mind.

Somewhere just before lunch, as Ryan tuned out the drone of the chemistry teacher talking about molecular bonds—a subject Ryan had mastered in seventh grade—it finally dawned on him: The only worthwhile education he had ever received was the training he had from his skeptical, irreverent, sarcastic, earnest, reliable father.

What was that education? Question everything, but keep your word. Doubt everything, but never give others a reason to doubt *you.*

It all came together at lunch, when Ryan said to Bizzy, "Do you think you could come with me to my dad's job site right after school?"

Bizzy cocked her head. "What's the agenda?"

"Well," said Ryan, "I could say that I want my girlfriend to know my dad, but that's not the reason."

"You want your dad to know your girlfriend?"

"I don't need his approval to know how I feel and what I want," said Ryan. "It's this: My dad is the wisest person I know. When he gives me advice, so far it's always worked. At least, whenever I was smart enough to follow it."

"And you want advice about . . ."

Ryan gave her a trying-to-be-patient-with-an-idiot look. "Stepping in front of a car was an impulse from my micropower. Walking up to the driver with no idea what to say to him, that was my clueless self coming into play. I think we need some kind of plan, some kind of best-case scenario we could be working toward, instead of reacting to threats all the time."

Bizzy nodded.

"I don't think he'd *know* what we should do," said Ryan, "because I don't think he even knows about micropowers. I haven't told him, and Mom has no idea, so she hasn't told him. He'll be hearing it all for the first time."

"You haven't told your mom?"

Ryan thought about that for a second. "Instinct," he said. "Dianne and I don't tell Mom stuff that will make her crazy."

"And what stuff is that?"

"Anything that matters," said Ryan.

"Come on," said Bizzy.

"You're right. What we don't tell her is anything that will make her think we're accusing her of something, or anything that will make her feel like she's not in control of everything about our lives."

"So . . . you don't tell her anything that matters," said Bizzy.

"She doesn't know about my micropower."

"How would that make her crazy?" asked Bizzy.

"She'd try to take control of it. She'd try to get me to demonstrate it. She'd try to set up situations to trigger it."

"Like Indefensible did," said Bizzy.

"Except her schemes would be pathetic and would never work. Defense's did. When my mom's attempts failed, she'd accuse me of deliberately *not* using my micropower because I despise her. Or something."

"You sound angry with your mother," said Bizzy.

"I don't think I am, though," said Ryan. "I'm just used to her and tired of what happens when one of us triggers her, so . . . Dianne and I both use avoidance as our make-life-at-home-livable strategy."

"You'll tell your dad," said Bizzy, "because your mom *would* believe it and make everything crazy, but your dad *won't* believe it and so he'll be helpful."

"Unless you've got a micropower yourself," said Ryan, "it's pretty hard to believe."

"Maybe he has one," said Bizzy.

"If he does, he isn't talking about it."

"Add in my mother's ability to curse people, then top it with the Slovenian witch hunters. That's kind of a lot for a rational person to absorb," said Bizzy.

"My dad *is* a rational person," said Ryan. "But he'll ask questions, maybe even questions neither of us had thought about. You know? I think it's worth a trip. I'll go alone if you can't get permission from your mom, or if you don't have the time. But I'd really like to have you there."

"Because you want him to meet me."

"Because he won't believe that I could ever have a girlfriend like you unless he sees for himself."

"I can believe that," said Bizzy. "Nobody else here at school can believe it, either."

"Especially not Defense," said Ryan. "And no, I'm not going to kiss you right here after we both just got through eating school lunch. Especially not when I'd have to lean over a table and probably knock something over or get food on my shirt, and then somebody might look at me and say, 'Clumsy of you.'"

"Got it," said Bizzy. "You're afraid *I'd* do those things and you were taking it on yourself to spare my feelings."

"Sweet of you to pretend to think that's possible," said Ryan.

It took two bus rides, but by now Ryan and Bizzy both had their youth passes for the bus system, so being broke was no barrier. Right now Dad was doing a remodel on a fast-food place, which had cars going through the drive-through while the dining room was still under construction. That meant a working kitchen with a lot of plastic barriers up to keep construction dust from getting into the food.

"This doesn't seem like a good place for an after-school snack," said Dad.

"Not here for the food," said Ryan. "Someplace private and quiet?"

Dad led them out to his camper in the parking lot, behind a bunch of cones. "Sorry to interrupt you at work," said Ryan. "Without, you know, checking first."

"It's fine," said Dad. "You've never brought anyone with you before, so I'm guessing this meeting matters."

Ryan indicated for Bizzy to sit at Dad's worktable, which she did, as smoothly as Ryan expected. Ryan, not so smooth, pulled out a stool and sat, much lower, across from Dad.

"Dad, this is Bojana. She goes by Bizzy. With a 'Y.' She lives in the new half of our house."

"Bizzy Horvat, right?" asked Dad, offering a hand. "I met you at the lease signing."

"Yes, sir," said Bizzy.

"She's also my girlfriend, Dad," said Ryan.

He had never said that sentence to his father before. He wasn't sure whether his father would say something supposedly witty that ridiculed Ryan somehow, or would instead be gracious and supportive.

"I didn't know Ryan moved in circles where such a thing would be possible," said Dad.

What, Ryan wanted to say. You thought I was gay?

But he didn't actually say that. It was what he *would* have said if Bizzy hadn't been sitting there. It was what he was *going* to say if Father teased him later.

"Mr. Burke," said Bizzy, "the social circle that brought Ryan and me together was the back deck you installed on our side of the house. Ryan sits on the bottom step and says smart and funny things, and I sit on the deck and try to keep up. And because we're both saturated with adolescent hormones, and the moon is often out, it was inevitable that we would fall in love."

Dad laughed out loud. "Okay, Ryan, I like her."

"Dad, I *did* want you to meet her, and her to meet you, but Bizzy and I have a real problem, a serious one, because we are both micropotents."

"A term needing definition," said Dad.

Ryan proceeded to define micropowers and tell about GRUT and Dr. Withunga and Aaron Withunga. He told the story of the bees, and then the story of stopping Errol from killing Defense. He did not tell about Jannis healing both Defense and Errol. He did not tell about Bizzy's power. Because that one was far more convincing when you saw it than when you told about it.

So when Ryan's stories were done, and Dad asked some questions about Dr. Withunga and then sat there nodding thoughtfully, Bizzy said, "I think you need to see my micropower."

He looked at her.

When nothing happened, he looked at Ryan.

"Keep looking at *her*," Ryan said.

Dad looked at her again. And then his chair toppled backward against the wall behind him. Then the chair slid out from under him, jamming one leg into Ryan's shin across from him.

Ryan jumped up, dealing with his own pain while trying to help his dad get back on his feet. Ryan picked up his father's chair, set it in place, and even got Dad to sit back down—but through it all, Dad couldn't keep his eyes off Bizzy's face.

"Maybe you should relax a little," Ryan said.

"Not possible," said Dad.

"I meant Bizzy." Ryan watched as Bizzy relaxed all the things she did to make glamor-face.

"And you can just do that," said Dad. "Whenever you want?"

"She rarely wants to," said Ryan. "It kind of stops traffic. Nobody's seen that face at school, for instance, except maybe just glimpses."

"I couldn't help thinking, the yearbook staff is going to want pictures of you on every single page," said Dad.

"I'm hoping for no pictures of me at all," said Bizzy.

"What matters here, Dad, now that you've actually seen a micropower in action, the reason we came here, is that Bizzy isn't the only one in her family with a micropower."

And Bizzy told him about her mother's "clumsy" curse. And her "you're so pretty" curse that only worked on Bizzy.

"She actually does that to you?" asked Dad.

"When I really annoy her," said Bizzy.

"Who would do that to their own . . ." His voice trailed off. Ryan didn't know why, but Dad's eyes teared up a little. They got a little shiny.

"In Slovenia," said Bizzy, "if you can mutter a curse and then bad things happen to the person you cursed, there are people who take note. People who hunt for witches."

"Burn them at the stake?" asked Dad.

"They don't care how they kill you. Belief in witches is different in Slovenia. At least among the *lovece*."

"Loveks," said Ryan. "Hunters. Witch hunters."

Then Ryan told about his conversation with the watcher in the RAV4 that morning.

"Do you believe him?" Dad asked.

"He was talking in a monotone," said Ryan. "He was looking straight forward through the windshield, not at me. He has a Slovenian accent, way stronger than Mrs. Horvat's. So I don't know whether I would have any ability to detect a deceptive pattern. I think it's possible that he means no harm, because, you know, he's done no harm. He might have been watching out for Bizzy like he said, driving back and forth. Or he might have been setting up the conversation we had, and it's a lie designed to get him inside the Horvats' house without getting himself a clumsy-curse."

Dad immediately started asking new questions. "Does anybody else in the GRUT group have some micropower that might protect you?"

Ryan shrugged. "We don't know a lot of the powers. The guy who knows where all the spiders are, that's not much help."

"But Flower Girl—Dahlia?" suggested Bizzy.

Ryan nodded, then explained to Dad. "Dahlia can make people yawn. She sometimes goes with the police. Even people crazy on drugs can't put up much of a fight or run away very fast if they're constantly yawning."

"So that's good," said Dad. "She doesn't have to say anything? No audible curse?"

"When she does it, people don't have any idea why they're yawning," said Ryan. "She's done it to me, even though she knows Dr. Withunga forbids using our micropowers against each other."

"Dahlia's a yawning rectum," said Bizzy. It sounded so pretty when she said it.

"But she'd help," said Ryan. "She helps. So that's a good idea."

"I think she secretly has a crush on Ryan," said Bizzy.

"In all my life," said Ryan, "only one person has ever had a crush on me."

Bizzy looked at him in surprise. "Who?"

Dad laughed again.

"So the real question is, Bizzy, would your mom let one of these supposed protector guys into her house? Like Mr. RAV4?"

"Maybe if he passed through a Transportation Safety Administration gate first, to make sure he wasn't armed," said Bizzy.

"I think that if Mrs. Horvat knew that we could disable anybody who tried anything, she might. I mean, she lets me walk Bizzy to and from school, because she knows that I only barely kept myself from killing Errol Dell. So she knew I could protect Bizzy."

Dad shook his head. "Not from a sniper bullet."

"Her feeling was," said Bizzy, "that sniper bullets could have ended the story back in Slovenia or anytime at all here in the United States. She was more afraid of kidnapping. A hostage situation."

"Why did you come to me?" asked Dad. "You know I'm not former military or anything."

"He says you're very wise," said Bizzy. "He says you ask good questions."

Ryan was glad, because her saying that meant he didn't have to, which would have embarrassed Dad.

"It sounds as if your mother is betting her life on this decision," said Dad.

"She believes she is," said Bizzy. "I don't have any evidence to contradict her belief."

"And I don't know anything," said Ryan.

"You know what your GRUT group can do."

"But I don't want to put the people of GRUT into a position of danger. I mean, what if they come in, guns blazing, and all we've got is yawning and belly-button detection?"

"And you," said Dad, "doing whatever it takes to keep Bizzy safe."

"Maybe what it takes to keep Bizzy safe," said Ryan, "is not to let this Slovenian clown troupe anywhere near the Horvats' house."

"The *prevent* defense," said Dad.

"A term from sports?" said Bizzy.

"Yes," said Dad.

"And you think Ryan will understand it?" asked Bizzy skeptically.

"He's been my dad all my life," said Ryan. "I understand most of his sports references."

Dad grinned. "You don't," said Dad. "But I'm touched that you think you do."

17

When Ryan left Bizzy at the Horvats' and came over to the Burke side of the house, Mom wasn't home, but Dianne was.

"It's all over school," said Dianne. "You and Bo-nana."

"Her name is Bizzy," said Ryan. "Please don't be annoying. I like it better when we don't fight."

"What's *with* that? I used to be able to get into a fight with you just by looking at you funny," said Dianne.

"I'm trying to grow up," said Ryan.

"How's that coming?" asked Dianne.

"Mostly okay," said Ryan. "Don't you have homework?"

"Already done, while you and Bo-nana were off doing whatever you do when you're pretending to walk her home."

"I actually walk her home, Dianne," said Ryan. "I've got an assignment due in chem tomorrow."

"A pipe bomb?"

"We don't do explosives," said Ryan. "What is it you *want*?"

"We need to talk."

"Not about Bizzy," said Ryan. "I don't owe any explanations to you or to her little brother."

"He may have a six-pack, but he's such a tool," said Dianne.

"My opinion, too," said Ryan.

"You think I'm a tool, too? Does Bizzy?"

"This may be hard to believe, Dianne, but we don't actually discuss you."

"Never?" asked Dianne.

"Not once," said Ryan. "What's your agenda here, Dianne? You can't really be trying to pick a fight with me, because Mom's not even here to see it."

"You're being nice to me because Dad told you to."

"Dad and Mom have told us not to fight since we were little."

"So why did it work this time?" asked Dianne.

Ryan didn't know what would come from telling her. But why not? "He said that he wouldn't give me a job until I could prove that I would get along with my coworkers. And he said that the proof I was ready would be if I could stop letting you goad me and just . . . not fight."

"So I'm part of your job application to Dad," said Dianne.

"Being able to control my temper is part of my job application," said Ryan. "And here's the weird thing. Since I stopped yelling at you and figuring out ways to make you sad or angry, I've discovered a remarkable thing."

"That life at home is boring now?"

"That you're nice. And funny sometimes. And I like watching rom-coms with you and Mom."

"So you decided not to be a man?"

"So I decided not to be a jack-in-the-box that you can wind up and set off whenever you feel like it," said Ryan. "I decided I wanted to be a guy who could be patient."

"But not for a job with Dad, now, right? Now you just want to be nice in order to impress Bizzy."

Ryan shook his head.

"Don't deny it," said Dianne.

"I'm not denying it. But being nice to impress a girlfriend is easy, compared with being nice to a little sister."

Dianne sat down on the sofa that in a couple of hours was going to be Ryan's bed. "We need to talk, Ryan."

"We could have skipped the whole trying-to-get-me-to-fight-with-you routine," said Ryan.

"I needed to know if I could actually talk to you," said Dianne.

"So . . . something serious?"

"Mom's not here," said Dianne. "We need to talk about Mom."

Ryan felt his gut twist.

"Don't panic," said Dianne. "But Mom and Dad are splitting up, and it doesn't make any sense."

"I don't have any more information than you have," said Ryan.

"I know," said Dianne. "But I have information you don't have."

"What? Mom doesn't keep a diary, so you can't have been reading it."

"Ryan, listen," said Dianne, and now there was no teasing in her voice at all. "I have information that you don't have because you're a boy, and therefore you don't notice anything, or if you do, you have no idea what it means."

Now he knew why she had tested his resolve not to fight. Because a statement like that would have set off a huge fight only a few weeks ago.

"Okay," said Ryan. "I accept that possibility. What did I either not notice or not understand?"

Dianne indicated for him to sit down. He did, and they each twisted around on the couch to face each other.

"When did they get mad?"

"About a day before Dad moved out," said Ryan.

"And up till that day, did you notice anything different about them?"

Ryan tried to think back, but it wasn't as if he had his memories all organized into a calendar so he could remember what happened just before something else.

"Dianne, just tell me, please. Don't make me try to discover it in my own memory, because I'll never be able to do it."

"I know, I'm sorry, I just—I'm sure of what I saw and what it meant. I just don't know how it all connects up."

"Tell me," said Ryan. "Because she's going to come home, and I'm guessing that's the end of this conversation."

"Okay," said Dianne. "For about ten weeks before the big implosion, they were all lovey-dovey."

Ryan tried to think what that meant.

"Dad would come home from work," said Dianne, "and he'd go straight to Mom and hug her and kiss her."

"I always try not to see that."

"They weren't subtle, Ryan," said Dianne. "You saw it. You even made icky faces at me."

"I was younger then," said Ryan. "I didn't know what kissing was for."

"And now you do?" she asked.

"Don't get distracted," said Ryan. "And, yes, now I do."

Dianne sighed, sat up straight, and then relaxed back into a confiding posture. "There was other stuff I noticed that I'm quite sure you didn't. First, sometimes Dad would come up behind Mom and instead of just hugging her, he'd put his hands—"

"Oh, please," said Ryan.

"Listen," she said. "He'd put his hands on her abdomen."

Ryan realized that yes, he had seen that.

"He wouldn't say anything, but he'd lean his head in and nuzzle her neck while his hands stayed there. If you think, you'll know what that meant."

"He loved her?"

"During that same time, Mom started throwing up every morning. Does that mean anything to you?"

"Flu?" Ryan asked.

"She was perfectly healthy after she ate dry toast and drank warm water. Not tea, not honey-lemon, nothing she drinks when she's sick. Just dry toast and warm water in the morning."

"I don't know what kind of coded message that information contains," said Ryan.

"Bizzy would know," said Dianne.

"But she isn't here," said Ryan.

"Ryan, Mom was pregnant."

"She's not pregnant," said Ryan.

"I know she *is* not pregnant. But she *was* pregnant. And Dad was glad about it."

"They would have told us," said Ryan.

"Eventually," said Dianne. "But in health class, they tell girls stuff that they don't tell boys. Like, what pregnancy means and stuff. And one thing my health teacher said last spring really rang a bell. She said that when women are older, pregnancy is a lot riskier. Chances of having a baby with birth defects are much higher. And chances of a miscarriage. And she said that's why older couples often don't tell anybody they're pregnant for a few months, because they aren't sure it's going to last. See?"

"But Mom's not that old."

"Late thirties," said Dianne. "That's a lot riskier than early twenties, like when she had us."

"Mid-twenties," said Ryan.

"Whatever," said Dianne. "They didn't tell us, but she was puking. That's morning sickness. I could hear her in their bathroom in the mornings—my wall is right next to—"

"I know where your room is," said Ryan. "Was. And I heard it too, sometimes. It wasn't subtle."

"Exactly. But after Dad moved out, did she ever throw up like that again?"

"I don't keep a calendar in my head," said Ryan. "So just tell me. Did she?"

"The pregnancy was over. She threw up in the morning about a week before Dad moved out. But not after that. Not at all that last week."

"And you were actually keeping track of that?" asked Ryan.

"When I realized she was pregnant, yeah, sure, I was tracking it. You'll never be pregnant, but there's a decent chance I will, someday. Maybe I'll be a puker, like Mom. If it just stops after a while, that's a good thing to know. If pregnancy means I puke for two months, but then it stops."

"So you were tracking it."

"Last vomity morning, and then a week later, they have a huge fight, of which we do not hear a single word because it was the worst fight of their whole marriage and they didn't want us to hear it."

"A silent fight, and the marriage is over."

"And Mother wasn't pregnant anymore."

Ryan leaned back on the couch. "You think Dad *did* something to her that—"

"No, moron," said Dianne. "*Think!* You know Dad isn't violent; you know he never hits us *or* her, no chance of that. Haven't you ever heard of a miscarriage? Suddenly Mom's not pregnant anymore. And a week later, Dad moves out."

Ryan sat there, processing this. "But if it wasn't Dad's fault, why did she kick him out? Why that crap about Dad caring about another family more than us?"

"You think I haven't been guessing, *trying* to guess how it all fits together? We know Dad wasn't having an affair, we know he wasn't taking care of another family, and a couple of days ago, it finally dawned on me what Mother meant when she said those nasty things."

"You always blamed Mom," said Ryan.

"I still do," said Dianne, "but that's not what this is really about. I'm trying to *understand*, and here's my guess. Mom lost the baby, because, you know, late thirties. It's just the odds. But Dad says to her, fine, babe, we'll try again. We'll get pregnant again."

"And Mom . . . what, she says no?"

"I don't know why, I don't know what led up to it, but I think maybe Mom says, let's not try, it'll just be another miscarriage, I'm too old, I don't want to try, we've got these two kids and that's fine, that's enough."

Ryan thought that sounded believable.

"But *Dad* wants to have a family with three children. Instead of *this* family with *two* children."

It finally dawned on Ryan. "He cares more about a different family. The version of the Burke family that has three children, instead of this one."

"So Mom mutters, 'He cares about another family more than this one.'"

"So Mom isn't lying, but the other family doesn't actually exist. It's the family Dad wants, the one Mom doesn't want to try for anymore."

"Maybe that was really a big deal for Dad. Maybe having more than two children was important."

"It was a long time to wait between you and Baby Three."

"Maybe there were miscarriages before. Back when I hadn't had health class yet, and we were both too young and ignorant to realize Mom was pregnant. I mean, maybe this was the third or fourth or fifth miscarriage, and Mom was done trying."

"And Dad wasn't."

"From there," said Dianne, "I don't understand what happened. But you know Mom. Even if Dad is being all understanding, she *sees* that he's really hurt and disappointed, and you know how that—"

"Mom gets mad."

"She gets mad because she thinks his being hurt is an attempt by him to manipulate her, because when *she* acts hurt, it *is* an attempt to manipulate somebody. Us, or him."

"Story of our happy family life," said Ryan.

"So the fight is because he isn't happy enough about knowing she's not going to try for another baby."

Ryan continued her scenario: "So it doesn't matter that he would probably have accepted it in the long run. *She* starts being furious because *he* isn't happy with just two kids, *he* wants to be with a larger family and—"

"And she gets so mad she says, 'Maybe you ought to go live where you don't have to keep seeing this disappointing family all the time.'" Dianne's imitation of Mother's sarcastic voice was spot-on.

"I can't see Dad moving out because Mom had a miscarriage," said Ryan.

"But can you see him moving out because Mom was being a total . . . fishwife about him still wishing for more children? If she *tells* him to move out? If she tells him, if you want a big family, there are plenty of women who'll pop out as many babies as you want, pop pop pop."

Ryan couldn't help but laugh at Dianne's imitation of Mom saying that. Still, "This is so not fair," said Ryan. "We don't know what she said, *if* she said anything at all like that. We don't *know* anything."

"Correct," said Dianne. "Except a week after Mom stopped puking, Dad moved out, and Mom was muttering all that crap about Dad caring about another family more than us."

"And you've been brooding about it—"

"Because I knew Mom had been pregnant, and you didn't," said Dianne.

"And finally you've come up with a pretty believable story—"

"Because we've both lived in this family long enough to know how Dad and Mom *both* act," said Dianne, "and the ridiculous way they fight without fighting, and—"

"And even though we have no idea if they even had these conversations," said Ryan, "we know that these are the kinds of conversations they might have had, and whatever got said, *something* happened, *something* was said that put Dad out of this house and got them to file papers because they agreed that the marriage was over."

"Exactly," said Dianne. "That's the crucial thing. Neither of them has said or hinted anything about wanting the other one back. They both know we think this is a stupid lousy thing for them to do to us, but neither of them is explaining anything, except for Mom's veiled accusations. They're just moving ahead with tearing up our lives, and *that's* not like them."

Ryan nodded. "Mom should be defending herself even though nobody's accusing her, because that's what she does, only except for those mutterings, *nothing*. And Dad should be defending Mother, the way he always does, being totally understanding and explaining to us why Mom is so mad and how it's probably inevitable now for the marriage to end, yadda, yadda, without ever blaming Mom for anything."

"That's what's missing here. Dad's not defending Mom, and Mom's not defending Mom, and yet Dad's living in an apartment which we're never invited to visit, and all we get is texts from him because Mom won't take his calls—"

"I know," said Ryan ruefully. "I tried calling her on Dad's phone and she texted back, 'Die.'"

"I've seen worse," said Dianne. "It's pure rage. Mom is walking around so tight with rage that *anything* might set her off. I know you feel it, I know that's part of why you've been so nice, doing the garbage, putting away dishes, *washing* dishes, being this model son. You even stopped sleeping naked on the couch. You wear actual pajama bottoms now, you pervert."

"I knew it bothered Mom," said Ryan.

"You used to do it *because* it bothered Mom—and me, too, I might add. I know you have a butt, but you don't have to keep proving it—and then you stopped sleeping naked—"

"Because I was trying not to be a jerk anymore," said Ryan.

"And succeeding. You've been succeeding. I have actually gotten some idea of why a cool girl like Bizzy would actually find you acceptable boyfriend material."

"Thank you for that," said Ryan. "And thank you for telling me what was going on last spring. I almost said, I can't believe I didn't notice Mom was pregnant, but of course I *can* believe it. What would have been unbelievable was if I *did* notice. So thank you. For helping all this crap in our family make a little sense."

"But they're still being childish," said Dianne. "I still don't buy it that they'd break up the family over this. Mom can be a loon sometimes, but come on, would Dad's disappointment really set her off so much, so *long*, that she'd let the family break up over it?"

Ryan sat there, thinking. "But that was your story," he said.

"It fits, but it doesn't fit well enough. There's something else."

"I can see why you refused to blame Dad, because you knew he hadn't had an affair."

"You knew it, too. You just thought from what Mom said—and heck, Ryan, at least with an affair their splitting up would make some kind of real-world sense."

"So I was blaming Dad, and you were saying he didn't do *that*, because you knew about the miscarriage—"

And Mom walked into the room.

How had she gotten the front door open without them hearing her?

Because Ryan never closed it when he came in. He and Dianne had started almost-fighting immediately, and he set down his backpack but didn't close the door. So Mom could walk up onto the porch and stand there and listen . . .

Mom didn't erupt. She didn't yell. She didn't say some vicious, sarcastic thing.

Instead, she closed the door behind her.

Then she walked up and stood behind the back of the couch. Neither Ryan nor Dianne turned on the couch to look at her. They were both looking down at their laps, waiting, waiting.

Mom's voice was quiet. "You were very observant, Dianne," said Mom. "And Ryan, I appreciate your effort to be loyal to me."

Then silence. A long silence.

"Was Dianne right?" asked Ryan.

"About what?" asked Mom.

"That you were pregnant last spring."

"She was right. Your father and I had always talked about having four children. Two of each gender would be nice, but we'd take whatever came. But Dianne was a tough delivery and some other things went wrong and I required a couple of surgeries, so for a long time we held off, and then we just kept holding off, but last winter we decided to try again, and within a couple of months, there I was. Pregnant again. Puking again. That's what pregnancy has always meant to me. And this time I really couldn't handle it. I *hate* being nauseated, I *hate* throwing up, and so I'd wake up in the morning having a panic attack because I could feel that I was going to throw up, and Dad would bring me toast and warm water, try to settle my stomach, but I'd puke anyway. He'd help me in there, he'd keep me from panicking, or he'd help me get over the panic attack. It was just hell on wheels, but he kept saying, it's gonna be worth it, the baby's gonna be wonderful like the two we already have, you know it'll be worth it."

It sounded like Dad.

Dianne said, "And that worked?"

"No," said Mom. "He did everything he could, but it didn't work. And I kept thinking, I'm too old to chase a crawler or a climber all over the house, that was fifteen years ago, thirteen years ago, but I can't do that this time, I'm going to be a horrible mother to any baby that comes along now, this was a stupid, stupid mistake, and all the things your father did to try to help, they just made me angrier and more panicky and I hated it all."

Another long silence. The fervor in Mom's voice, the naked emotion— that was familiar, but somehow it didn't sound like one of her diatribes. It was a memory. She was telling them how it felt.

And then Ryan understood what she was saying. Why she was saying it. Because . . .

"It wasn't a miscarriage," said Ryan.

"No," said Mom.

Another long silence.

"It was an abortion," said Dianne.

"It was a termination of an unwanted pregnancy, still in the first trimester," said Mom.

"Whatever," said Dianne.

And Ryan said, "But you didn't tell Dad till after it was done."

"I had my tubes tied. I didn't tell him that, either. I said 'miscarriage' and he didn't doubt me. Until he saw the denial-of-coverage letter, even though I had specifically asked the doctor *not* to file with the insurance company. Dad asked me to explain what medical expense I had and why the letter said I had not asked for coverage."

"So it was the lie," said Ryan. "And no possibility of another try."

"It was the fact that I got pregnant as part of a decision we made together, but I ended it on my own," said Mom.

As far as Ryan could remember, this was the first time Mother had actually taken responsibility for anything she did wrong. That was something she just didn't do. Except for this time. Maybe because this time, it was so huge it was tearing up the family.

"If I had told him I wanted to terminate the pregnancy," said Mom, "he would have talked me out of it."

Ryan knew it was true. At least the first time she proposed it. Though if Mom kept trying, she usually got her way.

"And I didn't want to be talked out of it," said Mom. "I didn't want any more panic attacks. I didn't want any more bending over the toilet and puking up my spleen. I was done."

Ryan got up from the couch. "This is my bed," he said. "If I had another, I'd go to it and think about things while I tried to go to sleep. But I've got nowhere else to go."

Dianne got up. "Mom, thank you for telling us."

"I know you hate me now," said Mom in a very small voice.

"You're the only mother we've got," said Ryan. "We know you and we love you and—"

"I don't hate anybody," said Dianne.

"I *know* that I'm a loon," said Mom.

"She didn't mean that," said Ryan.

"Emotions just . . . it's hard not to just let them go, let them out," said

Mom. "I'm not . . . contained, like your dad. I just can't, I'm not—I think I loved him because he not only contained himself, he could contain *me*, most of the time. *All* the time, until . . . this last thing."

Ryan walked around the couch. He was so angry and hurt and . . . mostly angry. Because doing what she did without telling Dad, and then lying about it—he knew what that had done to Dad. He didn't even have to talk to Dad about it. And because she had also lied to Ryan and Dianne, with her mutterings that implied adultery or bigamy or *something* that made it Dad's fault, Mom had made Ryan be angry with Father, and that was wrong.

Hardest thing he ever did, or close to it, was walking up to Mom that night and holding her in his arms and hugging her while she sobbed against his shoulder.

Because with Dad gone, that was his job now. Taking out the garbage, emptying the dishwasher, and holding Mom when she was falling apart. Always used to be Dad's job, but he wasn't here.

How is love even possible? Ryan wondered. How can you promise loyalty forever, no matter what? How can anybody ever say words like that?

Only because they don't know what they're saying, thought Ryan. Because even a word-keeping man like Dad can say them and mean them, and then one day something happens that he just can't bear. Something that tears up his promise without him being able to stop it. Something that tears up his love.

Or was Dad over in his camper, his movable office, somehow forgiving Mom and figuring out a way to make it all better again?

It could never be *good* again. The betrayal, the lie, would always be there, it wouldn't be undone, it couldn't be. How could Father forgive it?

If anybody can, thought Ryan, Father can.

If Bizzy did that to me, could I forgive her?

He felt a rush of emotion. His love for Bizzy. Tears came to his eyes. I hope I could. I hope I'd be man enough to forgive her, and take her back, and . . . and forgive her. Really make it all better again.

I hope Father can, thought Ryan. But I have no right to ask him, or prod him, or anything. That's something inside him, something he has to figure out, if he even *wants* to get his marriage put back together. I'm not part of that. I'm never even going to hint that I *know* what really happened. Dad has to work it out alone.

The two people I loved most in all the world, before meeting Bizzy, they're going through a soul-wrecking emergency, and screw my stupid micropower, I did *nothing* about it. I had no heroic rescue in my toolkit. There was no bee I could put in my mouth, no stinger I could flick away, no evil enemy I could jab in the throat, not even a car I could step in front of. My micropower was useless, *is* useless, in the worst crisis of my family's life.

But Bizzy loves me, thought Ryan.

Mom stopped crying, pulled out of Ryan's embrace, patted his shoulder. "So many tears on your shirt," said Mother. "I'm sorry I leaned on you like that."

For a mad second, Ryan thought of singing, "Lean on me, brother, when . . ." No, those weren't the words. "You just call on me . . ." The fact that he couldn't remember how the old Bill Withers hit went saved him from the humiliation of trying to sing it to his mother. In front of his sister.

Dianne whispered, "I'll help you carry on." Those were words from the song. She was thinking the same damn thing. Ryan looked at her and winked. Dianne grinned.

This had been terrible, but it had gone way better than they feared. Way better than they could have imagined. What would happen tomorrow was impossible to guess. But tonight, their private conversation that ended up being overheard, it was exactly the right thing, because nobody was attacking Mom to her face; they were just trying to work out what happened, and Mom was able to listen to it and decide to tell them the truth.

Without blaming Dad.

Such a milestone for Mom. Such a hurdle to get over. Ryan was proud of her.

Proud of Dianne, too.

And, yeah, why not. Proud of himself.

Not a micropower. Just learning to be a decent human being. Learning to be a grownup. Maybe I can do this thing. Life. Maybe I'll even be good at it.

18

First thing in the morning, Ryan called Dr. Withunga. She wasn't thrilled about a six AM call, but when Ryan explained, she listened. "One of the people watching us—well, watching Bizzy—he confirms that the loveks exist, though he claims *he's* trying to help protect the Horvats. Now he wants to come talk to her without getting himself cursed to oblivion."

"And you don't know whether you can trust him."

"I kind of do trust him," said Ryan, "but it's not my life on the line, and my dad said, is there anything that GRUT can do to help Mrs. Horvat be safe?"

"Excellent question," said Dr. Withunga. "To which I don't know the answer. I know all the micropowers discovered in our area so far, but whether they can be adapted to defensive use, and whether the micropotents are willing to try, that's not mine to say."

"Meaning not yours to ask of them," said Ryan.

"I can inquire," said Dr. Withunga, "but in a context where it's easy for them to decide not to speak up."

"I get that," said Ryan. Even though he thought Dr. Withunga might have *tried* to urge them instead of making it easy for them to—no, she was right. Every micropower was personal and some of them were terrible, like Bizzy's. How would he feel if Dr. Withunga tried to pressure her to do something dangerously public with glamor-face? People needed to be able to choose what risks they were willing to take, what costs they would pay for someone else's benefit. Superman in the comics could do whatever was in his power, because bullets couldn't pierce him, falling wouldn't kill him, and also he didn't actually exist. All the micropots did, in fact, exist, and were vulnerable in ways that most humans were not.

"That doesn't mean it isn't worth trying," said Dr. Withunga. "The GRUT group that meets at your school is too small and they've already made the drive once this week. Do you think you and Bizzy could ride with me to Danville?"

"That's a couple of hours each way," said Ryan.

"I'm not Uber, you ride for free," said Dr. Withunga. "I can assemble a much larger group in Danville, though most of them will have to drive at least an hour to get there. And I'm quite sure some of them—many of them—will try to think of ways to help."

"Which is more than I could do for any of them," said Ryan.

"Oh, I think you'd try, Ryan," said Dr. Withunga. "We can't be *sure* that you have to really know and love somebody before your micropower kicks in. And if someone was in real danger, I think you'd be willing to try."

Ryan wasn't sure of that at all, though it was nice she thought he was that altruistic.

"Shall we leave from your school straight after the last class? You and Bizzy?"

"Give us time to go to our lockers and the restroom, and yes, sure. Let's say, after the buses all go."

"I'll be in the turnaround at the front of your school."

"What kind of car do you drive?" asked Ryan.

"The kind that has me sitting in the driver's seat."

Ryan thought of scanning cars to see if Dr. Withunga was driving, instead of somebody's mother. If he could look, so could some weird stalker. "Everybody will see us," said Ryan.

"Everybody sees everything," said Dr. Withunga. "That's human life."

On the way to school that morning, Bizzy agreed that going to a big GRUT conference in Danville might be the best thing they could do, and not telling her mother in advance would also be a good thing. "She'll curse you when she finds out," said Ryan.

"Not if we bring her serious protection," said Bizzy.

"Yeah, that's right. *Your* mother is rational, now that we know this lovek thing isn't paranoia."

"Just because they're really after you doesn't mean you're not paranoid," said Bizzy. "And speaking of paranoid, what is it you're not telling me?"

Ryan had no answer.

"Your silence is a confession that there *is* something you're not telling," said Bizzy. "But I already knew, because you and Dianne had this long family conversation with your front door standing open. Guess who else's front door can be left open a few inches?"

"You listened in?"

"You didn't close your door. No expectation of privacy."

"The Supreme Court ruling on this is fascinating, but—"

"Ryan," said Bizzy, "my eavesdropping ended when your mom went inside and closed the door behind her. So just tell me this. Was Dianne's scenario right?"

"Not completely," said Ryan. "But mostly."

"What made it 'not completely'?"

"It was an abortion," said Ryan, feeling as if he was betraying his family by saying so.

Bizzy said nothing.

"She told Dad it was a miscarriage," said Ryan.

"I don't need to know any more," said Bizzy. "Thanks for trusting me with such a hard secret."

After telling Bizzy, Ryan felt a lot better, because she *was* his best friend now. Ryan could never have said anything about secret family stuff to Defenseur because the boy was terminally indiscreet. And Ryan couldn't have taken the inevitable teasing. He hadn't really known what a true friend was until Bizzy.

He went through school in a kind of daze, even more than usual, because he was worried about his parents, sick at heart especially about his dad.

On top of all that, there was the lovek problem, and the upcoming meeting with a big GRUT conference, and what he would say to them to explain the problem, though it wasn't really his place to say anything because it was about the Horvats, and Bizzy was way better at explaining things than Ryan was, so why had he thought it would somehow be his job?

Right after the last bell, Ryan called his dad. "Yes, I'm in GRUT, so you win, but Dr. Withunga is taking me and Bizzy to a big meeting in Danville because we're hoping to assemble a team to deal with stuff for the Horvats. We won't be back till ten at the earliest."

Of course Dad asked if Ryan had notified Mom.

"I have not, Dad. We have to leave right away and I don't have an hour to deal with Mom's resentment and anxiety and whatever."

"Your one hour becomes two hours and a lot of screaming if I try to do it for you."

"Thanks, Dad," said Ryan. "I owe you a big one."

"Kid, you already owe me everything you are and ever will be. This is a drop in the bucket."

"Dad. Seriously. I'm grateful to you for coming through for me, even for stupid selfish lazy stunts like dumping this on you."

"I hope whatever you're doing works out. And if it turns out this was just a scam for you to get *some* alone time with the girl next door—"

"Dr. Withunga will be in the car. Maybe a couple of dozen people in the meeting. No alone time."

"I'm glad I built the Horvats a deck so you can get *some* alone time with her."

"I think Mrs. Horvat is always in the kitchen listening to everything we say."

"Then she's a good mom," said Dad.

"Thanks for signing that permission slip against my will."

"I aim to please. Have fun. Be safe." And he hung up.

Ryan turned around to find Bizzy standing right there. "Is it your plan to keep Dr. Withunga waiting?"

* * *

The drive down to Danville was excruciating, mostly because Ryan wasn't free to talk to Bizzy about all the stuff that was on his mind. But it was okay because Bizzy and Dr. Withunga did girl-talk stuff in the front and Ryan mostly vegged out in the back seat and looked at all the trees and the occasional houses and gas stations and villages they passed.

Getting around Lynchburg was always tricky, because the highway designers constantly tried to send you to Appomattox, and you had to keep exiting from the main highway to stay on US 29.

Ryan was about to warn Dr. Withunga about the treacherous highway design and inadequate signage when he saw she was executing the route flawlessly, without resorting to GPS. She must make this drive all the time, thought Ryan. In fact, she actually lives in . . . where? He didn't really know. It was surprising how incurious he was about adults who didn't actually matter to him personally. Yes, he trusted her. He relied on her enough that calling her was his first thought this morning, before even peeing or brushing the morning breath out of his mouth. But that didn't make her an important *person* to him. She was in the category of resource. Or teacher. She was Mr. Hardesty, pretty much. At the top of the teacher list.

They were meeting at an elementary school in Danville. "I have arrangements with schools in all the cities in my area," said Dr. Withunga. "I even have keys to some where a custodian isn't there after hours."

"That's trust," said Bizzy.

"I keep waiting for a micropotent to show up who can open locks without keys and then lock them again." Dr. Withunga sighed. "You can't file a request for particular powers. You just take what comes."

"Bummer," said Ryan.

"Well, *you* are the scariest micropotent we've had so far, Ryan. The only one whose power includes astonishing violence."

"It sure astonished *me*," said Ryan.

"*I'm* pretty scary, too," said Bizzy, feigning umbrage.

"Scary in a different way, but yes," said Dr. Withunga.

"She's got thermonuclear beauty," said Ryan.

"How many megatons do you think glamor-face delivers?" asked Bizzy.

Dr. Withunga laughed. "Oh, come now, beauty isn't measured in nuclear terms. The measure of Bizzy's glamor-face is at least one full Helen."

"Helen?" asked Ryan.

"Helen of Troy. Referred to as 'the face that launched a thousand ships.' Therefore, a milli-Helen is officially enough beauty to launch *one* ship."

Bizzy hooted with laughter. "And a micro-Helen?" she asked.

"I think that after the milli-Helen, we start moving toward faces that *sink* ships, and those are measured in Bags, not Helens."

"Oh come on," said Ryan.

"Ordinary ugly people are one-baggers—they can only safely go out in public with a bag over their head," said Dr. Withunga. "A two-bagger means one bag over the ugly person's head, and then another bag over your own head as insurance in case the ugly person's bag breaks or blows off."

Ryan and Bizzy both laughed, though Bizzy said, "Cruel."

"You don't ever say it to somebody's face, because that would be unkind," said Dr. Withunga. "Besides, most people keep in mind that in someone else's view, they themselves might be a one- or two-bagger."

"Not Bizzy," said Ryan.

"I would say that Bizzy's normal face is around four milli-Helens," said Dr. Withunga, "which gives her a decent shot at being in a magazine ad. But that glamor-face—I'm not sure if a full Helen really covers it. After all, Paris was able to run away with her and make it all the way to Troy without anybody killing him to get to her."

"Are we really discussing these milli-Helens as if they were a meaningful unit of measure?" asked Bizzy.

"I did a paper in sociology class as an undergrad, about deliberately ridiculous systems of measurement. You should google 'FFF system'—that's three 'F's'—and remember that there really are computer geeks who carry out some serious measurements in, for instance, 'furlongs per fortnight.'"

"That's very slow," said Ryan.

"Let's see if I can remember this. The speed of light comes out as, like, one-point-eight-oh-something times ten to the twelfth furlongs per fortnight, or one-point-eight-something megafurlongs per microfortnight."

Ryan hooted.

Bizzy said, "I guess computer geeks had to do *something* back in the days when programs were on punch cards and they had to sit around three hours waiting for their programs to compile."

"FFF?" asked Ryan.

"Furlongs, of course, fortnights, and—"

"Fathoms?" asked Ryan.

"No, fathoms are just six feet of water, and a furlong is one-eighth of a mile. Both lengths. A furlong is supposedly how long an ox can pull a plow through a furrow without stopping to rest. An acre is an area one furlong in length and four rods wide, which is sixty-six new feet wide."

"*New* feet?" asked Ryan.

"Look it up, Ryan," said Dr. Withunga. "I wrote a paper about it, but I didn't memorize it. The English foot used to be about ten percent longer than it is now, so when they changed to our current shorter foot back in the thirteen-hundreds, they didn't change the furlong or the rod, they just added more feet to make up the distance."

"You've done a very good job of distracting Ryan from all his worries," said Bizzy.

"How about you?" asked Dr. Withunga. "Have I distracted you at all?"

"Oh, Ryan was my main worry, so yes, you've eased my worries by distracting him from his."

"How am I your main worry?" Ryan asked her.

"As your official punca," said Bizzy, "it's my job to keep you contented."

"There are so many overtones to that word," said Ryan, "that I'm not sure it actually applies. Let's stick with girlfriend."

"But in America," said Bizzy, "the job of the girlfriend is to keep you guessing and lead you around by the nose until you lose all your guy friends and barely have any testosterone in your system."

"Where did you get *that*?" asked Dr. Withunga.

"Observation," said Bizzy and Ryan simultaneously. They all laughed.

But apart from that it was mostly silence from Ryan, and girl talk—woman talk?—in the front seat. Ryan was surprised to learn that Bizzy was completely competent with woman talk that consisted of information acquired from *People* magazine and various celebrity-oriented websites and clickbait sources. The English royal family came up more than once, and both women seemed to be on a first-name basis with all the royals.

Ryan's eyes glazed over whenever he tried to listen. Someday I'll be married to an actual woman, he thought. Maybe Bizzy herself. Am I going to have to be able to take part in conversations like this?

As they got into Danville, Dr. Withunga began to talk about the work they were there to do. "Of course I keep a list of all the micropowers I know of, whether the micropotent is in one of our GRUT groups or not. But for our purposes—trying to keep Mrs. Horvat from being punished as a witch—we need to try to imagine a way to turn at least some of these micropowers into defensive weapons."

Ryan said, "I think the first thing we have to face is the biggest problem. These loveks aren't just hunting down Mrs. Horvat. If we confront them with a house full of micropots, they're going to think they just hit the witchcraft jackpot."

"Mother doesn't want anyone else in jeopardy. She hates it bad enough that *I'm* at risk because they know about her."

"The powers of micropotents do increase in the presence of at least a few others, so if all we did was increase your mom's powers, Bizzy, somebody else would have to be there."

"Do you mean that because Bizzy is present whenever her mom punishes her with the you're-so-pretty curse, Bizzy is making her mother's curse stronger?"

"Probably," said Dr. Withunga. "And didn't you tell me that the last time that happened, you were there, too, Ryan?"

"Oh, great," said Ryan. "I made it worse."

Bizzy laughed. "Come on, Ryan. You make everything better."

"Good try, punca," said Ryan.

"No, I was being a *girlfriend* right then."

"I think it's only right to separate the two issues. First, find out what might be weaponized. Whoever has a micropower like that, they'll need to work on it, to try and hone it. The way Bizzy learned to do her plain-face."

"No, I've got an ugly-face now," said Bizzy. "It's a weird combination of a couple of traits from glamor-face and a couple from plain-face. It looks like a really strange Halloween mask."

"Please don't demonstrate," said Ryan.

"Dr. Withunga," said Bizzy, "I don't want to demonstrate glamor-face in front of this group. Too many people have already seen it. I want to do ugly-face, and make the transition in front of them. They'll see I'm really a micropotent."

"They'll take my word for it," said Dr. Withunga. "You don't have to demonstrate anything."

"Glamor-face makes some other girls feel homicidal. Or suicidal," said Ryan.

"So she should show them ugly-face to help them feel better about themselves?" said Dr. Withunga. "You just don't know how depressed girls think, Ryan. They see ugly-face, and they'll probably say to themselves, yes, that's exactly how everybody sees me."

"Really?" said Ryan.

"Insane boys think God finally got the guy-design right when he made them. But crazy girls think God ran out of good parts and made them out of scrap."

"I don't think you're being fair to depressed guys," said Ryan. "We can hate ourselves every bit as much as depressed girls."

"Maybe," said Dr. Withunga.

"I get depressed sometimes," said Bizzy, "but I'm not crazy enough to have body image problems."

"So nobody's ever told you that you were fat?" asked Ryan.

"Not funny," said Dr. Withunga.

"She knows she isn't," said Ryan.

"Nobody knows any such thing," said Dr. Withunga. "Teasing a slender girl about being fat might make her hate how skinny she is, especially if other people laugh at your 'joke.'"

"Nobody has a sense of humor anymore," said Ryan.

"Jokes like that were never funny," said Dr. Withunga. "Not to the people being mocked. Oh, sorry, I meant 'being teased in a good-natured way.'"

Ryan felt as if he had just failed about three tests, but he still followed them into the school. There were no kids at all. Ryan asked about that.

"No classes today," said Dr. Withunga. "It was a teacher workday."

She had a roll of masking tape and four signs. She knew right where she wanted them. Each one said "GRUT" with an arrow pointing down a hall, except the last one, which just said "GRUT." She put it on the door and led Ryan and Bizzy inside.

They were the first ones there, and Ryan and Bizzy helped set up chairs in rows like a regular lecture class. "Not a circle?" Ryan asked.

"Too many. A circle for everybody who said they'd come would make it so you had to shout at the people on the opposite side."

"Rows work?" asked Bizzy.

"I've been working on GRUT for more than a decade now. I find that the people who stick with GRUT are very helpful and cooperative, no matter how I configure the chairs. And most twelve-step meetings use rows—I think because a lot of people are terrified to sit anywhere but the back row when they're new to a group."

It made a kind of sense to Ryan, though it would also have made sense if they had made three concentric circles of chairs. Though rows were way easier to line up evenly.

When the chairs were set up, Ryan and Bizzy sat down together and held hands. Dr. Withunga made a face. "Come on," she said. "You can't keep from touching each other for the duration of a meeting?"

"Since we made our mutual confession of undying love," said Bizzy, "we haven't actually *tried* not touching each other at every opportunity."

"Well, thanks for confining it to hand-holding," said Dr. Withunga.

Since hand-holding was all they had *ever* done except for a few kisses, Ryan let go of Bizzy's hand easily. "Dr. Withunga," said Ryan, "I'm so nervous now. Would *you* hold my hand?"

"Shut up," said Dr. Withunga cheerfully.

It turned out that the first person to arrive was Mitch—spider-boy. When Ryan looked surprised, Mitch laughed. "I live in Lynchburg. It's about as far for me to come to Charlottesville as to come here, so who cares?"

"Have you figured out how to weaponize spiders?"

"It depends on how creeped out a person is to have spiders on them," said Mitch. "And how big the local spiders happen to be."

"Can you make the spiders bite?"

"Spiders don't regard humans as prey. But if you start slapping spiders, they can get scared and take protective action. Unfortunately, hardly any spiders are able to inject humans with any kind of venom."

"Just wondered," said Ryan.

"Considering that you put bees in your mouth," Mitch said.

"Not as a matter of habit," said Ryan. "And if it had been a tarantula in her hair, I'm afraid Bizzy would have been on her own."

But imagining Bizzy with a huge hairy spider made Ryan feel a powerful impulse to do *exactly* what he had done with the bee, combing it out of her hair with his fingers. But in his instantaneous imaginary plan, the spider ended up on the ground with a big stomping foot on top of it.

I can imagine my way into seeing what I would do. Could do. Should do? That was a good thing to understand about his own micropower.

Meanwhile, Bizzy was shuddering. "What's the protocol for having a massive hairy spider on you. 'Stop, drop, and roll'?"

"I think it's 'screech, dance around, and pee yourself,'" said Mitch.

Dr. Withunga joined in. "And you know that because . . ."

Ryan and Bizzy both cried triumphantly, "Observation!"

Mitch laughed.

Pretty soon, though, the room began filling up. People who knew each other gathered together, and Dr. Withunga nodded to each new arrival and called some by name. A couple of them came up and handed her an envelope. Probably not packed with cash, thought Ryan; Dr. Withunga almost certainly was not using this GRUT thing as a front for dealing.

He was embarrassed that the thought even crossed his mind.

Finally it was time for the meeting to begin, though Dr. Withunga assured Ryan and Bizzy that quite a few would probably straggle in late.

"Nobody's late," said Bizzy, "if they show up at all."

"Most of you don't know a couple of new members. This is Ryan, whose micropower is falling in love way too easily . . ."

That got some laughter, including from Ryan.

"And this is Bizzy, spelled with an 'I,' two 'Z's,' and a 'Y.'"

"What's her micropower?" somebody asked.

Dr. Withunga answered with a chuckle, "Not important for our purposes here, because it's her mother who's—"

A gasp from several of the GRUT members caused Dr. Withunga and Ryan to turn and look at Bizzy. Bizzy's face was in mid-transition to ugly-face, and Bizzy had been right. It was way more disturbing than the transition to plain-face.

"Don't keep doing that," somebody called out, "or your face will stick like that."

Bizzy grinned and her face snapped back to normal. For a split second, Ryan was afraid it would revert all the way back to glamor-face, but no, Bizzy had it under control.

"I have an idea of all of your micropowers," said Dr. Withunga, "but I don't know where all of you are in working on them. For instance, Tay, you were trying to get beyond guessing passwords."

"Pretty good at names," said Tay. "About half the time."

"Guessing them?" asked Bizzy. "What do you start with?"

"Their face. Race. Age. Culture." Tay shrugged. "I know how people name their kids in my culture. I'm not as good with whites and I suck at Asians, but I'm getting better with practice."

"Not sure how to turn that into a defensive weapon," said Dr. Withunga.

"I was just thinking," said Bizzy. "My mom usually only curses people who are alone with her. There's no ambiguity about who she's talking to. So if she's talking to a crowd, it gets diluted and pretty much nothing happens. But if she knows a name, *says* the name, then she can direct it to an individual."

"Okay, that might be useful," said Dr. Withunga.

Tay shrugged. "What kind of curse? Maybe I don't want her to know *my* name."

"She won't curse you," said Bizzy. "She's usually careful who she hits with a whammy."

Ryan had a vague idea that "whammy" was a term from some ancient comic strip. Surely they didn't have American comics in Slovenia. But why not? They had *Star Wars* and *Friends*.

"I loosen bricks," said one kid. "But I have to be so close to the bricks that if a wall comes down, it's usually on top of *me*."

"Dangerous," said Dr. Withunga, "unless you can refine your micropower to a point where you can do it from twenty feet away."

"No bricks in the duplex," said Ryan.

"Still, we'll keep it in mind, because if you can loosen bricks, then, maybe stones? Maybe nails or screws?"

"Worth a shot," said the kid.

And so it went, people offering their micropower and other people chiming in with ideas on how to weaponize it. Some of them also told about the micropower of someone who wasn't actually there. "I can't think of any way that Linda's ability to detect the ripeness of fruit could be weaponized."

Ryan laughed. "Well, if it comes to a food fight, she'd be ideal. She could pick the most splattable fruit."

Ryan half expected Dr. Withunga to tell him to get serious, but when she explained the rules for good brainstorming at the beginning, she made a huge point of how even jokes could trigger a good idea in someone else, so the one thing you were forbidden to do was imply that somebody's idea was dumb or useless. Even when it was.

"Can Linda *make* fruit get riper?" asked Bizzy.

Linda's friend cocked his head. "I don't know if she's tried. For all I know, that's what she really does all the time, maybe without even knowing it. I've just seen her hold up a canteloupe or a honeydew and say, 'Found a ripe one.' She's always right."

"Does she hire herself out for grocery shopping?" asked Bizzy.

Aaron Withunga was there, in the back, as usual. Must have arrived late, because Ryan hadn't noticed him come in. "There are a few people who are maybe too shy to speak up," said Aaron.

"That's their privilege," said Dr. Withunga.

"I know," said Aaron. "But some micropowers are kind of weird to talk about, so I won't name any names, but let me just put some micropowers out there, and if somebody wants to claim it, fine. If not, fine."

"Aaron never tells," said Dr. Withunga.

"He tells *you*," said somebody.

"No," said Dr. Withunga. "Not if the person asks him not to."

"Go ahead and tell us some micropowers, then," said Ryan. As if he had any authority here.

"We've got one person who can unfasten things. *Not* door locks. So far, it's only stuff on cloth. They discovered their power because they could make snaps unsnap from a few feet away. Sort of a practical joke. But recently, with practice, buttons will pop off. And hooks and eyes will slide open."

Ryan had seen enough bras hanging up to dry to know the immediate application of that one. Groans from girls confirmed his assumption.

"They can't undo belts, because those are metal and leather, not thread, though they're trying to find a way to work the buckle loose from the end of the belt, without unfastening the buckle. I'm thinking, if a bad guy's pants start falling down, maybe he'll get distracted," said Aaron. "But since this person is not speaking up, I figure they'll either talk to you separately, or they just don't want to do it. Because some people seem to have thought badly of his ability with hooks and eyes."

Some nervous laughter.

"Potentially very useful, in an oblique kind of way," said Dr. Withunga.

Aaron wasn't done yet. "And there's one person whose grandfather lived with the family, and grandpa's alimentary system got stopped up a lot."

Murmurs of "ew," "gross," "yuck."

"This person took pity on their grandfather and discovered the ability to break up the blockage and loosen the old man's bowels. This person sticks around home because the old man is grateful to get relief once a day."

"I'm assuming you're telling us this," said Dr. Withunga, "because this person can loosen *anybody's* bowels."

"'Loosen' is an understatement," said Aaron. "This person probably won't come forward right now, either, but I'm thinking, a bad guy who's about to shoot a gun or throw a knife or strangle somebody is going to get seriously distracted if his bowels let fly and he's got poo slopping down his legs."

More exaggerated grossed-out reactions from people in the group.

"You have such a practical imagination, Aaron," said Dr. Withunga.

"I try to make you proud of me, Mom," said Aaron.

Another kid raised his hand. Young, maybe still in fifth grade, but probably sixth. Must have a parent waiting outside, or an older sibling in the group. "I've got one," the kid said.

"Go for it, Wye," said another kid halfway across the room.

"We got a baby brother about a year ago, and when he started toddling around, he fell over, and he hated doing that, so he stopped trying to walk or even stand by himself. My parents talked about it, but what I noticed was that when he was holding *my* hand—just a finger, really, and I wasn't holding him at all—he never fell, he never even wobbled."

"So when he was holding on to you," said Dr. Withunga, "he could balance."

"He's walking now because he practiced his balancing with me. It's the only time he stood up, was with me. And now he can walk."

"So have you tried that with anybody else?" asked Dr. Withunga.

"Who?" said Wye. "Everybody else walks fine."

"Can you make people *lose* their balance?" asked Bizzy.

"Never tried," said Wye. "Because that would be mean."

"Don't practice on cripples and old people," said Bizzy.

"There are plenty of games on playgrounds where people expect to fall down a lot," said Dr. Withunga. "You might just pick some people and make them lose their balance. Nobody high on the monkey bars, nobody running across a street—"

"Yeah, I get it," said Wye. "I know how to play nice."

Dr. Withunga kept the session going a long time. There were a lot of micropowers that Ryan barely even understood—like the girl with hypervision. "Not X-ray vision," she insisted, "not like an MRI. I can't burn people with it, no lasers, nothing like superpowers in the movies. I just focus. I can see from really far away and make out letters on license plates or street signs."

Somebody who knew The Lord of the Rings said, "Like elf eyes."

The girl shrugged. There was nothing particularly elfin about her. "But I don't know how my hypervision could possibly help."

"Me neither," said Dr. Withunga, "but it's a cool power, and we'll keep thinking about it."

"It wasn't always cool," said the girl. "I saw a lot of things very clearly when other people thought nobody could possibly see."

"There's always a learning curve," said Dr. Withunga. "And a price to pay, unfortunately."

"I don't have supersharp vision," said a young man on the back row. "I just know what's written."

"Not sure others will know what you mean," said Dr. Withunga.

"I needed glasses when I was little. I mean, I needed them really badly. But I'd go for an eye test, and the doctor would say, tell me the letters you see on the chart from left to right, so I'd tell him. All of them, right down to the tiny ones. I couldn't actually *see* any except the big tall 'E' at the start. But because I named them, no glasses. My parents were told I had amazing vision."

"How did you finally get those Coke-bottle lenses, then?" asked Ryan. "Very *attractive* Coke-bottle lenses."

"I was about eight, and I figured it out. They didn't want me to *tell* them the letters—the doctor already had the chart memorized. They wanted to find out which letters I could actually *see*."

"So you can read letters that aren't visible to you," said Bizzy.

The boy shrugged. "Yeah."

"But the letters have to be in plain sight, right?" asked Bizzy.

The boy shrugged again. "Usually."

"Ever see the letters on a paper that was folded?" Bizzy asked.

The boy shrugged. "Sometimes."

"Well," said Dr. Withunga. "I'm surprised this didn't come out in a session before this."

"Wasn't sure I wanted people to know that I could read a sealed letter or a closed book," said the boy.

Somebody whistled. A few people said wow.

"Don't tell the CIA about him," somebody said.

"Wouldn't matter," said the guy. "I don't spy. I don't cheat on tests. Wouldn't be fair."

And so on. And so on. Ryan began to realize that every micropower had a story behind it. Things that could go wrong, that had gone wrong. The kid who could make cars go out of gear since he was three—his parents *still* didn't know it was him that did it, and he wasn't going to tell them, now that he was a driver himself, now that he knew how many thousands of dollars they had spent on completely unnecessary transmission work back when he was little. Dr. Withunga asked, "Do you ever do it now?"

"No."

"Can you shift from one gear to another, instead of just to neutral?"

"Easy," he said.

"Into reverse?"

"That can go bad really fast," he said.

"Do you have to be inside the car to change the gears?" asked Dr. Withunga.

"No," he said.

"That's scary," said another kid who was old enough to drive.

"I'm not out to hurt people," said the gear shifter.

"But you could stop a getaway car," said Ryan.

"If I'm close enough to it, for long enough. Just takes a couple of seconds, but cars passing at freeway speed, I don't have time to find the gearbox before they're gone."

"Maybe now it's time to say," said Dr. Withunga, "that any of you who have powers that might be helpful, you all know that being with a group of micropots strengthens you and sharpens you, right?"

Yeah, of course, they all knew that.

"But we're looking to protect a micropotent who has been chased by some seriously scary people from her home country," said Dr. Withunga, "and we don't know how dangerous they might be, or what form the danger might take. Ryan and Bizzy both asked me to warn you, anybody who might be willing to help, that you might be putting yourself in harm's way, and even if everybody uses their micropowers with skill, we haven't heard of any micropower that evaporates bullets in the air or turns knife blades to rubber."

There was a long silence.

"Some of you are kids," said Bizzy. "And even if you have the best, most useful power in the group, we're not bringing kids into this."

"Define 'kid,'" said a kid who looked to be twelve.

"You're one," said Dr. Withunga.

"I bet I'm as old as Ryan," said the kid.

"Fifteen," said Ryan.

"Well, dang," said the kid. "Try to look older next time."

"I'm growing my beard," said Ryan. "Can't you tell?"

That earned a chuckle from a bunch of people.

It still took half an hour for the brainstorming to end. After that, about two dozen GRUT members had short private conferences with Dr. Withunga, and a few people—mostly girls—wanted Bizzy to show them what she actually did with her face.

Ryan listened in and was surprised that Bizzy really didn't hold back. "It's like learning to wiggle your ears," she told them. "You find some facial expression that just naturally makes the movement you want, and then you work on isolating it. It takes a lot of practice at first."

When they found out she didn't know how to wiggle her ears, she made Ryan demonstrate.

"The only one moving is your left ear," said one girl.

"If you blink just *one* eye," said Ryan, "that's a wink. It means something. But if you blink both eyes, that's just blinking, doesn't mean a thing."

"So what does raising your left ear up and down without moving your right ear mean?" another girl asked.

"That I'm a truly intriguing and attractive person," said Ryan, deadpan.

"No it doesn't," said the second girl. And they all went back to Bizzy, getting more demonstrations of some of her individual changes. Through it all, Ryan saw how she showed them none of the movements that were part of shifting to glamor-face. There were things that weren't good to pass on or reveal.

It made Ryan wonder if glamor-face might be teachable. What if Bizzy could make millions of dollars posting videos on the internet demonstrating how to get from normal to glamor-face, a step at a time?

No, Ryan decided. Bizzy was only recently coming to understand just what she did. She had only just learned how to move to any face *other* than glamor-face. But the power she started with, what she used to do as a little kid, going straight to glamor-face—that just came naturally. And Ryan was willing to bet that perfect symmetry and proportion was not teachable or even, for most people, attainable.

Finally, the last of the lingerers broke away and Dr. Withunga asked what fast food they wanted for supper. It was after eight p.m. and they had two hours to drive before they got back to Charlottesville.

"I am so in trouble," said Ryan. "Even if Dad *did* call and warn her. *If* she picked up the phone when he called."

"I thought your dad couldn't call her."

"He probably texted something like 'Call me to find out why Ryan won't be home before ten.'"

"That would work?"

"My mom loves me. Another proof she's crazy."

"Why will you be in trouble, then?"

"Because Mom's already on edge. We had that conversation last night. And then the next night, I don't come home till way after dark?"

"So she's going to react to her anxiety rather than to what you actually did."

Ryan sighed. "She doesn't really know about my micropower."

"Nobody told her?" asked Bizzy.

"Who? Defense? She thinks he's an idiot."

"Well," said Bizzy.

"He's actually not. And he's my friend. I think she hates him because I really care about him."

"She didn't figure out that you saved his life by being, you know, sort of marginally super?"

"My dad also called your mom," said Ryan. "Or he was going to."

"I called her, too. She's fine. She knows you're with me, and she figures your warlock powers, used on my behalf, will keep me safe and maybe take out a few of the loveks, if they actually make a run at me."

"Warlock," murmured Ryan.

"I already reserved the word 'witch' for my mom," said Bizzy, "and I can't call you a 'wizard,' because it makes me think of Michael Gambon."

"He's a very attractive guy."

"No he isn't," said Bizzy, "so you're much prettier. Not pretty, but closer than he is."

"Never wanted to be pretty."

"Good thing," said Bizzy.

Ryan switched back to actual conversation. "The thing is, if I get home at ten, they'll assume I got you pregnant by nine-thirty."

"Or vice versa," said Bizzy.

"No, they won't actually think you got *me* pregnant," said Ryan.

"I thought you said your parents were crazy."

Instead of carrying on the playful argument, Ryan just kissed her lightly and then said, "*You're* crazy."

"That's what you love about me," said Bizzy.

"I'm so sick of you kids," said Dr. Withunga. "Are you going to chew each other's hamburgers and then spew them into each other's mouths while kissing?"

Bizzy answered, "Except for the part about it being so disgusting that we'd both end up puking—"

At which Ryan said, "*Into* each other's mouths—"

"It sounds kind of romantic," Bizzy finished.

It was the drive-through at a Dairy Queen near Lynchburg that got their business. Dr. Withunga refused to buy any milkshakes or ice-cream products.

"Oh, you need a permission slip from our parents to buy us anything sweet?" asked Ryan.

"I don't care what kind of crap you eat," said Dr. Withunga. "I just don't want anything sticky and cementlike getting spilled inside my nice clean car.

Dr. Withunga seemed pleased that she was dropping them both off at the same house. "One-stop dropping," she said.

"We climb the stairs with a wall between us, and dream about each other all night," said Bizzy.

"I have no doubt," said Dr. Withunga. "We'll talk tomorrow after school. When I've had a chance to collate the whole list of volunteers and their powers."

"My mom's going to hate all of this," said Bizzy.

"And I'm going to hate dodging all my mom's questions so she doesn't know that a bunch of Slovenian witch hunters are going to be targeting our house," said Ryan.

Dr. Withunga clucked her tongue. "Think again, Ryan," she said. "If you don't tell your mom *and* dad—and I mean tonight—I'll tell them about the loveks first thing in the morning."

"And here I was just thinking that you *weren't* a petty tyrant," said Ryan.

"I'm sure you meant that in the nicest possible way," said Dr. Withunga.

"But of course," said Ryan.

"I prefer '*first-class* tyrant' anyway," said Dr. Withunga. "Nothing petty about *me*."

"My mother won't be cooperative," said Ryan.

"That's her privilege."

"My micropower belongs to me," said Ryan. "It's not her decision."

"I *am* a mother," said Dr. Withunga, "so I'm on her side."

"The battle lines are drawn," said Ryan.

"I already won the battle, so comply with the terms of your surrender tonight," said Dr. Withunga. "Now go inside, both of you. It's cold with the doors open like this."

Her car was gone before they got to their front doors. So when they kissed good night, it absolutely was *not* to show off in front of Dr. Withunga. It was just for them. And that made them keep at it until the Horvats' door opened.

It was Jake. "Mother says that she's fine with you kissing on the porch because you're standing up, but it's too cold to keep at it any longer."

"She really said that?" Ryan asked Bizzy.

"Sounds like a direct quote to me," said Bizzy. "Should we show Jake how kissing works?"

"I know a lot more about it than clown boy does," said Jake. He closed the door.

"It wouldn't have helped him anyway," said Ryan. "Kissing *you* doesn't teach him about kissing ordinary girls."

"You forget what an incredible stud my little brother is," said Bizzy. "I think the only thing wrong when he kisses girls is that they can't stop squealing in excitement, which means that they're always blowing down his throat, which makes a horrible burping sound."

"Seriously?" asked Ryan.

She clamped her mouth over his and squealed. The air she expelled made a burping sound going down his throat.

He pulled away from the kiss. "You have now officially ruined kissing," he said.

"You don't want to do it anymore?" she asked.

"You weaponized kissing," he said.

"I won't do it again," she said.

"You *say* you won't," said Ryan.

"If I say I won't, then . . ."

"You'll decide I need to be punished for some terrible offense."

"Solemn vow," said Bizzy.

"Good night, my love," said Ryan. "May flights of angels sing thee to thy rest."

"Now cracks a noble heart," said Bizzy, showing off, as usual, that she actually knew the whole quotation more correctly than Ryan.

"That's just what a woman who blows down your throat would say," said Ryan.

Bizzy opened her door and went inside.

Ryan stood outside in the cold. Tomorrow was Halloween, wasn't it? Or was it the next day? How could he have lost track of Halloween?

It never snowed on Halloween in Charlottesville. October was way too early. But the air smelled really cold and crisp. It smelled as though it wanted to snow.

Everybody wants snow at Christmas, thought Ryan. But nobody wants it at Halloween. If it does snow, somebody on TV is going to blame it on climate change. Are Bizzy and I going out trick-or-treating? Is she going to wear glamor-face and pretend that it's a mask? Or ugly-face?

And what face am I going to wear? Ryan wondered. The one Defenseur says I have—the I'm-so-in-love-with-Bizzy-I-can-hardly-walk-face?

Does Defense think I'm trick-or-treating with him? Is he going to think I'm still punishing him if I don't? Or will he know that when you have a girlfriend, you have to trick-or-treat with her? Or is fifteen too old to trick-or-treat?

Too old. That's my excuse. No trick-or-treating, because I have to do the thing that we're asking everybody else to do. I have to see if I can go into super-protector mode for somebody I don't know or like. Which means I can't be with *either* Defenseur or Bojana, because I know them both too well and care too much about them, even if Defenseur *is* a git.

19

In the end, it was Defense after all. Bizzy didn't want to go trick-or-treating, Defense did, and it seemed like the best way to reaffirm his friendship with Defense under circumstances where Defense could show whether or not he was trustworthy. Halloween was always when Defense thought of his most creative—and therefore offensive—pranks. It would be the ultimate test of his pledges.

Defense swore he had no pranks planned. But since he always swore that, this was nothing unusual. What changed it was Ryan saying, "Is that the same swearing you did when you promised never to try to manipulate me again?"

Defense paused for a moment and then said, "No. That was, like, serious. But this is, you know, Halloween."

"So go right ahead, have your Halloween, prank away, but I won't be there."

Defense looked utterly crestfallen.

"Your pranks are going to make somebody come after you, Defense, and then I would have to come to your rescue, and I told you, I'm not going to be there again when you provoke somebody."

"I don't *mean* to provoke—"

"Yes you do," said Ryan. "I have enjoyed being your friend, Defense, and I really don't want to stop, but I'm not going to be with you when you goad somebody else into mayhem."

Defense stood there thinking. He looked especially stupid, considering that he was wearing a full-on Daffy Duck costume.

"Where did you even get that?" asked Ryan.

"There's a costume rental place in Manhattan."

"Let's see, two hours to DC, but you go all the way to Manhattan?"

"Mail order," said Defense. "I mean, you know, online and then mail."

"Craigslist?" asked Ryan.

"No, I Googled 'Goofy costume' and I got sent to a bunch of sites with cartoon characters and superheroes and I didn't like their Goofy after all, plus it was Disney so I was afraid I couldn't post any selfies because, you know, copyright, so I went for Daffy Duck."

"Because you have the fantasy that Warner Brothers doesn't care about copyright?"

"Because my skinny legs were going to look a lot better in a Daffy Duck costume," said Defense.

"So what am I supposed to be, Elmer Fudd? Because you know we don't own a shotgun. Or a gun of any kind."

"Your dad's in construction and he's not into guns?"

"You're only now noticing that my family is strange?" asked Ryan.

So that's how, after a quick call to Bizzy to make *sure* she didn't want to come with them, Ryan ended up trick-or-treating with Defense. Ryan quickly realized that his makeshift account-executive costume, assembled by finding one of his dad's oldest and skinniest suits in the storage space just inside the attic, where there was actually a bit of floor, and then knotting a tie—this costume did not look like enough of an effort to most people who came to the doors. If Defense hadn't been with him in a full-out cartoon costume, Ryan had no doubt that most people would have turned him away with some comment like "Trick-or-treating at your age is just begging."

In fact, once that thought played out in his mind, Ryan began using it as his door mantra. While Defense was struggling to get anybody to under-stand a word of his very bad Daffy Duck voice, Ryan would simply say, "I'm way too old for trick-or-treating, so I'm just flat-out begging." That got him chuckles and handfuls of candy. One old lady even said, "For a growing boy with oversized chutzpah."

It took Ryan and Defense a couple of minutes to remember the difference between "putz" and "chutzpah."

"Either way," said Defense, "it was kind of a compliment."

"This is the last year," said Ryan. "Next year, go by yourself."

"Or I'll go with somebody who cares enough to have a costume."

"I have a costume," said Ryan. "It's not store-bought, but it's sincere. I never dress this way. It's a costume."

"You're such a hypocrite," said Defense. "You already knew how to tie a double Windsor, so it's not really a costume at all."

"Well I'm not going to tie a single Windsor, because you have to manually untie them instead of just pulling out the skinny end."

"What I'm saying, Ryan," said Defense, "is that you've stopped being fun."

Ryan nodded. "Because I don't want to have to kill the people you target with pranks and goading?"

"Because you fell in love," said Defense.

"You're going to blame everything on Bizzy?"

"Yeah," said Defense. "It's not gallant of me, but it's true. She made you get all serious and responsible."

"I was already serious and responsible. My dad told me I had to be serious and responsible in order to get a job with his company so I could earn enough to buy a car *and* the insurance *and* gas and maintenance."

Defense shook his head. "So to get a cool car so we can ride around and have fun, you have to turn yourself into the kind of responsible adultish person who it isn't worth riding around with because you're no fun."

"Not Bizzy's fault," said Ryan. "My father's."

"Whatever you say, boss. Do I get your Kit Kat bars?"

"Do I get your Twix?" asked Ryan.

"My Twix are not making it home alive," said Defense. "If I have any left in my pillowcase, sure, I'll give you a few of them."

"So I'll see if I have any Kit Kat bars at the end of the night."

"Do I have to beat you up *every* Halloween, Ryan, or will you just wise up and fork over?"

"You have never, not even in your dreams, beaten me up."

"Okay, beat you *down*, which is more accurate."

"What was your big prank going to be this year?"

"No prank," said Defense. "I made my best friend a promise, didn't I?"

"Which means you not only *did* have a prank, but it's a doozy, and you're still going to do it, and it's against me."

"I gave you my solemn oath."

"But you've already done it, so you can keep the oath because you won't do a *new* prank, you'll just wait for me to discover the pre-oath prank."

"You'll never discover it," said Defense.

"I always do."

"Because I've always wanted you to. But not this time."

"Tell what it is," said Ryan.

"There's no prank at all. You're way too suspicious, Ryan."

"Tell," said Ryan, "or we're not friends."

"You're going to play that not-your-friend card once too often," said Defense.

At that point, they were walking along a commercial street with a couple of establishments that sold alcohol. They were restaurants, but they had bars inside, and not everybody came out feeling completely ambulatory.

Defense startled Ryan by grabbing his arm and setting off in pursuit of a guy who was reeling and careening along the sidewalk, alternately bumping into parked cars and building walls.

"Why are we following this guy?" asked Ryan. "We do not mug drunk guys."

"Only high school football heroes," said Defense.

The drunk guy stopped at a car parked at the curb. He carefully made his way to the driver's side.

Defense pulled out his phone. "I'm watching an obviously drunk guy get into his car." He named the street and described both the car and the guy. He recited the license number. Then he exploded. "Twenty minutes? Do you think he's still going to be sitting at the curb? He'll already be out there trying to kill himself and everybody else on the road!"

Ryan was looking around. "Couple of cops over here," he said.

Defense looked where Ryan was pointing, then hung up on the 911 operator. Defense bounded over, doing his best Daffy Duck walk, and started telling his spiel to the policemen.

Ryan came up, trying to increase the urgency. "He's falling-down drunk and he's going to drive away. You've got to stop him *now*."

One of the cops shook his head. He held out his badge and ID. They looked like dime-store props. "Halloween," said the cop. "Costume."

They were pretty good police costumes. For a moment, Ryan wondered if they were just trying to avoid working by pretending they were wearing costumes.

Then a police car pulled up, partly blocking the drunk guy's car from pulling out. Apparently the 911 operator's estimate had been on the high side.

The cop car whooped the siren and blinked the lights for about two seconds, to get the drunk's attention.

The pedestrian cop pointed. "*Those* are cops," he said.

Ryan looked carefully at the uniforms of the cops getting out of the car and realized that on several key points, the guys there on the sidewalk were wearing uniforms that didn't pass muster. They *were* just cops for Halloween. "Plus," said the cop who hadn't said anything yet. "Puh-luss, we are more drunken than that poor stupefied dude."

Ryan sniffed at their breath and laughed. "Yeah, you probably are."

"But we will not drive," said the fake cop.

"Good thing," said Defense.

"We won't drive either," said Ryan. "Neither of us is sixteen yet."

"We're also not drunk," said Defense.

"You are good citizens," said the talkier cop.

"Trying to warn us," said the other cop.

"Good night now," said the first cop, and then they were in motion again, staggering down the street.

"Ain't friendship a grand thing to see?" asked Defense.

"The friendship of drunks who need somebody to lean on must be one of the great blessings of alcoholic life," said Ryan.

"It's getting dark, and we don't have half enough candy."

"You don't believe in the concept of 'enough candy,'" said Ryan.

"Yes I do," said Defense. "And besides, you're begging for three now."

"Three!"

"Isn't she pregnant?" asked Defenseur.

"Not by me, anyway," said Ryan, getting angry.

"Stand down, sailor," said Defenseur. "I'm not insinuating anything. Just making a bad guess, okay?"

"Those were pretty good cop costumes," said Ryan.

"I saw costumes just like that in the shop in DC where I got my—"

"Ah, DC. *Not* Manhattan."

"Yeah, well, I thought Manhattan sounded cooler. The prices weren't even bad. But I couldn't bring you to see it, because then you'd guess the game."

"What's the game?" asked Ryan.

"To see how many ridiculous stories you'd believe."

Ryan thought back to all the stories he'd been told so far today. "You've been running everything all day."

"I have not," said Defense. "It has been fate alone that chose your path through Charlottesville."

They quit, as they always had before, in the Burke kitchen, where Dianne tossed in her night's catch and the three of them divvied up the spoils. Only Ryan didn't really want any of the candy. He just wanted to finish up and get over to see Bizzy.

"Ryan's getting impatient," said Dianne. "He wants to finish up so he can see Bizzy."

In the old days, Ryan would have flown into a rage and shouted Dianne out of the kitchen.

Instead he just laughed and said, "Smart girl."

"Do you get what Bizzy sees in him?" asked Defense.

"A bodyguard," said Dianne.

"Because he's so big and strong," said Defense.

"Because he's a puppy dog," said Dianne.

Ryan didn't mind the teasing, because it wasn't in front of anyone else.

"Maybe the loveks will show themselves tonight," said Ryan.

"What's a lovek?" asked Defense.

"Bogeymen," said Ryan.

"Slovenian hit men?" asked Defense.

"Olympic-level flatulentes," said Ryan.

"What's that?"

"Farters," said Ryan. "At an international competition level."

"So all the time I've know you," said Defense, "you've been practicing for an Olympic team and you didn't even tell me."

Ryan smiled. "If you couldn't interpret the evidence . . ."

Dianne pushed herself between Ryan and Defense, looking Ryan in the face. "So what was the prank this year?"

"None so far," said Ryan. "That I've detected, at any rate."

"So the prank wasn't to get you out trick-or-treating with Daffy Duck?" asked Dianne.

"That's not a prank," said Defense. "That's a blessing. I blessed him with that."

"True," Ryan agreed. "We only came back with candy because of Defense Duck."

Dianne turned to Defenseur. "Was *that* the prank? To get Ryan to say 'Defense Duck'?"

"He called me that the instant he saw the costume," said Defense.

"Or was it to pry Ryan away from Bizzy long enough for her to have a tête-à-tête with her real boyfriend from Slovenia?" asked Dianne.

Ryan laid a firm hand on the nape of Dianne's neck. "I bet you were hoping that the link between your head and your shoulders would remain in place."

"That was *your* prank," said Defense to Dianne. "I'm not dumb enough to try to make him doubt Bizzy's adoration of his adorable self."

Ryan steeled himself not to strangle Dianne or punch Defense. It would only be his normal weak moves, because he knew nobody was being threatened, so no micropower.

"I was just kidding," Dianne told Ryan.

Ryan shrugged, because he didn't trust himself to speak without betraying emotion.

Dianne turned back to Defense. "I know your prank couldn't be destructive, like that time you cut out the crotch of all Ryan's underwear."

"Worth it," said Defense.

"You had to buy all new underwear for him," said Dianne.

"Twice," said Ryan.

Dianne looked at him quizzically.

"Defense's mother agreed with our mother that a dozen pairs of pink panties would not make up for the destroyed tighty-whities," said Ryan.

Dianne laughed. "Expensive, Defense."

"To quote myself, 'worth it.'"

"You still have those panties, don't you," Ryan said to Defense.

"I put them in Dianne's drawer."

"You did not," said Dianne. "I never got a deposit of unfamiliar pinkies."

"Made you think, though, didn't I," said Defense.

"Defense thinks that when I get a little older, I'm going to go out with him," said Dianne.

"Duh," said Defense. "Who else?"

"Anyone," said Dianne. "Everyone."

"She's playing hard to get, but she's secretly intrigued, wondering just how creative and adventurous being my girlfriend would turn out to be."

"You've jumped from fantasy dating to *girlfriend*?" asked Dianne.

"She thinks," said Defense, "that she's going to be able to date the boy next door, Bizzy's godlike brother."

"She does not," said Dianne. "She has no idea of dating anybody, least of all somebody she's seen picking his nose."

"I didn't pick this nose," said Defense.

"She means Bizzy's brother. He's a frequent nose picker," said Ryan. "And when he isn't picking his nose, he needs to, because there's always a booger just inside one nostril, ranging from a dangling goop like a nasal uvula to a full load of green mucous that forms bubbles whenever he breathes out through the other nostril."

"Disgusting and untrue," said Dianne. "He is always fastidiously clean."

"Because he lives with his face in the mirror," said Defense.

"Because he can *face* the mirror without a mask," said Dianne.

Defense lifted off the Daffy Duck head. "No boogers. You can check."

"Why would I do that?" asked Dianne. "If I don't find boogers, then I lose. And if I *do* find boogers, I *really* lose."

"I've already lost," said Ryan, "because I'm with two people who like to talk about boogers."

"He used to wipe them on the wall by his bed," Dianne confided. "Then Dad moved the bed out from the wall and saw, like, four years of accumulated dried-on boogers. He made Ryan sand down the wall so it could be repainted."

Ryan had to do something, go somewhere, to keep himself from going insane with anger that Dianne would tell that to anyone.

"You went too far, Dianne," Defense said.

"But I know you'll protect me," said Dianne.

"From *him*?" asked Defense. "I was counting on you to protect *me*."

Ryan went to the door. "I'm going to see how Bizzy made it through Halloween."

"He's already putting his hands all over me!" Dianne called out to Ryan.

"Bite them off," said Ryan. "Or better still, sand them off." Ryan momentarily wondered if Dianne wasn't speaking some deeper truth; Defense had told him last summer that Dianne was growing up to be really hot. Was it possible that he really had designs on her, that this wasn't all stupid banter, and Dianne was realizing that Defense had intentions, and they weren't particularly honorable?

But Defense knew that Ryan would protect Dianne. He wouldn't put his hands anywhere near her.

On the front porch, a man was ringing the Horvats' doorbell.

The door opened, and Bizzy stood there with a bowl of candy, about to serve some into the trick-or-treater's bag. Only there wasn't a trick-or-treater.

"No treat," said the man to Bizzy.

"No trick, either," Bizzy said to him coldly.

"Invite me in," the man said.

Ryan wasn't going to continue being ignored. "Bugger off," he said.

The man's hand flew out toward Ryan's face. Depending on where he meant it to land, it would have blacked Ryan's eye or given him a bloody nose.

Instead, though, the man's hand hit the edge of the Burkes' storm door, which Ryan had partly closed to bring it right to the place where the man's fist was going.

Ryan had done it with the same unplanned, preternatural speed he had used in combing out the bee and jabbing Errol's throat. So his micropower could also show up for use in self-defense. That was *very* useful knowledge.

Meanwhile, the man was crying out in agony. The storm door was good-quality metal—Dad would never put up anything less—and as Ryan tried to glimpse the injured hand, he thought he saw blood and broken bones.

"Since you were so rude about demanding to go into the Horvats' house," said Ryan, "and even ruder in attempting to hit me in that clumsy, ill-thought-out manner, I think that instead of waiting for us to call an ambulance to deal with that hand, you should find your own way to a doctor or emergency care facility."

The man did not seem to be hearing anything except his own agony, but he got the idea and stumbled away from the porch, still holding the damaged hand in the other and wailing softly in a foreign language.

"Is he speaking Slovenian?" asked Ryan.

"Probably," said Bizzy, "but I'm not understanding any of his words."

"So not Slovenian, then."

"Probably Slovenian," said Bizzy, "but not words that my parents would have allowed me to learn."

"Maybe the next guy they send will be polite to the neighbor boy and ask you nicely to let him in," said Ryan.

"Maybe the next guy will have a submachine gun, which he starts firing at the house before he gets anywhere near the porch."

"So we live in two separate fantasy universes," said Ryan.

"That move with the door was very clever. How did you know that his jab would reach that far?"

"I didn't," said Ryan. "I just knew I needed to move the door to that exact position."

"Your micropower?" Bizzy asked.

"Could have been," said Ryan. "But did I do it to protect myself, or you?"

"You were the one about to be poked," said Bizzy.

"But yours was the door he was trying to get through, and he didn't get through it."

"Want some candy?" asked Bizzy, holding out the bowl. She had asked him a few days before what treats kids around here would like. He told her that Twix bars were always the first to go. So all that was in the bowl were lots of little baby Twixes.

"No thanks," said Ryan. "Got Twix of my own."

"By now," said Bizzy, "I bet you don't have any."

Ryan thought of Dianne and Defense together in the kitchen. "Probably not," said Ryan. But he still held up a hand to stop her from pushing the candy bowl any farther his way.

"On a diet?" Bizzy asked.

"I just shattered a man's hand," said Ryan. "That sort of thing kills my appetite."

"He shattered his own hand," said Bizzy. "Don't get all pacifist on me."

"I knowingly put a metal door edge where his hand was going to be," said Ryan. "The fact that my face was supposed to be there doesn't make me any prouder that I did that to his hand."

"It makes *me* very happy," said Mrs. Horvat, who had come up to the door without stepping into the light.

"Did you know him?" Bizzy asked her mother.

"He was from the university library," said Mrs. Horvat. "I'm afraid he was bringing me something from your father."

"Isn't Dad coming home tonight himself?" asked Bizzy.

"I asked him not to," said Mrs. Horvat, "because there's such a good chance of awful things happening here."

"Why does your dad have a library friend who lashes out at boys from next door like that?" Ryan asked Bizzy.

It was Mrs. Horvat who replied. "Because he's a lovek that befriended my husband to try to get to me. I suspect he was going to tell me that they're holding the dear man and will send me body parts until I give them what they want."

"And what is that?" Bizzy demanded.

"Me," said Mrs. Horvat. "Or, failing that, you."

"And he was going to give you what, a ransom note?" asked Ryan.

"I don't know," said Mrs. Horvat. "But my husband and I already had this conversation. He told me to give them nothing. If they ever had possession of him, I should presume that he is already dead or will certainly be killed trying to escape. So even if I capitulate, all they could return to me would be a corpse."

Ryan believed that Bizzy's father might have said that. But maybe he was tied up somewhere wishing he had left his wife a more conciliatory path. Maybe he was saying, go ahead and bail me out of this, if you can.

Or maybe he was getting grim satisfaction out of knowing that his wife was tough enough not to budge an inch.

"I'm sure you know that the police have telephones," said Ryan.

"I still have hope that we'll get Ciril back undamaged," said Mrs. Horvat. "Since he didn't actually deliver his message, it's possible he was just here to tell us that Ciril was going to be late."

Ryan ran his finger down the bloodied and very slightly dented edge of the door. "That was quite a blow for a guy with a message of love and peace."

"I said 'possible,' not 'likely.'"

Ryan nodded. "Otherwise, how has your Halloween been?"

"Candy's two-thirds gone, and the trick-or-treaters seem to have gone in out of the cold," said Bizzy.

"Wanna come out on the porch and kiss standing up?" asked Ryan.

"Very funny," said Mrs. Horvat. "I know I can't stop you, but at least I don't have to watch."

"He's kidding, Mom," said Bizzy.

"He's pretending to be kidding," said Mrs. Horvat, "but he's really hoping you'll do it."

Bizzy looked inquiringly at Ryan.

Ryan shrugged. He could deny it. But he didn't want to actually say it.

Bizzy stepped toward him, still holding the bowl of tiny Twix bars. She leaned in to kiss him. As his lips met hers, he felt the Twix bars land on his head, followed by the plunk of the metal bowl.

He did not break the kiss. Not for a good long while. Then, as they parted, he said, very mildly, "Owie."

"You were supposed to jump away and laugh," said Bizzy.

"The choice was kissing you or jumping away and laughing. Didn't I make the right choice?"

She grinned at him, and suddenly her face went beautiful. Ryan could hardly breathe.

"Not on the porch, you boneheaded girl," said Mrs. Horvat from the shadows inside the house. "You know they're still watching."

"So is Ryan."

"I know you're trying to be nice," said Ryan, "but that face just terrifies me. I mean, I love you, I love how beautiful you always are. But when you really pour it on, I feel completely unworthy."

Bizzy's face relaxed back to normal. "I love you, fant."

"Keep feeling unworthy," said Mrs. Horvat.

"I thought you didn't want to watch, Mother," said Bizzy.

"I thought you knew better than to show that face outdoors," said Mrs. Horvat.

"Says the woman who cursed me to a couple of days of compulsory beauty," said Bizzy.

"You should have stayed home."

"With the woman who cursed me? Have you heard of 'sanity'?" asked Bizzy.

"Whoever sent him," said Mrs. Horvat, "his actions show that violence is already in their hearts. Will you please come inside so I can lock the door?"

"Come in with us," said Bizzy to Ryan.

"So you two can kiss on the sofa for hours, passing Twix bars from mouth to mouth?" asked Mrs. Horvat.

"I hadn't thought of that, Mother, but it's a good idea."

"I need to call Dr. Withunga," said Ryan. "We need her to get her list done and bring some people over."

"I have not given my consent to anyone coming over," said Mrs. Horvat.

"But you will," said Ryan, "because that guy was scary strong."

"And a big baby when he got hurt," said Mrs. Horvat.

"Everybody's a big baby when they've got a few broken bones," said Ryan.

"They aren't coming tonight," said Mrs. Horvat.

"And you know this how?" asked Bizzy.

"Because they sent only him," said Mrs. Horvat. "And they saw that

Ryan was able to stop him by shifting a door about twenty centimeters in a split second. So when they come back, it will be in numbers, and with strategies and tactics."

"Or 'shock and awe,'" said Ryan. Father had made that a family slogan in memory of whatever war that had been a catchphrase in.

"They will try to be clever," said Mrs. Horvat. "They will try to get somebody into the house before I know who it really is."

"I assume your plan is to let nobody into the house," said Ryan.

"That seems the safest course to me," said Mrs. Horvat. "But they'll try to find a way around that."

"But not tonight," said Bizzy.

"No," said Mrs. Horvat. "Ryan, go back into your family's home and sleep well. There is still school tomorrow. I'm going to turn off the porch light so trick-or-treaters don't come anymore."

Ryan kissed Bizzy again quickly and started to head inside.

"Aren't you going to help me clean up this scattering of Twix?" asked Bizzy.

"I will if your mother says I may," said Ryan. "Mother, may I?"

"I know that you are mocking me with the name of a children's game in America," said Mrs. Horvat. "And the answer is yes, you may."

She let the door close behind her. Ryan got down on hands and knees and helped Bizzy gather up the fallen Twix bars. He got about twice as many into the bowl as she did, because she kept stopping to kiss some unexpected part of his head—ear, nape of the neck, eyelid, cheek, chin. He never thought that having Bizzy kiss him could possibly be annoying, but now he knew that it could. And that she *wanted* to annoy him.

So he annoyed *her* by not letting her kisses distract him from his task *or* goad him into showing annoyance.

They were soon done with the task. The bowl was full.

"If we didn't get them all," said Bizzy, "eat whatever you find."

She got up and went inside without a final kiss or a backward glance. Was she pouting about something? Why would she be pouting?

He found four more Twixes on the front walk and in a bush. He placed them in a little row just beside the outer bottom corner of her door.

Opening the storm door would not move the bars, and nobody taking a step through the door would step on them. But they would be easily noticed. Ryan wanted the candy to convey a very clear message: I will give anything good that I find to you. And I will not be ordered about.

He went inside and got into his pajamas for bed. Mom and Dianne had apparently gone up to bed, so Ryan padded around in a quiet kitchen, went to the bathroom, and then came back out and flopped down on the sofa that he slept on.

The sofa gave a muffled cry.

Ryan got up and removed cushions until Defense was revealed, curled up and moaning. "You're so fat and heavy," he said.

"I'm not fat and I'm very light for my height," said Ryan. "You're an idiot to sneak into my bed."

"It wasn't actually a prank," said Defense.

"Obviously," said Ryan. "It was an act of self-destructive stupidity."

"It didn't cause anyone to get angry with me and try to attack me," said Defense. "So you didn't have to defend me."

"True," said Ryan. "Which means you lied to me about not having a prank, but at least you kept your word about not manipulating me into killing somebody."

"I'm trying," said Defense.

Ryan reached down and hauled him up out of the base of the sofa. When he put the cushions back down, it was obvious that there was way less support from the springs and such. Defense had probably broken the sofa and it would be even more uncomfortable to sleep on.

Not Ryan's fault. Mom or Dianne had let Defense in, so they were responsible.

It didn't make the couch any more comfortable that night, however, knowing it was their fault.

20

The day after Halloween, morning came too early. Ryan saw two big bowls of candy on the table, which meant that Defense had taken his candy home. Ryan knew which bowl was his, because it was the one with only crap candy in it, the stuff people bought in bulk and without the slightest concern for what children actually liked. Which was perfectly fair, because Ryan was not a child and should not have been trick-or-treating.

Ryan took the bowl of crap candy and poured it into the kitchen garbage. Then he pulled the bag out of the container, tied it off, replaced it with a new one, and then carried the one with all his candy in it out to the bin.

I could have donated it to children somewhere, he thought. But by throwing it away, I'm helping preserve the health of their teeth. Altruism, thy name is Ryan.

He greeted Dianne cheerfully for breakfast. She looked at the candy bowls. "Did I guess correctly?" he said.

"No," she said. "I left all the good ones for you."

"Well, now they're yours."

"What happened to the crap bowl?" asked Dianne.

"I ate it all."

"And you're still eating breakfast?"

"There's always room in my tummy for good food."

Mom spoke up from the kitchen, where she was finishing up with Dianne's lunch. Dianne preferred Mom's sandwiches to anything at the middle school cafeteria. "I'm glad to hear that," said Mom. "But it would reassure me more if I knew you did not really eat that entire bowl of candy."

"It's in the outside garbage," Ryan said, deciding that the joke had gone on long enough.

"Ha-ha," said Mom.

"Honest truth," said Ryan. "Happy All Saints' Day."

"You never cease to astonish me, Ryan Burke."

"And vice versa, Mother," said Ryan.

"Are you going to be safe today, Ryan?" asked Mother.

"Why would you ask?" Ryan replied.

"Because you seem to be leading a watchful, dangerous life these days," said Mom.

"I will be safe today, Mother," said Ryan.

"When I get to high school," asked Dianne, "will you walk me to school the way you walk Bizzy?"

"No," said Ryan. "Because you wouldn't want me to stop every twenty steps and kiss you."

"Excuse me, Mom, but is it all right if I vomit up every bit of breakfast right now?"

"Not at the table, dear," said Mother.

"If I puke, Ryan made me do it."

"Thanks for breakfast, Mom," said Ryan, getting up from the table and carrying his plate to the counter by the sink.

"I love you, Ryan. Have a nice day."

"It's already nice because you were in it," said Ryan.

"What a suck-up," said Dianne.

"And I'm glad you're in my life, too, Diagonal," said Ryan.

"Now I really will throw up."

Ryan was smiling as he went out the front door. Bizzy was sitting on the top step. "Took you long enough."

"Mom cooked breakfast."

"Hard to chew?"

"So delicious I couldn't leave any of it behind."

"Oh, so we're being officiously cheerful today, is that it?"

"I'm worried that something ugly is going to happen today."

She stopped on the sidewalk and turned to face him. He expected ugly-face, but instead it was pure glamor.

Then she let her face glide back to normal.

"Wow," he said.

"Every now and then," she said, "I like to give my fant the best I've got."

"Was that so I could die happy, knowing I was loved by the most beautiful girl in all of history? Was that why you showed me that kilo-Helen face?"

"Only a thousand Helens?"

"A tera-Helen. Peta-Helen. Zetta-Helen."

"Zetta?" she asked.

"Not an exaggeration. It's only a thousandth of a yotta-Helen, anyway."

"And you're way smarter than a yocto-Plato," she said.

"How smart was Plato, really?" said Ryan. "And you made up that smartness measure, anyway."

"IQ is so passé," said Bizzy. "I think Einstein is overrated or I would have used his name for the measure. And Newton is already used for a unit of measurement. Did you eat all your candy yet?"

"Threw it away," said Ryan.

"Self-control. That makes you a deci-Gandhi."

"I thought Dianne had left me a bowl of all the crap candy. Instead, she was giving me all the good stuff."

"She said."

"She was telling the truth," said Ryan.

"Now you have another micropower?"

"I've lived with that girl her whole life," said Ryan. "She was telling the truth. Which meant she was trying to be nice to me. Her reward was that she ended up with all the good stuff anyway."

"What's going to happen, Ryan?" asked Bizzy. "That guy coming to the house. You breaking his hand."

"*He* broke his hand," said Ryan. "I just provided the edge of a door for him to break it on."

"Things are violent. He meant for that blow to hit *you*."

"So I figured," said Ryan. "People sometimes offer me gifts I don't want."

"You aren't a superhero. Stopping a kid from kicking another kid, you were magnificent, of course, all the videos on the internet confirm that, but still, these guys probably have guns and that guy proved they aren't afraid to cause serious injury. That blow would have decked you."

"I don't know how far my micropower goes," said Ryan.

"How strong does it make you?" asked Bizzy.

"I don't think it gives me any more strength than I would have with a full dose of adrenaline and perfect aim."

"And speed," she said.

"I don't know if I'm faster than I would be on adrenaline. I just start sooner."

"Because you think faster?"

"Because I just know. I don't stop to think."

"What if you're wrong?"

"Was I wrong about Door-Hitting Clown?"

Bizzy said, "I don't want you to die for me, Ryan."

"Your mother does. That was the deal. She spelled it out for me."

"I bet your mother would offer a counterargument," said Bizzy.

"Not sure of that," said Ryan. "Not sure how much she actually loves me."

"She loves you," said Bizzy.

"Maybe she wishes she had aborted me, too," said Ryan.

Bizzy said nothing to that. They walked the rest of the way to school in silence.

Ryan went to her locker with her. Then she went to his locker with him. Because he wasn't going to let her out of his sight, and she thought that was a good policy.

The day's events began in Mr. Hardesty's class, when he was tormenting a student who had no idea of the answer to a fairly simple question about the Emperor Diocletian. The door to the room opened, and a man in a dark suit stepped in.

"I beg your pardon?" asked Mr. Hardesty.

"I'm Lieutenant Alford of the FBI," the man said, holding up a badge.

"I'm Professor Hardesty of Yale, emeritus," said Hardesty. "I carry my credentials in my brain."

Ryan was already on his feet when Alford of the FBI turned to face the class. "I'm here to bring Bo-JAY-na Horvat to the front office to be signed out of school by her parents."

Bizzy was rising to her feet when Ryan pushed past her and stood halfway between her and Alford of the FBI. "She's not going," said Ryan.

"What are you, her master? Is she on a leash?" asked Alford.

"Her parents aren't in the front office."

"Let's go there and see," said Alford.

Hardesty chimed in. "Mr. Burke, I'm sure Bizzy doesn't need your protection."

Ryan paid no attention to Hardesty. He just stood there between Alford and Bizzy.

"I think I should go," said Bizzy.

"I think not," said Ryan.

"Boy, he sure takes being a boyfriend seriously," said Kit, one of Bizzy's friends.

"It's a Slovenian thing," said Ryan.

"You're not Slovenian," said Defense.

"But Lieutenant Alford is," said Ryan.

Alford's eyes got a tiny bit narrower. His brow creased a tiny bit more deeply. He was getting angry.

"I'll go, really, Ryan," said Bizzy.

Alford held out a hand as Bizzy started to step around Ryan.

Ryan stepped farther forward and took hold of Alford's hand. It was strangely clammy. "I stay between you and Bizzy the whole way."

"You're not invited to this meeting," said Alford.

"I'm her plus-one," said Ryan. "Let's not quarrel."

Alford shrugged and walked up to stand against the chalkboard. He waved Ryan past him.

Ryan maneuvered Bizzy to the front and guided her out the door of the room. Alford was right behind him.

Ryan could see the flexing of Alford's muscles. His distribution of weight between his feet. He could see Alford's intended move as soon as the door closed.

So Ryan didn't wait for the door to close. As Alford got exactly in the middle of the door frame, Ryan struck him in the side of the head with all the force of his open hand and extended arm. Alford's head crashed into the metal door frame. His head did not bounce off. Instead, it sort of stuck there. Then Alford slid down the door frame as if his skull were on a track. A thick streak of blood trailed after him.

Bizzy gasped.

Ryan said softly, "The FBI has no lieutenants. Only special agent on up to special agent-in-charge."

The door couldn't fall shut behind them, what with Alford-not-from-the-FBI sitting there on the floor with his head welded to the jamb. Ryan looked up and down the corridor and saw a man in a black suit at either end. They probably had seen what Ryan did, because they were beginning to walk very briskly toward them, reaching for guns in shoulder holsters.

Ryan dragged Bizzy back into the classroom. Everyone was looking at him in shock. "He wasn't an FBI agent. He was a Slovenian terrorist, and he's here to kidnap Bizzy and eventually kill her and her whole family." He pulled Bizzy toward the wall of windows. She was a little bit shocked, it seemed, but even walking like a zombie, she followed his lead readily enough.

Ryan pushed open the transom at the base of the window. He knew from experience that he could fit through it, but he had never analyzed Bizzy's body with this aperture in mind. He lifted her up and fed her feet through the window.

"No," she said.

Ryan tossed her in the air just a little, to flip her over so that she would go through facedown. "It's not a long drop to the lawn below," he said. He pushed her through until her center of gravity was beyond the sill. Then he opened the window next to that one and squeezed himself out as easily as ever. He reached the ground before her.

"That just scraped up my whole front," Bizzy said.

"Whiny baby," said Ryan. He took her hand again and led her off along the side of the building, heading toward the gym. He figured the agents were all over inside the main building and watching the exits. He began jogging and Bizzy kept up just fine.

They made it to the gym unseen, apparently—at least, nobody shouted There they are. Ryan pulled her around the building and over to the woods that came up against the school grounds. He was hoping that the Slovenians didn't have a helicopter watching—he couldn't hear anything in the air, and anyway, this was obviously a completely incompetent group. "Lieutenant Alford" had a perfect mid-Virginia accent, as if he had grown up around Charlottesville, and pronouncing Bojana as bo-JAY-na was a nice touch. But they couldn't even prep him with a proper FBI-sounding title? They didn't warn him of what Ryan could do? Amateur hour.

"I think you killed him," said Bizzy, as they walked carefully through the woods.

"I think so, too," said Ryan.

"Was that your plan?" she asked.

"My plan was to keep you from going three feet with him. He was ready to knock me down as soon as the door closed. But I didn't care who saw what I did, I just knew I had to strike first."

"But to kill him?"

"Look, Bizzy, this micropower is new to me. I was on course to kill Errol that day, aiming right at his larynx. I had to *try* to redirect my blow so it wouldn't kill him. Even then he needed a tracheotomy. So apparently my micropower sets me in motion to eliminate threats to people I love."

"He was going to hit *you*," said Bizzy.

"If he knocked me down, who would have protected you?" asked Ryan. "I'm not sure what your qualms are about. These guys plan to kill your mom, don't they? And kidnapping you would just have been part of accomplishing that—after which they would have killed you, too. Is my assessment incorrect?"

"No, I think you're right. But killing is so . . . permanent."

"While saving you is apparently quite temporary," said Ryan. "I think the guy at the east end of the corridor had his hand in a big thick bandage. I think he's the guy at the door yesterday."

"You're thinking you should have killed him, too?"

"I had nothing to kill him *with* that night," said Ryan. "Bizzy, I don't plan these things. That's the whole essence of my micropower. I notice things unconsciously so I just *know* what's about to happen, and I am already taking preventive measures before I realize what I just unconsciously sensed. It happens like inhaling or digesting—I'm not choosing to do it, it already chose itself. So I was smashing his head into the door frame before I knew I was going to strike, and when I did realize it, I was afraid I wouldn't be strong enough to incapacitate him. I thought the most I could do was knock him to the ground with a headache."

"I think you slotted his head," she said.

"Maybe he had an unusually flexible skull. I don't know that he's dead, and neither do you, but I must admit that if he *is* dead, then I feel pretty good that he probably won't be coming after you anymore."

"Yeah," she said. "Me too." She squeezed his hand. "I never said I disapproved."

Only then, with her consent, or forgiveness, or whatever—only then did he realize that yes, indeed, he probably had killed a man with a single blow from his left hand, his nondominant arm.

Walking through the woods, he thought of the possibility of legal trouble. Assaulting a federal officer—that's what the kids in the room probably thought. What Mr. Hardesty thought. Of course, the real FBI would immediately realize that he was a fake, but meanwhile the police might put out the news that two fugitives, one of them a murder suspect and—heck, they probably assumed Bizzy was his hostage. That's how it would go on a cop show.

"We're not calling your mom for a ride home," said Ryan.

"They're watching her, I'm sure, and she'd lead them right to us."

"But we need to call people," said Ryan. "Dr. Withunga. We need to get a group of micropots together so we're all strengthened."

"You were pretty strong alone," said Bizzy.

"I had another micropot with me," he said.

She didn't say anything.

"You," he said.

"I don't have a micropower," she said. "I just have a thing I do with my face."

"And I just did a thing with my left arm," he said. "I had you with me."

"Where are we going?" she asked.

"We're already there. Standing here at the edge of the woods. Right down there is a bus stop. When we see the bus coming along the road, we run down and get on, just in time. You have your youth pass?"

"In my purse," she said.

"You have your purse?" asked Ryan. She held it up. "In plain sight."

"I wasn't looking," said Ryan. "I was watching our path through the woods so neither of us would twist an ankle or anything."

"Always looking out for me," she said.

"I believe that's accurate, yes, ma'am."

The bus came along a few minutes later. It was a busy route, and Ryan didn't care which bus they were on. They sank down in the seat so their heads wouldn't show through the window. Only then did Ryan figure out what route they were on so he could figure out where to get off in order to catch a bus that would get them to Dad's work site. If he could only remember which job he was on today. Not the McDonald's. It was a house. Adding a second story, and the new footings were already done, so Dad would be there taking the roof off so they could put up the walls and getting the new roof on before it could rain again. And that house was . . .

They got off the bus. They retreated between two commercial buildings until the bus they wanted came along. They were at Dad's project before a full hour had passed since Ryan killed Lieutenant Alford. What a shame that the poor man would be stuck with that pathetic false identity in Ryan's mind forever.

Dad wasn't there. But Niddy Adams was. "I need my dad," said Ryan.

"Your girlfriend?" asked Niddy.

"Yes sir," said Bizzy. "But we really need Ryan's dad."

Niddy looked back and forth between them. "Emergency, I take it?"

"Life and death," said Ryan.

"Literally," said Bizzy.

Niddy had his phone out already, was selecting who to call. "Anyplace we can hole up, out of sight, till he gets here?"

"You don't want to talk to him?" asked Niddy.

"If you tell him I need him here, now, then he'll come," said Ryan.

"I think he will," said Niddy. "Just go in the house. The walls are still up on the downstairs floor." His attention turned to the phone. "Ryan and his girlfriend are here and they need you right now . . . Yes, sir."

And that was it. The conversation was over before Ryan and Bizzy were three steps away.

"Is that your dad's boss?" asked Bizzy as they went through the garage and into the house. There was no furniture; it had been completely emptied. So they sat on the carpeted floor, out of sight from any windows.

"No," said Ryan. "He works for my dad. My dad *is* the boss."

"And he just ordered your dad to come?"

"He told my dad that I needed him. *We* needed him."

"And your dad will come?"

"He trusts Niddy," said Ryan. "And Niddy trusted me."

"We'd have to burn down the house to get my dad out of the university library," said Bizzy.

"Let's not do that," said Ryan. "Unless his micropower is to completely disarm anyone with hostile intent toward his family."

"I wish," said Bizzy.

"Do you think your dad *has* a micropower?"

"The ability to concentrate so completely on his scholarly undertakings that he wouldn't look up for a nuclear explosion."

Ryan chuckled, but it died at once. "I'm scared," Ryan said.

"I'm not," said Bizzy. "I have *you*."

"That's what scares me," said Ryan. "I know something much bigger is coming, and as far as I know, I've already used everything I've got."

Bizzy sat still for about a minute and then said, "I think you've got more in you than that."

"Why do you think that?" asked Ryan.

"Because you still love me," she said. "So you'll have whatever you need." She kissed him then.

"That's very distracting," said Ryan, when he was able to breathe again.

"I'm a girl, looking at a guy, asking him to—"

"No movie lines," said Ryan. "No jokes. What are we to each other,

Bizzy? When this is over, when all the bad guys are dead or locked up, when you don't need a protector anymore, what are we?"

"You're seriously asking that? Now?"

"Do you love me? Or just need me?" asked Ryan.

"I need you. I love you. Will you be my valentine, Ryan?" She kissed him again.

"That's not an answer," he whispered. "But I understand. It's all you can give me right now."

"You should ask yourself the same question. If this ends happily, and I don't need you to protect me anymore, will *you* still love *me*?"

"I loved you before I knew you needed me," said Ryan.

"Also not an answer," she said. "But it'll do."

The door opened and it was Dad.

"So what is it?" he asked. "Bad guys chasing you? Or the police?"

"Probably both," said Ryan.

"Definitely the bad guys," said Bizzy.

"Can I use your phone to call Dr. Withunga?" asked Ryan. "We need to get some micropots over to the house."

"Our house?" asked Dad. "You want to assemble people there? Isn't that kind of ground zero?"

"Exactly," said Ryan. "When micropots gather together, all their abilities increase and have greater focus."

"Any of those micropowers include tear gas? Flame throwers? Automatic weapons? Grenades?"

"No," said Ryan. "I do know a guy with a nail gun."

"Which you don't even know how to operate," said Dad.

"Not my fault," said Ryan. "But I *can* take out garbage and put away dishes."

"Come on and get in my car," said Dad.

They got up and followed him out the door.

"You think I should bring some of my guys along?" asked Dad.

"No," said Ryan. "If they have micropowers, we don't know what they are, and if they don't, there's no reason to put anybody else in jeopardy."

"And what about your mother and Dianne?" asked Dad.

"Dianne's in school, and Mom's . . . at work."

"Ah, yes," said Dad. "Work."

"My mom will be there," said Bizzy.

"I imagine so," said Dad. "Isn't she the actual target?"

"*She* thinks so," said Bizzy.

"Any reason to think she's wrong?" asked Dad.

"None," said Ryan.

"Apart from the fact that she's a lunatic witch, no," said Bizzy.

"Lots of that going around," said Dad.

Which was as close as Ryan had come to hearing Dad say anything disrespectful about Mom.

21

Once Ryan had Dr. Withunga on Dad's phone, Dad reached for it and Ryan handed it over. He had serious misgivings about Dad and Dr. Withunga talking together, though he wasn't sure which he was afraid of—that Dad wouldn't get what Dr. Withunga was trying to do with micropotents, or that Dr. Withunga would look down on Dad as a nonuniversity guy who built things with his hands.

But apparently they got along perfectly, or at least understood that this was a serious problem they were working on together. "I don't think you want to bring your people through the front door," Dad said, right at the start.

"All I know is the front door," said Dr. Withunga.

Dad told her the streets that would get her and her crew parked on the street behind. Fortunately, Dad and the back-door neighbor got along well enough that there was an unlocked gate in the fence, and Dad said he'd call the guy and tell him that a bunch of people were coming through and please don't call the cops on them.

Then they talked about what they'd do inside the house. "Here's what I think," said Dad. "I know that house. I know every route from one place to another inside it. If all you really need right now is proximity, so their super-powers—no, right, micropowers—so they're augmenting each other, right?"

Apparently Dr. Withunga said yes.

"Then I think we should try to bring you all in more or less secretly, depending on how close a watch they're keeping on the house. And inside the house, I want everybody to stay with me."

Ryan was surprised that Dad thought he was part of this.

Bizzy apparently felt the same, because she raised her eyebrows at Ryan.

"Um, Dad," said Ryan.

"I'm on the phone here, Ryan," said Dad, in a voice Ryan hadn't heard since he was five.

"But I didn't want you to—"

Dad put the phone on speaker. "Hush up, please, Ryan," said Dr. Withunga. "Of course your father will be with the rest of us. *You* have to stay with Bizzy and her mother. So you can't be with the rest of us."

Ryan hadn't really thought it through. He thought he would be in charge of getting everybody set up, but no, he would be in the Horvats' living room and there he would stay, because if anything could activate his micropower, it would be any kind of threat against Bizzy and her mom.

Bizzy reached out her hand and placed it over Ryan's. It had a cooling, calming effect. She thinks it's okay this way, so that's enough, thought Ryan. Enough for me.

Dad had the phone off speaker mode now, and he was describing where he would put the GRUT volunteers. And Dr. Withunga told him which powers she had invited. "Once you've got the first group into the house from the back," said Dad, "then you go out to the street behind and wait for the others, lead them to the gate in the fence. When you've got them all through, come on in yourself. I don't think they'll make their move till dusk. At least that's when I'd make *my* move, if I were trying to get into the house."

When Dad disconnected the call to Dr. Withunga, he said, "Okay, you heard that?"

"Your side of it," said Ryan. "Till you went on speaker."

"You've got enough to worry about," said Dad. "Dr. Withunga and I will do crowd control. The crowd being your fellow micropotents."

"Makes sense," said Ryan, though he still felt a little embarrassed that Dad thought he could just take over something he hadn't even been a part of. It was my show, Ryan heard himself thinking, like a petulant child.

Well, I *am* a child. But Dad's a lot more experienced than me in pretty much everything. He's led bunches of people before, and I couldn't even lead Defense. If I can handle myself, then it's a good thing I won't be distracted by having to worry about where other people will be.

"One thing to keep in mind," Bizzy said. "Once my mother has any of the loveks within earshot, she can curse them and mess them up. So they'll be trying to be as stealthy as possible in their approach."

"Or sly," said Ryan. "Remember the driver of that car? How he said he was from a faction that didn't want your mother killed? Maybe he was telling the truth, or maybe it was a con to try to get into the house without a curse. Ditto with the guy who broke his fist on the door."

"What's been going on around here?" Dad muttered.

"It's all hell, Dad," said Ryan, "and I think it's going to break loose tonight."

"Do you think they'll try another trick to try to get in?" asked Bizzy.

"If I were them," said Ryan, "I would take three failures as a sign. Car guy, door guy, the fake FBI guy at school—I think they've shot their wad on subterfuge."

Bizzy shrugged. "I didn't even believe they were real till we started seeing people showing up more than once, stalking us."

"Funny thing is that the first stalker I spotted was Aaron Withunga, so, not a bad guy at all."

"But it made me start to take Mom's paranoia seriously," said Bizzy.

"Strange how parents aren't always wrong," said Dad.

"Yeah, yeah, the generations don't understand each other," said Ryan.

"No," said Dad. "Your generation doesn't understand *mine*, because you haven't lived long enough yet. But I was your age. And I remember."

Ryan wanted to give a snotty answer about how being older didn't mean he understood anything, it just meant that he *thought* he did.

Then Ryan thought about taking out the garbage and putting away dishes and getting along with Dianne, and how much more peaceful the house was, and how Mom didn't always look so tired and frazzled. And he also thought about how doing all those things made Ryan feel a stronger sense of responsibility for his family. He no longer did those chores and showed patience with Dianne because Dad asked him to, or because he wanted to prove to Dad that he was ready to work for him. He did those things because they were the right things to do for the family.

So yeah, Dad did in fact understand some things about life that Ryan didn't know yet, and when Ryan listened, even for selfish reasons, life got better for everybody.

I need Dad back in my life. Back in the house. Mom needs him too, and Dianne. We need to get Humpty-Dumpty back into his shell. And I have no idea how to do it. Somebody has to swallow their anger and pride and just accept that some bad crap happened and people were hurt but not so much as to make it worthwhile to break the family apart.

And again Bizzy took Ryan's hand, as if she knew the anxiety churning inside him and understood.

I should be thinking about Bizzy and Mrs. Horvat and how I'm going to protect them. But by now I know that I'm not capable of making any kind of rational plan, because it always just comes to me in a rush, faster than I can hear myself think it. And it'll be something I would never have thought of, never would have believed I could do. Like pushing Lieutenant Alford's skull into the doorjamb and making a nice slot for the jamb to hold the man's head in place.

I killed a man today, thought Ryan. He began to tremble.

"You'll be okay," whispered Bizzy.

Ryan realized that she had felt his trembling and thought he was afraid. "I'm not worried," said Ryan. "I'll do whatever needs doing."

She held his hand more lightly, so that it trembled in hers.

"I killed a guy, Bizzy," Ryan whispered.

She nodded and gave an oh-that's-it face.

From the driver's seat, Dad—who apparently could hear all whispers—said, "Did the guy need killing, Ryan?"

"I don't know," said Ryan. "I didn't plan to kill him. I just had to stop him, and I couldn't wait until he started using combat moves on me. He had me by six inches of reach and probably fifty pounds of muscle. Or more. I don't have a lot of muscle."

"You had enough," said Bizzy.

"Hey, Bizzy, was it bloody and disgusting?" asked Dad.

"Yes, sir," said Bizzy. "And Ryan was bloody wonderful."

"Just remember, Ryan," said Dad. "The police have a lot of forensic ability these days. Not as much as on TV shows, but enough that when this is over and they interrogate you, the only thing that will help you is the truth. Because if you try to lie or hide anything, they'll see a pattern of deception, and they'll start to zero in on you as a bad guy."

Ryan nodded.

"If you're nodding," said Dad, "I can't hear the rocks rolling around inside your skull, so use your words, please."

"Tell the truth, conceal nothing," said Ryan.

"You're still a minor," said Dad, "and you were protecting yourself and your girlfriend from a kidnapping attempt back at the school."

"And what am I doing tonight?" asked Ryan.

"Defending your home and theirs from a criminal invasion. Between Mrs. Horvat's curses and your rapid forward defense moves, I think you might not even need the other micropots tonight."

"We need them," said Bizzy, "because they make *our* micropowers a little less micro."

"Yeah, that," said Dad. "I wonder if I've got a micropower."

"Yours is obvious," said Ryan.

"Oh really?" asked Dad, sounding amused. But Ryan knew he was actually taking this seriously.

"It's knowing the right thing to do."

Dad thought about that a while. Then he said, "Man, I wish that was true. Wish I always knew."

"Close enough," said Ryan. "Even if you haven't done it yet, you know what it is."

Dad thought a little more. "Not talking about the invasion of the loveks now, are we."

"Not entirely, anyway," said Ryan. "But no pressure. Now that Mom finally told Dianne and me the truth, we get it. The whole thing is above our pay grade."

"Above mine, too," said Dad. "Bizzy, you in on this?"

"I overheard the whole conversation," she said.

"I didn't make the walls that thin," said Dad.

"Open doors make the walls kind of irrelevant," said Bizzy.

"And I told her everything she didn't hear," said Ryan.

"Sir," said Bizzy, "I thought we were going in from the back of the house."

"That's for the micropots and Dr. Withunga," said Dad. "*We're* coming through the front. Because we want them to know that we're there, and to have an idea of our numbers."

"What are they going to think about you?" asked Ryan.

"That because I'm a blue-collar guy, I probably belong to the NRA and they're going to have to shoot me pretty quick."

"Do you even have a gun?" asked Ryan.

"Not in the house," said Dad. "And they'll never see me, so there'll be nothing for them to shoot at."

"Except Mother and me," said Bizzy.

"Depending on if they're in shooting mode or kidnapping mode."

"I think that if they get close to Mom without being cursed, they'll kill her as fast as they can, before she can get a curse out of her mouth."

"Wouldn't it be nice," said Dad, "if your mother could curse them in her mind, without actually talking."

"Who knows?" said Bizzy. "With a bunch of micropots in the house tonight, maybe she can."

Dad parked in front of the house. "Remember, we're not hurrying," said Dad. "Don't look furtive. Don't do anything different from what you usually do."

"Except that we're all going into the Horvat side of the house," said Ryan.

"I'm not," said Dad. "And I'd appreciate it if you'd stay with me on the Burke side for just a couple of minutes. I want to show you what I'll be working with when the others get here."

"I don't like being away from—"

"I'll come with you," said Bizzy. "Mom isn't home yet, her car's not here."

"Good idea," said Dad. "Besides, we don't know but what some lovek is already hiding inside their house."

So the three of them went into the Burke side of the house. Dad was as good as his word. He took the stairs two at a time and then pulled down the attic access stairs. He led them up the ladderway into the attic and then showed them how to walk on the ceiling joists while balancing themselves with their hands on the jack rafters overhead.

The only light they had was from the window in the gable end on the Burke side of the house. The attic roof on the Horvat side ended in a hip roof, so there was no window. It was too dark to see much of anything, but then Dad took out one of his tiny LED flashlights and shone it down at a place where a bit of plywood had been laid out like a floor, with an opening in the middle.

"This is my secret passage," said Dad.

"You're kidding," said Ryan.

"It leads from here all the way down to the crawl space."

"There's no room for that."

"In my office, where the built-in shelves weren't so deep. Now the microwave is mounted on the wall in front of the passage. It's just a ladder, nothing fancy."

"So if you need to get out," said Ryan, "you can lead them all down to the crawl space."

"If they start to set the house on fire," said Dad, "I don't want us all trapped in the attic."

"Why would you build this?"

"I read *Nancy Drew and the Hidden Staircase* when I was about six or so," said Dad. "Always wanted a secret passage. So when I was remodeling to build my office, I put one in."

"You think you know your parents . . ."

"Cool," said Bizzy.

"I told you," said Ryan.

"He told you that I was cool?" asked Dad, chuckling.

"He told me you were crazy," said Bizzy, "but he was obviously proud of you for that, so I took it the right way."

Now Dad laughed out loud. "I'm not going to take you down the secret way, I just wanted you to know that we'll have a way out. Up to the attic, over to this end, down the ladder, and out through the crawl space. So you won't be distracted by worrying about me and the others."

"Very thoughtful of you, Mr. Burke," said Bizzy.

"I don't want anything to interfere with Ryan's ability to protect you and your mom."

"And we're pretending," said Bizzy, "that protecting *both* of us is going to be possible. Because I love my lunatic witch of a mother, and I know that if Ryan has to choose which of us to save, he'll pick me, and if my mother dies, it'll break my heart."

Emotion was seeping into her voice, and Ryan put his hand on hers now. "I'll take care of both of you," he said.

"You can't promise that," said Bizzy. "You don't know what the threat will be, or what it will even be possible to do."

"I know," said Ryan. "But I do get some discretion. I don't turn into a robot."

"I'm just afraid that by trying to protect us both, you'll fail at protecting yourself *and* us, so we'll all croak."

"*Croak?*" said Dad. "Really?"

"Mother's favorite word for dying," said Bizzy.

"Weird what people pick up, learning English as a second language."

"Sixth language," said Bizzy. "But everybody in Slovenia is multilingual."

"Now we learn the other secret passage," said Dad.

"Come on," said Ryan. "Really?"

"This one you know about because you saw me building the wall between the two halves of the duplex."

"Oh, you mean the passage under the stairs," said Ryan.

Dad led them back down out of the attic. He left the attic stairs in place instead of raising them back up into the ceiling. That way if they needed to go that route, pulling down the stairs wouldn't make a lot of noise. Dad was thinking of everything.

Dad opened the well-oiled door leading into the closet under the stairs on the Burke side. Then they wound their way among the two-by-fours until they were at the panel under the Horvats' stairs, leading into their living room.

"I didn't know this was even here," said Bizzy.

Dad reached to each corner and turned a flange so that there was nothing locking the panel in place. "It's a snug fit, so it won't just fall out into the room. But if you have to get out from the main floor, it'll be easy to lift this out pretty quietly. Then lean it against the wall and get through to the Burke side and then get up to the attic and down into the crawl space."

"They'll just follow us," said Bizzy.

"I suggest you move quickly if you ever need to do this," said Dad. "Just stay ahead of them. In the attic, do you think you can find that secret ladder in the dark?"

"Yes," said Ryan. "Piece of cake."

"Just don't put your foot through the ceiling. Make sure you walk on the joists."

"Tricky, but yeah," said Ryan, "we'll be mountain goats."

"And the other guys won't," said Bizzy, "because by then my mom will have clumsied them out the wazoo."

"We hope," said Dad. He led them back out into the Burke living room. To Ryan's surprise, the next thing Dad did was to hug him. Long and tight. "I love you, son," he said. "I'm proud of you. Proud of what you've already done, proud of what you're going to do."

Then Dad let go of him. "Both of you go out, open the front door, and let them see that you enter Bizzy's side of the house. Then when your mom comes, Bizzy, I'm betting it won't be long before they make their move."

"And you'll be on this side?"

"When you open the front door, I'll let them see me standing in here, so they'll think this is where I am. And it'll be true for a while, because I have to get to your back door, Ryan, so they don't all get up onto the Horvats' deck and try to go inside from there."

"Ah," said Bizzy. "Yeah, that's the most obvious back entrance."

"And it helps shield our back door from view, because it's at ground level," said Dad.

Ryan noticed that Dad slipped from "your back door, Ryan," to "shield *our* back door from view." In his heart, Dad still lived in this house. It was still "our" door.

22

Dad had done a good job of providing sound insulation between the two halves of the duplex. He must have done it while Ryan was at school, because for Ryan, the division went from bare studs to mudded wallboard between leaving for school and getting home. Yet despite knowing that he had never heard a sound from the Horvats' side since they moved in—not through the walls, anyway—Ryan still kept straining to hear the GRUT members getting drawn into the Burke house.

All he heard was Mrs. Horvat's nervous grumbling or cursing or—it was conceivable—praying. If she *was* praying, she didn't use a very deferent tone of voice with the Almighty. She pretty much talked to him the way she talked to Ryan—as if she was constantly choosing between talking to him and slapping him really hard.

But Ryan wasn't offended or even annoyed. Mrs. Horvat had plenty of reason to be afraid. Ryan was pretty sure he hadn't overreacted this morning at school—that fake FBI lieutenant was about to lay him out on the floor and quite probably kill him. This would have removed him as a possible obstacle to abducting Bizzy, and it would have shown Bizzy that her abductors weren't shy about being brutally violent, so she would probably be more cooperative. Especially because Dead Ryan wouldn't have been much help to her. So Ryan knew he had been right to use maximum force on the guy. He had no way of knowing that the "maximum force" he could exert from his skinny body might possibly be lethal.

And what about now? How would he protect them now, with himself inside the house with them? He couldn't even *see* any threats until they got inside, and that might be too late.

Of course, for all he knew, these guys weren't loveks after all, or Mrs. Horvat didn't know what they were really about. Maybe they wanted Bizzy as a hostage so they could force Mrs. Horvat to work for them. If they wanted to assassinate somebody without being detected, having her be near them and mutter, "Awfully clumsy of you," might be lethal, and it would *be* an accident that killed them, so nothing would have to be faked or covered up.

But it would be good to stop Mrs. Horvat from being forced into a killing spree. Stopping these guys from kidnapping Bizzy and controlling Mrs. Horvat was every bit as essential as stopping them from killing the Horvats.

In his mind, when he tried to think of them as the Horvats, he always felt like he was lying. They weren't "the Horvats" like any common neighbor. They were the woman he loved and his potential nightmare of a mother-in-law. They were Bizzy and, oh yes, Mrs. Horvat.

But it wouldn't keep him from doing what it took to protect them both. They were his responsibility.

There was a knock on the door.

Bizzy started to get up.

"Sit down," said Ryan. Since Bizzy wasn't used to obeying him—or anybody, really—he had to stand up, hook her arm in his, and wheel her around and push her back on the couch.

"What am I here for?" he asked her sternly. "To watch you get abducted from the front door and then wring my hands and say, 'Dear me, dear me, who'da thunk they'd be so bold, those bad men?'?"

Bizzy chuckled as Ryan went to the front door.

It was Defense. "Nobody answered your door," he said.

"Nobody's answering this door, either," said Ryan. "Go away."

"Yeah, I know, I'm always dropping in at the wrong time."

"This is the time when guys with guns might burst in at any moment," said Ryan. "And of the people in this house right now, *third* on my gotta-save list is you. Third out of three."

Defense caught sight of Mrs. Horvat and Bizzy. He waved.

"Did you notice that I haven't invited you in?" asked Ryan. "I'm not joking. Bullets. Guns. Defense la morte."

"Frenchmen don't talk like that even with three cigarettes in their mouths at once," said Defense.

Mrs. Horvat spoke loudly from the couch. "Get the little idiot through the door and out the back," said Mrs. Horvat. "Everybody here is a hostage."

Defense came in and Ryan closed the door behind him. "Nobody wanted you here, Defense."

"That only proves how much I was *needed*, to help expunge their anti-Defenseur prejudices."

Ryan led Defense around behind the couch. "You see these throw pillows on the floor? Please arrange one tightly over your mouth and nose, then press down until you can't breathe."

"Do your own homicide, Ryan," said Defense. "If you want me dead, be man enough to—"

"Shut up," said Bizzy.

"Someone is coming up the walk," said Mrs. Horvat.

Ryan returned to his place by the door. Two man-size shapes appeared through the translucent windows in the door. "Charlottesville Police," said one of them. "Please open the door."

Ryan saw that they were indeed in uniform. Ryan opened the door as he was saying, "Nobody here called the police and I know we're not making too much noise," but before he got half of that out, the two policemen had pushed past him into the room.

"We've had reports of men with concealed weapons in this neighborhood," said one of the cops. "We have reason to suspect a home invasion might be taking place in one of these houses."

The other cop said, "Since they might be holding one of you hostage, we have to check every room."

"Where's your son?" asked the first cop. "Our records show you have a boy and a girl."

Ryan glanced at Bizzy and saw she was wearing her plain face. Neither ugly nor glamor.

Then Ryan noticed some details of the police uniforms. Identical to the fake cop uniforms on Halloween. Good fakes, but not actual Charlottesville uniforms.

So they weren't cops. One of them was already heading past the couch toward the back. But the other was directly in front of the couch, and Ryan saw his arm flex and his hand reach for the handgun at his belt.

That was apparently all that Ryan needed—he was already in motion. As the fake cop was drawing the gun, which Ryan knew he was going to use to kill Mrs. Horvat and Bizzy, Ryan got his own hand onto the gun and squeezed a shoulder nerve in the guy so that his grip on the pistol suddenly let go.

Ryan raised the handgun and shot the guy square in the shoulder. It was a heavy bullet fired at close range. The guy dropped like a rock, screaming and rolling on the floor. Meanwhile, Ryan was clearly aware of the bullet, which had passed clean through the shoulder, flying into the wall dividing the halves of the house, just in front of the stairs.

By now the other fake cop had turned around and was drawing his pistol. Ryan was nowhere near close enough to do anything. But he had a very powerful projectile weapon in his hand, so he took aim at the guy.

He meant to shoot him in the right shoulder, because that was the arm he was using to hold the gun. But at the last moment Ryan redirected his aim and shot him in the left shoulder, through and through. It had the desired effect, sending him to the ground without firing his weapon.

"Defense, I saw you thinking about being brave. Thanks for not blocking my shot."

"Brave would have been stupid," said Defense.

"Be brave enough to get his weapon," said Ryan. "Don't fire it. Don't fiddle with it. Just slide it far away from his reach."

"Weapon," said Defense. "You said 'weapon,' like a soldier. They've been trained not to call personal weapons 'guns' because that means artillery."

Ryan understood the nervousness that made Defense babble. Two pistol shots had just brought down two uniformed policemen. Ryan didn't make him shut up, because he was kicking the gun away from the guy while he babbled.

"Just so you all know, those aren't real Charlottesville police uniforms. They're costumes. I saw a couple of guys wearing them as costumes on Halloween."

"Oh, yeah," said Defense.

"We saw the costumes and real cop uniforms within seconds of each other. So I noticed the differences."

"You just shot two guys," said Bizzy.

"They were going to shoot the two of you," Ryan said. "And I didn't have time to get my lightsaber, so I used the tools they brought me."

"Very ecology-minded," said Mrs. Horvat. "Don't buy things when you can use what's already at hand."

"I'm not just shooting fake cops," said Ryan, "I'm protecting the environment."

"Does anybody else notice that this isn't funny?" said Bizzy. "Those were two very loud gunshots, which I'm assuming could be heard outside the house."

Thinking of people hearing gunshots, Ryan thought of a bunch of micropots huddling upstairs. But by now they'd already be headed down, wouldn't they? Dad wouldn't keep them upstairs with gunplay going on.

Ryan looked toward the far wall of the kitchen-that-used-to-be-Dad's-office and imagined people climbing down the concealed ladderway.

Then he realized that the second fake cop had been standing in such a place that if the bullet had passed clean through his gun-holding shoulder, it still would have been going very, very fast when it struck the thin wall of the secret passage. Ryan could easily have shot and injured, or maybe killed, somebody going down through that passage.

But he must have realized this at some level, which was why he changed his aim at the last moment. The bullet that went through the guy's left shoulder ended up embedded in a wall of the living room. It didn't make it into the kitchen at all.

Since the guys on the floor were still making a racket with all their complaining about the pain, Ryan let them both see that he still had the pistol. "I'm jumpy and I'm nervous," Ryan said. "You can see how my hands are shaking, right? I may need to start shooting again, just to let off some of this energy. I might want to use a couple of bullets to let all the gas out of your intestines to shut you up."

And Ryan pointed the barrel of the pistol at the belly of the first guy he shot.

"Can I use this other gun to shoot this guy?" asked Defense.

"Weapon, not gun," said Ryan. "And no. Because he's quiet now, see?"

"Of course he's quiet," said Defense. "While you were waving your weapon at that guy's gut, I kicked *this* guy really hard in the head."

"Is he unconscious?"

"Either he is, or he wishes he were," said Defense.

The panel under the stairs fell open. Defense rushed over and helped Dr. Withunga into the room.

"Before I left the premises, I thought I should warn you that I counted about thirty belly buttons approaching the house rapidly but carefully. Most of them are crawling, but they'll be here soon."

"Everybody's okay?" asked Ryan.

"Dahlia refused to leave the attic," said Dr. Withunga. "She was having fun making all these guys yawn their brains out. Everybody else is still trying to do whatever they can, but from under the house instead of at the top."

"How are you going to get under the house without going outside?" asked Ryan.

"The trapdoor under the stairs on your side of the house, of course," she said.

So Dad hadn't shown Ryan *all* the secret passages.

Dr. Withunga went back through the passage behind the stairs. Defense took a moment putting the panel back in place.

Someone was pounding on the front door. A window broke in the kitchen.

"They're he-ere," intoned Defense.

"I hope you feel as useless as you are," said Ryan.

"Oh, much more useless than *that*," said Defense.

When the front door shuddered open, Ryan aimed his pistol at the first man to come through. He was yawning, his mouth so wide open his eyes were closed. Same with the guys behind him. Thanks, Dahlia.

No fake police uniforms this time—just shabby business suits. When he got his eyes open, the first man saw one of his compatriots on the floor and screamed as if in agony, "Why did you kill them!"

"He isn't dead," said Ryan, "but I'm perfectly willing to kill *you* if you don't stop where you are and lie down on the floor."

In reply the man drew a weapon and began to raise it to aiming position. He was slowed down, however, by the fact that he was yawning again, his eyes pouring tears down onto his cheeks.

Ryan did not believe in playing fair when the other guy is holding a pistol, so he didn't wait till the guy's yawning stopped. He fired his pistol and the man sprouted a hole in his forehead and dropped like a rock.

"Was that where you were aiming?" asked Bizzy.

"I didn't expect to *hit* what I was aiming at," said Ryan. His gun was still pointed at the door, where two more yawning men came through, their guns already out and vaguely pointed—not at Ryan, but at the women on the couch.

At that moment, the couch rocked backward and so did Bizzy and Mrs. Horvat. Ryan didn't have time to look, though, because he was shooting at the two guys who now didn't know where to aim. They dropped to the ground, probably not dead because Ryan's shots took them in the knees. They were screaming in pain, while yawning.

Then there were flashing lights outside and somebody was yelling over a loudspeaker, saying something about "weapons down," "lie on the ground," and the last two guys coming through the doorway knelt down and lowered their guns.

Four uniformed Charlottesville cops—not costumes, real uniforms, Ryan noted—came through the door.

"Don't shoot him!" yelled Defense. "He was protecting us from the intruders!"

Oh, yeah, Ryan realized. Cops just came into a place where shots were fired, and I'm holding the gun that fired them. Ryan set down his pistol.

"I think that guy might be dead," said Ryan. "But these other two were only shot in the shoulder."

"And who shot them?"

"Ryan Burke!" shouted Defense. "He was great! He never fired until they had their weapons out aiming them at people. But the dead guy, he was aiming right at *me* and Ryan had to save my life!"

Ryan wanted to tell Defense to shut up, they were all supposed to tell the truth. But when he turned, he saw that the couch was upright again and Bizzy and Mrs. Horvat weren't in the room.

Defense was leaving them out of it. He had tipped the couch over—he used to do that at parties, especially when some couple was kissing on the couch. He flipped over the couch to take Bizzy and Mrs. Horvat out of the line of fire, and then as the real cops came in, he must have pushed Bizzy and her mother through the passage under the stairs. Nobody would be asking questions of people they didn't know had been present.

Defense had his uses.

"Officer," said Ryan, using his toe to touch the pistol lying on the floor beside him. "I got this pistol from that guy," he said. "I really don't want to hold it anymore."

"You disarmed a guy and shot him with his own pistol?" asked one of the cops.

"It was the only weapon I could reach at the time," said Ryan.

"Any idea who these guys are?" asked the other cop.

"Sure seemed to be a lot of them," said Ryan. "But these two are just wearing cop costumes. Pretty convincing fakes, though."

"We're going to track down the source of these costumes and get an injunction to stop renting them out. Very confusing and could cause fatal misunderstandings."

"He just shot me in the shoulder without provocation!" shouted the guy on the floor in the other room.

"Didn't I kick you hard enough in the head?" demanded Defense.

"And this one kicked me in the head! Really hard!" the guy shouted.

"Sounds like a good day's work, guys," said a cop to Ryan and Defense. "You both fifteen?"

"I'm thirteen," said Defense. "We're both in eighth grade. But he's fifteen. He was held back twice."

"We're both students at Vasco da Gama," said Ryan, "and we're both fifteen."

"And you live here?" asked a cop.

"In this building," said Ryan, "but my family lives next door."

"So *you* live here?" the cop asked Defense.

"Sure do," said Defense.

"He does not," said Ryan. He gave Defense's name and address. "The Horvat family lives here. My dad is their landlord. They asked me to watch the place so I was going to do my homework over here and then I got interrupted."

"So where is your homework?" asked the cop.

Ryan blushed. "All right, I was going to play games on their iPad." Bizzy had left her iPad on the couch when she disappeared.

"And nobody in that family was here?" asked a cop.

"They didn't answer when I came in," said Ryan, "but maybe upstairs?"

A couple of cops dutifully started up the stairs.

That was just the beginning, because one of the guys on the floor had to say something about the Horvat women being right on that couch, that's why they came, to . . .

"To what?" asked a cop.

"I'm sure they were just early for a dinner party," said Ryan.

"Bet they were surprised to find you here instead," said a cop.

"No, *I* was surprised. I've never handled a gun before. A weapon, I mean."

The cops had already looked over the dead guy and the injured ones. "Were you aiming for their shoulders?"

"I was, like, ten inches away," said Ryan.

"From this one. I'd guess about twelve feet from that one."

"The stupid one kicked me in the head!" That One complained.

The cops shook their heads and started handcuffing the injured men and hustling them out to waiting squad cars.

There soon came a time when Ryan, unarmed now, was alone with Defense. "Where are they?" Ryan whispered.

Defense grinned. "Who? There wasn't anybody here."

Just at that moment, the two cops who had gone upstairs came clattering down. "The attic access was open," said one of them, "but there was nobody up there."

Dahlia must have gone down the secret ladderway when the cops got things under control, Ryan decided. By staying in the attic till the last second, she had kept the bad guys yawning while they entered the house. That probably saved Ryan and the Horvats, and also saved the last couple of intruders from getting shot by Ryan. Ryan wondered if she had kept all the loveks outside the house yawning, too. Probably, he decided. Probably right up until they were cuffed and being read their rights.

While the forensics guys were still working on Dead Guy, and Ryan and Defense had been answering questions for a half hour or so, Ryan on the Burke side and Defense on the Horvat side of the house, Dad came to the front door—with Mrs. Horvat.

Dad could hardly say a word before Mrs. Horvat was through the door, demanding of Ryan, "What brings all these policemen here! What were you *doing* in our place! Were you doing drugs?" And then she seemed to suddenly realize, "Oh, oh! My little girl! My Bojana!"

"She isn't here," said Ryan, falling in with the improv. "She must still be at school."

"You're supposed to walk her home!"

"I can't walk her home while I'm watching your side of the duplex, now, can I?" demanded Ryan.

"How old is she," asked a cop. "Your daughter?"

"Fifteen," said Mrs. Horvat.

The cop rolled his eyes.

Mrs. Horvat rushed from the Burke side out onto the porch and then into the other side. Ryan could hear her yelling, "You! Strange useless boy! Who invited you! You are not welcome here!" Apparently she had seen Defense, but whatever it was that made her so hostile to him . . . No, Mrs. Horvat was a good actress, and she was just improvising fake wrath at Defense.

The next day, after Ryan had made his deposition at the police station, with Dad sitting beside him the whole time and Mother needing sedation out in the hall—she was that frantic, until a woman clerical worker took her home—the detective leaned over to Ryan and said quietly, "Son, I know you're the one who put the da Gama kicker in the hospital. And now you've sent four of these home-invading terrorists to the hospital and another's in the morgue. Two, counting the fake FBI guy at the school. So let me ask you one last question. Are we going to have to worry about you putting on spandex and playing vigilante all over Charlottesville?"

"Spandex makes me itch," said Ryan, "and I didn't actually like killing those guys. I don't get in fights and I think *you're* the ones who should fight crime. So no, I'm not going to go all Spider-Man on you."

"I think that most of the things you told us are true," said the detective. "I think you acted entirely in self-defense and in defense of others. I don't know how you got the Horvats out of the house without us seeing, because this place was surrounded by bad guys and then by cops, but I can't shake those guys' story about Mrs. Horvat and her daughter Bojana being on that couch in the room with all the shooting. I think that for some Slovenian reason, these guys came to kill them or, who knows, kidnap them. I think you were protecting them. So tell me, are they safe?"

"Ryan hasn't seen the Horvats since yesterday when Mrs. Horvat came home," said Dad. "But I have. And yes, they're safe, though they're in a dither about bullet holes in their walls. And, you know, blood on the floor. But I'm the landlord. I'll get it cleaned up as soon as your crime scene guys give me the all clear."

"And you didn't see them on that couch?" asked the detective.

"Sir," said Dad, "I've seen them on that couch many times. But I'm a working man. I was working. Haven't you checked with my crew?"

"Of course we did," said the detective. "I think that even if we caught you up to your elbows in somebody's bowels, those guys would alibi you out of it."

"They're honest men," said Dad. "If they lie, they don't work for me."

The detective smiled. "Sounds like you both put in a good day's work yesterday."

"Any charges?" asked Dad.

"The DA wondered why I even had to consult him, it's such an open-and-shut case of self-defense. Especially because the only weapon the kid used belonged to the bad guys. He came unarmed to a gunfight. So you're free to go. No charges. And, you know, good job, kid. Let me know if you ever want to get some police training or do a ride-along. The force could use somebody who knows how to protect people. Especially people who aren't even there."

He left the door open behind him.

Ryan was about to burst out with thanks to his dad and a lot of questions, but Dad covered his mouth and led him out of the room and then out of the station before he finally said, "You know they have recording devices in that room, don't you?"

"Well, I do now," said Ryan.

"I know I told you truth was best. But I also know that the Horvats did not need to have their names in a crime report. You kept them alive, and between Defense and Dr. Withunga and me, we got them out of the house. And just so you know, I let them out of their lease. Dr. Horvat will be back to pick up their clothes and a few other things, but Bizzy and Mrs. Horvat are not going back there again."

"I . . . I didn't think that—"

Dad flung an arm over Ryan's shoulder. "I think we can be pretty sure their enemies have that address. The Horvats are going into hiding again. They can't leave an address with us. Bizzy says to tell you that you'll hear from her when . . ."

"I'm okay, Dad," said Ryan.

"She thinks that she nearly got you killed," said Dad.

"What, she's never going to see me again to keep *me* safe?"

"Like that," said Dad.

"Load o' crap," said Ryan. "I served my purpose."

"Oh, come on, don't go trying to tell yourself that it was never love."

"She can just walk away?"

"Her parents are terrified of what might happen to her," said Dad. "And I'm terrified of what might happen if you stay in the protecting-Bizzy business."

"I wanted that to be a lifelong career."

"And maybe someday it will be. Come on, Ryan. You're both alive. You won't be minors forever."

"I'm not sad, Father. I'm glad she's safe. I'm kind of excited about what we learned about GRUT and micropowers and stuff. I can't wait for the next meeting, except that Bizzy won't be there. I mean, I've got a lot to think about, a lot to do. But it all worked. And you're welcome for not putting a bullet through the secret passage."

"Oh, was that in the cards for a while?" asked Dad. "Yes, indeed, thank you for being careful about that."

"And now we've got a lot of work to do," said Ryan. "On the house."

"Not that hard to putty over bullet holes and repaint a little," said Dad.

"But it's a lot of work to take out unnecessary walls and unnecessary kitchens and stair units."

Dad didn't answer.

"Come on, Dad. You still love Mom, and she's not just crazy, she's so lonely and terrified that it hurts to see her. It hurts *you*."

"I don't know if I can do it, Ryan."

"Do what?"

Dad opened the car door and Ryan got in. Then Dad walked around the car and got in the driver's side. "I don't know if I can live with it," he said. "What she did. That was my baby too, we decided together, it was *ours*, and it's dead now, and we'll never have another, and I didn't even get a vote." And Dad broke down and wept, right there in the car, his forehead on the steering wheel.

Ryan didn't have any answers. He knew what he wanted—he wanted his parents to forgive each other and come back together and make the world all right again.

But he also had no idea how Father would ever get over this enough to be able to stand living with Mom again.

So after a minute or so, Ryan laid his hand on Dad's back and said, "Whatever you do, Dad, we'll be all right. Dianne and me. You're the kind of man who loves his children even before they're born. Dianne and I got the benefit of that all our lives, and we always will. So whatever you do, Dad, we're all right with it. But we miss you. That's all. I miss you."

23

When they got home, Mom was sitting at the kitchen table. She looked up and seemed to see only Ryan. Ryan looked behind him and saw that Dad had not come in with him. Must have gone into the Horvat side. So there wouldn't be a fight with Mom right now. Or at least not one between her and Dad.

"I come home yesterday to find crime scene tape everywhere," said Mom. "I didn't know if you and Dianne were alive or dead."

"She was at school through the whole thing," said Ryan.

"You could have been full of holes from those . . ."

"They're calling them terrorists for now," said Ryan.

"You could have been—"

"But I wasn't," said Ryan.

"Don't cut me off like it doesn't matter what I say!" shouted Mother. "I know you weren't hurt, but you didn't know you weren't *going* to get hurt."

She was right, of course. Ryan didn't know yet if his micropower gave him any kind of protection, but judging from the outcome yesterday, it seemed possible.

"I didn't exactly choose for them to—"

"I think you did," said Mother. "I think you wish for excitement and danger. I think you wanted to show off for your Slovenian girl-next-door."

"That's true enough," said Ryan, because he knew from long experience that agreeing with his mother calmed things down way faster than arguing with her. "Not so much wishing for danger, because I don't. I like safety. But she was in danger."

"And brave Ryan *saved* her and slew the mean dragons and—"

"Yes, Mom," said Ryan. "You say it sarcastically, but in fact I did save her life, and her mother's life. Without getting injured myself in any way."

"So where are they! Why aren't they here on their *knees* thanking you, weeping and thanking you."

"I don't need any weepy thanking," said Ryan.

"They're ungrateful! Like the nine lepers!"

Oh, no. Mom was starting in with scripture references. It was going to be a long one.

The door opened and Father came into the foyer.

"The boy had a hard couple of hours answering questions at the station," he said. "Let's give him a chance to recover a little."

"Oh, well, Mr. Absentee Father wants to intervene to protect his—"

"Yes, I do, my love. I am intervening to protect him from being harangued by you for the terrible sin of saving lives yesterday in a situation he didn't ask for. Our boy is a hero, and maybe he shouldn't be punished for it."

"So my talking to him about how frightened I was counts as punishment?"

"Yes," said Dad. "The very worst of punishments, because you sound very much as if you're holding him responsible for the whole thing, when in fact he saved the day. And yet, because you're his mother he can't answer you by pointing out how selfish it is for you to think only of your fears instead of the fear he must have felt yesterday when he saw that these clowns were about to start killing people, including the girl he loves."

"The girl he *thinks* he loves," said Mother scornfully.

"The girl he loves," said Dad. "I don't understand the distinction you think you're making, between thinking you love somebody and actually loving them."

"He's too young to love somebody for real," said Mother. But her voice had steadily grown quieter since Dad arrived in the room.

"Perhaps we all are," said Dad. "Perhaps our whole lives. And yet we do extraordinary things for the people we *think* we love."

Mother was now down to muttering mode. "Like move out of the house because of one little—"

"Maybe Ryan and Dianne would like dinner," said Father.

"Are you reminding me of my parental duties?" asked Mother. It sounded like an ultimatum. Or a declaration of war.

"I was offering to go get dinner. Pizza maybe. Chick-fil-A."

"I, on the other hand, was planning to prepare actual food," muttered Mother as she got up and went to the kitchen.

As soon as she was gone, Ryan looked up at Dad and mouthed the words, "Thank you."

Mother's voice was already coming from the kitchen. "That's right, Ryan, thank your father for shutting me up."

Ryan knew that Mother couldn't possibly have heard him or seen him, but somehow she knew. Was *that* Mother's micropower? Or did all mothers know how to do that?

Ryan opened his mouth to answer, though he had no idea what he would say. Father made an erasing motion with one hand and shook his head. Don't answer, he was saying. And Ryan knew that he was right.

"And now he won't let you sass me for saying that," said Mother loudly from the kitchen. Pans clattered.

"Aren't you glad Dad stopped by just in the nick of time to keep you and me from quarreling, Mom?" asked Ryan. Father was shaking his head sadly. But Ryan knew just how much sass he could give without triggering an eruption.

She kept muttering amid the pan-clattering, but she was genuinely talking to herself; it wasn't meant to be overheard. Ryan didn't know what she was doing, but she *never* clattered pans like that when she was cooking. "Smart-mouthed little . . . clone of his father . . . people thinking they can talk to me any way they want . . . teach his children to respect their mother? No, that would be too hard . . ."

By then Father was leading Ryan out the front door to sit beside him on the porch.

"Couple of things," said Dad. "First, is there any chance that Bizzy is pregnant?"

"Not by me," said Ryan. "We haven't . . . you know."

"I assumed, but I wanted your word on it so we could plan accordingly. Bizzy told her mother the same thing, so it means there's no reason for them not to go into hiding."

Father said that as if their going into hiding were a good thing. "Witness protection?" Ryan asked.

"You and Defense set it up so they apparently didn't witness anything," said Dad.

"Defense did that," said Ryan. "Didn't even cross my mind."

"So Defense actually served a positive purpose," said Dad, letting a touch of wonder into his tone. "The Horvats are gone, Ryan. Mr. Horvat is sending a couple of guys over to pack everything, but in fact they don't have much. The furniture is all rental stuff that I'll take care of returning now that they're gone."

Ryan was stunned. "I didn't know that I'd lose her," he said.

"Haven't lost her," said Dad. "I think she's crazy in love with you."

"But she's going into hiding," said Ryan.

"Maybe she'll write," said Dad.

"And maybe somebody will check our mail looking for her return address or a postmark or something," said Ryan. "She can't write."

"I meant by email."

"Oh, good," said Ryan. "Because nobody knows how to intercept and track down emails."

"Please don't be sarcastic with me," said Dad, "even though you're in the process of losing the love of your life."

"So you admit that that *is* what's going on," said Ryan.

"It sure looks like it, and so it feels like it. But you're not going anywhere for a few years. Maybe the loveks will give up on trying to kill them. Maybe they can come back sometime."

Ryan admitted that it might happen, but it didn't feel likely to him. It felt like the Horvats would never come back. It was already a deep ache, losing her.

And yet not as painful as he had feared. Somehow it was just . . . inevitable.

Ryan wondered, but did not say, does this mean that what I felt for her was just a stupid crush?

But Father answered as if he heard. "The two of you are really in love. Your ages don't matter when it comes to that."

"How did you know I was—"

"I've been in love too, you know," said Dad.

"But not with a Slovenian witch's daughter," said Ryan.

Father nodded. "No matter how it all turns out in the long run, please don't close the door in your heart. Because you don't know but what there'll be a way to open it again. For someone. For some love. Maybe even for Bizzy, someday. If not soon, then maybe not too much later."

"Why did you come back here?" asked Ryan.

"I was inspecting the damage on the other side," said Dad. "I heard your mother going after you."

"She was just upset," said Ryan.

"I know," said Dad. "I know her better than you do. But she also knows better than to take her fears out on you kids."

"Mom knows better than a lot of things she does," said Ryan, "but still she does them."

Dad nodded. "As do you. As do I." He looked sad, but he didn't look like he was going to cry again. He was his calm, controlled self again. "Your GRUT team—they really came through, it seems to me."

"I don't know who Dr. Withunga ended up bringing. The yawns were Dahlia, but I don't even know what else the others might have done."

"And having them in the house," said Dad. "Do you think it helped you?"

"Yes," said Ryan. "It made my micropower work even faster than usual. So I was already shooting those guys in the shoulders before I knew I was going to. And the first guy through the door, putting a bullet through his head while he was still yawning and trying to talk. I didn't know that was coming. Even though my finger pulled the trigger, I didn't have a chance to argue with myself about it."

Dad said nothing, just looked forward at the street, where drivers were still slowing down their cars to look at the crime scene tape and police barriers that were still scattered around.

Ryan knew that when Dad was silent like that, it meant Ryan was supposed to think of something Dad didn't want to have to tell him.

"All right," said Ryan. "Maybe I did know. In time to change my aim. Maybe I always have time to change my aim."

Dad nodded.

"I knew shooting their shoulders would stop those fake cops. I knew that it would put them on the ground. In stupid movies, heroes get shot and they keep on fighting because of, like, adrenaline and they're superheroes or whatever. But real people can't take a bullet in the shoulder and keep on doing stuff."

"Didn't stop them from talking," said Dad. "That one guy couldn't keep his mouth shut. You need to teach Defense how to kick people harder so they really do stay shut up."

"I'm not going to help Defense acquire any skill I don't want to see used against people I care about, because Defense is an idiot."

"He showed up to help you," said Dad, "even though he doesn't have a micropower."

"One more proof of his idiocy."

"A good friend," Dad pointed out.

"Always has been," said Ryan. "And an idiot."

"Not mutually exclusive," said Dad, grinning.

"Are you staying for dinner?" asked Ryan.

"Your mother didn't ask me," said Dad.

"Oh, come on," said Ryan. "How much pride does she have to swallow?"

"All of it," said Dad. "Every bit of it." He rose to his feet.

"What about you?" asked Ryan. "Don't you have to swallow some?"

Dad didn't turn back as he walked to his truck.

So Ryan jumped up and ran to him. "Answer me," he said to his father.

Dad climbed into the driver's seat, but he didn't close the door. "I'm still chewing hard and trying to gag it down," he said. "But I'm the one with . . . I'm the one with the broken heart," he said.

"Not the only one," said Ryan. "I think Mom's heart is broken too. I think she hates what she did as much as you do. I think she hates losing you. I think that scares her so much she can hardly breathe. And Dianne and I, we've had our hearts broken some this past six months, too. Not on a scale like the two of you. But, you know, just saying."

Dad nodded. "I love you, Ryan. I'm proud of you. Now get out of the way so I can close the door and drive."

Ryan rested his hand for a moment on Dad's forearm as Dad reached out to pull the door closed. Father paused a moment. Then pulled the door closed as Ryan stepped back out of the way. Dad drove off.

As Ryan walked back toward the house, Dianne showed up, walking from the direction of her school. "Did you go to school today?" she asked him.

Ryan shook his head. "I had to get interrogated down at the police station."

"Interrogated! Are they arresting you for something?"

"Maybe I was only being debriefed. But they had some penetrating questions, and they seemed to want to catch me in a contradiction."

"Kind of cool," said Dianne.

"Less cool than you might think," said Ryan.

"Why?" asked Dianne. "It's not like you were in any danger of getting arrested."

Ryan sat down on the front porch step. Dianne set down her backpack with a thunk.

"It was self-defense, of course," she said.

Ryan shook his head.

"Wasn't it?" asked Dianne.

Ryan didn't know what he meant by shaking his head.

"Weren't they going to kill your girlfriend and her mother?" she demanded.

Ryan shrugged.

"Come on, you were saving lives," she said.

Ryan suddenly found himself crying, and in a moment he knew why. "Dianne," he said, "if it was all self-defense, if I was only saving people, why am I the only person in this whole thing who killed people? I killed two people and nobody else killed *anybody*."

Dianne didn't make any answer. Just sat there as Ryan kept crying into his hands.

"I hope you plan to wash all the snot off your hands before you pass any food to me at dinner," Dianne finally said.

"I was thinking I could wipe it off on you," said Ryan, "but you'd probably tell Mom."

Dianne reached out and grabbed his hands and wiped them on his jeans. "Snot goes on your own clothes," she said. "There are rules of civilized behavior."

Ryan smiled. His crying was over.

But it didn't change anything. He understood now what was bothering him all day. The cops gave him a pass, Dad gave him a pass, Dianne gave him a pass, but Ryan knew he was a killer. His micropower led to death. His move against Errol to save Defense, he was aiming right at Errol's larynx. It would have killed him if Ryan hadn't been able to make a tiny directional change at the last moment, and even then it might have caused permanent maiming damage.

The fake FBI guy in Hardesty's class, Ryan had killed him with one bare hand right in the open doorway of the classroom. This was going to be all over the school: Ryan Burke is a killer. Some people would think it was cool, but those weren't the kind of people Ryan wanted to have admire him. And that bullet hole in the one guy's forehead—was there a moment in which Ryan could have aimed somewhere else? He couldn't remember. Maybe. Everything had been so quick. Because the house was full of micropots?

If they hadn't been here, could I have still saved the Horvats?

If they hadn't been here, could I have maybe saved them without killing anybody?

24

When Ryan called Dr. Withunga and asked about the next local GRUT meeting, she said, "A lot of micropots laid themselves on the line for you the other day, Ryan. We owe them a big meeting where you tell everybody the outcome. Don't you think?"

Ryan thought that sounded fair. If he had come along to a support group project where somebody was actually shot and killed, he'd want to know what happened. Not be left in the dark like he wasn't really a participant.

Besides, Ryan wanted to know what they actually did. Besides Dahlia, because the yawning thing was obvious.

"I can't bring Bizzy," said Ryan.

"I can imagine she doesn't want to go out in public," said Dr. Withunga.

"She's moved out," said Ryan. "I don't know where she is or how to contact her."

"Oh," said Dr. Withunga. "That must be hard on you."

"Hard enough," said Ryan. "So it's just me."

"Meet after school for the drive to Danville?" asked Dr. Withunga.

"Aaron going with us?" asked Ryan.

"Always best with a third party in the car," said Dr. Withunga.

"Was he there at the, uh, home invasion thing?" asked Ryan.

"He had this crazy idea of watching out for me," said Dr. Withunga. "As if anybody could sneak up on me."

Ryan chuckled.

"But he reminded me that if someone kills me, it'll probably be somebody with a navel, and knowing that his navel is there won't save me."

Ryan said, "Boy loves his mother."

"Yes, he'll be riding with us," said Dr. Withunga. "Because you're known to have a violent streak."

Ryan knew she thought she was making a joke, but he couldn't find any kind of laugh that he could give her right now over the phone.

It was a long, quiet ride to the meeting in Danville, because Aaron had never been chatty, and when anybody brought up anything the conversation petered out in a couple of minutes.

Since Dr. Withunga and Aaron were both in the front seats, with Ryan in back, Ryan thought that if he seemed to be asleep they might talk more readily with each other. But when he leaned against the door and closed his eyes, they didn't start talking, though he heard Dr. Withunga ask quietly if he was asleep, and Aaron answered with "Maybe. Looks like."

Then, when Ryan woke up, because pretending to sleep was a pretty good way to fall asleep, they still weren't talking. So he assumed they hadn't said anything the whole time he was sleeping. He couldn't imagine being alone in a car with either of his parents and having complete silence reign for hours on end. Dad wasn't as chatty as Mom, but neither of them could tolerate silence for very long.

Neither could Ryan. But now his heart was heavy and his mind was full and he had nothing to say. He was afraid of crying like he had with Dianne. He also knew that he simply didn't want to talk about things.

No, he knew he had to talk about almost all those things in front of a fairly big group of micropots, but that would be different. And because he was going to do that, he wanted to do it only the once. Talk only one time about his day of killing.

Everybody was already in their chairs in the same room as before, when Ryan and the Withungas came in. Nobody milling about. The whole attitude of the room was different. These were the people who had already committed to helping. Who had already done it.

"The outcome was pretty clean," Dr. Withunga said, to start the meeting.

"These bad guys, whoever they were, came into the house with guns and there was shooting. All of you who came did so in the hope that your micropower might be useful, but we also know from our previous experiments that having several micropots in attendance increases the powers of all of them. So just by being there, even if things were out of the scope or range of your micropower, you were still helping. Thank you for that. Because it *was* a dangerous place, and you came anyway, and you stayed, and nobody freaked out, and everybody followed instructions, which included climbing down a ladder in the dark and crawling under a house."

People laughed and groaned, either remembering or imagining what had happened.

One kid spoke up. "Wish I could have been there, but always knowing what time it is in any time zone on Earth didn't seem to have any application."

"We may find some way to extend its utility," said Dr. Withunga. "But we know you would have helped."

A girl spoke up. "I just wonder if my power actually worked. I *thought* I was causing one bad guy to grow hair really rapidly, and—"

Ryan stood up and went up beside Dr. Withunga. "I talked to the police, and when you say you can make hair grow—"

"On myself," said the girl. "Just on my face. Not very practical, when I only wanted to *stop* it from growing. But with everybody there, it felt like I could cause it to happen on somebody else, so—"

"Eyebrows?" asked Ryan. "Were you growing his eyebrows?"

"Yes!" she said triumphantly.

"The police talked about—well, not the detective who was . . . debriefing me, but I overheard one talking about a guy with such long eyebrows that he didn't know how the guy could see."

The girl grinned and could hardly bring herself to sit down.

"So maybe one guy couldn't see where he was going," said Dr. Withunga. "And now you know you can make other people grow facial hair. Good work."

A guy spoke up. "No way to know about my power, I guess," he said. "I can bring my own eyes into really, really sharp focus. Without corrective lenses. But I was trying to take their eyes *out* of focus, and how will I know if it worked even at all?"

Ryan immediately said, "I didn't hear any cops talking about it, no, but when people—like, home invaders—came in, they looked kind of confused. And now I think back on it, the last few guys through the door were squinting as if they were trying to focus their eyes. I know that doesn't prove that it was you doing it, but it *might* have been, anyway."

The guy nodded. "Good enough for now. Since it might actually work, I think I won't try it on people who are operating heavy machinery." A few laughs.

"I could use that," said a girl. "Make guys' eyes go bleary when they're looking at things I don't want them looking at."

"They go bleary anyway when they do that," said another girl, and several people laughed.

"I can't see either of you from here," said Ryan, "so apparently you're blearing my eyes right now." A little more laughter.

"What else did you try?" asked Dr. Withunga. "Ryan here is the only witness, since *we* were all in the attic and then finished up in the crawl space."

"I only saw what happened inside the Horvat house," said Ryan, "and because I was sometimes busy shooting people, I couldn't see all of that, either. But I did hang out at the police station the next day, for obvious reasons."

There was an outcry about that, along the lines of they have to know it was self-defense, those guys were attacking the house, how stupid are the cops.

But Ryan calmed them down with a gesture and then said, "They weren't planning to charge me with anything, but come on, that was pretty crazy. Home invasions are usually a couple of guys bursting in and taking hostages, not a whole—what, not an army, but—"

"A squad," suggested a guy.

"A tactical team," said another.

Ryan shrugged. "They had some tactics. Pretty good Charlottesville police costumes, but not really up-to-date. They had some people who could talk like somebody from our part of Virginia, instead of sounding foreign. The cops think some of them were local recruits, or else maybe people with immigrant parents who already belonged to the group. But I hope that any military group of *ours* will have better training than those guys."

Aaron Withunga spoke up for the first time. "I'm glad they weren't particularly well trained."

There was general assent to that.

"How do you know they weren't?" asked a girl who looked college age. "It's not like an *ordinary* fifteen-year-old beat them. It was a guy with a killer micropower, augmented by being in the same building with a slew of other micropots, plus the rest of us were doing our best to confuse them."

"I had quite a few of them winking their brains out," said a girl who looked too young for her parents to have let her take part.

"I wonder if the other guys thought the winkers were trying to tell them something," said the college girl.

"It would have felt like their left eyelid was having spasms," said Winking Girl. "I've never winkled so many people at one time."

Another girl spoke up. "I know I can make people drop what they're carrying in their dominant hand."

"Did it work that night?" asked Dr. Withunga.

"I couldn't see. I just know that I kept making people let go of things."

And Ryan thought: If you had made me drop the gun I was holding, that bullet hole wouldn't have blossomed in the middle of that guy's forehead.

And immediately the rational part of his brain answered, And Bizzy and Mrs. Horvat might be dead. Somebody would have been dead. All I did was pick who.

A guy raised his hand. "Um, Ryan?" he said.

Ryan pointed to him. It was weird, being in the teacher position, calling on people with raised hands.

"You see or hear anything about people falling down because their knees and elbows went all double-jointed on them?"

Ryan had to shake his head. "It was getting pretty dark when the main mass of them started attacking the house. A lot of them just fell down, the detective told me. Not shot or anything, just fell down and lay there moaning. So maybe when they interview everybody, they'll find out about a bunch of them whose knees suddenly gave out in the wrong direction. Is that what your power is?"

"Well, I found I could go double-jointed myself, just the hinge joints, like fingers and knees and elbows. Not shoulders and ankles and necks. And jaws—I don't know what a double-jointed jaw would even do."

"But you were trying to do it to other people?"

"I kind of worked my way into it. It used to really hurt, but now my hinge joints are all used to going the other way, when I want them to. And I know I can do it to at least one other person, because my brother—"

"That is just sad," said Aaron Withunga, "to think of that terrified little boy—"

"My *older* brother," said Hinge Boy. "He had it coming. It was self-defense."

And even though most people laughed or chuckled or at least smiled, Ryan couldn't help but think, yeah, self-defense is also an excuse for tormenting other people. But is that what these powers are even for?

They're not *for* anything, thought Ryan. Just like the ability to memorize things, or to draw recognizable portraits. It's not like a person has such abilities because somebody bestowed them. They just got sprinkled randomly through the population. It's an illusion to think they have a purpose. But it's really depressing to think they *don't* have a purpose.

There was silence for a minute.

"Well," said Dr. Withunga, "not everybody who came out that night had a power that we thought had much chance of *directly* helping. Kinsey, what about you? Did you find anything?"

"There weren't any cats around close enough for me to sense them," she said. "And it's not as if I've ever been able to get a cat to do anything. Knowing what they want doesn't mean I can *influence* what they want."

"It was fun to imagine a herd of cats flying out of the darkness to land on their heads," said Dr. Withunga, "but cats do what cats do."

"So true," said Cat Reader.

Another girl said, "I always know whether the lights in my own house are on or off, but I can't change their state, and I couldn't tell anything about the lights in the duplex that day."

Ryan nodded his head. "That's okay. I don't know if it would have helped us to have lights blink on and off."

"That's what I thought," said On-Off Girl. "So I kind of didn't try very hard."

"But you were there, lending strength," said Dr. Withunga.

"Look, that's the thing I wanted to talk about," said Ryan.

Because he had been the hero of the hour, everybody seemed willing to defer to him.

"I think you really did enhance my micropower. In past times, I've either been alone or I had Bizzy with me or near me. And so it was always the same. I saw a crisis, a danger to somebody I was responsible for. But before it even registered in my conscious mind, I was already taking action. Already reaching out to grab a bee, or leaping to punch a guy before he could kick my friend in the head. Like that. And I could control it enough that I never killed anybody. Not even the bee."

Everybody waited silently for him to go on.

"But in the Horvats' living room that evening, I saw the danger *way* before I could actually see it. I mean, I knew the fake cops were going for their guns before there was any physical sign of it. Not that I was aware of it consciously. I was kind of *too* quick. So the one fake cop was only just getting his hand on his gun in its holster when my own hand was in the perfect position to glide it out from under his hand and there it was in my hand, pointing at him, my finger on the trigger, and I still don't know how. I just did it without knowing I was going to do it, without deciding."

A couple of low murmurs.

"Are you saying *we* did that?" asked On-Off Girl.

"No way," said Ryan. "It was me. But my micropower was, like, super-charged. Moving too fast for me to *know* what it was going to do. I never decided to go for the gun because I'm not stupid. What kind of stupid person goes for somebody else's gun and thinks he can get to it first? Only I did, and at some level I must have known I could do it. I was doing it, not anybody else, but *I* wasn't doing it, not my conscious mind."

They were really quiet now.

"Those fake cops—my micropower didn't push me to kill them, like it had done a couple of times before. If it had, I don't know if I could have stopped it, because it was the fastest it's ever been. I aimed at the one cop's shoulder and just shot, because I knew it wouldn't kill him, but it would knock him down, and it did. So, fine. The other fake cop, he was raising his gun to shoot at me, and I was going to shoot him in the shoulder of his gun hand, and believe me, I wish that drop-things-in-the-dominant-hand thing had been working right then—"

"I didn't dare use it inside because I couldn't tell who was who," said the girl with the micropower. "I was afraid I'd disarm the good guys."

Wish you had, thought Ryan.

"I'm not criticizing," said Ryan. "We were all doing our best. But here's the thing, I pointed my pistol at his gun-hand shoulder, but then I switched my aim to his other shoulder and shot that one, even though it wasn't the arm with the gun."

"It's still pretty distracting to get shot anywhere," said Aaron Withunga.

"I know, right?" said Ryan. "I knew that, because that actual thought went through my head *after* the guy dropped the gun and fell to the ground and started complaining about everything."

"Why did you change shoulders?" asked Dr. Withunga.

"I was not conscious of any reason. My hand suddenly was aiming at the other shoulder. But right after, I realized that if my bullet had passed through his right shoulder, the bullet would have gone straight on to the center of the secret passage, right when some of you were almost certainly climbing down. I might have actually killed or wounded some of you."

The reaction was vocal. Some gasping, some sighing.

"Look, maybe it was my unconscious mind, because my dad showed me where the passage was, and I knew what the wall unit around it looked like, I *knew* it was there, so maybe it was my unconscious mind doing it. But maybe not. Maybe *that* move came from you. Maybe the fact that you were there, you unconsciously sensed the danger I was putting you in, and maybe you caused me *not* to shoot in that direction. Could that be possible?" Ryan looked to Dr. Withunga for an answer.

"I'm not going to say it's *im*possible," she said.

"That's a cool thing, if you can unconsciously protect yourself from other people's micropowers, don't you think?" asked Ryan.

There was some assent, but many of the people still looked worried.

"But here's the big one. To *me* the big one, anyway. I turned to the door because loveks were coming through, and the first guy, he was yawning but trying to talk through it—thanks, Dahlia—"

Several people applauded.

"But without my being aware of deciding it, I pulled the trigger. I didn't work at aiming, I didn't think *anything*, I just shot and it got him right in the middle of the forehead, in mid yawn."

"I don't know what the problem is," said Hinge Boy. "He was armed, right? He was threatening you or other people in the room, right?"

"I'm not asking about self-defense," said Ryan. "My micropower doesn't get me to do things that don't qualify as self-defense or protecting others from immediate threat. That's not what I'm thinking about. It's that I don't—"

He couldn't find words for a moment.

"Look, when Bizzy's mother accepted me as her . . . bodyguard. She asked me, would you die for her? But I knew soon after that her real question wasn't do you love her enough to lay down your life for her, because a lot of people, the real heroes, they do that for complete strangers, and I was in love with her, so, duh. Yeah. Or at least I thought I would. But that wasn't her real question. Her real question was—"

Aaron Withunga interrupted. "Would you kill for her."

Ryan nodded. "And on that day, on two separate occasions, I found out the answer to *that* question. When the fake FBI guy was ushering us out the door of history class, I had a split-second opportunity, when he was in the door frame and I was just outside, to straight-arm him and bash his head into the doorjamb. I realized that while my hand was already flying out, all the strength of my arm and my upper body behind the blow, and I jammed his head into that metal doorframe so hard that his skull was crushed on that side, fragmented, so it was reshaped to fit the jamb. I didn't know I was that strong. I didn't think *anybody* was that strong. And the only micropot near me was Bizzy. That wasn't your powers plus mine. That was mostly just mine."

"You don't want to kill people," said Aaron.

"I don't," said Ryan. "I don't want to enhance my power if that means I'll kill people by reflex, without even thinking. Because that's not a superpower. Or maybe it is, but it's not the power of a superhero. I think my micropower makes me a super*villain*."

Dead silence.

"But," somebody said, "you only killed bad guys."

"How did I know they were bad guys? I don't know even now. They seem to have been part of a group, or so Mrs. Horvat told me, a group that had devoted themselves to tracking down and destroying people with . . . well, with micropowers. Witches, people who could make things happen at a remove. Maybe they wouldn't care about making other people wink, but making their joints work backward? Oh, I think they'd call that witchcraft."

"I think people like that would be pretty quick to call winkling other people a kind of witchcraft," said Winking Girl.

"They have no right to kill people, especially people who aren't doing any harm with their micropowers, so please understand, I'm not saying they *aren't* bad guys. But did they deserve to die, just because they knew micropowers existed and they were scared of them?"

A murmur of quiet conversation among the micropots.

"Here's what I've decided. For *me*. I don't know what any of you ought to do, because so far none of you has the power to kill anybody, and nobody else has a trail of corpses and mayhem behind them. Only me. What I'm doing is, I'm dropping out of GRUT. I don't want to refine my powers any more."

"Not even to slow them down?" asked somebody.

"How can I practice it?" asked Ryan. "Somebody has to be trying to harm somebody I feel responsible for. After this, maybe I'd feel responsible for every one of you, but how many of you want to be in a situation so dangerous that my micropower kicks in so I can save you?"

A few people chuckled, but the consensus seemed to be no, thanks.

"I can't practice my micropower until and unless somebody I care about is in mortal danger."

"So you don't want to study it or practice it," said Aaron.

"I have a father, a mother, a sister," said Ryan. "One really dumb and completely brave and loyal friend. Before I met anybody from GRUT, before I met Bizzy and fell in love with her, that's what I had. Bizzy has left town, she and her whole family, and I don't expect to see her again. So I'm back down to my core group. And as far as I know, *nobody* except for a few random bees has ever tried, or would ever try, to kill anybody in my family. So if my family is careful, I will never need to harm anybody again, still less kill anybody, because that's what my micropower is."

"You're disarming," said Aaron.

"You found me, Aaron," said Ryan, "and you were right, I needed to be in GRUT. I needed all of you, I needed to know that what was happening to me was real, and I needed your support that terrible day. So thank you. I owe you. And if any of you ever needs me, or thinks you might need me, I owe you protection, I really do. I'll stay in touch with Dr. Withunga. If she calls on me, I'll try to come through for you like you came through for me and Bizzy. But I'm not in that business. I'm not *hoping* to get better at it. I'm already as good as I ever want to get. So think of me as the GRUT of last resort. I'm not abandoning you. But I'm . . . taking early retirement."

Then Ryan realized he had said everything he had to say, so he walked from the lectern and sat down.

Dr. Withunga was coming back to the lectern, but before she could say anything, the whole group started clapping. A lot of them stood up. It lasted about thirty seconds, that ovation. Ryan didn't know what it was for. And when it ended, the meeting broke up. No final remarks after all. Nobody rushing up to talk to Ryan, though a few came up and clapped him on the shoulder, and a couple of girls gave him a hug, and one guy said, "The power to kill with your bare hands, and you're giving it up. Dude." It seemed to be a favorable "dude," so Ryan took it as praise.

On the way back to Charlottesville, when Ryan asked what the clapping had been about, Dr. Withunga said, "Could have been they knew you were through talking, and they wanted to applaud you for saving lives that day. And also for all the people your micropower wanted you to kill, that you didn't kill."

"They were saying they were on your side," said Aaron. "Your decision to try not to kill again. To stay out of the way of life-and-death defenses."

That left a silence in the car, while Ryan tried to digest it. Finally he said, "So they were applauding *everything*? The times I killed, the times I didn't kill? Using my micropower, and now my *not* using it?"

"Yep," said Aaron. "That's how it looked to me. Nobody was angry with you, nobody looked sad. Some a little awestruck, because face it, among micropots you're kind of a rock star."

"Hope not," said Ryan.

Dr. Withunga answered him. "Come on, Ryan, almost all of them have told me at one time or another that they wish they didn't have their micropower. Even the ones who've found a real use for it, a way to genuinely help other people, they still want to hide it, to protect themselves from their own micropower. But you, you're the only one who has to work at *not* using it to help other people, because you hate the harm you do along the way. So they envy you the decision to walk away, and they also envy you the intensity and effectiveness of your micropower. Both at once."

Only when the car pulled up in front of the duplex did Ryan say what he assumed would be his last words to them. "Maybe I'll hear from you again," he said, "because I made a promise down there in Danville. But you won't hear from me. So this is my last chance to say thank you, Aaron, for finding me and talking to me. And thank you, Dr. Withunga, for helping me understand what I am and what I can do. I think you're doing good things, and whatever it means that micropowers are in the world, thank you for helping people find ways to use them and control them."

Dr. Withunga nodded. "I'm glad you see the value in the work."

"It's had value for me, too. And, uh, thanks for the ride to Danville."

Aaron laughed.

Ryan got out of the passenger seat and heard the car whoosh away almost the moment the door closed behind him. He didn't look, because his eyes were on the front of the house.

He had hated having two doors inside the front door, instead of one, when Dad first split the house. But then Bizzy. Knowing she lived behind the door on the right—that made it kind of like a magical fairy door in a tree in the park, a place he couldn't go through but knew it held all the treasure that mattered in the world.

But now it was a dark door. There was nothing behind that door. He wanted it to disappear. He wanted the house to go back the way it was.

25

As November went on, Dad was over at the house more often. He always started in the Horvats' side of the house, getting furniture ready to return to the rental people; patching, spackling, and painting bullet holes; and doing other jobs that involved some hammering, some sawing, and a lot of drilling and screwing stuff in.

And then Dad always sort of had something to do or check on in the Burke half of the house, too, before he left. It was almost always some kind of errand or fix-it job—the dishwasher not doing a good job of grinding up food left on plates, for instance, for which his first repair was to say to Dianne and Ryan, "Why are you putting dishes in the dishwasher with food on them anyway?"

Dianne replied sweetly, "I read the manual, Father, and it says that we can because it has a marvelous food-grinding component that works even better than the average sink garbage disposal."

"And you believe that?" asked Father.

"I believe that if you have to wash dishes before you can put them in the dishwasher," said Dianne, "you don't *have* a dishwasher."

"I thought your mother gave birth to two perfectly adequate dishwashers," said Dad.

"Are you going to repair it or not?" asked Ryan. "I'm fine either way. I just don't need to be treated as if the defect in the dishwasher is somehow my fault for expecting it to work as advertised."

Dad looked at him for a long moment. "I already brought the part to fix it," he said.

"So the lecture to us about prewashing dishes, that was just a bonus?" asked Dianne.

"Yes it was," said Father. "And you can expect a lot more of those lectures in the coming weeks and months."

"So you're moving back in?" asked Dianne, in her most sarcastic voice.

"Your mother and I have decided to give it a try. Thanksgiving, you know."

Which laid Ryan out, so to speak. That had not seemed possible, not after everything that had been said and done. Had Father actually *forgiven* Mom? Or had Mom actually—what did Dad want?—apologized in some particularly abject and sincere and non-Mother-like way?

"So everything's back to normal?" asked Dianne.

"Nothing will ever be back to normal," said Father, "*if* anything ever *was* normal."

"It was normal enough," said Ryan.

"This wall in the entryway is coming down. As of December first, this edifice will no longer be listed with the city as a duplex."

"Does that raise or lower the property taxes?" asked Ryan.

"It lowers them, but so little that it won't mean a rise in your allowance."

Ryan answered, "Since I don't get an allowance . . ."

"Since your mother and I both provide for your every need . . ."

Ryan then asked, "If you're back, can I go back to only taking garbage to the curb once a week?"

"You can always do that. Or you can do nothing at all to help at home," said Dad. "You've always had that option, though for the past couple of months you've chosen not to exercise it."

"I don't actually *want* to quit garbage detail," said Ryan. "I just wanted to make sure I wasn't preempting a job you missed doing and wanted to have back."

Dianne got up from the table, where she was doing homework, and hugged her father long and hard.

When the hug was over, Dianne sat back down. Ryan stayed sitting at the table, where he had been reading a book that he wasn't enjoying much because it had been assigned for English class. Father took a step and laid a hand on his shoulder. "Since you aren't walking anybody home from school," said Dad, "I wonder if your schedule has opened up enough for you to come apprentice with one of my guys."

Was Father giving in to everybody? "My schedule is as open as it needs to be," said Ryan. "Which guy? What trade?"

"Wallboard and spackling," said Dad. "Starting you on the stuff that, when you screw up, it'll be easiest to redo."

"I'll try not to screw up."

"Except, of course, when the job *is* to screw things to other things," said Dad.

Dianne had not actually returned to doing homework. "Dad, when do the walls come down? Between the halves of the house?"

"Tonight," said Dad. "It takes a few more people than just me to walk the walls down so we don't damage the floor."

"You mean me and Dianne," said Ryan.

"If you're willing."

"And when is this event planned for?" asked Ryan.

"Now would be convenient," said Dad.

Ryan stood up, and Dianne did, too. "What do you mean, 'walk the walls down'?" asked Dianne.

"I'll cut through the wallboard on this side, and then I'll call to Ryan to push from the other side. You and I, Dianne, we'll keep the wall from just crashing to the floor. We'll walk backward, letting our hands walk up the wall as it sinks toward the floor, and when it's close, I'll tell you to drop it, and you'll jump backward so it doesn't take off your shins when it falls the last couple of feet."

"That sounds way more complicated than just dynamiting it," said Ryan.

"It'll take a lot of force to get it started. You have to overcome a lot of friction. And try to press only on the studs, not on the wallboard in between."

"You're saying you don't want me to punch holes in the wallboard, you want me to push the whole *wall* down? That's not at all what I thought we were doing. Somebody went to a lot of trouble to frame in this wall, and we're just going to undo all that work, in one push?"

Father didn't rise to Ryan's bait, but he also wouldn't wait forever for Ryan to stop pointing out how unnecessary Father's instructions had been. "It won't take me long to cut this, Ryan, so get on over to the other side and listen for me to tell you to push."

Father started cutting with a keyhole saw, and Ryan asked, "Are you leaving both staircases in place?"

"I'm not taking down the walls upstairs," said Father, "so we'll need both sets of stairs."

Ryan took that in and made no answer. The house was *not* being reunited, not really. And Ryan instantly guessed that Dad would move into a room on one side, and Mom would be in a room on the other. Separated at night, separate sleeping.

But maybe this also meant Ryan could have a bedroom again. No more sleeping on the couch. A reason to be thankful at Thanksgiving.

When he got to the Horvats' side, Ryan realized that Father really *had* been hard at work. The walls were completely repainted, and there wasn't a stick of furniture. He did think he caught a food smell from the kitchen, but Dad wouldn't have repainted there. It wasn't the Horvats' house anymore. There was no trace of Bizzy here now. It cut him to the heart. It was also a great relief. He wasn't sure if those emotions should go together. They didn't really fit well.

Dad's sawing went on. The wall that was coming down no longer had wallboard on this side. Father had pulled up the nails that had held the stud wall to the floor. Pretty soon Dad called out, "Push!" and Ryan started pushing. Nothing happened. "Pretend you're playing football!" Dad called.

Ryan had about six smart answers to that, but the main thing was to get the wall down. He knew what Dad meant—he had seen the football players pushing those padded frames along the practice field. But he also knew his shoulders weren't padded. So he pushed only with his hands, but got his whole bodyweight behind them and dug in his shoes on the floor, and the top of the wall moved out just a little. Just a jot. And then he pushed again, and this time, maybe an inch. On the next push, five or six inches.

"Almost there, Ryan," said Father.

Ryan pushed again and it gave much more easily. Too easily. He was afraid the whole thing was going to collapse on the floor. But that's when Dad and Dianne caught it. It kept sinking toward the floor, but it was controlled now.

"I hope it's okay that I stopped pushing it," said Ryan.

"Excellent plan," said Dad. "Gravity is doing the job, and we're slowing it down."

Then the wall got even lower, and Father yelled, "Jump back, Dianne!" Then, with a loud *fwump*, the wall crashed onto the floor.

Dianne was against the far wall. She apparently took "jump back" like an Olympian.

As Ryan stepped between the studs on the wall section lying on the floor, Dianne said, "I bet you're wondering . . ."

Ryan laughed at the old family joke. Maybe he laughed a little harder than usual, because reuniting the house was pretty emotional, even if it wasn't a complete restoration of unity. Dianne's laugh also had a kind of crazy excessiveness. They stopped laughing and grinned at each other. They were, for once, apparently thinking and feeling the same thing.

"Good job, kids," said Dad. "I'll take this apart the rest of the way tonight. But now it's time for dinner."

"Mom's not here," said Dianne. "You calling out for pizza?"

"Mom's here," said Dad. "She and I discussed it, and she decided she liked the new kitchen better." Father led Dianne in walking over the fallen wall and into what used to be the Horvats' side. Only now did Ryan register that the cooking smells on that side of the house were fresh. How could he not have noticed that?

Mom was in the Horvats' kitchen. "Our table is still on the other side, so we'll load up our plates and carry them over, okay?"

Mom wasn't actually singing, but to Ryan it sounded like that. The world had changed. Dad was still going to keep a wall between them at night, maybe, but the house wasn't a duplex anymore, and Ryan could extrapolate that the whole divorce thing was off the table. For now, anyway. And Mom was happier than she had been in eight months.

It was shepherd's pie, which was basically hamburger in brown gravy and vegetables, with mashed potatoes on top. A family favorite.

Dinner was good. And since it would be Thanksgiving the day after tomorrow, this probably meant that Mom and Dad would do their Thanksgiving Ballet, as Dianne had named it years ago, where Dad cooks turkey and dressing, and Mom makes gravy and cooks vegetables and rice, moving around each other in the kitchen and never getting in each other's way. Dianne and Ryan always tried to help, setting the table and folding napkins and such, just so they could watch how Mom and Dad fit together perfectly. Surely they would do it that way again this Thanksgiving.

And at Christmas, they would all be there. Ryan had been dreading Christmas without Dad in the house, without Christmas in the house. That's what it would have felt like. And now . . . not.

"This is delicious, Mom," said Dianne when they were back in their side of the house, sitting at the table.

"Best ever," said Ryan.

"Why thank you, delightful children, your voices are music to my heart," said Mom.

Dad said nothing. Just silently ate his shepherd's pie and looked up now and then, not at anyone in particular, just taking in the three people sitting with him at the table.

* * *

By Thanksgiving, Dad and Ryan had taken time for a bit of a chat going to and from work, when Dad picked Ryan up after school. Ryan had been afraid Dad would make him take the bus, which would cut out an hour of work, depending on where the job was. Having Dad drive him meant a much shorter travel time. And they could talk.

"There's still a lot of pain between your mother and me," Dad said when Ryan asked him directly. "It can't go back to how it was, not yet. Maybe not ever. For now, she's moving into the Horvats' old master bedroom." Which Ryan knew had been Dad's and Mom's room back in the day, only it had shrunk to accommodate an extra bedroom on that side, and another full bathroom.

So Dad would get the room Mom had been sleeping in during the duplex days, which had once been Ryan's room, and Ryan would be sleeping in . . .

"Dad, I don't know which bedroom used to be Bizzy's room."

"Doesn't matter," said Dad. "Your mother and I decided that you're getting the room Dianne has been sleeping in, next to my room, and Dianne will pick one of the rooms the Horvat kids were using. I don't know which one was Bizzy's, either, and it doesn't matter."

With Dianne sleeping on that side, Dad was right. It didn't matter. It would only have mattered if Ryan might have ended up sleeping there. He didn't know if he wanted to sleep in Bizzy's old room, or stay as far from it as possible. Now that he knew he wouldn't get a vote about it, he felt a stab of regret that he couldn't share even that pathetic level of vicarious closeness with Bizzy. But he also knew that sleeping on the other side of a wall from where she used to sleep was an excellent plan. The best possible plan.

All the sleeping arrangements, including some new beds, were completely settled and set up by Thanksgiving morning, with Ryan and Dianne making their own beds and loading up their own dressers while Mom and Dad got the dinner started. Mom was making her rolls this Thanksgiving, which meant she was doubly busy and would start baking them as soon as Dad got the turkey out of the oven and started carving it. Then she'd produce batch after batch as dinner went on and they would run out of room in their stomachs for more bread but they'd keep on eating it until they almost wept with fullness because those rolls were too good to stop eating them, either slathered with melting butter or swashed across the gravy on the plate.

And tonight, after everything was cleaned up, after they played some games and some Christmas music, they would all go to bed in their new rooms, in a house that was still sort of divided but was nevertheless all one again.

* * *

It was well into December when Dad picked up Ryan after school to take him to the job but instead took him home. "Go inside and get cleaned up," said Dad. "And I mean shower, and wash your hair, I don't care if you did it already this morning, you don't look like you did, and put on clean clothes. Not jeans. Am I clear?"

"You want me in basketball shorts with wet hair," said Ryan.

"I'm taking you somewhere and I want you to look nice. As nice as you *can* look, given your slovenly personal habits."

"What about Dianne and Mom?" asked Ryan.

"They will have to beg in the streets until somebody feeds them," Dad said.

"Meaning they're going somewhere, too," said Ryan.

"Somewhere much nicer than where *we're* going, because Dianne cleans up better than you do."

Where they ended up going was Outback Steakhouse, and because they got there about five-thirty, it wasn't too crowded yet. Plus it was Wednesday, which wasn't the biggest restaurant day of the week. Ryan winced as Father told the hostess, "One adult and one child, but no high chair. Probably won't need a booster seat, either." The hostess smiled—she had *never* heard a joke like that before, Ryan was sure—and led them to a booth. Which was already occupied.

Father stood at the end of the bench and beckoned Ryan to slide on in. Then Father walked away. If he was eating there tonight, apparently it would be at another table.

Ryan was sitting opposite a girl. Blonde hair, blonde eyebrows even. It was a very good dye job. Not a wig. And she wasn't wearing any face Ryan had seen before. She had gotten very good at changing her face, but it didn't even slow Ryan down. He knew who she was. He knew it from her posture, her size, and above all the smile in her eyes when she saw him.

She reached a hand across the table. He took it.

"All I wanted to do," she said softly, "was kiss you."

"Thanks for not saying anything to make me crazy," said Ryan.

"I still love you, Ryan Burke."

"I still can hardly walk and talk for thinking about you," said Ryan. "And missing you."

"Your father said the house isn't a duplex anymore," said Bizzy.

"Close enough," said Ryan.

"This is our last meeting, Ryan," said Bizzy. "For a long, long time."

Ryan took that news in silence. He had already known it. In fact, he hadn't imagined he would get *this* meeting with her.

"Mom and Dad won't tell me," said Bizzy, "but they got me an updated passport with a picture that actually looks like—well, not *me*, but the face I'm wearing right now."

"It's a nice face," said Ryan. "But I've seen better."

She smiled. The smile made her face look just a little more like glamor-face. But it also made it look a little more like Bizzy's natural face, which Ryan liked best.

"How's Defense?" she asked.

"He's made printouts of his Christmas wish list and he's giving it to everybody in school, including the teachers and the counselors. I don't think he actually wants anything on the list, he just wants to amuse people with the ridiculous variety. And some of the things are just not obtainable, so . . ."

"Still Defense," said Bizzy.

"I don't have a Christmas wish list," said Ryan, "because the only thing on it is already sitting across the table from me at Outback."

"I'm having the prime rib," she said, "because they do it pretty well here."

"I hope you're having it with horseradish," said Ryan, "because if you don't like horseradish on prime rib I'll be disappointed in your degree of acculturation."

"I'll try it," said Bizzy.

The waitress came by and got their drink orders—water for Bizzy, ginger ale for Ryan, because that's what Dad always got when Ryan was little. And pretty soon the mini-loaf of black bread showed up, along with a couple of knives that weren't quite sharp enough to slice the bread without crushing it and were way too serrated to be good for spreading butter. They sliced the bread, crushing it, and then spread butter on their own pieces.

They had never eaten out together at a place where waiters brought the food. Ryan felt like he was catching a glimpse of a whole life that might have been, a life in which he was able to court her, to drive her to the movies and someday to the hospital to give birth to their child, and strap car seats into the back of the car until the kids were old enough to sit up safely on their own, four of them in the back of a six-passenger SUV, while Ryan drove the Prius to work during the day, whatever kind of job it was he did to support the family.

And every couple of years, a bunch of guys would show up to hurt the family and Ryan would kill every last one of them. Every time. Because nobody hurt the people that he loved, not while he was around.

"Ryan," she said, "I had a long talk with my parents before they called your dad. And they had a long talk with him before he would agree to this meeting."

"And I was last to know."

"You understand why," said Bizzy.

"I understand that everyone is deciding what's best for me, while I don't get a vote, because I could never cast a vote that didn't include you in my life."

"That's exactly why you don't get a vote," said Bizzy. "Because I saw your face when you killed that fake FBI guy in the doorway of Hardesty's room. I saw your face after you shot the guy coming in the front door. I saw devastation in your face, Ryan. I saw despair."

"You did not," said Ryan, "because Defense had tipped the couch over and you and your mother were hustling through the panel to the other side of the house."

"I saw your face," said Bizzy, "and I knew that I would never again be the cause of your having to kill somebody."

And there it was.

"I can learn to control it, so I stop people without killing them."

"He came in the door with a gun," said Bizzy. "He was too far for you to reach him in time with anything slower than a bullet."

"What if I hadn't had a gun?" asked Ryan. He thought she would realize that he would have found a way.

She did. "You would have stepped between the bullet and me," said Bizzy. "You would have died to save me."

She was right.

"I love you at least as much as you love me," she told him. "That's what I came here to say. I love you so much that I can't bear knowing that your love for me made you kill two men. I knew it would tear you up inside—it's still tearing you up and I think it always will because you're not a man who kills people."

He could feel the tears spilling out onto his cheeks, but he didn't try to wipe them. He didn't have to pretend to her that he wasn't crying.

"I love that man, the one who doesn't kill people. I love him so much that until and unless the danger to me and my family goes away, I'm going to stay far enough away that he never again has to kill someone in order to save my life."

Ryan started to open his mouth, though he really didn't know what he was going to say.

"Don't argue with me," said Bizzy. "You know that I'm right. You might have spent a lot of time thinking about me and missing me. I'd be disappointed if you hadn't. But you also spent a lot of time brooding about those dead guys. Thinking about how there was a lot of danger that day, but the only person who killed anybody was you."

He had lost it that day, talking to Dianne, but he wasn't going to lose it here, with Bizzy, in the Outback. He only nodded.

"Here's how much I love you," she said. "I will not see you again until I know it's safe. For me, for you. And if it's never safe, then you will remain my most treasured memory. My first love. My true love. The man who saved my life, at any cost."

She squeezed his hand.

It took Ryan a while before he could speak.

"I go out onto the back deck sometimes. It's cold there these days. I sit on the bottom step, and I imagine that you're up there behind me, just looking out at the same scenery as me. I know you're not there. You never come out. But as long as I'm sitting there, you *could* come out, you *might* come out, and then we'd just talk about stuff, about nothing, about big ideas, about dreams and plans. Like the friends we were. Like the lovers we are."

He knew it was daring to say "lovers" because he knew that in some key ways they weren't, and would never be. But they loved each other and so it was the right word.

And she didn't contradict him.

She let go of his hand.

He looked down at the table in front of him. "We aren't going to eat together, are we?" he said softly.

She didn't answer.

He looked up and Father was sitting there. "I told her to order the prime rib," said Dad. "I knew you'd make her get horseradish."

Then Dad handed a handkerchief across the table. Ryan turned toward the corner of the booth, and then lowered himself down onto the bench and cried.

When he was done crying, and the handkerchief was soaking wet, he sat up and the food was on the table in front of him. "Got to eat," said Dad. "Put the handkerchief in your pocket. Always return handkerchiefs clean and dry."

"Thanks, Dad," said Ryan.

"Bizzy was afraid this would hurt you too bad, but I said you could take it. Was I right?"

Ryan nodded. "Far as I know."

"And Bizzy was afraid she couldn't take it, but I said I didn't care, she owed you a goodbye."

"She did," said Ryan. "But I do care, and I think she took it fine."

"So I won't tell you that she was crying into her napkin on the way out to her parents' car because sure, she can take it, she'll take it fine."

"She'll marry somebody else someday," said Ryan.

"If she does, you won't know it, because it will only happen when she knows that she can never come back to you, so she'll never tell you."

"Will I ever love somebody?" Ryan asked.

"Yes," said Dad. "Because you're a good man, and there are women who are looking for a good man and know one when they see him, and the right one will be what you're looking for, too."

"But Dad," said Ryan. "I'm still me. And if I love someone, then if anybody tries to harm her . . . I'll kill them."

"You'll stop them," said Dad. "And if they die, that won't be your intent."

"No, it won't," said Ryan.

"Your steak is getting cold," said Dad.

Ryan looked down at his plate. At his baked potato. He started mashing the butter and sour cream into the potato and then dug in and ate everything on his plate.

Apparently he still had an appetite.

Apparently, even though Bizzy was gone, probably forever, he still wanted to be alive.